Praise from her

for MICHAEL JECKS's extraordinary
KNIGHTS TEMPLAR MYSTERIES

"Michael Jecks has a way of dipping into the past and giving it the immediacy of a present-day newspaper article . . . He writes . . . with such convincing charm that you expect to walk round a corner in Tavistock and meet some of his characters."

Oxford Times

"Involving and memorable . . . The whole series belongs in any collection where historicals are popular."

Library Journal

"Old hands welcome Sir Baldwin Furnshill and Simon Puttock as reliable old friends . . . Jecks is an authority on medieval history . . . His intimate knowledge of the countryside, customs, and lifestyles of the period are authentic, and bring it vividly to our minds in both its beauty and brutality."

North Devon Journal

"Memorable characters, steadily absorbing period background . . . a commendable achievement."

Kirkus Reviews

"His research is painstaking down to the smallest detail, his characters leap alive from the page, and his evocation of setting is impressive."

Book Collector

"Michael Jecks gave up a career in the computer industry to concentate on writing . . . It was a good move."

Brentwood Gazette

Books by Michael Jecks

THE BUTCHER OF ST. PETERS
THE CHAPEL OF BONES
THE TOLLS OF DEATH
THE OUTLAWS OF ENNOR
THE TEMPLAR'S PENANCE
THE MAD MONK OF GIDLEIGH
THE DEVIL'S ACOLYTE
THE STICKLEPATH STRANGLER
THE TOURNAMENT OF BLOOD
THE BOY-BISHOP'S GLOVEMAKER
THE TRAITOR OF ST GILES
BELLADONNA AT BELSTONE
SQUIRE THROWLEIGH'S HEIR
THE LEPER'S RETURN
THE ABBOT'S GIBBET
THE CREDITON KILLINGS
A MOORLAND HANGING
THE MERCHANT'S PARTNER
THE LAST TEMPLAR

The Crediton Killings

A Knights Templar Mystery

MICHAEL JECKS

AVON BOOKS
An Imprint of HarperCollins*Publishers*

This is a work of fiction. Names, characters, places, and incidents are products of the author's imagination or are used fictitiously and are not to be construed as real. Any resemblance to actual events, locales, organizations, or persons, living or dead, is entirely coincidental.

AVON BOOKS
An Imprint of HarperCollins*Publishers*
10 East 53rd Street
New York, New York 10022-5299

ISBN-13: 978-0-06-084654-1
ISBN-10: 0-06-084654-2
www.avonmystery.com

First Avon Books paperback printing: January 2006

Printed in the U.S.A.

10 9 8 7 6 5 4 3 2 1

For Rachelle, Vicki, Chris,
Gwynn and Alan.
With love.

The Crediton Killings

1

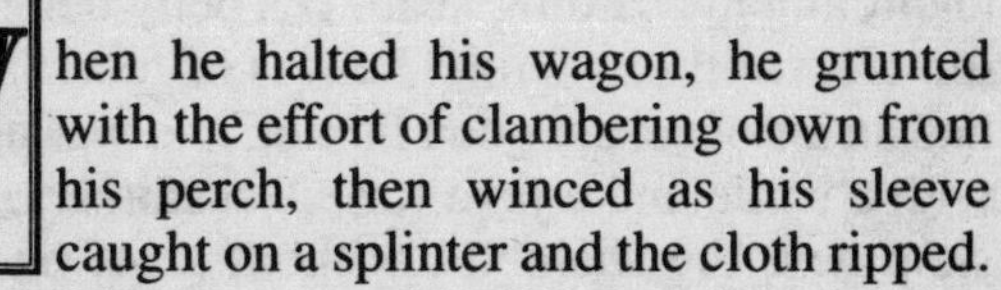

When he halted his wagon, he grunted with the effort of clambering down from his perch, then winced as his sleeve caught on a splinter and the cloth ripped. The short, chubby man stood by his horse inspecting the tear disconsolately. That, for his wife, would be the last straw, he thought.

Sensing her master's wandering attention, the horse dropped her head and began to crop the grass. The man glared at her; the sound of stems being ripped drowned out the faint musical tinkle at the extreme edge of his hearing. He slapped the horse, but she ignored him, used to his clouts and curses.

He was not overly bothered. On the busy road from Exeter to Crediton there were all manner of travellers; this jingling sound probably heralded another fishmonger, or maybe a party of merchants. Shrugging, he flattened a horsefly that had settled on his forearm, then stood scratching idly at a flea bite on his neck, hands and nails stained orange-red from the blood, while he squinted back along the road.

Other sounds distracted him too: the chattering of the birds in the trees, the chuckling and gurgling of the stream, and the rustling of the leaves overhead as the breeze gently teased the branches. He turned his eyes skyward, and wished that the draft would reach down and cool *him*. Even under the trees, the heat of the August sun was stifling.

Kneeling by the stream, he scooped water over his head, rubbing it into his face, puffing and blowing with the sharp coolness. He came upright slowly, shaking his head, a stout man in his early thirties, round-faced and heavy-jowled, with a thin covering of sandy hair encircling his balding head. His belly demonstrated all too eloquently how fond he was of food and drink. He had an air of robust good humor, and was always ready with a smile and a joke for his customers; few left his shop near the shambles without grins on their faces. His business was still young, and he was keen to make sure that all who visited him wanted to return.

Remembering why he had stopped in the first place, he lifted his tunic and turned away from the roadside, morosely contemplating the rippling stream before him while he gratefully emptied his bladder. He should never, he thought, have accepted all that ale from the farmer . . .

He straightened his hose reflectively. His wife would be bound to be irritable after waiting so long. He had promised to be back quickly after picking up the two calves' carcasses which were now in the back of the wagon. He glanced at the sun and grimaced. It must be midafternoon at the earliest! Mary's tongue would be strengthened and matured with the passage of time like a strong cheese—and all her bitterness was sure to be focused on him.

"Hah!" he muttered under his breath. "If a man can't take a drink with a friend when he's tired, what is the point of life?" Scratching at another flea bite on his chest, he lumbered back up into his seat and retrieved the reins, snapping them. His old horse tore up a last mouthful of grass and leaned forward in the traces, jolting the wagon and making the man swear. "God's blood! You old bitch, be easy! Do you want me to fall off?"

The rumble and clatter of the wagon as it jolted along gradually eased his tension, and he slumped, hardly taking notice of his direction. There was little need, in any case. The old beast knew the way home to Crediton, and did not have to be touched with the whip or reins to take the correct path. Flies left the calves' carcasses behind as the wagon bumped, and he swore as he waved them away.

Adam was no fool. He knew full well that he was not an ideal husband, and he could easily imagine that Mary had been nervous when they first married, but he judged that his solid career and the money he lavished on her were together enough to please her. Small in stature, she reminded him of a bird, with her slender figure, tiny bones and bright eyes. She was even shorter than he, by at least half a head, and he enjoyed the sense of control this height difference gave him, though he was quick to admit, if only to himself, that he would never consider using it, he was too fearful of hurting her feelings. Adam was not like other men he knew: he did not believe in beating his wife.

The horse was toiling up the hill now, and there were only another three or so miles back to town. Sunlight sprinkled through the branches above to form golden pools on the ground, and he allowed his eyes to ease themselves shut as his head nodded under the soporific effect of the regular hoofbeats. It was the ale, he thought to himself. He should never have had so much. Belching, he began preparing excuses in case Mary was in a bad mood. Merely saying he had accepted the farmer's offer of a drink after a morning's hot and sweaty work would be unlikely to win her over.

At the top of the hill the horse paused; he was about to snap the reins in irritation when he heard the noise again, and turned in his seat to stare behind him. This time it sounded like a troop of soldiers, he thought, but he could see nothing. The road twisted too tortuously between the trees for him to be able to see more than a few tens of yards. Giving a suspicious grunt, he jerked the reins and set off down the hill toward Crediton. He did not want to meet with armed men so far from home.

The trees opened out a little now, and over on the opposite hill he could see the outskirts of the town, with a couple of farmhouses showing stark and white under their limewash. Smoke rose behind them from the dozens of fires in the town, and Adam smiled at the sight. His spirits always lifted on seeing his town, surely the oldest and best in Devonshire, the place where St. Boniface had been born. His eyes were fixed on the horizon as he trailed down the road until he was back under the cover of the trees once more, and the view was obscured.

It was here, near the sluggish river, that he saw the Dean. Adam quickly reached down and slid his purse out of sight behind his back. He had no hesitation in offering a few coins for the assistance of the church, especially since the canons were good clients, but he objected to giving alms on the road.

The man heard him approach and turned, peered shortsightedly. "Adam. How are you?"

"Well, Father," Adam said, ducking his head reverentially.

"A beautiful day, my friend."

"Oh yes, Father," Adam sighed. If the priest wanted to talk he could not ride off rudely. Peter Clifford was an important man in the area. Then he brightened. The Dean was an excuse whom even Mary could not ignore.

"Where have you been?" Clifford asked, seeing that Adam had reined in and seemed willing to talk. Inwardly, he too sighed. He was a kindly man, but he knew Adam to be a boorish fellow, and did not greatly wish to speak to him. Still, he forced a smile to his face and tried to look interested as the butcher told of his journey to the little farm in the east to collect the two calves. The buzzing of the flies over the back of the wagon added a touch of verisimilitude to the tale, Clifford thought with a pained wince. They were rising in waves and resettling on the carcasses.

"And who are these, I wonder?" he murmured.

"Who?" Adam asked, his train of thought broken. Turning, he could see at last the source of the noise he had heard earlier.

Coming down the road toward them was a group of men, but these were no ordinary travellers, and Adam felt himself stiffen. They *were* soldiers.

Out in front were two riders on tired-looking but sturdy ponies. Both wore quilted jacks, stained and filthy from long use, over green tunics. One had on a basinet with the visor tilted up, and held a lance in his hand, while the other wore a long-bladed knife like a short sword. Both stared at the two men by the road, and the helmeted one winked at Adam before passing.

Behind them came another, seated on a massive

black stallion which gleamed as if it had been oiled as it passed among the pools of daylight. It was this man who immediately caught Peter's eye.

He was huge, at least six feet tall, and his demeanor showed he was used to commanding men. It was there in his self-awareness and stillness, in the way he scarcely glanced at the strangers by the side of the road, but rode on, his frown fixed ahead as if searching out new battles. His tunic showed the effects of days on the road, but was made of expensive cloth and bore no device to show his allegiance. Crediton was renowned for its wool, and Peter, like most men from the town, could recognize quality material. This man's was very good. Light, soft, and fine woven, under its layer of dust it was the fresh crimson of a good, full-bodied wine. Whoever the man was, he must surely be wealthy.

Adam's glance fell on the men behind. Three more were on horseback, but behind were at least another twenty, and wagons trailed along in the rear. He could not help cringing away. Warrior bands were too unpredictable for his liking.

As the stallion came level with him, Peter Clifford stepped forward. "Good morning, sir. Peace be with you."

The little column of men and horses stopped, and there was silence for a moment. Then the man's head snapped to Clifford and stared at him unblinkingly. The priest smiled, but his face slowly froze under the intense gaze of the pale gray eyes. They were wide-set in the square face, and held no compassion, only contempt. Unnerved, the priest nearly retreated under their sullen scrutiny. He had no idea what he had said to cause so much offense. As he opened his mouth to speak further, the knight spat at his feet.

"There, *Priest*!" he said. "So much for your peace!"

"I meant no insult, sir, it was merely a greeting—"

"No insult?" he thundered, and his horse stamped and blew as if it too felt the depth of the slight. This time Clifford could not help himself taking a quick step back. Adam felt a prickle of cold fear wash his back as, suddenly, the man leaned down until his elbow rested on the horse's withers, and he looked back at the men on foot. " 'No insult,' the little priest says. 'No insult,' " he sneered, and faced Clifford again. "Do you think we are friars, Priest? Do we look like monks? Or maybe you think we're weavers and millers looking for a new market. We are *soldiers*, man! We fight for our living. We don't want peace! In peacetime we starve. We want *war*! The pox on your peace!"

Adam watched as the furious man jabbed spurs into his horse's flanks and jerked its head back to face the road, the men-at-arms trailing after, one or two throwing him and the priest a casual, uninterested glance.

"Father, who on earth does he think he is, that he should dare to insult a man of God?" Adam asked, breathless in his horror.

Clifford smiled thinly and shrugged—a tall, ascetic man of a little over fifty, with hair that was now a faded reflection of its past redness. He stood, silently watching as the men marched past, followed by lurching wagons laden with chests and strongboxes.

Though still tall, Peter Clifford was stooped, and this together with his slitted eyes made some of his parishioners scared of him, thinking him aggressive. In reality, both were the result of reading too often by weak candlelight. His skin had paled to the color of old parchment, showing how little time he spent in the open air away from his studies. There was a tautness in his figure to prove he still rode regularly, though he could no longer enjoy hunting and hawking as often as he had in his youth. The crow's feet at either side of his intelligent dark eyes hinted that he was a good and cheerful soul, but now he was troubled, peering after the dust-shrouded men as they passed round a curve in the road and out of sight.

Turning to Adam, he smiled sadly. "They are men of war and violence. Soldiers—*mercenaries*! They can have no understanding of the pleasures which I enjoy in serving God. All they know is how to slaughter. Kind words come hard to such as them." He stared after them as the last of the wagons passed by. "I wonder where they are going?" he muttered to himself.

"Aye. And let's hope they don't want to stay here long, Father," said Adam emphatically. "I've seen enough like them before now, and we don't want their sort in Crediton for long. There'll be trouble."

"No, there shouldn't be. If they make trouble, the town can defend itself. There were only some thirty men, all told, and the town can protect itself against so few. But you're right, they are unsettling, and it would be better if they were not to stay." Clifford put them from his mind and set off toward the town. "In any case, I have too much work to do to remain idly wondering about a group of rude travellers. I must get back to Crediton to prepare for the Bishop."

Adam coaxed his horse into movement and rattled along beside him for a while. "Bishop?" he enquired.

"Yes, Walter Stapledon has been to visit someone in Cornwall. He let me know that he is to stay with us shortly—on his return journey to Exeter. We must get things ready for him."

"I . . . er . . . Will you need meat for him? I have these two calves, and—"

"Possibly. I will have the cook come and see you," said Clifford absently. It was obvious even to the butcher that the priest's mind was on other things, and soon Adam whipped his horse into a faster pace toward home. News of the band of soldiers would probably calm his wife's temper a little, he reflected.

The trees gave way at last to open land, and Adam could see the men and women in the narrow fields. A group stood in a corner, drinking ale and eating as they took their rest, while others carried on with their work. Adam could see that the harvest was good. The weather had for once been kind to the farmers, and the wheat and barley were standing tall and proud in the strips. He turned in, leaving the main track and taking a shortcut to avoid meeting the soldiers again. Soon he was at Crediton's outskirts. He passed old cob buildings and entered the busy thoroughfare which ran through the center. Here the noise and bustle of the little town dispelled the last residue of languor from the ale and he sat a little straighter in his seat.

Crediton was always busy. The birthplace of St. Boniface had a thriving religious community; the abundance of farms ensured the profits of the merchants and tradesmen, and proximity to Exeter guaranteed the availability of rare foodstuffs and precious goods which could be purchased with the money earned from the cloth-makers.

Now, in the late afternoon, there was a busyness about the town which many lords in other areas would envy. Adam had been raised on an estate west of here, but had been permitted to become an apprentice, so he knew the difference between urban life and that of the peasants in the country. Towns were not feudal or rural, and the restrictions which were imposed on others did not exist in places like Crediton. Here business and crafts could thrive, the only rules being laid down for the benefit and advantage of the population.

And thrive it did, if the crowds were any sign. Milling at either side of the road, avoiding the dung heaps where horses or oxen had passed, keeping clear of the open sewer which travelled down the middle of the street and trying not to step into the puddles of urine from beasts or men as they went on their way, the people of Crediton were not calm and quiet: they hurried. Adam saw one man, who must have been wealthy since he wore a fur-lined cloak tossed casually over a shoulder despite the heat, stumble and fall. The butcher joined in the general amusement, guffawing as the poor individual knelt upright in disgust, shaking his hands free of ordure, whether human or animal Adam could not see. The man was beside himself in rage and frustration.

Only a little way farther on, Adam saw Paul, the innkeeper, standing under his new alestake, and the two near-neighbors nodded to each other as Adam, still grinning, turned off to the left, up the street beside his shop. His apprentice was in the hall, dutifully breaking the neck of a goose; he'd placed its head under a broom handle, on which he stood, while jerking the legs upward. Adam's smile broadened. For all his efforts, the boy was too weak in the back and shoulders, and had to reach high over his head as he tried to kill the alarmed bird, while feathers flew from the rapidly beating wings. Stifling a guffaw, the butcher dropped from his perch and took the bird's legs from the boy. His single upward tug almost jolted the boy over as the strong neck lifted the broom handle before snapping with a dull crack.

"You see to the horse and get the carcasses inside," he said, jerking his thumb behind, and the boy scampered out gladly.

"Well? What have you been doing then? Why did it take all day to fetch and kill two calves?"

"The mercenaries are back!"

Then she was suddenly still, forgetting to rail at him for his lateness, as he told her who he had seen on the road to Crediton.

~ 2 ~

The innkeeper was pleased with his new advertisement. The old "bush," which had been literally a small blackthorn bush tied to a pole, had lasted some months, but had eventually disintegrated, and when twigs and a part of the old pole had fallen on Tanner, the Constable, Paul thought he'd better get a new one quickly before Tanner could express his indignation. Rather than use another bush, he had decided to purchase an alestake. Now a large cross of timbers swung gently in the wind above him, hanging from its new, stronger pole by chains like an X, and he watched it for some minutes with arms akimbo. No one, he thought with satisfaction, could fail to recognize his inn with a clear sign like that one.

He was about to turn and re-enter his hall when he heard something strange in the bustle of the street. The cheerful cries of the water-carriers and hawkers changed, sounding more muted. People stopped their hurried rushing and stared; urchins craned their necks to peer past adults standing in the way, forgetting their games; a maid from the house opposite appeared, bowl in hand, and was about to throw the contents into the sewer when she stopped and gawped.

Following her gaze, Paul found himself wishing he did not have quite such a prominent alestake after all, but he took a deep breath, squared his shoulders with resolution, and scurried inside. "Margery? Margery, where are you?"

"What is it?" His wife appeared from the buttery, wiping her hands on her tunic. She was in the middle of boiling wort for the next brew of ale and could do without her husband bellowing. Eyeing him with long-suffering exasperation, she was about to give vent to her feelings when he waved excitedly at the door.

"There's a troop of men-at-arms arrived with their captain. Quick, get the girls to help us; there are too many for us to cope with on our own."

"We only have room for five—"

"They can't stay, but we can at least provide them with food and drink. Food! I wonder if Adam has anything we could buy? Otherwise we'll have to rely on the cookshop."

She glanced from him to the door, her mouth opening, and then was still.

"Good day," The confident tone of the knight's voice pulled the innkeeper's thoughts back to the present with a shock, like a running dog reaching the full extent of its leash.

"Master, how can we serve you?" Paul said quickly, and moved back to invite the man inside. While his wife watched, he led the stranger to the best seat in the hall, bowing and smiling all the way.

"This looks a comfortable enough inn. My troop and I are bound for Gascony but need to rest awhile. Soon we will continue on our way to the coast."

"Ah, to join a great lord, I expect."

"I would hope so. We came back to join the King in

the north. Took a ship to London, and we missed him, so we went to York, and met with some of the commissioners, but they seemed to prefer raw youths rather than trained men-of-war. Well, they may regret that choice!"

"They refused you?" the innkeeper asked, with a flattering note of surprise in his voice.

The captain nodded curtly. "They rejected us out of hand, so we came back. But London was full of rumors of war. There were no ships to take us across to Gascony, for all vessels were heading north with extra provisions, and the prices were ruinous, so we decided to come this way. We'll catch a ship from the coast in a few days."

"I'm afraid we don't have enough rooms for all your company, but there may be other places in the town where they can be quartered."

"I would prefer them to stay here with me."

"Of course, of course. But I fear we do not have room for them. No matter, I'll seek out what can be—"

Catching sight of the captain's unblinking gray eyes as he looked at her husband, Margery froze. The way he twitched his short cloak aside was unmistakably threatening, as was the way he rested his hand on the hilt of his sword.

"I feel sure that your guests will understand my wishes, and will be happy to allow my men to take over their rooms. Now, I would like a quart of ale for myself, and I'm sure my men would also like some."

"Yes, sir, of course," Paul hesitated. "But I must say again, I am afraid the inn is quite full."

"We shall see." The captain turned away; the meeting was at an end. "A quart of ale. Now."

Leaving her husband to serve him, Margery hastened from the room and, lifting her skirts, rushed through the yard behind the inn, her mind whirling. In residence at the inn was the family of merchants, the cloth-buyer and his wife and daughter, and the goldsmith and his apprentice among others. What would they think of sharing their rooms with the motley troop of men-at-arms? She preferred not to dwell on it. And then there were the girls, too: Cristine, Nell, and young Sarra. A sour grin lessened the solemn set of her features for an instant as she thought of Sarra: if Margery knew the girl at all, she would be pleased with the attention of thirty fit and randy troopers.

At the back of the yard, she paused at the bottom of the steps to catch her breath, then clambered up to the room over the stables and hammered with her fist on the door. "Sarra, are you there? Sarra!"

There was a grunt, then a groaning enquiry. Margery cursed under her breath. "Open the door—quickly! You must come and help us. *Sarra!*"

A bolt shot back, then the door creaked open to reveal a peevish-looking figure. Margery pushed the door wide and stepped into the room. Sarra had been late to her bed the previous night, she recalled. The girl had been serving guests until the early hours, according to Paul, and had been near the goldsmith's apprentice almost the whole night. The innkeeper had been amused to see how she tried to engage him in conversation, commenting on his clothing, on his enamelled buckle, and when she ran out of ideas, on the weather. The miserable youth, tongue-tied and self-conscious, had gone puce with embarrassment. To Paul he had looked thoroughly unimpressive, but apparently Sarra had formed the opinion that he was sure to become a wealthy and successful smith, and thus worth the investment of a little of her time. When he and his master had gone to their chamber after saying barely a word to her, she had flounced from the room with a face like thunder. Sarra had never hidden her ambition to marry while she was still young.

And she should succeed, Margery thought to herself, eyeing the young girl. She was not the type that Margery favored usually: she was too long in the leg and small in the bosom for a serving girl, but there was no denying that she had the right glint in her eye when a man took her fancy, and her face was that of an angel—though now it was the face of a disgruntled angel, with the indignant sharpness of someone woken too early.

"Well, what is it? I cleared up this morning and did my chores, so what's the matter? Aren't I allowed to have a rest before the evening trade?"

Her tunic was thin, and Margery could see the slimness of her body in the sunlight streaming in from the doorway behind. Where it touched her ruffled hair, it made the honey-golden mane glow like a halo. Her neck was bare and it struck Margery how vulnerable the girl looked. For all her desire to wed while she was still young and not wait until she was "old," as she put it, no doubt thinking of Margery as the symbol of decrepitude, she was still practically a child, and when the innkeeper's wife thought of the quality of man which was at this moment settling into the hall, she had a pang of conscience. The girl would be thrown to them like a scrap to a pack of hungry hounds.

"Well?" Sarra's voice was irritable.

Briefly, Margery explained about the men who had arrived. Even as she spoke she saw the girl's eyes light up, and could read the direction of her thoughts: men, and a wealthy captain at their head—surely a fellow of influence and power to have the control of thirty others. He was bound to be impressed by her calm and mature demeanor. Margery sighed. "Sarra, don't start thinking you can run away with men like these. They're not the kind to want to marry a woman and raise children."

"Oh no?" There was a sneer in her tone.

"No!" Margery snapped. "I know more about men than you." The disdainful curl of Sarra's lip implied that with the difference in their ages, that was no surprise, and the innkeeper's wife felt her cheeks flame with resentment. "I've seen their kind before: they're the sort to take a tumble with a maiden, then rush off without even a farewell. Their captain is as bad as the rest, or worse."

"Worse—how?"

Margery paused and stared at her. "He feels nothing for anyone. All he knows is how to wage war. I promise you, Sarra, these men are no good. Serve them, but don't try to flirt. It's too dangerous."

The girl tossed her head, then ran her fingers through her hair, pulling out the knots and tangles before absent-mindedly plaiting the thick tresses. When she spoke her voice was suspiciously meek. "Very well, Margery. I will be careful."

"Do. Not for me, but for yourself, Sarra. You're far too good to waste yourself on the likes of them. You spend more time with the apprentice if you want to marry, and leave this captain to Cristine. She knows how to control men like him."

After she had gone, the girl stood for a moment or two, staring into the middle-distance while her fingers deftly arranged her hair. Then, giving a short giggle, she tugged off her tunic and dressed in clean shift and skirts.

Sir Hector de Gorsone sat back and let the warmth of the alcohol seep into his tired frame. His men were seated all round, with pitchers of beer before them. It was too late in the summer for wine to be available; that would not be shipped in until later, when the weather was cooler and the drink would not spoil so quickly. Ah, how he looked forward to returning to Gascony where the wine would be fresh and strong! After so many years on the continent, wine suited him better. Ale bloated him.

The hall was like any number of inns he had stayed in, and to his way of thinking, they were all hovels. He was too used to good French buildings. Long and ramshackle, it was filled with the vinegar-sweet stench of stale alcohol and rotting food, which lay on the rushes where it had been tossed by other diners. Dark and comfortless it looked to the knight, but the glow of the braziers and sconces created islands of cheeriness. Benches and tables stood haphazardly, and round these the serving-girls and the innkeeper circulated, trying to satisfy the guests by keeping pots filled with ale and trenchers with pottage and bread. The shutters were tightly barred to keep out the night's chill, and only their rattling proved that there was a strong wind outside.

Sir Hector yawned, then turned his attention back to his thoughts. He was determined, once he had power or wealth enough, to possess a property in the country, away from the squalor of urban life. He wanted a place with extensive buildings to house his retinue. In towns the amount of land available was restricted by the burgesses, so that all should have adequate space. Sir Hector wanted none of that. He was after an estate, with a good-sized manor house at the heart of it, where he could take a wife and begin his family. The road to success and riches which he had trodden was losing its luster. He was tempted to try a life of peace, and start a new dynasty. But first he needed more money.

He sat at the end of the hall, from where he could see his men and the doorway to the screens. There was no chimney; the fireplace in the middle had access to the roof, in which there was a simple pottery louvre to allow the smoke to escape. The wind was gusting, and added another unpleasant aspect to the hall as smoke fitfully wafted around the room, making Sir Hector cough.

His men were determined to enjoy themselves, he could see. There were three girls, and they ran the gauntlet of ribald jokes and grasping hands wherever they went. Two, he saw, were practiced tavern wenches, slapping at unwanted hands or offering quick responses which inevitably made the men howl with laughter, usually at another's expense. Every now and again one of his men would offer a fresh sally, and then redden or roar as it was rebuffed. The scene was one he had witnessed in taverns and alehouses from London to Rome, but the sight still brought a faint smile to his otherwise ill-humored features.

One girl caught his eye. She looked younger than the others and less worldly-wise. Where the older women used stinging rebukes to respond to the offers made at each table, this one moved quietly from place to place, apparently embarrassed at the more personal questions hurled at her. She was less experienced at avoiding the hands which reached for her, and seemed nervous of resisting forcefully. She reminded the knight of a hunted deer held at bay, aware that the end must be soon, but not knowing which of the slavering monsters would be first to reach her.

As he watched, he saw the two talking. Henry the Hurdle and John Smithson were ever together, always acted in concert. Now Henry stood as the girl approached down the narrow aisle formed by two long tables, and under the lewd encouragement of his mates, he moved toward her. She could only stand, staring at him with fear in her eyes. When she turned at last to flee, John was already there, cutting off her escape.

One of the girls tried to get to her, but she was blocked by men who grinned through their beards, hoping she would try to break through them to reach her friend so that they could manhandle her. Cristine was crippled by indecision: should she run and get help, or fight her way to Sarra to protect her? While she deliberated, Henry moved the pots from the table before him and smiled at the girl. Then he gestured at the empty space, inviting her forward.

"Stop!"

The single word, not bellowed, but merely spoken with authority, sliced through the noise and tension like a sword of war cleaving bone. For Sarra, it was like hearing the war-cry of a protective knight-errant, and she looked at the knight by the fire with a rising hope. Her heart was thumping painfully, and in the quiet she felt it was deafening her; she was convinced that all in the hall must be able to hear it. The jug which she gripped with both hands was shaking, and she carefully set it down on a table nearby. There was an emptiness in her belly which would soon rise to sickness, so great was her relief at being saved. That she had been going to be raped she did not doubt.

"Leave her. You, girl! Come and serve me here. Bring ale."

Sir Hector watched her retrieve her jug and approach. When she was close he held out his pewter jug imperiously, and studied her face as she poured. There was a light down on her arms and face, he saw, and her lips, though tightly pursed, were full and moist. When his mug was filled, she stood a short way back and met his gaze. His eyebrows rose. He could see that she was not scared of him—of the men under him, yes, but not he himself, and he admired her spirit. Her eyes were the light blue-gray of a winter's sky, and a little of her golden hair escaped from her net. She was not the heavily-built peasant girl he would have expected to find in a small town, but a radiant young woman who would grace the hall of a wealthier man than he.

"Stay here, and serve me," he said gently. "Do not fear my men. They will leave you alone now."

She nodded in slow and thoughtful agreement, and then gave him a smile of such warmth that he had to return it.

Outside, the innkeeper let his breath escape in a whistle of relief as he slumped back against the wall. Margery rushed up breathlessly. "What's happening? Is she all right?"

"Thanks be to God! Yes, she is. The knight protected her; called his men off."

She peered round the doorway. "She's lucky. With that lot, there's no telling how far they'd have gone."

"No. But at least she's safe enough for now."

"Right. Well, I'd better get back in there."

The innkeeper nodded glumly as she passed by, freshly filled jugs in each hand. He watched as she poured with the quick efficiency of a practiced alewife, neatly sidestepping to avoid a dozen ambushes as she made her way along one side of the hall. He had more pressing difficulties. Sir Hector still insisted on keeping all his men with him, and no suggestions as to where they could be housed carried any weight with him. For the innkeeper, the thought of standing up to the knight and refusing to allow his men to remain was not one to make him feel entirely at ease. Usually Paul would place additional guests in the hall, where they could use the benches or even lie under the tables, and any overflow could use the stables, but with men like these he was sure that such simple solutions would not suffice: the newcomers would demand the best beds, but the existing guests would complain about being evicted from their accommodation.

Leaning against the doorway, his eyes fixed on the hall as he worried over his problem, he did not notice the men who entered from the stableyard. The hall comprised one half of the main building, the other consisting of kitchen, buttery and stores area. Splitting the building was the screens passage where the innkeeper now stood, and from this corridor two doors led to the hall itself. To his horror, he now saw three men stride in. Two were the goldsmith and his apprentice; he did not recognize the third. Stupefied, he could do nothing but stand and watch the disaster unfold before him.

Sir Hector saw them at the same time. He paused, his mug held out to Sarra as she filled it, studying the newcomers with interest. His face registered only mild amusement while he took in the rich fabrics of the goldsmith, the fur trimming on his coat and the heavy rings on his fingers. Walking in briskly, his attitude proclaimed him to be a self-important, busy man with no time to spare for the pleasures available to commoners. Following on close behind, head down, clad in simple hose and shirt, was his apprentice. Sir Hector gave a small smile and motioned toward Henry, who nodded and made his way to the two men.

Sir Hector sipped his ale. His men were a rough group, he knew, but at least a few of them knew how to obey. Henry was a good man when he was properly directed. So long as he knew what was expected, he could achieve results. As a soldier he was excellent material, due in large part to his cruel nature, but also to his greed. He was one of the mercenaries who had swiftly realized that the best way to get rich was by holding the surrounding areas to ransom. Extortion, and the constant threat of a *chevauchée* to destroy all the crops and village stores, were Henry's more effective methods of squeezing a profit even from the most desolate-looking districts. It was Henry and his friend John who had helped in the last few campaigns in Gascony, always seeking out the best hostages to ransom, the most promising buildings to raid, the richer merchants to rob. Their zeal for relieving others of their possessions had helped Sir Hector to build up his own fortune, but they did not begrudge him his wealth. They knew they were indispensable to him and, as such, were safe. He would not want to dispose of them while they continued to enrich his coffers.

That mutual reliance was the reason why Sir Hector often gave them special tasks, treating them as his trusted sergeants. He glanced up to see the goldsmith, now ashen-faced, rushing from the room amid the jeers and catcalls of the other men sitting round. The sight made him give a dry smile.

The innkeeper had been called to the buttery and, leaving it, he nearly collided with the goldsmith. "Ah, master, hello. Would you like some—"

"How much do I owe you?"

Paul's face fell. The goldsmith was trying to smile, but his quivering mouth told the lie. "Are you well, sir?" His voice hardened. "Is it something those buggers in there have said? If they've been threatening you, I'll—"

"No, no. It's nothing like that, it's just that I have to leave Crediton. A matter of business, you understand. I . . . er . . . I have to get to Exeter. Some problems there. I—" He broke off, noticing the apprentice sulking nearby. "I told you to go and get our things: see to it at once! *Apprentices!* All they ever think of is food and women," he added restlessly, feigning a world-weary distraction in an attempt to cover his agitation.

Paul was irritated by the goldsmith's pretence that he had no fear of the mercenaries and plenty of time to discuss insignificant points with an innkeeper.

The man gave a sickly smile. "I fear you may not have noticed, but he has been making a complete fool of himself over that young wench of yours. Stupid, I know, but there's little I can do about it."

While Paul tried to persuade the smith not to leave, though not too enthusiastically because he feared the mercenaries' response should they find their plans thwarted, Sarra glowed with pride at the right hand of Sir Hector.

It was all very well for Margery to tell her to leave

the soldiers alone, but the captain had already taken an interest in her, and anyway, Sarra was sure that Margery's warnings were prompted more by jealousy than genuine concern; the jealousy of an older, careworn woman for a young girl. Why should Sarra not get attention—for she was surely the most attractive of the women at the inn. Margery's problem was she was so old she had forgotten what it felt like to be young and desired. And Sarra had a businesslike streak to her thoughts: all her friends had to work until they were almost thirty, trying to save some money to be able to marry upon. They were almost past child-bearing age already before they wed. Sarra wanted none of that. She was young and wished to marry before she grew much older, so that she could bear lots of children and enjoy the rewards a wealthy husband could bestow. This man was surely the wealthiest she had ever known. She had seen the chests of silver and plate being carried to his room. A person with so many valuables must be rich beyond her dreams.

If she had been given even a little education, Sarra's life might have been very different. Her brain was quick and intuitive, and she often offended others unintentionally by slicing through their long preambles when she could see their point in a few words. Work for her was a tedious exercise, necessary to keep her clothed and fed until she could find a husband, but her mind constantly sought diversions. Through the boredom of days with little to do, she had enjoyed a recurring daydream: a wealthy lord would arrive at the inn, maybe wounded from a fall, and only she could bind his wounds sufficiently to save him. Afterward he would be so devoted to his savior that he would press his suit upon her. There were endless permutations to the basic theme, involving her protecting him from robbers or assassins, to the most basic in which she spurned his expressions of adoration only to be persuaded when he carried her off to his castle.

Her ability to invent and add to her store of pleasant fantasies was one protection from the dullness of her toil, and now there was a possibility of the realization of her dreams. She glanced into Sir Hector's eyes as she poured more ale. Catching her look, he subjected her to a serious study for a moment.

She was certainly comely, he thought. Her hair was rapidly coming loose from its moorings, lending her firm and youthful body a deliciously wanton look. Her eyes were bright and swift to smile, if not bold or experienced. He could not wish for a better companion for a couple of days, and when he saw her eyes fall and the blush rise to her neck and cheeks, he felt sure that her thoughts had turned the same way. Her response delighted him, and he turned away confident in the knowledge that his bed would be warm that night.

Henry had not yet returned to his seat, he saw, and a quick frown crossed his brow. The third man who had entered with the goldsmith was still by the doorway, staring at him.

This was no wealthy merchant or burgess. He stood clad in a simple tunic and short hose, both of a green turned pale by overuse. A russet cloak was draped over his shoulders, and a hood darkened his features. No sword hung from his belt, only a long knife. He appeared to be hesitating, and Sir Hector watched his indecision with amusement. He was sure it must be caused by the revelry in the hall; the newcomer must soon decide it would be better to leave and find another tavern.

To his surprise, the man started moving toward him, weaving through the throng of soldiers with casual self-confidence.

"Are you Sir Hector de Gorsone?"

- 3 -

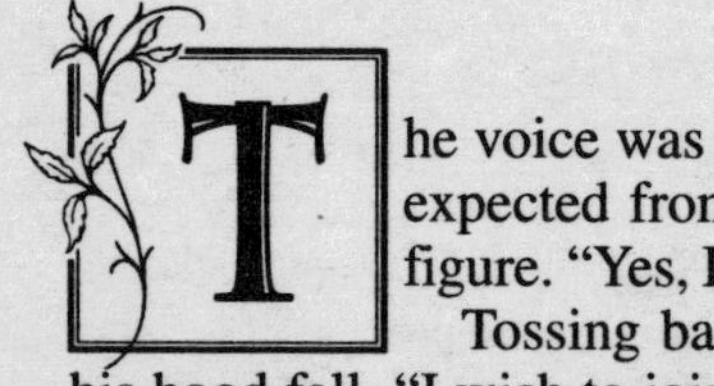

The voice was more youthful than he had expected from such a broad-shouldered figure. "Yes, I am Sir Hector," he replied.

Tossing back his head, the visitor let his hood fall. "I wish to join your band."

For the second time that evening the hall fell silent. The knight found himself faced by a young man, no more than nineteen or twenty, with long wavy hair the color of unfired clay. His face was narrow and clean-shaven, with a high forehead and narrow nose which was marred by freckles. A thin mouth pointed to obstinacy of character, and the wide-set green eyes showed that he had a serious nature, not given to jokes.

"I have enough men already," said Sir Hector dismissively.

"One more can always be of help at need."

"Have you been trained to fight?"

"No, sir. But I am young and strong. You can teach me."

"Why should I? There are others I could pick from."

"I'm healthy and loyal. I want to go with your band and learn your ways. I am sick to death of farming. Let me come with you."

Sir Hector opened his mouth to refuse the insolent puppy, but then allowed himself to reconsider. The young man was a tempting addition to the band. He was solidly built and looked capable of using his hands. There was a determined cast to his mouth, the captain saw, a look of resolution. He carried himself well, straight and tall, moving with an almost feline ease and sureness, and the breadth of his shoulders pointed to strength. He was still now, one hand resting on his dagger-hilt, the other on his purse. There was an aura of purpose and dignity about him which, as Sir Hector knew well, many abbots would do well to emulate.

Out of interest, he let his gaze wander over his men. They sat quietly, for the most part, watching their captain and waiting to see how he would react. One or two were grinning, obviously expecting him to issue a devastating rejection. The look irritated him. He had selected them all in similar ways: he had never felt the need to seek out new recruits—they accumulated round a successful captain as a matter of course. All the men in this room had come to him after hearing about his triumphs, just like this new one. Why should he throw him out when he had accepted them?

"You look brave enough," he said at last, slowly. "It takes courage to enter a hall like this and ask a favor in front of men you know nothing about." The stranger inclined his head in acknowledgment, a curiously cynical smile twisting his mouth.

"Come here." Passing his mug to Sarra, the knight leaned forward and motioned the newcomer to his knees. When he knelt, Sir Hector took both his hands between his own. "Swear to be loyal to me and to take orders from me and no other."

"I so swear."

"Good. Henry? Take this man and show him how we are organized. See to his weapons."

"Thank you, Sir Hector," the youth said as he stood.

The knight raised a quizzical eyebrow. "Do not thank me yet. I can be a hard master, but if you show loyalty and are prepared to follow my commands, I will be good to you."

Sarra watched as the stranger walked away with the man who had tried to attack her. He was a handsome lad, she thought. It was a shame that he was going to be indoctrinated by an evil oaf like Henry.

"So what's your name?" Henry was intrigued by his new charge, who hardly glanced at him as he answered: "Philip Cole."

Some echo in the name made Henry give a fleeting frown, but they were at their table, and Cole was maneuvering himself into a gap at the bench so he missed the brief grimace. Henry barged in to sit at Cole's left, while to the young man's right sat a rough-looking rat-faced fellow with hair as black as a crow's feathers. His amber eyes roved restlessly around the room as if looking for someone more interesting to talk to, and the candles and sconces reflected in them. To Cole they looked alive with devious, glittering intelligence. Together with the blackened teeth in a slack and dribbling mouth, he possessed an air which gave Cole a feeling of revulsion. His frame was whip-thin and wiry but there was strength and cruelty in the long fingers that tore at the chicken before him.

Henry introduced him. "This is John Smithson. He's like me, one of the old men of the band."

"That's right. We were two of the first to join Sir Hector."

"That was back in 1309. In Gascony."

Cole accepted a pot from a passing waitress. "So you must have fought in many battles?" he asked, carefully keeping his tone level.

John smiled. "Yes, all over. For one master and then for another."

"It's a good life," Henry sighed, taking a huge draft of ale and belching. "Others are told to join an army and fight, but we can go where we want and fight for whoever we want. We are more free than any burgess or farmer."

"Yes—and we can make more money from it," said John slyly.

His friend laughed. "Aye, and keep it!"

"What do you mean?" asked Cole.

"Just this," Henry said, leaning toward him. "In a lord's army, if you were called up to fight, you would be there because of your master and fighting for him. Any money you won would be his; any hostages you wanted to ransom would be his—you would have no rights. With us, we fight for ourselves. If we win a prize, we keep it. Any spoils go to the winner, and the devil with the losers."

"They rarely live anyway," said John casually as he bit into a haunch of chicken.

Henry noticed Cole's expression. "Don't worry, Sir Hector is a good master. He doesn't lose, and has few men hurt under him. He's more likely to change sides when the wind blows sour than stay and be hacked to death. There's no profit in winning a coffin."

Cole held his tongue, but nodded as if eased.

Turning to his food, Henry hid a smile. Philip Cole had the typical look of a peasant, one of unfocused goodwill, with bovine slowness of thought and general dullness. Laughing, Henry slapped the recruit on the back. "No need for the long face! You'll soon find yourself rich enough to be happy." Henry had open, friendly features which had deceived more experienced men than Cole, and the thick shock of sandy hair made him look much younger than the scars and wrinkles promised; his age was only given away by his strength. Though his arms were short, ending with stubby little fingers, they held enough power to make Cole think, when he was thumped genially over the shoulders, that he had been buffeted by a benign but clumsy giant. "Don't worry—if Sir Hector isn't there, John and me'll look after you, won't we, John?"

"Oh, yes."

"Uhn . . . thanks," said Cole, feeling that some response was required.

Glancing round cautiously, Henry leaned nearer. "So why did *you* want to get away?"

"Eh?"

"Why did you want to get away? Everyone has a reason. I had to run because I killed a man—in a fair fight, you understand, but the hue was raised after me."

"And I had to get away because my master's wife fancied me. I was apprenticed to a smith, and when I rejected her, she told him I'd put my hands up her skirt and tried to tempt her into my bed. I had to get away before he could catch me. He was going to kill me," John added in an aggrieved tone. "With an axe."

"So what made *you* want to run? We all tell each other everything here. There's no need to be shy." Henry smiled encouragingly.

"I . . . I was to become a father."

"Ah." Henry winked knowingly.

"And I did not wish to marry."

"A girl from your own village, I expect. Where was that? Are you from round here?"

"No. I come from north and east of here, a short way from Exeter—a village called Thorverton."

"Ah yes. Is it far from here?" asked Henry.

Cole shot him a glance, wondering if his story was being checked. Before he could respond, though, the rat-faced one nudged him, pointing with a chicken bone.

"Well, if you want to try some of the women here, just make sure you don't touch her."

He followed the line of the bone. Sarra was laughing at a remark made by the smiling knight. "She's his, is she?"

Henry's voice was somber. "There's one thing you must learn quickly, Philip. Our master is a good warrior and leader, but he won't have anyone messing with his belongings. It doesn't matter if it's his money, horses, or women. If he finds someone near any of them he's likely to reach for his knife. No, I'd leave her alone until he tires of her. He always does, sooner or later."

"You stay with us. We remember what it's like to be new, that's why Sir Hector usually asks us to look after the recruits. He knows we'll show them all the ropes."

"Yes. For instance, your purse looks quite full. There're some would try to take it, just to see what's inside."

"There's only money in it," Cole said easily.

"God's blood! Well, don't tell any of the others!" Henry whispered urgently, and sat back, perplexed. "There are men here who'd cut your throat just for *thinking* you had something there. If you don't go carefully, you'll get yourself hurt."

"He's right, you know," John muttered darkly, eyes flitting over the other figures in the hall. "Some of the men here, they can't be trusted. They'd sell their wives—some of them probably have—for a purse like yours. I reckon you'd best stick with us, let us look after you for a bit."

"Yes. I mean, where you came from, Thorverton way, I expect you never had to worry about thieves or murderers, did you? When you left your girl . . . what was her name?" Henry asked, but his mind was fixed on the purse. If Cole was a mere peasant from a small village, he could not have collected so much money.

"Who?"

"Your woman. The one you left home for."

"Oh." He wavered a moment. "Anne. Anne Fraunceys."

Henry did not miss the slight hesitation, and his grin broadened. It pointed to invention, and if that part of the story was invented there was sure to be a better secret, a more valuable one, behind this young man's decision to join the company. Henry intended to root it out, but he could already guess that there was a theft at the bottom of it. A runaway farmer would not legally be able to get his hands on enough money to make a wallet the size of his bulge so attractively.

"Well, when you left your Anne, you were just a free man with little fear of the world, weren't you?" he said genially. "At your home you could walk around without a sword or axe and know you'd be safe, couldn't you? Here, though, you're with a troop of men-at-arms, and some of 'em are dangerous. You waving a purse under their noses is like showing a dog a bitch on heat. They'll have to try to take it, see? You stay with us, though. We'll look after you."

"Yes. We'll protect you like you were our own family." John smiled, displaying his noisome teeth once more.

Cole looked from one to the other, and when they slapped him on the back in a show of good-natured friendship, he smiled back gratefully. A few minutes later he bent to eat, and Henry and John exchanged a look over his back. Slowly, John winked.

Paul, the innkeeper, was unable to sit down in the buttery until well into the night. The cries and laughter had gradually faded as men fell asleep—some, like the captain himself, staggering to individual rooms. Sir Hector had gone at least three hours ago, Paul thought distractedly, wiping his forehead with his towel, so *he* at least would be asleep by now.

A step behind him heralded the arrival of his wife. "Margery? I thought you'd have gone to bed by now."

She sank down onto the bench beside him, gazing round the little room with its wreckage of empty barrels, pots and jugs. "I'd better start a new brew tomorrow," she said tiredly. Her face was gray even in the yellow candlelight, and the lines at either side of her mouth were like slashes in her skin. Even her green tunic and off-white apron hung dispiritedly as if overfatigued. She pulled her wimple free and scratched her hair loose.

He put out a hand and touched her arm. "I'm sorry I couldn't get some of them to move, but at least they've not caused any trouble. There's not been any fighting or anything."

"What of the other guests? What happened to them?"

"They've all decided to go. The goldsmith and his apprentice were first, then the burgess from Bath, then the merchant and his family . . . They all found they had important business elsewhere and had to move on—always shortly after one of the captain's men had spoken to them. I suppose we should be grateful no one was hurt. There was no violence."

In answer she shrugged, a tiny gesture of exhaustion. "No, and they've done little damage—just some broken jugs, and they can soon be replaced. Let's hope they'll be gone tomorrow."

"I don't know about that. I heard one of them talking earlier, and he was saying they might stay for a few nights more."

"I hope not!"

He could sympathize with her hostility. They were used to quieter guests: merchants, clerics and burgesses. It was rare for them to have more than ten staying at the inn, and a group of thirty, all men-at-arms, was unheard of. The money would be welcome, if they did not argue too much about the charge but, as Paul knew, this kind of client was all too likely to balk at the real cost of the stay. Soldiers were prone to preying on the fears of peaceable folk to try to force large discounts. Paul sighed; he would have to add a goodly portion to the amount they had drunk so that he could haggle over the final reckoning. Otherwise he would end up subsidizing their stay, and that was something he could ill-afford.

His wife's mind was on the same problem. "It's not just the food and drink, is it? We've got the fodder for their horses to buy in as well. What if they refuse to pay enough?"

"We'll have to see," he said comfortingly, patting her knee.

She smiled, but then her face hardened. "You know where Sarra's gone?"

"Sarra?" He could not meet her gaze.

"With him," she said. "With their captain. She's gone to his chamber with him."

Paul sighed. "She's old enough to know what she's doing, Margery."

"Old enough? She may be old enough, but she obviously doesn't realize!" his wife said hotly. "You know how hopeless she is: her head's up in the clouds most of the time. And what about *him*? You know as well as I do what sort of man *he* is. He's just taking advantage of her, and she'll get nothing from him."

"Margery, she is old enough to know her own mind," he repeated. "And if he is taking advantage, what can we do?"

"She thought he might marry her; you know what a romantic fool she is."

"In that case she was trying to take advantage of *him* as well," Paul said reasonably.

"But what if she gets with child? He won't want to help her then, will he? We'll be the ones left holding the baby!"

The innkeeper squeezed her hand. "We'll just have to see what we can do for the best if it comes to it."

"But what if she *does* have a child? She can't look after it, can she? And I wouldn't want to see her on the street like Judith and her poor Rollo." Her eyes widened. "Rollo! You know what they say about the boy. Perhaps . . ."

"Enough, Margery," he said and stood up. "It's time we were going to our own beds. It's late, and we have much to do in the morning to get this mess straight. If there is a child, we'll see what should be done then. I'm not going to worry about it now. Come, let's go to bed."

She stared up at him, a little angry at being put off, but then gave a self-mocking smile and rose. "Very well, husband. But I'd be happier if that stupid girl had left him alone."

"Maybe she'll have cause to regret her actions too," Paul said, glancing in the direction of the room where Sarra and the captain now lay, as if he could see through the wattle and timber. For some reason, he had a hollow feeling in the pit of his stomach; he recognized it as a premonition of something evil about to happen, and the awareness made him shudder.

- 4 -

It was two days later that the knight of Furnshill, Baldwin, strode out into the sunshine with a feeling of impending doom. The morning was clear and bright, small clouds like freshly cleaned balls of fleece hung suspended in a deep blue sky, and the sound of larks singing high overhead, the chirruping of the tits in the bushes, and the raucous, chuckling sqawks of blackbirds scurrying off, flying inches from the ground in urgent panic at his appearance, gave him a momentary respite from his black mood.

Tall, with brown hair shot through with silver and a neat black beard which just followed the line of his jaw, Baldwin was an anachronistic figure for a modern knight. Most men went cleanshaven these days, like his friend Simon Puttock, the bailiff of Lydford; few sported even a moustache. Nor did his dress follow the latest fashion for ostentatious display, for he preferred to appear in a stained old tunic which hung loosely until nipped in at his belt. Other knights would have commented on his shabby old boots, which hardly had any toe at all, and did not match the modern courtly trend for elongated points curling back toward the ankle. A long scar marked Sir Baldwin's cheek, stretching from temple to jaw; the sole remaining evidence of a lively past.

As his attire showed, Sir Baldwin Furnshill was not like other men in this increasingly secular world. He had been a warrior monk, one of the Knights Templar, until the Order had been disbanded; with its destruction his own faith in the church had been shattered. Now forty-six, he was well into his middle age and content to spend the remainder of his life as a rural knight, leading a quiet existence, avoiding the pomp of tournaments and other royal festivals. The supposed excitements of life at the center of politics bored him, not because he disliked power, but because he saw those that sought it to be manipulative and unprincipled. His own experience had led him to doubt the honor of those at the very pinnacle of political and religious authority, and the thought of circulating among men who were, to his mind, corrupt and dishonest was unattractive to him.

At a time when King Edward II was so ineffectual, this was not a common point of view. Many wished to get close to the monarch, hoping that by proximity they would be able to snatch the control which constantly eluded Edward himself. Baldwin Furnshill was happier leaving such machinations and knavery to others. For himself, he was content to stay in Devon and find satisfaction in his work, leaving the administration of the nation to those who felt they had an aptitude for it.

But there were times when he could not help becoming involved, and this was one of them. As he thought of his meeting, his face took on a glowering aspect, and the beauty of the countryside ahead could not relieve his sudden ill-humor.

This was usually his favorite position, before his old long house, looking down to the south. The building itself was on rising land, and in front the ground fell away for a short distance. Apart from a small hillock, there was nothing to obscure the view, and Baldwin often came out here to sit on the old tree-trunk to consider any problems he had, letting his mind range over issues and solutions while he gazed into the distance.

Today he knew he would not find peace. He seated himself, resting his arms on his thighs and staring, but could not see a way out of it.

The problem had its roots in his acceptance two years before of the position of Keeper of the King's Peace. At the time he had been wary of taking on the responsibility, knowing that it must inevitably embroil him in any arguments or disputes which exercised the local population, but holding magisterial powers meant that he could at least display a little restraint with some of the more paltry of crimes, and he had managed to help in two serious investigations over the last two or three years, bringing two murderers to justice. That was the positive side; the negative side lay in the inevitable calls to meet others who felt he was important enough to be courted.

And now he had been asked to go to Peter Clifford's to meet Walter Stapledon.

He sighed, forcing himself to sit upright and scowling at a house so far off near the horizon it appeared as a mere splash of white among the green of the trees which surrounded it. If there *was* a way to avoid the meeting, he failed to see it.

It was not that he disliked Stapledon—he had never met the man—but the Bishop of Exeter was an astute politician, not a mere priest. In late 1316 Walter Stapledon had helped create a new movement which strove to break the deadlock between the King and his cousin, Thomas of Lancaster. Acrimonious disputes between Edward II and his Steward of England had led to the brink of civil war, and Walter and his friends had managed to avert it only through skilled negotiation.

And now Baldwin was invited to meet him . . . The knight set his jaw: there was only one reason why the Bishop would want to meet *him*, and that was to force him to declare his allegiances. Baldwin had few loyalties: in the main he recognized a commitment to his villeins, but that was as far as his convictions took him. From his bitter experience, prelates and kings were equally capable of squashing people with as little compunction as they would a flea if there was a profit in it, and he saw no need to ally himself to any of them. He was reluctant to meet the imposing Bishop and be questioned, but there was no way to evade the invitation; he would have to go.

There was one silver lining to this storm cloud: his old friend Simon Puttock would also be there. Peter Clifford's messenger had taken special care to mention that the bailiff to Lydford and his wife would be visiting Peter at the same time. This carefully appended comment showed how alive Peter was to the knight's antipathy to politicians, and Baldwin had nearly laughed when the youth had recited his message, frowning with concentration: "And my master said to be sure to tell you that Simon Puttock, bailiff of Lydford, will also be there, and his family. He knows you will want to see them. They will be joining my master for supper."

Baldwin snorted.

Yes, he would have to go and meet this Bishop—but

he must be alive to the risks and take care not to become embroiled in any political matters.

As it happened, the meeting with Stapledon was the least of his difficulties that night.

Peter Clifford's house was a pleasant, airy building near the new church, which was still some way from being completed. Piles of rubble and masonry waiting to be dressed lay all round in untidy heaps as if a siege had been in progress with heavy artillery. When Baldwin arrived at a little after noon, his servant by his side, he gazed about the place with interest.

The walls of the new church looked to him like the wharves of a busy port: the scaffolding rose on all sides like the thrusting masts and flag-poles of a fleet in harbor. He paused at the sight, studying the grotesque structure of the scaffolding, all bound together with hemp and with walkways of flimsy timber, with a wince. Baldwin feared no man alive—he had witnessed the worst sufferings that men could inflict—but he had a dislike verging on loathing when it came to heights. He could not understand how men could scramble along such insubstantial planks like monkeys, putting their faith in the strength of knots tied by others. Too many regularly died, proving that such faith was misplaced.

"So, Baldwin. You've not lost your distrust of English workers then, to judge from the disgust on your face?"

Just by his stirrup was a tall, dark-haired man with a square face burned brown from sun and wind and, as Baldwin turned, he gave a slow smile.

"Simon!" The knight passed his reins to Edgar, his waiting servant, and dropped from his horse. In a moment he was shaking hands and grinning, but the expression on his friend's face made him hesitate. There was a pinched tiredness in Simon's grin which he had not seen before. It looked as if the bailiff was concealing a secret pain.

"Baldwin, it's good to see you again."

"It's good to see you too."

Pulling away, Simon said thinly, attempting humor, "Oh yes—just so you have someone to talk to while the good Bishop is spouting forth about affairs of state, you mean?"

Baldwin grimaced shamefacedly. "Well, not entirely, old friend, but your company would help to—perhaps—divert the conversation from some of the more serious affairs of state."

"I hope so," Simon laughed. "If not, Margaret will slit my throat."

"Margaret is here?"

"Where else should my wife be, but at my side? Yes, she's here."

While Edgar led the horses away to the stables, they walked to Peter's house, but before they arrived at the door Baldwin took his friend by the arm and halted, studying him. Simon had lost weight; his face was thinner than Baldwin recalled, and lines of strain were etched deep into his forehead and at either side of his mouth. His dark hair had begun to recede, giving him a distinguished appearance, but his gray eyes, once sparkling with intelligence, were now dim and vapid. "Simon, tell me if I am prying where I'm not wanted, but is there something wrong?" Baldwin said gently.

"You're my closest friend," Simon said, and the other man was shocked to see his eyes glisten. "I . . . You can't intrude, Baldwin, I have no secrets from you." He looked away and said in a broken voice: "It's Peterkin, my boy."

The knight frowned in quick concern. Peterkin was Simon and Margaret's son, a lad of just over a year and a half. "What is it, Simon?"

"He's dead."

"Simon . . . I'm so sorry."

"It's all right. I'm almost over it. It has been hard, though. You know how much we both wanted a son, and to have lost him like this is very cruel."

"When? I mean, how did he die?"

Simon made a futile little gesture. "Three weeks ago. He had been fractious for some time, crying and whining, but we didn't know why. For a day and a night he had a fever, and wouldn't eat, diarrhea all the time, and then . . . And then he was dead."

"My friend, I . . ." Baldwin murmured, but Simon shook his head.

"It's all right, Baldwin."

"And Margaret?"

"She has taken it cruelly. It's not surprising." His voice was taut.

"Let us go inside," said Baldwin. Simon's anguish, though he tried to keep it under control, was painful to witness. The knight could feel his misery.

They walked into the house. Inside, Baldwin saw Simon's wife sitting by the fire, her daughter Edith at her side. Behind them was Hugh, Simon's servant, and a short way away Peter Clifford sat on his chair. Baldwin was glad that the Bishop had not yet arrived—a stranger's presence would have inhibited Margaret. As it was, she had little desire to talk. The knight nodded to Peter, who gave him a twisted grin. He had been a close friend of Simon's since before Baldwin had met the bailiff, yet he found it difficult to know what to say to them. Peter had never married, and consoling those who had lost their children was, he felt, beyond his powers. It was a relief for him to see another friend arrive.

Rather than greet the priest, Baldwin walked over to Margaret and knelt before her, his sword scabbard clattering on the flagged floor as he took her hands in his. "Margaret, I have just heard about Peterkin. I am terribly sorry. There's nothing I can do or say which will ease your loss, but you know you have my deepest sympathy."

"Baldwin, thank you." She gave him a fragile smile. "Of course we miss him awfully. We can only hope that God grants us another son to take his place."

Peter Clifford leaned forward and patted her hand. "He will, my dear. He will. Keep your faith, and He will send more children to lighten your life."

Margaret sat still and made no comment, holding Baldwin's gaze. To him she looked like a tragic figure from a Greek play. Usually tall and willowy, with the pale complexion and long fair hair that Baldwin associated with the women of the Holy Roman Empire, now she seemed shrivelled and wasted. Her skin, once soft as a fresh peach, looked dry and brittle, her hair, which he had only ever seen carefully braided and held in its net, straggled carelessly, making her seem much older.

"He was our first son," she murmured. "After seven years, we had managed to have a brother for our daughter. And now he has been snatched away from us."

Baldwin wanted to console her, but could think of nothing to say. He got up, staring down at her, while she, as if unaware of his presence, gazed at the floor. Across the room, Simon stood, wretched. The bailiff was transfixed by his wife's heartbreak, but trapped by his own feelings of loss, he had no idea how to soothe her.

The knight quietly stepped away from Margaret. Now he was glad he had come, if only to protect Margaret and her husband from any comments made by the Bishop. As he moved away he saw her hand grip her daughter's convulsively. It looked like a desperate attempt to hold on to her, as if by doing so she could protect Edith's precious life and save her from being stolen away as well.

Walter Stapledon arrived an hour after Baldwin, but the atmosphere had not improved. Peter Clifford was out of the room when Baldwin heard the blowing and stamping of horses in the yard, and he noticed a nervous young canon leaping to his feet in alarm at the realization that Peter was not there to welcome his guests. Motioning to him, Baldwin said, "Fetch your master. I will entertain Bishop Stapledon." The lad immediately ran from the room, and Baldwin, sighing, left the Puttocks and their servant alone for a moment. His own servant, Edgar, followed along behind him.

Outside, he found a fair retinue of six men dismounting from their horses, grumbling and muttering as they rubbed sore backs and stretched stiff joints. There was one clerical type he could see, a man in a plain robe, climbing down from a wagon, and Baldwin made his way to him. "Bishop?"

"Not him. *I* am Bishop Stapledon."

Baldwin spun round. Behind him was a man in his sixties, wearing a plain cloak and tunic, both of good quality and cut. At his belt was a short sword, the grip worn from regular use. Graying hair cut fashionably sat atop what looked like a warrior's head, and Baldwin was reminded of the leaders of the Templars. He had the same aristocratic haughtiness, bred of a long family history and awareness of his power. When Baldwin glanced down he was not surprised to see that the Bishop's boots were light and fashionable, the point rising elegantly, as befitted a courtier. It made him sigh.

"My Lord Bishop, Godspeed." Not knowing the man, Baldwin preferred to bow a little and give him the customary formal greeting.

"Godspeed." The Bishop had keen green-brown eyes which were perpetually on the brink of smiling, as if he was genuinely happy with his lot and saw no reason to be otherwise; Baldwin found himself liking the look of him. While the knight introduced himself and explained that Peter was supervising food in the kitchen, Stapledon nodded absently and issued a string of commands to his men. In minutes two servants were leading horses to the stables, while others lifted chests and bags from the wagon and carried them inside.

It was just as he was about to walk in that Baldwin asked him for a word in confidence.

"Of course, Sir Baldwin. What is it?"

The green eyes held his while he explained. "My friend Simon Puttock, the bailiff of Lydford Castle, has just lost his son, my lord. I fear it is not a cheerful gathering you have come to."

"How old was the boy?"

"Eighteen or twenty months."

"Good God! Ah well, we must see what we can do to divert them in their sadness, mustn't we, Roger?"

This was addressed to a young man, clad in simple

clerical gear of cassock, gown and hood. He was introduced to Baldwin as Roger de Grosse, the son of Sir Arnold in Exeter. Baldwin had heard of Sir Arnold de Grosse; he was a patron of a number of churches in Devon and Cornwall. Now, it appeared, he had decided his son should become a rector.

"Do you have a church selected for you?" Baldwin asked.

"Er . . . yes, sir. Callington. We have just been visiting it in Cornwall. I hope to be confirmed in my position soon," he said nervously, casting a sidelong glance at the Bishop.

Baldwin indicated the entrance and they made their way inside. Trailing along behind the great politician and man of God, Baldwin had a twinge of doubt as to whether he had done the right thing in warning him about Simon and his wife, but the fear was dispelled as soon as they went into the hall.

Peter had returned, and stood, flustered, as the Bishop walked in. They exchanged greetings, but then Walter went over to Margaret. "My lady, I am so sad to hear of your loss. I promise you, I will remember him, and you, in my prayers. You are an intelligent woman; you know that nothing I can do or say will reduce your grief, but think on this: although God has seen fit to take your boy from you, and that is for some reason we cannot yet comprehend, He did at least give you the gift of the boy in the first place. He might never have done that. That He did so means He may intend giving you another, and this one you may keep." As he stopped, her eyes filled with tears, and at first Baldwin was worried that he had upset her more, but then he saw her attempt a smile, and breathed a sigh of relief.

* * *

As midday crept into the afternoon, Paul sat in the inn's buttery, carefully totting up his profits. Though he could neither read nor write, he had no difficulty in calculating bills, and could keep a tally of six simultaneously when he needed to. With all his space being taken up by the captain's men-at-arms, he anticipated a cheerful reckoning at the end of their stay.

He was absolutely exhausted. The girls had run themselves off their feet, all but Sarra. He had quite failed to get the lass to bestir herself. The stupid girl had insisted that she was too tired to get up and work, when he went to her room—and when he roared that it was her fault for escorting the captain to his bedchamber, she had screeched at him to leave her alone or she would speak to Sir Hector about him. The threat was enough. His sole Parthian shot had been to point out that the captain and his men would soon be gone, and if she wanted to make sure she still had a job afterward, she should get out of bed and roll up her sleeves. It had not worked. He had not truly expected it to, for he knew how pig-headed she could be.

Soon he would have to go to the cookshop and collect the evening food. The captain and his men demolished stews, pottages and hams as if they had starved for months, and it was hard keeping up with them. What was even more difficult for the stressed innkeeper was trying to adjust to their hours. He, like most others in the town, relied on religious schedules for his meals. Up at dawn, he would have a short breakfast, ready for his main meal at nine and a supper in the afternoon. Rural lords would eat later, but they did not have to worry about fitting the regular round of jobs into their day and could afford to have others work to prepare their food. The captain and his men seemed happier rising late, the knight at nine, while some of his men were still abed at ten; they preferred their last meal to be both more substantial than the others and served later—much later. If the previous night was anything to go by, any time up to the middle of the night was fine.

Hearing a step, he glanced out into the screens and gave a wry smile. "Hello, Sarra."

The girl had not seen him, and he was surprised at the way she jumped when he called out. He was hidden slightly in the darkness of the buttery, while she was walking along the lighted screens: he must have surprised her.

"Did you have to do that?" she demanded, and to his amazement she was shaking with anger, white-faced and wide-eyed.

"I'm sorry, Sarra, I had no idea you'd be scared. I was only saying hello."

"I wasn't expecting you."

"No. Well, I'm sorry."

She flounced away, out through the door and into the bright sunlight of the yard behind the inn. Crossing it, ignoring the catcalls of two mercenaries at a table, she made her way to her room, and only when she had shut and bolted the door and could stand with her back to it, safe and secure once more in her old room, did she let her breath escape in a long hissing sigh of relief.

The fool had almost made her leap from her skin, the way he had called out to her. He wouldn't dare do that to anyone else, it was just because he thought of her as a silly wench, good only for serving and flattering the customers. It wasn't as if he had ever given her any responsibility, even.

Gradually she felt her heartbeat slow and could move from the door to the mattress, where she dropped down, and huddled miserably.

That first evening had been a long, slow anticipation of a delightful, sensual experience. In her dreams she had elevated her meeting with a suitable man to the level of a courtly love affair. There were many songs of how knights would vie for a lady's love at tournaments, trying to win renown to honor her . . . and during that evening she had invented dire situations from which Sir Hector would save her, his lady, while in reality she stood beside him refilling his tankard. Her old fantasies had been reinvigorated by his presence, and she had saved him from miserable circumstances time after time while she stood, head bowed, the jug held firmly in her hands waiting for him to hold out his mug again. But instead of finding love, she had been taken like a prize of battle.

She had thought she would be happy with Sir Hector. He had been quiet in the hall, reserved and undemonstrative, not pawing at her like others she had known. At one stage she had wondered whether he was going to show any interest in her after all. But that had changed once they entered his chamber. She had expected compliments, some well-chosen phrases of flattery such as a well-educated knight might use to his chosen lady, but no. Sir Hector had battered at her as if she was a city to be conquered. He had no finesse, no interest in her whatsoever: she was there to satisfy him, and that was all. When once she tried to refuse him, he struck her. Not hard, but painfully. She could still feel the lump on her ribcage where his fist had landed with that short blow.

In the morning she had been roused and evicted. Always before, she had been woken tenderly by her lovers, gentled and teased into wakefulness. Sir Hector had risen and dressed while she was still asleep, then kicked her foot to wake her, laughing at her tousled appearance. She felt used and angry at such treatment, and almost decided not to show him any favors again, but then she began to have second thoughts. A quiet, calm voice at the back of her mind told her that she should not give up immediately, for he could still fall in love with her. Was it not often said that women were the cleverer sex? That, although men might have the brawn and muscle, women controlled them through their brains? If a woman knew what she wanted, she could surely achieve her aims and ambitions.

Sir Hector would be no easy conquest, that was plain. In the afternoon she had prepared for him, dressing carefully and smiling alluringly, and gone to him. To her amazement, he had at first ignored her, then waved her away with every expression of revulsion. This sudden rejection had confused her. There seemed no reason for him to have turned against her, and yet he had refused even to speak to her, choosing instead to go out for the evening. At first she had wondered whether the man who had tried to rape her, Henry, might have poisoned his mind against her, but her man had been out of the inn most of the day, while Henry and his friend, when she asked Cristine, had been in the hall or the stables: they had been nowhere near Sir Hector. They could have had nothing to do with his change of heart. It must be something else.

Her eyes narrowed. She must have a rival—he had said as much, though it was hard to accept. Another girl had managed to win him and would make him her husband. Was it Cristine? The thought was a dagger-thrust in her brain, and she caught at her temples with the sharp pain. Shame was not something she was used to, but being spurned for a woman ten years older, made her feel close to sickness.

She *must* win him back! Tonight she would dress in her finest and make herself so tempting that he could not look at another.

Sarra was in many ways a simple girl, and she was used to being the woman in town whom men leered after. It was a position she enjoyed, knowing that she could make a man's head turn even when his wife was with him, and the idea that a man who had enjoyed her company could go on to desire another was intolerable.

Then a new thought struck her. She had dreamed of saving him, of performing a service for him which snatched him from a vile end, and surely if she was to do so he could only feel a new passion for her. If he knew he was in her debt, he must look on her in a different light.

She wrapped her arms round her legs as she considered, chin on her knees, in what possible way she might be able to win him back. One thing she *did* know was that Henry and his friend were evil, and must surely be bad for him. Her face lightened as she as she recalled overhearing a whispered conversation. All at once her ever-inventive mind began to sparkle with plans.

- 5 -

It was hard, especially when it was so late in the evening that the shutters had been slammed and locked hours before, but Margaret tried, for the sake of the others, to do justice to the meal. Peter had taken great care over it, and she did not want to hurt his feelings. She had dressed in her favorite green tunic with her hair carefully braided and decorously tied under her net. Simon was similarly attempting a brave face, but he avoided her eye, and she soon looked away.

He had been quiet ever since their son's death. Whereas she wanted to talk to him and try to make some sort of sense of their loss, he had taken his despair and shackled it deep inside himself. It made her feel as though she had not only lost her son, but her best friend as well. His face, she could see, still had the drawn-out look which reminded her of badly cured leather stretched too tightly over a frame. In the past his gray eyes had always shone with love for her, but now their light had been blown out like a candle-flame in the wind. Sometimes she thought it would never return. Losing his heir had hit him very hard.

Her gloomy thoughts were not helped by this meal;

it was such a large affair. They were seated at the head table on the dais, and below them, on her right, were all the men, Stapledon's as well as Peter's. Hugh and Edgar sat at a table not far away, Edith with them. She had wanted to sit with Hugh rather than on the dais, under the gaze of all the servants, and Margaret had readily agreed. To be seated at the head table was to be on display, and she did not want to put her daughter through that. It was hard enough for Margaret herself to keep calm.

The noise of the servants and guests made listening to the Bishop's comments difficult. Though the men were not rowdy, over forty people eating made quite enough din to smother the conversation of those at the head of the table. Their talk and the clatter of knives against trenchers and spoons on table-tops echoed into the rafters high overhead. The tapestries which lined the walls, darkened by years of smoke and dust, deadened the row a little, but Margaret could feel a headache beginning, and knew she would sleep badly, if at all, after eating so late.

In honor of his guests, Peter had allocated one mess between two at the top table, but Margaret could see that the servants were all seated four to a serving dish. Courtesies were observed, and the men carefully spooned the correct portion on to their trenchers without fighting, though she observed Hugh surreptitiously seeking out the tastiest morsels from the bowl. She stiffened, thinking he might embarrass Simon if it were noticed, but then relaxed when he doled the portion into Edith's bowl.

The panter arrived again, removing her bread trencher, which had become soaked in juices and sauces from the meat, and replaced it with one freshly sliced from the loaf. At the same time the bottler refilled her goblet. She had hardly tasted the wine, but the staff had all been exhorted to show the best manners possible while the Bishop was staying with Peter, and it would be an appalling *faux pas* to allow any guest's goblet to become empty. From the set smile on the bottler's face, Margaret could see that the injunction was proving difficult to obey. She could feel some sympathy for him, used as he was to a quieter life normally, but his difficulties were at least transitory, she reminded herself.

"Margaret, how has Edith been?"

Baldwin's soft voice at her side was a welcome interruption to her thoughts. "She is well—she's too young to really understand. She misses Peterkin in the way she would miss a favorite pet. Perhaps she never got to know him."

"You *will* get over it, Margaret."

"Yes—but how long will it take?" Her brimming eyes slid back to her husband.

"Not long. He needs something to occupy him," said Baldwin, noticing her look and understanding. "He will be the same Simon you remember."

"I hope so."

The knight looked at her anxiously. In the three years he had known Simon and Margaret, he had thought them to be the perfect example of a well-matched couple. Simon had even reduced the number of trips he was supposed to make away from Lydford, so as not to be separated from his young family too much. That this death would have upset them both he could understand, but that it could have broken them to such an extent was grievous.

"So, Sir Baldwin, what do you think?"

The Bishop's words made him look up. "My apologies, my lord, I was speaking to Margaret and missed your words."

Stapledon's eyes flitted to her and back to Baldwin, and the knight could see that he felt a quick pang at interrupting. He cleared his throat. "I was talking about the state of the country. Now that the Ordinances are confirmed, do you think the people will be calm again?"

Baldwin pulled at a hunk of bread on his plate. This was just the kind of discussion he wanted to avoid. "I think that while the leaders of England want to discuss issues and avoid bloodshed, the country will be calm."

"Ah! You pick your words carefully Sir Baldwin. Enough caution, we're among friends here. What do you really think?"

"My lord, I am only a poor rural knight. I have no interest in matters of state. The state, happily, leaves us alone here to carry on with our lives as we see fit, and that is how I like it."

"I see." Stapledon nodded sympathetically. "And comprehend. It would be better for all if matters could be directed so that the King could leave the people in peace, as you say. Yet I fear it will not be so."

"Why do you say that?" asked Peter Clifford, finishing his goblet of wine and holding it out for more.

"Thomas of Lancaster wants power. Last year, the King and he exchanged the kiss of peace after they agreed their treaty at Leake, but he only truly won a pardon for himself and his friends. Nothing more. When he went to the Parliament at York last October, he demanded the right to nominate those he considered suitable to the offices he felt to be the most important in the land, initially the Steward of the Household.

Well, he was put off then, but he returned to his demands this year when the Parliament met again at York. He wanted the King to grant *him* Stewardship of the King's Household."

"Isn't that sensible? He is the Steward of England, and it might make sense for both posts to be merged," said Simon.

Stapledon smiled gently. "It might seem so, but no. If he was to win both, he would have complete control over the King. In effect, he would have authority over all the King's advisers. That is too much power for one man."

"In any case," Baldwin said off-handedly, "it hardly seems very important now. The Bruce has taken Berwick and the King's army is attacking. Petty politicking will not help anyone. There is a war to be fought, and the Scots need to be given a bloody nose."

"I think you are wrong." Stapledon chewed carefully at a morsel of meat, smiling good-naturedly at the implied snub. "Whatever happens in the north will not last. What will take place when it is over? We all know the King is in a weak position—the Treaty of Leake, which was supposed to have settled matters between him and Lancaster last year, was really a negotiation between Lancaster and other barons. The King had little to say in the affair! No, this issue must be resolved between others, Pembroke and Lancaster in the main."

"Then there will be civil war again," said Baldwin, and sighed heavily. He had not realized that he had spoken aloud, but the sudden hush made him realize his mistake. Looking up, he saw the Bishop peering at him with keen interest. Baldwin met the stare resolutely. He knew full well that his words could have offended, but he was not prepared to deny the truth of his view.

"You speak your mind, Sir Baldwin. Yet," his voice was low as he picked at the fruits in the bowl before him, "yet I fear you could be right."

"And what will you do if it comes to war again?" Baldwin pressed.

"I will ask God for guidance. And then fight for whoever seems to me to be best for England."

The knight was about to reply when he heard a knife clatter on the table-top beside him. "My friends, please . . ." Margaret stood, pale in the flickering candlelight. "I feel weak, I think I must . . ."

Seeing her sway, Baldwin quickly took her arm, and supported her. Simon joined them, his face haggard. "I'll take her to her room. She's probably tired. Don't worry, I'll look after her."

Baldwin watched as the bailiff assisted his wife from the room, Peter Clifford leading the way with a candle.

"Their misery is very great, isn't it?" Stapledon said.

Sitting once more, the knight could not help saying, "To hear talk of war so soon after her son's death may well have upset her."

"Perhaps you are right to chide me," the Bishop said, and then leaned forward, his voice harsher. "But look at me, Sir Baldwin. Do I look like an insensitive fool?"

The knight stared, and the Bishop's tone became calmer as he spoke quietly but with great seriousness. "I know she is sad, and if I can do anything to ease her depression, I will. But I have other things to consider—such as whether this country of ours should be riven by disputes which must lead to war. Mark my words, Sir Baldwin, when the army comes south again from Scotland, there *will be* war, and when that happens, many more women will be bemoaning the loss of their children, their fathers, their lovers and husbands. It may take one year, it may take two, but war there must be if Lancaster's power is to be curbed."

"And who would you have in his place?" Baldwin asked pointedly.

"Pembroke is safer," the Bishop said.

"Perhaps."

"Another thing I must consider is the loyalty of the knights in the country. Maybe you could answer me this: where would a good knight like you stand if it did come to war?"

Baldwin saw Peter return, and was grateful, for it meant that this interrogation must soon be ended. He had been cornered, as he knew he must be, but his answer was ready. "With the man to whom he gave his oath—he could stand by no other, whether it be his lord or his King," he said heavily, then poured wine and handed it to Peter. "How is she?"

"Resting," The priest dropped onto his seat with a sigh. "She asked to be left alone."

Stapledon looked as if he wanted to continue with the talk, but as he opened his mouth there was a rising chorus of noises from the street—cries and yells, a clattering of hooves, then a scream and more shouting.

Baldwin glanced enquiringly at Peter, who shrugged with evident mystification. Feeling gratitude for whatever might have caused the interruption, Baldwin excused himself, then stood and made for the door. Edgar immediately followed. Baldwin's servant had been with him for many years, since the days when he had been a man-at-arms in the Order of the Knights Templar, and in all that time he had never lost his utter loyalty to his knight. If Baldwin were to get involved in a fight, Edgar would be there with him.

Two of Peter's men were at the door before them, one grasping a cudgel, ready to protect the hall against any invasion by rioters, and Baldwin and his man had to push between them. Outside they found a scene of confusion.

In the dark street, men scurried to and fro with burning torches. Commands were bellowed, and men-at-arms stamped up and down, gesticulating threateningly when they felt their orders were not acted upon fast enough. A thin woman in dusty gray robes knelt at the roadside, cradling a screaming child, a boy of five or six who had been knocked down, while men on skittish horses jostled, iron-shod hooves ringing on the cobbles. More people poured from houses, many in degrees of undress, while the clamor rose. Horses whinnied, there was a thunder of slamming doors; urgent questions flew as people tried to discover the cause of the disturbance. The air was tainted with the sharp fumes of burning wood and pitch, and filled with the hoarse cries of confused and angry men.

The knight watched for a moment, then made his way over to a rotund figure leaning laconically against a wall. Baldwin recognized him in the glare from a passing torch: it was the butcher. "Hello, Adam, what's all this about?"

"There's been a robbery, I think. Someone at the inn's had his chest stolen. All his plate and stuff's gone."

Baldwin groaned as the butcher shrugged unconcernedly, then gulped at a large pot of ale. This was turning out to be a worse evening than even he had anticipated. Seeing a man-at-arms approach, he gestured. "You! Who has been robbed?" The man gave him a sneering look, and from his expression was about to snarl an insolent response when he caught sight of the sword at Baldwin's waist. *"Well?"*

"It's my captain, Sir Hector de Gorsone. His chest of plate has been raided, and much of his silver has gone. The chest needed three men to carry it, it was so heavy, yet it's all gone."

"God's teeth!" This was all Baldwin needed. First Simon's child, then being roped into politics, and now a theft, with the hue raised to find the thief. He rubbed at his temple, then: "I am the Keeper of the King's Peace here. I do not want anyone hurt without reason. Where is your master?"

"My captain's over there."

Following the finger, Baldwin saw the mercenary leader. He was standing under the new alestake, arms folded, glowering at his men. As Baldwin approached, Edgar warily trudging close behind, he could hear the man bawling: "I don't care if he went to Scotland. I want him caught and brought back here! Just find him and fetch him to me."

"Wait!" Baldwin shouted, and held a hand aloft.

"Who are you?"

"I am the Keeper of the King's Peace. I'll not have bloodshed. Who is it you seek—one of your men?"

"Yes. He only joined my band the night before last, and tonight he has robbed me!"

"What is his name?" Baldwin demanded.

"Philip Cole."

"What does he look like?"

Sir Hector gave a short description. It was not easy, for he had only remarked the lad briefly on the night when he had asked to join the band, and Sir Hector had already been drinking for some time by then. Inwardly he was fuming that a mere yokel lad could take advantage of him so quickly and with such apparent ease. He slapped a fist into the palm of his hand. "He must be from around these parts; he joined my band here, while we were staying at the inn, the bastard!"

Another of his men standing a little away interrupted: "Thorverton—he said he came from Thorverton."

"There you are, Keeper of the King's Peace," Sir Hector sneered. "A local man! One of your own. I'm glad you manage to keep your precious peasants under such good control."

"The local hue will find him for you." Baldwin ignored the jibe and kept his voice reasonable. He had no wish to antagonize Sir Hector, for the captain could create mayhem in the little town. In any case, if he had been robbed, he had every right to demand to see the culprit caught.

"My men can save you the trouble."

"Oh yes?" Baldwin gauged the heavily armed men around him. "They will promise to bring him back alive for questioning?"

"They will bring *him* back, *and* my silver!"

"I am sure they would."

"It will take ages for you to organize a posse, and by then Cole will have escaped. It's better that my men ride on now."

He was about to issue more orders, but Baldwin's calm, firm tone made him pause. "Your men would certainly bring him back, of that I have no doubt, only I wish to see him while he is alive. Can you say you saw him steal from you? No? In that case, I'll not have him lynched or stabbed before he has had a chance to defend himself. You!" His finger jerked out and pointed to the butcher still lounging against the wall.

Adam started. "Go to Peter Clifford and ask him for some men to help us search. We'll need as many as he can afford. Ask Bishop Stapledon whether we may use some of his entourage as well."

"But Cole is getting away while you ask me to wait!" Sir Hector sputtered furiously while the man hurried off.

"Did anyone here see him leave?"

"No, I don't think so."

"Did he take a horse?"

Sir Hector scowled, then pointed with his chin to an ostler. "Well—did he?"

"No, sir. All the horses are still there."

"There's your answer."

"Yes." Baldwin gave a quick frown. One man on foot could not carry away a chestful of silver on his own, not when three men had been required to bring it inside. He shrugged. "If he is on foot, a delay will not signify. If you want to catch him, you'll need more men. There are two main roads leading east and west out of Crediton, and more to the north and south. We need several teams looking for him, and men to search all of the routes out of the town. He will not get much further in the ten or twenty minutes it will take to assemble my men, but with them we will be more likely to find him. I can double the hunting parties."

His speech done, Baldwin smiled reassuringly. "Have no fear, Sir Hector. We will find him—*and* your silver."

"You had better. I hold you responsible for this delay, Keeper. If he escapes, I will demand you compensate me."

The men around Baldwin had a threatening air, as if they too blamed him for the slowness in setting off after their quarry, and the mood could soon have become ugly. He knew Edgar was still behind him, but if the two of them were attacked by so many, they would be in a futile position. He was relieved when he heard the sound of horses in Peter's yard. Soon there was a jingling of harnesses and squeaking of leather as the group approached.

To his surprise, the men were led by Simon. He rode up, leading Baldwin's horse, and passed him the reins, giving a dry smile at the look on his friend's face. Baldwin took them and swung into the saddle, then gave Simon a questioning glance. "You do not have to come, old friend."

"I need the exercise."

Baldwin nodded gravely, and Simon knew precisely what he was thinking: the bailiff should have stayed with his wife. But Simon was not going to discuss the matter here in the street.

Surveying the men available, Baldwin began mentally pairing them off; he was about to begin ordering them to specific routes when he realized Simon was no longer beside him. Turning in his saddle, he saw the bailiff riding toward the woman and her child. Cursing under his breath, Baldwin spurred after him.

A man-at-arms on horseback was pushing at her with the butt-end of his pike. "Out of the way, bitch, before you get run down."

She wailed even louder, clutching the child to her. "He's hurt, I say—by one of the horses."

"*Move!* Out of the way, you old sow. And take that brat with you or I'll give him something to scream about!"

Simon forced his horse between them. "Leave her alone," he hissed.

"Who are you to tell me what to do?" the man demanded, holding his polearm aggressively, ready to swing it like a club at the bailiff's head.

"He's my friend, and I'm the man who could have you put in jail for a week," said Baldwin. He had arrived behind the mercenary, and now sat threateningly, one hand on his thigh, near his sword. "Leave us—and leave her alone."

Muttering, the man went, his eyes going from one to the other, but Simon ignored him. As soon as he was out of the way, the bailiff dropped from his horse. "He's not badly hurt," he said, after examining the lad. "Just bruised. I would go now, though, before that guard returns."

He watched her as she shyly took her son from him, ducking her head nervously in the manner of a peasant who finds herself in the presence of a lord. The little matter had enraged him, and the tension, now it was released, left him feeling tired out, and with a hollowness in his belly: she could go home now, her child by her side. Baldwin watched as he clambered aboard his horse again, picking up his reins like a man exhausted after a long race.

A little later they had finished dividing the men. Baldwin had insisted on four main groups, one to search each of the roads out of the town, and he ensured that there was a good mixture of Peter Clifford's and the Bishop's men in each. He did not want a preponderance of mercenaries in any company; he was sure that Sir Hector's men would want to kill Cole on sight to satisfy their master, and Baldwin was determined to prevent that. Peter and his guest had not joined them, but there were enough men to match the mercenaries, and that was all he wanted.

Upon reflection, he decided to ride with Simon. He commanded the others to their allotted routes, and then set his face to the south and moved off.

Simon rode stiffly. His servant Hugh, at his side, seemed to exude disgust. Lean, dark-haired, and with the keen sharp features of a ferret, he had for years yielded only under protest to the need for travelling, and had never enjoyed the experience. At long last he was beginning to get used to riding, and Simon knew that his moroseness tonight was due to having to leave Margaret alone with Peter Clifford. The servant had been devoted to their son and felt the loss of Peterkin as deeply as the parents. Living with them full-time, serving them, eating with them, he was a member of the family. He would have preferred to remain with Margaret to try to ease her desolation.

The bailiff had hoped that this chase would give him some relief from his misery, but all he sensed was the disapproval of his friends and servants; their censure was a weight he could hardly bear. If only, he thought, if only they could understand. He knew he could not help his wife. No matter how long he spent with her, he could not explain his feelings, and listening to her going on and on about how they had found poor Peterkin lying in his bed, cold and blue, merely added to his anguish and frustration. If he spent too long with her, he wanted to hit her, just to make her quiet. His own despair at his loss was hard enough to carry; he did not have the strength to support her as well. Peterkin had died, and Simon could not think of a future without his son. Without an heir.

Nearby, Baldwin forced his mind to the search. There was not much chance, he thought, that the thief would be down this way. Still, they had to cover all options. If the lad was local, from Thorverton, there was no reason for him to head down toward the moors. If he had any sense, he would have gone east, to Exeter, where he could hide. There were smiths there who would ask few questions about where silver came from, if the price was right. He pursed his lips. Yes, if he had to guess, he would say the boy had gone that way.

But Baldwin kept an eye on Simon as they rode. The knight could not understand why Simon did not stay with his wife. It was out of character, like his cold treatment of her earlier, and as such it was incomprehensible. Baldwin had suffered loss himself. In his experience, it always made him more dependent on his friends, not less, so Simon's apparent withdrawal from his wife was all the more baffling. If there was any fighting, Baldwin decided he must remain close to his friend. Whether from the urgency of the call to horse or simple absent-mindedness, he saw that Simon had forgotten his sword, and only wore his old bone-handled knife. Others in the party were better prepared. Roger de Grosse had joined them on a lively bay, with a short sword at his side. The rector looked flushed but excited, and Baldwin was amused to see such warlike enthusiasm on the face of a man who was devoting his life to God, though he could understand why. Of all prey, he had once heard someone say, the most invigorating to pursue was another man.

They came to a stream which lay still and strangely solid-looking, like a ribbon of polished metal under the bright moon. Their hooves churned it, creating a luminous spray, and to Baldwin it felt like vandalism to destroy the peaceful water, as if they were knights "riding out" on a *chevauchée,* leaving mayhem in their wake.

The destruction left him with a sense of impending disaster, as if their casual wrecking of such beauty and peace was about to bring doom upon them all. He shook off his black mood irritably. It was Simon's part to be superstitious, not his. He would not tolerate foolish premonitions.

A short way after the stream there was another road westward, and here Baldwin separated his force, grateful for the need for thought and action. Five he sent east while he continued south with the others, keeping Simon at his side.

The trees crowded round the lane like a suspicious army, and Baldwin found himself eyeing the thick trunks with trepidation. In previous manhunts he and Simon had been able to make use of hunters skilled in tracking, and rushing along the road like this made him realize just how much he had depended on them. There could be thousands of signs, even now in the dark, which the hunters of wolves and foxes would be able to discern and advise on. He glared behind. The eleven men of the troop were making so much noise that they could be heard by a man on foot leagues away. It would take mere seconds to duck into the trees and hide. He grunted as the futility of the exercise struck him. Whether the man was on this road or not, there was next to no chance that they would find him. It would take a miracle.

He was about to hold up a hand and halt the posse when a cry came from in front. Frowning as he tried to pierce the darkness, he set spurs to his horse and quickened his pace. The road bent to the left, gently dropping down the slope over the summit of a small hill. As they came round the bend, Baldwin saw three shadowy figures, one lying unconscious on the ground, two standing over him, a short distance from the verge. Automatically he slowed, feeling for his sword, aware of Edgar at his side. He was about to bellow a challenge when one of the men took a step forward.

"Thanks to God you're here! We've got him!"

"Who are you? Who have you got?" Baldwin demanded.

Two fearful eyes stared up at him, set in a weasel-like face. "Sir, we've caught a thief. This man stole Sir Hector's silver."

"Who are you?"

The other moved forward, a confident-looking, strong man, Baldwin thought. "I'm Henry the Hurdle, sir. This here's my friend, John Smithson. We're with Sir Hector's troop."

"And who is that?" he asked, pointing.

"Philip Cole, so he says, but I don't know if it's really his name. He only appeared the day before yesterday, and now he's stolen my master's silver. Look! We found this on him." He held up two plates and a small leather purse.

Baldwin took them and weighed them in his hand thoughtfully. "Why did you follow him? Did you know your master's silver was missing?"

"No, sir, but we spotted him skulking round the streets, furtive-like, so we thought we'd follow him, take a look at what he was up to. Then we saw him examining a silver plate, and I thought I recognized it as one of my master's."

Henry's face was earnest, his eyes compelling, and the knight nodded encouragingly.

"We called out to him, but he started running away, and we only caught up with him here. We had to knock him out to stop him struggling." He took a long, weary breath. "We were just wondering how to get him back to town, us not having a horse."

"You have done well. Your master will reward you, I'm sure," Baldwin said, staring down at the still body. The man would have to be tried, and Baldwin would be the man to pursue him in the court. But there was something not quite right about the stolen plate . . .

~ 6 ~

At Crediton they delivered their prisoner to the jail, much to the disgust of Tanner, the Constable. Edgar, who knew him, explained with a malicious smile that Tanner was friendly with a certain widow whom he knew to be lonely quite regularly, and this was an evening when she would expect him.

Their return had been slow, with the two men-at-arms walking. The thief's body they had slung, bound, over the horse of another trooper, who had led his mount on foot. By the time they got back to Crediton the prisoner was awake again, and had begun to shout and complain, but he was soon plunged into a horrified silence when he was told who had captured him and why. The prisoner's eyes were bloodshot, and his gaze wandered as if he found it hard to concentrate. Sir Baldwin knew that a hard knock on the head could addle a man's mind, and was sure that it would be more profitable to question him the following morning.

The two men who had captured Cole were unhappy about this. One, the weasel-faced soldier said, "Our master will want to speak to him."

Baldwin gave a curt shake of the head. "Sir Hector

may well want to question Cole, but he can wait. This man will have to be investigated, and if he is found to have been the thief, your master will see that our revenge is swift."

His response did not satisfy them. Their glowers indicated that their captive's guilt was plain enough given his decision to run away—especially since he had been found with some of the stolen items on him. They gave in with bad grace only when they realized that Baldwin would not be swayed. Hugh and Edgar were sent back to Peter Clifford's with the horses, while Baldwin and Simon went on to the inn, having first given instructions to Tanner to keep his charge in the jail *without* any visitors. The knight had a shrewd idea that one of Sir Hector's entourage might think he could earn favors by punishing the thief.

Baldwin had taken the recovered silver from the two, and he studied the plates with interest when he had an opportunity, standing with Simon in the hall of the inn near a guttering candle. The plates were doubtless of fine quality. Deep and heavy, adorned with leaves and a hunting scene, they were both beautiful and valuable. He turned them over and over, his mind far away. When his name was called, he came to with a start. A messenger was waiting to conduct them to Sir Hector.

Crossing the hall, Baldwin was struck by how deserted the place was. It was strange to see a room, normally so bustling and raucous, now empty. Most of Sir Hector's men were still out searching, and were unlikely to return until morning. They would want to make sure that they could see no sign of their quarry before risking their master's wrath, and it would have been impossible to send messengers after them to call them back: there were too many routes being covered.

Smoke hung lazily in the rafters, and the stench of rotten ale permeated the atmosphere. The inn stank of the men-at-arms in the mercenary band, of their unwashed bodies, of urine and sweat. A couple of dogs rooted among the rushes on the floor like hogs, searching out bones and scraps. One of the serving women tossed a crust to them, and then watched as they fought over it, laughing. To Baldwin, the dank and chill jail was more appealing than the inn at this moment.

They went through a door, which was concealed behind a tapestry at the back of the room. A room led off into a number of chambers, and Baldwin and the silent Simon were conducted to the one Sir Hector had taken for himself. The captain was alone in his chamber.

"So, Sir Baldwin. I didn't need to ask for your help in the first place, did I?"

Sir Hector eyed the knight and the bailiff with a sardonic smile. If only he had got the hue out immediately, he thought bitterly, he could have had the thief back here and punished without the unwelcome attention of the Keeper of the King's Peace. It still rankled that the man had appeared and taken charge, and it was aggravating in the extreme that he had been with the group that found John and Henry and their captive. Any other team would have brought Cole back to Sir Hector for immediate retribution, but this local knight, who looked like a hard-up merchant with his shabby tunic and scuffed boots, was too keen to keep a hold on his own power in this pathetic little town. Was it because he wanted to extort money from Cole in return for rigging the jury at his trial? It had happened often enough before, Sir Hector thought contemptuously.

"This is good plate, Sir Hector," Baldwin said politely, ignoring the sneering suggestion.

"I don't keep poor items."

"Is it English?"

"No. I won it in Gascony."

Baldwin nodded to himself. He knew that "won it" meant "stole it." For a man like Sir Hector, there would have been many chances for enriching himself. Few men would go to war for amusement. Someone like Sir Hector saw it as a uniquely profitable business which could offer excellent opportunities in exchange for short-term risks with the potential, providing the captain was bold enough for untold rewards: sometimes even the overthrow of a ruler and the theft of his entire kingdom. Incidents of that nature did not occur too often, but such had happened with the Grand Catalan Company, which had turned against its employer in 1311 and set up its own duchy in Athens. Poor laborers and peasants with the army found themselves in possession of wealth they could hardly have conceived of before. Baldwin knew that the Catalans still ruled there, and were likely to do so for some time: they had the arms, the power, and the will to use both to keep what they had won. It would take a strong army to dislodge them, and there was none which was prepared to try.

"Was this all that was taken?"

Sir Hector gave a short, annoyed shake of his head. "No, of course not!" he snapped. "The bastard took almost all of the plate from my chest."

"Yet this was all that was found on him," Baldwin murmured, studying his distorted reflection in the plate. "I wonder where he could have disposed of the rest?"

"He'll soon answer that, whether he wants to or not."

Baldwin glanced at the captain. "Perhaps," he said

mildly. "I suppose there is no possibility that you made an error? The silver *was* definitely taken?"

"Look for yourself." The captain waved a hand haughtily round the room.

There was, Baldwin had to admit, little likelihood that the silver could have been secreted in the room. Apart from the mattress, there were few items of furniture in the low-ceilinged room. Some heavy chests lay on the floor near the window, a chair among them, and a sideboard sat at the opposite wall. The floor was trodden dirt, and any digging would have been immediately obvious. No, the silver must have been removed.

Some of the captain's treasure still occupied the top of the cupboard, lying on a great expanse of cloth which made the jug, pair of mugs and saltcellar look lonely when compared with the empty space around them.

The saltcellar attracted Baldwin's attention. It was a great silver box shaped like a church without a roof, the four walls concealing the glass bowl which held the precious mineral. A tower rose at one end, while doors and windows were carefully and elaborately defined. It was the sight of this which removed the last vestige of sympathy Baldwin had held. Such a piece could only have been made for a man in Holy Orders or the patron of a religious order. No other would pay for such a costly item. Why had the thief not taken it as well as the rest?

"The whole of the top of that cabinet used to be covered in my silver. Plates, goblets, spoons—all of the first quality. And he took the lot."

"It's not in the cupboard?" Baldwin lifted a corner of the cloth and peeped under. The shelves were clear.

"Satisfied?"

"No, not at all. Did your silver fill one of these chests?"

"Yes. That one."

Baldwin nodded slowly as Sir Hector pointed. The chest was a good three feet long and over two feet in height and depth. "And I suppose all the staff here at the inn knew about it?"

"Do you think I'm a fool?" Sir Hector roared. "Nobody from the inn was allowed in here, and I made damn sure that my men were always outside in the hall to stop anybody walking in."

"I see. Tell me, when did you notice your silver had gone?"

Sir Hector was quickly becoming exasperated with the knight's steady questions. "What does that matter?"

"Possibly not at all, but I would like to know."

"This evening, after I had taken some food. I usually eat with my men late at night, but tonight I chose to dine earlier."

"Ah, and did you have your cellar with you when you were eating?"

"Where else would my salt be? Of course I had it on my table. Then later, when I came back to my room tonight, I found that my silver had gone." Bitterly he added: "And the man you want to protect from *me* had disappeared, too."

"How did you find that out?"

"I asked whether anyone had disappeared, and we discovered that Cole had gone," the captain said, adding with heavy sarcasm, "I suppose I was wrong to immediately assume that he might be guilty, but the fact that my silver was found on him makes me suspect my first thought was right."

Baldwin ignored the taunt and laid the two plates found on Cole back on their cloth. "Was anyone else missing?"

"Yes. The two who followed him, Henry the Hurdle and John Smithson, but they are long-established members of my troop. They would not have dared do this to me."

"I see."

Simon looked up. He had been preoccupied, thinking about Margaret again, but something in Baldwin's manner caught his notice. The knight was standing with his back to Sir Hector, who scowled at him from the chair. Simon could see that Baldwin was smiling to himself with a kind of world-weary amusement. Then he turned, peering at Sir Hector with a sudden sharpness. "Were you in here before your meal?"

"What is this? The lad was found with my silver on him! What's the point of these questions, Sir Knight?" Sir Hector spat, but Baldwin gazed at him imperturbably.

"The point, as you so elegantly put it, is this: you are asking me to believe that a single man could have taken all the silver from this room on his own, without a horse or assistance from another, when I have heard it took three men to carry your chest when full. I find that hard to swallow. Either he removed it piecemeal over a period, or he had an accomplice. If he took it over a period, it would be helpful if I knew how long he had to do so."

"Ah . . ."

"And *that* means I have to know how long this room was empty before you discovered your loss."

"It doesn't matter. We—you—have him. Interrogate him. He can give you the answers to your questions."

A trace of acerbity had returned to his voice. He stood, and the interview was over; the knight and his friend were no longer welcome.

"I will ask him, of course." Baldwin gave a smile in which there was not a hint of warmth. "And if there is something interesting which leads from that, I shall let you know, naturally." He nodded to Simon and made his way to the door.

The men had begun to filter back. Those who were less keen on the search had speedily decided to return, and the hall was already raucous with their laughter and swearing. Simon noticed one group grow quiet as he and Sir Baldwin appeared from behind the tapestry and crossed the floor. He thought he recognized the two who had caught Cole among them.

Baldwin had seen them too. They were being fêted as the heroes of the moment, and no doubt the story of the capture was being retold to an appreciative audience, with plenty of embellishments. On a whim, he motioned to one of the serving-girls and asked for ale. "Is your master here? It is Paul who owns this inn, isn't it?"

She gave him a bright smile. Cristine was a buxom, cheerful girl, almost thirty years old yet remarkably untouched by her life as servant and companion to travellers through Crediton. Pushing an errant lock of hair back above her forehead, she nodded helpfully and disappeared into the buttery. Soon she returned with Paul, directing him to their table before making off to fill more pots.

The innkeeper wore a harassed frown. His day had been, quite simply, awful. The headache his wife had woken with had not eased as the guests began to get up and demand ale and food, and Paul had felt himself flagging quickly before noon, exhausted by lack of sleep and the unaccustomed effort. His wife had disappeared in the early afternoon, snapping that she'd had enough and couldn't carry on without a rest, but Paul had to struggle on, enlisting the help of Nell and Cristine. Sarra was either refusing to answer her door or had gone out.

He had hoped that Sarra might want to try to help when she knew how pushed Margery was, but the strain of serving so many people soon forced her from his mind. Occasionally, as he stood waiting for the ale to flow from the cask and fill the jug, he remembered to curse her, but for the most part he was too busy.

He gave his most servile smile to the knight. "Sir, you wanted me?"

"Innkeeper, you look dreadful!" Baldwin gave him a faint, understanding grimace of sympathy. "These guests are working you hard?"

"Yes, sir," said Paul, and gratefully accepted the knight's invitation to sit. Checking briefly that there were no men complaining, he watching his two serving-girls for a moment. "But at least we have a full inn."

"You have been here all day, serving these men?"

"Oh, yes. I've not had time to sit until now. Missed my lunch, and all. It's been mayhem. And last night we didn't get any sleep hardly."

"The men stayed here all the day, did they?"

"Most of them. Running me and the girls off our feet."

"I suppose you've hardly had time to notice whether anyone left the inn at any time? Or if someone—a stranger—came in?"

Paul's eyes snapped to the knight's face. "If you

mean, did I see who went and stole the silver from Sir Hector—no, I didn't."

"Is there any other way into his rooms apart from through that door?" Baldwin asked, jerking his head toward the tapestry behind the dais.

The innkeeper shrugged. "There are windows in all the rooms, though no one can get in through them. They are kept shuttered during the day—Sir Hector's orders. Never mind the heat. I suppose he was justified, seeing what's happened."

"They are barred?"

"Yes. All of them."

"The windows open out onto the street?"

"Most of them. Some, like those in his bedchamber, look out over the stables and yard."

"And none, I think, open on to another alley or road?"

"No, the far end of the solar part of the hall was sold some years ago, before I came here. That's all owned by the butcher now—Adam."

"So someone would have had to open all the shutters and pass the silver out at the front or back, or carry it through the hall itself?"

"Yes, sir, but they'd have to be brave to take it through the hall."

"Why?"

"Because some of the mercenaries were there all day. It would have been hard to get past them, and they all know Sir Hector hasn't given permission for anyone to enter his rooms since he got here. I was only let in once, when I made sure he was comfortable just after he arrived."

Baldwin scratched his ear. "Could anyone have spent time outside his window without being seen?" he hazarded.

"What, in the yard? No." Paul was definite. "There's no possibility of that. The yard's in use all day, and even at night people are always going backward and forward. The girls have rooms out there above the stables, and they walk past those windows regularly when they go to the cookshop for pies and so on."

"You don't make your own food here?"

"Some of it, but not all. It's bad enough trying to brew ale enough for this number. We'll have a roast, a stew or pottage for guests, but when it's like this," he waved a despairing hand at the swiftly filling room, "well, we have to get extra from the cookshop. We couldn't cope otherwise."

Baldwin nodded. "So they would be passing by that window throughout the day?"

"Yes. Someone would have noticed if there was a man loitering."

"That wasn't what I was thinking," Baldwin said mildly.

"Eh?"

"Did you see all Sir Hector's silver?"

"Yes. He had the whole of the top of the cupboard filled, and a couple of shelves beneath."

"How could one man carry all of that out? Even if he had a confederate in the yard it would be quite a task, wouldn't it?"

"I see what you mean. He'd have needed a friend outside and a wagon or something." Paul looked around. The serving-girl was passing not far away, and she caught his eye. She finished pouring a pot of ale, slapped at a hand which was trying to lift her skirt, and joined them.

Simon glanced at her sourly, then sighed and rubbed his temples; while Baldwin wanted to keep interrogating the innkeeper, he felt duty-bound to remain with his friend, but this endless series of questions was surely irrelevant. The boy had been caught carrying some of the stolen plate, and he was a recent, unknown recruit to the band, with no loyalty or commitment to it. It was plain as a hog in a goldsmith's that he must have committed the robbery, and tomorrow they would begin to question him about his accomplice. Cole would answer or suffer the penalty. There was no point in this, Simon thought irascibly, and he had to bite back a few choice words.

Cristine looked at them, her cheeks dimpling. It was her duty to remain calm and happy, to make men relax and forget their worries, and she was good at her job. Under her look, she saw the knight shift uncomfortably on his seat, and she concentrated on him. He looked shy, she thought. And rather sweet.

Baldwin coughed. "Cristine, we're just trying to work out how the missing silver could have been removed from Sir Hector's room, because with so many men in here all day, no one could have carried it through the hall without being seen. We think someone must have taken it out through the window into the yard."

Grumpily clearing his throat, Simon said, "There're other windows in the solar block, Baldwin."

"Yes, Simon." Baldwin threw him a quick look. His friend was not as astute today as usual, but allowances should be made for his mood. "But they all give out on to the street, and someone would be sure to remark a man bundling goods through a window. I reckon it must have been out into the yard that the silver went. What do you think, Cristine?"

She gave him a long stare. Cristine was no fool, and

though she maintained her vacuous, happy smile, she was thinking quickly. "It would make sense. As you say, nobody could have brought it out through the hall here, not with all these men."

Simon poured himself some ale from Cristine's jug. "Why couldn't this man Cole have brought it all out through here?" he objected. "The men might not have noticed the silver if he concealed it on him; after all, he was one of them."

"Simon, think how much silver we're talking about here," Baldwin said with a degree of asperity. "He'd have had to bring it out piece by piece. Think of the size of the plates we found—only a few at a time could be carried without making him look suspiciously heavy—and what about sudden clanking noises? It would have taken five, or ten, maybe more trips to bring it all out. Three men were needed to carry the chest into the room, and the chest itself wasn't that heavy, it was the weight of the silver inside. And how would he have explained so many trips to his master's solar? No, I refuse to believe he could have done it that way."

"There's another thing, sir," Cristine said. At Baldwin's nod, she continued, "This man, Cole, was new to the group. Those chambers are only for Sir Hector and his closest men. I think if Cole went in there just once he'd be asked what he was doing. These soldiers don't seem very trusting."

"A good point, Cristine. So, to return to my idea, did you see anyone waiting outside Sir Hector's room today? A man with a horse, perhaps? Maybe a wagon?"

"No, sir," she said, her eyes round. "I went past there many times, and I never noticed anyone. I'd have said if I did."

"See?" said Simon. His friend ignored him.

"Other rooms behind the hall have windows which look out to the front, don't they? Cristine, would there be any surprise if someone was spotted waiting in the street with a wagon?"

"Of course. And they'd be told to move, too. The street's not very wide, is it? If someone sat there waiting, there'd be plenty would tell them to clear off."

Baldwin was about to ask another question when there was a series of hoarse shouts. Turning, he saw the captain emerge from his rooms, bellowing.

"What is it this time?" groaned Paul.

"Come on, Baldwin," Simon muttered, levering himself upright with difficulty. "It's about time we were back at Peter's . . ."

"Sir Baldwin!" Sir Hector pointed at them, and Paul the innkeeper felt his earlier premonition of evil return in full force at the sight of the man's ghastly face. "Sir Baldwin, come here! There's been a murder."

~ 7 ~

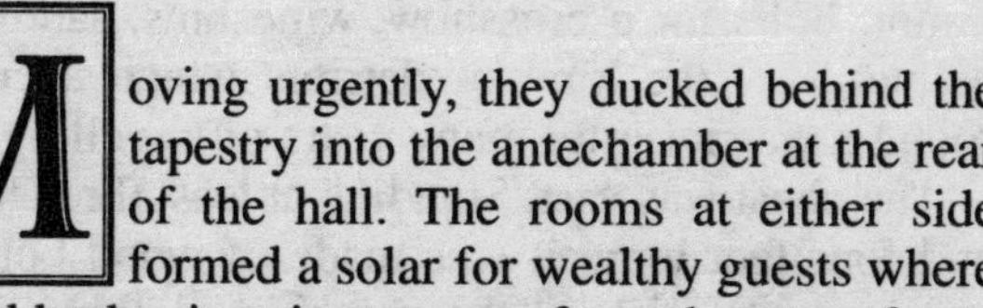

Moving urgently, they ducked behind the tapestry into the antechamber at the rear of the hall. The rooms at either side formed a solar for wealthy guests where they could relax in privacy away from the row of revellers at the inn. On the right was Sir Hector's bedchamber; to their left, storerooms. The captain led them inside one of these; a white-faced servant was waiting for them, gripping three smoking candles in his hand.

"I was looking for some clothes, sir," he explained to Baldwin. "My master asked me to fetch a fresh shirt, and when I opened the chest, there was a cloak on top, and then this serving girl!" With a trembling hand, he lifted the lid and Baldwin found himself looking down on the still, calmly beautiful face of Sarra.

Simon choked and turned away, stumbling to the window. It was not the sight of death—he was all too used to that—but the oval face with the narrow nose, surrounded by a mass of fair hair looked, at first glance, like his wife. The eyes seemed to stare directly at him, as if in rebuke for his behavior.

Ignoring him, Baldwin studied the chest and noted

the details dispassionately. He took in the general layout of the room before concentrating on the body before him.

The storeroom was low-ceilinged, stinking of damp, with a small window overlooking the road. It was ill-lit by the candles grasped by the servant, a darkly suspicious-looking man, with square features and a grizzled beard. In here were placed a number of chests which held some of Sir Hector's less valuable belongings. Many were open. Baldwin saw clothing, some armor, bolts for a crossbow, wineskins, saddlebags, a helmet . . . the kind of detritus which accumulates round a warrior after many years of travelling.

The chest was vast. Standing at least three feet high, and four feet long, it was made of wood bound with iron hoops, and held the captain's clothing. Baldwin leaned forward to study the interior while Simon groaned once more at the sight of the body inside.

Sarra lay twisted, with her arms hidden beneath her. Her knees were bent and turned to one side to allow the lid to close. Her posture was that of a young girl snatching a rest, but she was as lifeless as a rag doll. A strip of green cloth ran tightly from her mouth to the back of her neck, making caverns of her cheeks. Baldwin felt her forehead, but there was no heat. She had been dead some little time. Her breast too was still, with no motion as of breathing, and he sighed: another young life wasted. Feeling a quick anger, he drew his dagger and cut the gag, pulling it away. More cloth projected from inside her mouth, and he gently removed that. Whoever had wished to silence her had made a very competent job of it.

She was dressed in a light blue tunic, embroidered with tiny flowers. Touching it, he could feel that the cloth was expensive, and he noted the fact with a raised eyebrow. A serving-girl would not usually be able to afford such material. Her head lay on a bolt of fine, golden fabric which Baldwin thought could be gauze, and her hair mingled with it. She looked as if she had just awoken from a slight sleep, her eyes freshly opened, and he half-expected her to smile and welcome her visitors.

"Help me get her out," he said, and heard the harshness in his voice. It was one thing to find the corpse of a man, for men were born to fight and die, but quite another to find the body of a young and beautiful girl. The servant helped him, taking the knees and lifting while Baldwin grasped her shoulders. They set Sarra down alongside the chest, and Simon saw that her hands had been bound with another cord made from the same stuff as the gag. "So that's how you died, then," Baldwin muttered.

"How?" Simon asked, curiosity overcoming his squeamishness. Peering over the knight's shoulder, he saw the stain on the clothing in the trunk. "Stabbed?"

"Yes. And viciously, too. Look, the thrust of the blade went right through her and damaged the cloth behind her. She was in there already, then, before being killed."

Simon winced. "Why kill her?"

Baldwin glanced at him. "Why? Because she saw someone, I would imagine. She witnessed the robbery, and had to be silenced. What I would like to know is, why her killer bound and gagged her. Was he not going to kill her at first—and then something made him change his mind? No matter: she was stabbed and left to die alone in the darkness." He gently rolled the body over. "Bring the candles lower. Ah, yes. One knife-wound high in her chest, on her left side." He pursed his lips. "Another here, a little lower, just above the breast. From where they came out at the back, both were angled sharply." He studied the cloth carefully in the inadequate light, trying to make sense of the marks on it. After a minute or two he sighed and looked up. "I'll need to look more carefully in the daylight. It's impossible to see anything in here."

"The poor girl." Sir Hector was standing above Baldwin staring down at Sarra's body. The captain was clad in hose and boots, bare-chested, but wearing his sword—Baldwin assumed correctly that he rarely went anywhere without it. His torso was as white as a lump of goose fat making him look strangely young, but with livid pink stars and slashes of scar tissue from his career as a soldier.

"You knew her?" Baldwin asked coldly.

"She was a serving-girl here called Sarra."

"Did you see her today?"

"Not that I noticed."

"When were you last in here?"

Sir Hector looked round the little storeroom with distaste, "I am not in the habit of entering places like this. I watched to see that my chests were brought in yesterday when we arrived here, but I've not been in here since."

Baldwin spoke to the servant. "Has anyone been in here today?"

"I was here this morning, sir—it was when my master asked for his tunic before he went out—but she wasn't there then. I'd have seen her, and if I had, I'd have called for help as soon as I did, I'm sure."

"So she was not here earlier. She must have been killed today."

"Cole must have done it when he robbed me." Sir Hector's eyes were fixed on the body, but there was no mistaking his anger.

"Perhaps," Baldwin said musingly. "Though it seems odd."

"Sir, I didn't kill her! You must believe me, I—"

Holding up a hand, Baldwin reassured the panicking servant. "Don't worry, I'm only trying to see when someone might have come in here last. You say you were here this morning?" The man nodded, but his wary, dark eyes showed no lessening of his fear. "Early morning, or late?"

"It was early," Sir Hector interrupted. "As soon as I rose."

"Could anyone else have got in here? And if they did, would they have been seen?" Baldwin questioned, his eyes still on the servant.

"Anybody could have got in, but—" said Sir Hector heavily.

"Sir Hector, do you allow all your men to have access to your private chamber?" Baldwin asked coolly, spurred by the disruption of his questioning.

The captain hesitated. "No, but some of my men who are trusted can always gain admission."

"Such as?"

"Servants, my officers . . . a few people." He spoke reticently.

"And who are these servants and officers?" Baldwin asked suavely.

Simon wandered to the chest while Sir Hector, glowering, listed the men who formed his private guard, the men in whom he placed his highest trust, beginning with Henry the Hurdle and John Smithson.

The bailiff was, for the first time, feeling a prickle of

interest. In the past he had found getting involved with murder enquiries distasteful: as an investigator he sometimes felt tainted by the evil of the act. Too often he had been plucked from his comfortable, safe home-life, and tossed headlong into wild and conflicting emotions, for, in his experience, at the root of all murders were passions which, for some reason, suddenly spilled over and became extreme. Such ferocity had always been a mystery to him, for Simon's life had ever been moderate and relaxed.

However, since Peterkin's passing, the security and certainty of his whole being seemed ill-founded, as if the sickness which had killed his little boy was now gnawing at the vitality of his entire family. After his son's burial, Simon's desire to dispense justice had withered, for he had little concern for others now his own life had been so cruelly wrecked.

But there was a poignancy to this killing. It was not merely the superficial resemblance of Sarra to his wife, it was the manner of the girl's death. This murder was yet another proof of how unfair and cruel life could be. He had a sense that, if he could resolve it, he might in some way compensate for the unreasonably early death of his son. It would be a cathartic exercise.

Now that Peterkin was gone, Simon could feel the unnecessary death of another more keenly. If this had been a fellow who had died after a drunken brawl, or a man killed while arguing over a woman or a game, he would have remained unmoved, but the combination of the dead girl's visage and the demeaning cache in which she had been stored fired his anger against whoever might have committed this crime.

Baldwin had returned to his study of Sarra's body while Simon mused, and the bailiff watched with lackluster eyes as he used his dagger to slice through the cord binding her arms, then listened with half an ear while the knight talked to the captain.

"So we have to assume that this killing was done either by one of your trusted officers, or by a servant from the inn, *or* by someone who broke in through one of the windows." He wandered over to a shutter and tested the heavy baulk of timber which held the doors closed. Moving it, he found it was heavy and fitted closely in its rests. "Not easy to shift that," he muttered.

"It must have been one of the inn's people," Sir Hector growled.

"I doubt it." Turning, Baldwin stared at him. "You have told me that you only permitted your most trusted men into this area. You would not want to have strangers wandering round your private apartments, would you? No, the only people who would have come in here were your men."

"And her."

"Her?" Baldwin glanced down at the body. "You allowed her in?"

"Yes. I liked her." He stopped, looking at Baldwin as if expecting a rebuke.

"Hmm. I see, so she knew the silver was here, too. But unless she talked to someone, the most obvious suspects must be your own men."

"One of them: Cole," Sir Hector said between gritted teeth. "Otherwise someone from the town who thought they might be able to make a quick killing."

Simon shot a glance of loathing at him, but the captain appeared unaware of his pun.

Baldwin repeated, "Cole," thoughtfully.

Leaning down, Simon saw that the gauze was heavily stained with blood, and the firm imprint of the girl's body could be clearly perceived: her legs, her hands, her head. But there was a jutting edge in the clots which marred the outline and made him frown.

"Couldn't he have had an accomplice, waiting outside? Someone he could pass the things to, once he had murdered poor Sarra?" Sir Hector asked.

"I can't see how. It is the same as before, when we were thinking it was only a theft: anyone trying to get in from the street would have been noticed—this road is busy at all times of the day—and someone loitering on the other side of the window in the stableyard would attract attention from an ostler or one of the other innworkers. I suppose it's possible that it was a coincidence that the robbery and killing happened at the same time, but it hardly seems likely. Tell me, you say you liked the girl—are you aware of anyone who could have wanted to kill her? Someone who hated her?"

"Her? She was only a serving-girl from an inn, Sir Baldwin. How could someone hate a creature like that?" Sir Hector spread his hands in astonishment.

Baldwin nodded, his eyes straying back to the body before him. In life she had been pretty, and he was not surprised that the captain had "liked" her, a euphemism which left little to Baldwin's imagination, but he could understand that the captain would find it hard to comprehend an unimportant young wench might have enemies who could want to kill. The reasons were legion; a jealous lover; a jealous wife disposing of her husband's lover; a lover discarding his mistress because she had become an embarrassment . . . and so on. Still, as the man said, it was more probable that Cole had killed her. She must have discovered him taking the silver, and he stabbed her to ensure her silence.

While he ruminated, Simon carefully lifted the cloth by a corner, peering underneath. "Baldwin. Look at this."

"What? Ah, that *is* interesting!" Baldwin reached down. Beneath the cloth was a third silver plate. The knight bent and took it out. "There is the proof. The murderer *must* have been the thief. He killed Sarra because she had seen what was happening. She knew who he was."

"That bastard!" Sir Hector stepped quickly to Simon's side and stared at the plate in Baldwin's hands, tarnished where the blood had marked it. "So he killed her when he stole my silver."

"Yes," said Baldwin lugubriously. "Yes, it does look a little like that, doesn't it?"

There was nothing more to be said. Sir Hector left them a short while later, his face working with emotion, and Simon felt a certain sympathy for him. "He's mad about this," he murmured to his friend. "I thought he was angry before when it was only his silver which had gone, but now I bet he would lynch Cole without thinking twice about it. He must have been very fond of the girl."

Baldwin gave him a dubious look. "Perhaps, although it seems out of character. In any case, whatever Sir Hector does or does not think, we have the rule of English law here, and his suspicions carry no weight with me."

"Don't you think it was Cole then?"

"I suppose so, but I still have the same problem I had before. How was the silver removed? And how did he get in here in the first place?"

They left shortly afterward, but waited in the hall while Paul sent a messenger to fetch Hugh and Edgar.

When the two men arrived, Baldwin ordered them to guard the storeroom in which the dead girl's body lay. Nobody was to go in. Baldwin wanted to study the place again in daylight. Then he led the way outside. A few steps along the road he paused, then walked up to the closed outer shutters of the storeroom. Simon heard him mutter a short oath of disgust, for he'd accidentally stepped in a pile of rotting intestines and viscera—a pungent reminder that the butcher was next door. Through cracks in the old, untreated timbers, narrow beams of light escaped, and the knight tried to peer through, his eye close to the wood. Frowning, he walked back through the inn to the yard behind, and repeated the exercise, Simon trailing after him.

"That's one thing."

"What?" Simon asked, yawning.

"Whoever stole the plate did not see it through these shutters. This was no random, opportunistic theft. Not that I thought it would be, for who would dare to steal from a mercenary captain and his men? No, nobody could have glanced in and realized that the room held a great store of silver."

"So?"

"So, old friend, the thief must have been someone who was a member of the company, or was the friend of a member of the company. It would seem to bear out Cole's guilt—but who was his accomplice?"

The next morning Simon awoke later than usual with a vague sense of gloom. Margaret's body had left a hollow in the mattress beside him, but the dent was cool to his touch. She must have risen some time before. He sighed and rolled onto his back, an arm flung behind his head.

It hurt him so much to see her suffering—and yet he could not find the words to help her. His own desolation was so vast that he could not think how to bridge the chasm which had suddenly appeared and now separated them as effectively as the deep gorge at Lydford. He had no means of spanning it.

To his surprise, thoughts of the dead girl intruded. Her face, which looked as though it was better used to being happy and carefree, was so violated and shrunken in that meager coffin with the cruel band round her mouth, that he felt anger stirring once more against whoever could have inflicted so demeaning a death on her. No matter how hard Simon tried to put her from his mind, the girl kept returning, as if demanding revenge, staring at him accusingly with his wife's eyes.

He rose and dressed himself. The hall was along a short corridor, and there he found the table laid. Peter, Baldwin, Margaret and Edith were all present, as was Stapledon. Peter waved him to a seat, but it was the Bishop who spoke.

"Ah, Bailiff. I have just been hearing about the dead girl you found. Sad, very sad. To think a young man could do that—steal another man's silver, and kill an innocent girl as well. It is horrible to discover how dark a man's heart can be." He crammed a thick hunk of bread into his mouth.

Simon nodded and sat beside his wife. Margaret was pale, and her eyes looked red, though whether from lack of sleep or weeping he couldn't tell. While he gazed at her concentrating on her food, by chance the sun escaped from behind a cloud. From the windows high in the walls, sunlight entered at a steep angle, falling through the apertures like a luminous mist in which dust motes danced and whirled, forming pools of color on the floor. One fell near, and by its light Margaret's face was suffused with a golden tint which revivified her features, softening and smoothing her wrinkles, and renewing her youth. It made her hair glow, and she looked five years younger. To Simon it was as if the woman he had fallen in love with had returned, unlooked for.

Chewing, Baldwin was about to ask Simon whether he had any fresh thoughts on the dead girl when he saw his friend staring at his wife. She turned to catch sight of his expression, and slowly her taut expression eased into a smile, as though she had almost forgotten how to. To his secret delight, Baldwin saw Simon return it.

"Sir Baldwin," Stapledon said, waving his knife vaguely, "What do you think the boy has actually done with the silver? Could he have hidden it out on the road before he was captured?"

"No. That's inconceivable, according to the men who caught him. Apparently they had been following him for some time, after they saw him behaving oddly—I think they said 'furtively'—in town."

"They could have marked the spot where he hid it so that they themselves could return there and claim it."

"It's possible," Baldwin agreed.

"But you don't think so?"

Baldwin shook his head. "Sir Hector de Gorsone has some thirty odd men with him. He has undoubtedly fought in several campaigns, and his soldiers are battle-hardened. All can kill. It is quite feasible that these two men could have seen where the silver was placed, as you say, but what then? They would not have left Cole alive to say where it had been stored; they would have killed him immediately. Then they could go to it whenever they wanted. If they were to stay with Sir Hector, they would have a hard time explaining where any new wealth came from, but on the other hand, if they were to try to run away, where could they go? And don't forget they would have incurred the wrath of their captain. He would be bound to seek revenge, if only to reimpose his will on the other men. The two with the silver would find thirty or so highly motivated men chasing after them wherever they tried to go. I think that if they saw Cole making a fool of himself, then witnessed him hiding something, they would have told their master as soon as they found out about the robbery."

"What if they did not realize that it was their master's silver? Couldn't they have decided to profit by someone else's theft and hidden it to collect later?"

"That is possible, but as soon as they found out it was Sir Hector's treasure they would be bound to tell him where it was. They would be unhappy to steal from him, I would think, although they might expect a reward for bringing it back."

"People can react fast to changing circumstances," the Bishop said. "Perhaps they secreted it somewhere new, so they could go back to it later."

"Unlikely," Sir Baldwin decided. "In the first place, like I say, I believe they would have killed Cole to ensure that their secret was safe. Then again, they had no idea how long it would take for the robbery to be discovered, so they could not know how much time they had to hide the silver. I think they would have tried to capture the thief and deliver him up to their master. After all, even if they are mercenaries, they are still soldiers. Their whole life is tied up with their companions."

"I have known men-at-arms who have been disliked

by their companions and who have disappeared as soon as a good sum became available," the Bishop observed.

"So have I," Baldwin admitted. "But until I see evidence of that, I shall assume that these two have been telling the truth. And, of course, we do have a suspect in jail. Right now he is the most likely culprit."

Margaret leaned forward. "Why would he have killed the girl? There was no need, surely?"

"Possibly—and possibly not. There is one simple explanation. He went into the room to steal the silver and either she was there already or she came in a little later. Either way, he knew that if she spoke of him being in Sir Hector's room his life would be forfeit. He killed her to save his own skin, then hid the body so that he could make good his escape."

Roger de Grosse was sitting nearby, and he frowned at this. "Surely, Sir Baldwin, if he was intending to make his escape, he would have planned a better means than his own feet?"

"A very good point. But it is possible that in the first case he intended taking the silver and hiding it, so he could return to it later when the fuss had died down."

"How did he do it? From what you have said, he would have been seen leaving by the hall, and the shutters were closed. He couldn't have jumped from a window."

Baldwin glanced at Simon. "I have told them about our talks last night," he said. "That, Roger, is still the point which interests me. Again, we don't know how, but several explanations are possible."

"Could Sarra have been an accomplice? She might have opened the shutters for him and closed them after he left."

Baldwin smiled. "And afterward he wandered back in and killed her? No, all we know is that he must have taken the silver some time *after* Sir Hector rose from his bed, and *before* the captain returned from his meal."

The bailiff nodded. "I look forward to hearing how he did it."

8

The jail was a small building near the market, almost opposite the inn. Commonly it was used for victims of the Pie Powder courts, at which market traders were convicted for selling short measures or defective goods, but it also served for those committed for more serious offenses. Small, stone and square, it lurked malevolently near the toll-booth, a focus of fear for people of the town, for many of those who entered would only leave to make their way to the gallows.

It was only a few minutes' walk from Peter's house. Baldwin and Simon set off immediately after their breakfast. Roger had asked if he might join them, and Stapledon agreed that it could be useful for the rector to witness how investigations were conducted.

Even this early in the morning the street was busy. Hawkers strolled, yelling their offers to the world, horses clattered along the partly cobbled way, wagons thumped and rattled past, and Simon smiled to see the children running and jumping in and among the traffic. He saw the woman in gray, her child nearby, but she did not appear to recognize him. He did not blame her: it had been late when he helped her, and dark in the street. She stood quietly, a begging bowl in her hand, smiling pitifully at all who passed in a desperate attempt to win alms. Simon averted his gaze. There were so many, especially after the years of famine, who needed the charity of others to survive, yet the sight of beggars always made him feel uncomfortable.

All along the way Roger found his nostrils assailed by the fumes of the busy, growing town. Sharp woodsmoke gave a wholesome background, but more pervasive was the noisome stench rising from the open sewer in the street, to which the dung of horses, oxen, pigs and sheep all added their malodorous reek. As they approached the inn, the smells altered, subtly proclaiming the presence of the butcher.

They stopped to watch. The butcher's was on the corner of two streets, right next to the inn, and behind it Roger could make out the cookshop. A little beyond was the lane which led behind the cookshop, past the stables, to the inn's yard. Before the inn itself was the small pile of animal remains Baldwin had stood in the night before; now four stray dogs hovered over it, snatching what they could and snarling at each other.

In front of the butcher's itself Roger saw the rotund little figure of Adam at his work, a large knife in his hand, and dressed in his heavy old apron. The rector paid little attention; he was staring at a hawker further up the street when there was a loud, piercing squeal that made the hair on the back of his neck tingle.

When Roger turned in horror, he saw that the butcher had stuck a pig. It hung upside down from a tripod by a rope around its hind legs, jerking and twitching as the blood bubbled and gushed from the vivid gash in its throat, dripping into a large pot underneath. As its struggles decreased, the butcher slit it from breast to pelvis, and the entrails, massive ropes of yellow brown, suddenly slithered free like so many snakes from a sack. An assistant was already tipping boiling water over the animal and readying his razor to remove all the bristles from the body, and Adam had his hands inside the carcass pulling out the heart and lungs as he watched.

The smell of rotting flesh pervaded the street. Although many townspeople complained regularly to Baldwin about the smells and the flies, there was little he could do. If folk wanted to eat, the butcher must ply his trade. It was a shame that feces voided from the bowels of animals were dumped until they could be carried to the midden, for it created an unwholesome aroma, but the guts must be cleaned so that sausages could be made. Little if anything was wasted from a pig's carcass.

When the body had been carelessly shaved and carried away, a fresh hog was brought to its three-legged scaffold. Adam stropped his knife and waited while it was hauled aloft, squealing in rage and terror, its evil little eyes rolling wildly in fury. Seeing the three men watching, Adam smiled and waved, and Roger thought to himself how like a hog the butcher himself looked, with his little shining eyes and round features.

They walked on across the street. It was only a matter of yards from here to the jail, and Simon's eyes were on the small, squat building, but when he shot a glance at Baldwin, the knight was staring at the inn almost opposite.

"What is it?" Simon asked.

"Oh, I was just thinking that being here, near the market, the inn must often have wagons parked outside it. Look, one is there now."

"Yes." The bailiff could see the old cart, the horse standing slack and tired, thin and ragged from underfeeding and maltreatment. "So what?"

"I had thought it would be too obvious for Cole to try to get the silver out through a window on the street, but look! If a stranger parked a carriage of some sort here, it would be noticed immediately, but a man could wait nearby, and take the things from the window, couldn't he? If there was someone there now, he would be hidden from sight by the butcher's wagon."

"But if the silver weighed so much that three men were needed to carry it . . ."

"Oh yes, but he could have had more than one accomplice, or he might have passed it out in small parcels. That way his companion could have stood here for a few minutes, then gone to hide the silver and come back for the next instalment. Always hidden, always out of sight behind a wagon. It would be a perfect arrangement."

"There's one thing I don't understand."

"What?" Baldwin looked at him with a faint grin. Simon was a long way from being himself, he thought, but he did seem to be mending. It was not only the way he had smiled at his wife over breakfast; he had a different look to him. Last night he was peevish and complaining, but now that he had something to occupy his mind, he had almost become the cautious and thoughtful man whom Baldwin remembered. Apart from anything else, raising objections to Baldwin's ideas was a sure sign that the bailiff was improving.

"Let's say you're right and he had an accomplice out here . . ."

"He must have had an accomplice somewhere, whether here or out back, in the yard."

"Fine. If that's right, why did he still have two plates on him?"

Baldwin stopped. "I . . . What?"

"If you're right, then he must have passed everything out to his companion. So why did he have two plates on him when he was caught?"

"I suppose he might have discovered that his friend had gone so he had to take them out himself when he left the room."

"Through the hall, you mean? That makes no sense. If he was part of an organized group, the reason for having someone outside was so he didn't need to carry anything himself. Nor would he have left any spare things behind, like the saltcellar. If he was going to carry out something worthwhile, he'd have gone for that, but instead he took two plates, the last things I would have expected him to choose."

"It would have been easier to hide two plates. They are flatter," the knight suggested.

"True, but even better would be nothing. Why risk discovery by carrying them? Far better to leave them behind and make good his escape. Especially since you're supposing his accomplice had disappeared—in that circumstance, I would have expected him to get out and not take anything with him. His only interest would be in how fast he could vanish, not what else he could take with him. That's what I find so difficult."

"Why? He was greedy, that's all. He's a thief. All right, so his accomplice had to leave for some reason, or maybe he simply took too long to get back. Whatever, Cole found himself with the last two plates and decided to brazen it out."

"If you were him, would you have taken out those plates? Put yourself in his shoes. The whole theft has been thought out carefully, even down to the accomplice outside. And then the accomplice disappears . . . you don't know why, but surely you would suspect he had been seen. You still have to escape—and that means walking through the hall, under the eyes of thirty-odd men. You have two plates left out of God alone knows how many, and you are so blasé you decide to take them with you? I find that hard to believe!"

"Thieves can be irrational."

"Not so irrational, surely, that when they know they're being chased they keep some spoil on them! He would get rid of any incriminating evidence as soon as he discovered his pursuit."

"You might have a point, but think on this: you have just had to murder a girl as well. That has thrown your plans all awry. You hide the body, and then escape, taking the shortest route. It could well be that your accomplice never disappeared: after having to commit murder, you decide to get out through the window yourself."

"Somebody would see a man diving out through a window."

"Would they? If so much silver could be shoved out without being noticed, I doubt it. If somebody's carriage was in the way, maybe no one could see. Cole could have jumped out and remained hidden, then gone on later."

"But, Sir Baldwin," Roger interrupted, "who closed the shutters afterward?"

Baldwin found that he was frowning. Out of the corner of his eye he caught sight of a merchant staring at them. Grinning apologetically, he continued in a mutter, "I have no idea, but it is the best explanation I can think of for now."

"I want to know what really happened," Simon stated.

Baldwin raised a fist to hammer on the door. "Well, rather than speculating, let's find out. Simon, I . . . Where are you going?"

"Just a thought, Baldwin," Simon called over his shoulder.

The butcher had that minute stopped, and was sitting on a three-legged stool, a pot of ale in his fist. As people walked past, all had a polite word with him, Simon noticed, and all received a nod and a smile from the genial man. Children got a wink too.

Simon was aware of his companions joining him as he reached the other side of the road. The inn's hall ran parallel to the street here, the entrance almost in the middle. Here, almost opposite the jail, they were at the dais end, and to their left were the windows that gave on to the solar block commandeered by the captain. With the bustle and hubbub in the street, it was obvious to the two men that nobody could have taken anything from the inn unseen.

Walking slowly past the butcher's, Simon went to the road which led up the hill. Aware of the amused patience of his friend, Simon walked past the butcher and his tripod to the corner where the two roads met, and looked up the incline.

The butcher had storerooms and a small pen, and past that was the cookshop, and then the alley which led to the inn's yard. The road rose steeply after that, and was soon lost among the trees scattered on the hillside.

"Seen enough?" Baldwin asked.

"Yes, I think so." Simon gave him a long and thoughtful look, then smiled at the butcher. "A pleasant morning, isn't it?"

Adam smiled back. His back ached, his feet hurt, and he had nicked his thumb with his thin knife, but the sun was warm on his face, the ale tasted good, and there was little more for him to do that day. His apprentice could get on with things alone. "Yes, sir. It feels good to sit in the sun for a change."

"It must be hot work in this weather," Simon said, nodding toward the gantry where the apprentice sweated as he worked on the dead pig.

"Oh, not so bad, sir," Adam said indulgently, pouring himself more ale from a jug beside his stool. "It's all right out here. It's when we have to work inside it gets a bit warm."

"Are you out in the open most days, then?"

"Most mornings. Afternoons we spend indoors, jointing and cutting up. Then there's the salting of the pork, and hanging of cattle to make them tender, and preparation for smoking, and sausage-making, and all the other tasks. It takes ages. People always think the killing's the hardest part, but that's only the beginning for us."

Out of the corner of his eye, Roger saw the apprentice curl his lip as his master spoke. The rector was convinced that the "us" was not necessarily indicative of an equal share in effort. He restrained a smile with difficulty as Simon continued, "Were you here yesterday—last afternoon?"

"Yes, sir."

Baldwin tried to control his excitement as Simon casually asked, "Here in the street?"

"Yes, right here. My boy there," he jerked a thumb at the assistant, "was inside with some chickens and capons, but I had to take a rest. The noise they make goes right through my head."

"Did you see anyone up there, by the windows to the inn?"

"What, there?" Adam asked, pointing and squinting a little.

"Yes, outside the living quarters to this side of the hall."

"No. People keep away when there's bits of offal in the road. I wasn't here all day, but no, I didn't."

"Were you here for the early part of the afternoon, then?"

"I was here from about . . ." he glanced blankly at his apprentice as if for inspiration ". . . a couple of hours after noon, I suppose, until maybe four hours after. I got too hot then, and went in to the cool."

"What about you—did you notice anyone round here? Anybody who shouldn't have been here, or who was hanging around for some time?" Baldwin said to the apprentice.

"Me, sir? No, I was working in the room all afternoon."

"It doesn't look out over this street?"

The boy pointed to the window near Adam's shoulder. "Yes, sir, but I was working. I didn't have time to look out."

Adam was nodding contentedly as he spoke, and Simon had the impression that he would, for all his easy smiles and cheerfully rotund features, be a hard taskmaster. "Very well," he said with disappointment. "Thank you for your help."

"Wait!" Adam said, and both turned to face him once more. The butcher smiled and went into his shop, returning with a short string. "You'll try some of my sausages, gentlemen, won't you?"

* * *

Tanner answered the door quickly, a disgruntled, unshaven figure in dirty russet tunic and hose. A strong and stolid man, he had dark hair and a square jaw, which now jutted with irritation as the visitors pushed past him. He walked with them to the curtain at the back of the room.

Beyond was the trapdoor in the floor. It was held in place by a large iron clasp, and locked by a wooden peg. Tanner wandered over to it and kicked the peg free before bending and lifting the trap. He slid the ladder over and lowered it into the depths.

Roger winced at the stench coming up from the cell below. It was not only the cold, dank air, it was the scent of unwashed and fearful bodies. The town jail usually held people who were waiting for punishment, and all too often there was only the one punishment available. It smelled as if the fear of hundreds of prisoners over the centuries had impregnated the walls of the jail with their expectation and dread.

Philip Cole was different. In the past, when Simon had waited here and watched as a prisoner clambered up the ladder, he had felt sympathy wash over him. Philip Cole needed none. He hopped from the ladder with a degree of agility that surprised Simon, then stood silent and still beside it, staring at his interrogators.

Baldwin had learned over time to be wary of first impressions: in his experience people were rarely either as simple or as complex as they appeared, and yet . . .

This man was suspected of murder and robbery, two of the most heinous crimes possible, and if he was guilty, he should be betraying some of the symptoms of his conscience: nervousness, an inability to meet an official's eye, twitching and biting his lips. Baldwin had known some criminals who were practiced in their craft and who could keep their anxiety hidden, but they were rare and usually a great deal older than this man.

Philip Cole stood defiantly, his arms behind him, and met their stares with what looked like near-anger. He displayed none of the signs of contrition which were to be expected of a man who had murdered a young woman like Sarra. If he was a knave who had killed to hide a robbery, Baldwin mused, he was a very good actor. His forehead was unlined, giving him an air of probity, his eyes had a guilelessness which fitted well with his simple clothing, marking him out as a farmer, and the way he stared back at his three jailers held more contempt than remorse.

The knight had to remind himself that this man, even if not a murderer, was at best a willing mercenary; he had joined a band of men who were little better than outlaws who held legitimacy purely by the force of their arms.

"Well? Have you come here to release me?"

Simon moved over to join Roger by a wall. Tanner leaned against the doorframe in case the lad attempted to escape. The bailiff of Lydford had no authority here; this was Baldwin's area, and he must conduct the enquiry.

"You know why you are here?" Baldwin asked.

"Two men have accused me of stealing. It's stupid! Where is all this silver I'm supposed to have taken? Search my bags; look through all my things. I've got nothing to hide."

"The thief was well-prepared, even had an accomplice. Such a man would find it easy to conceal what he had taken."

"Oh? And where, then, am I supposed to have put all this silver?" Philip exploded. "I don't even know anyone here."

Studying his face, Baldwin still could not discern a trace of nervousness. He paused a moment. "Yesterday you were at the inn all day?"

"Yes." He sounded irritable, as if such questions were foolish.

"Yet last night you were found some miles from the town, on a road heading south. What were you doing there?"

"Nothing. I was attacked here, in the town."

"What?"

"I was attacked. Knocked on the head."

"Where?"

"At the inn, in the yard behind it. I was sitting near the rear door when I heard something out at the stables. The horses were making a racket, and I went out to see what was upsetting them. That's all I know."

"What happened?"

He shrugged, and for the first time looked a little ill-at-ease. "I remember crossing the yard. No one else was about, and I didn't hurry, there seemed no point. There's the one big door and separate boxes set out on the left, and I think I just got inside the door when something caught me. I fell, and I can remember being dazzled; it was dark in the stable, and I'd been trying to get used to it when I was struck. When I fell, I rolled, and the sun was in my eyes."

"Did you see who had struck you?"

Cole reached up and touched the hair above his left ear. "No," he admitted wryly. "I wish I had."

"Let me see." Baldwin walked over to him and peered at the man's head. He was not lying about being hit, that much was evident. Just over his ear was a tangled mess where the greasy hair had become matted. Baldwin probed, making Cole wince and hiss. There was a crust, Baldwin saw, and a little broke off in tiny clumps which he studied closely. In the dark of the jail it was hard to be certain, but it looked and felt like dried blood. He glanced back at the man's face. "Was there anyone else there who might have seen this happen?"

"I don't know." His impatience was reasserting itself. "I was unconscious. Someone must have seen me go in, I imagine."

Simon broke in. "When did all this happen?"

"Sometime in the late afternoon."

"We found you late at night. Do you expect us to believe you could have been out cold for that long?"

"All I know is, I went to see what was happening to the horses, and when I came to loads of men were staring at me like I was something that'd just crawled out of the sewer."

The bailiff subsided, looking at Baldwin, who recognized the other's expression: baffled confusion. The knight ventured, "If what you say is true, do you have any idea why someone could have tried to make you look like the guilty one?"

Cole glowered at the ground. "Yes."

"Could you tell *us,* then?" Baldwin prompted smoothly.

Cole hesitated. "I want to get him myself. It's me he's hurt—I want to have my own revenge."

"Do you realize the position you are in?" asked Baldwin in disbelief. "Your captain has had all his silver stolen—some of it was found on you—and a murder has been committed, probably during the robbery. Why should we listen to you when—"

"Murder?" His face had paled, his shock so palpable, Baldwin was convinced he had no idea that Sarra had been killed, though whether that was because he thought she had merely been injured and would recover, or because he knew nothing of the attack on her, was another matter. "What murder? Who's dead? This is a trick—you're trying to get me to confess to the robbery by threatening me with—"

"Shut up!" Tanner snapped curtly, but Baldwin held up a restraining hand. He surveyed the prisoner.

"This is no trick; we're not trying to trap you. All we want to do is clear up a particularly nasty murder, and right now you are the main—well, the only—suspect."

"But I know nothing of this. Who's dead? Is it one of the soldiers?" His face was ashen, and he reminded Roger of a sack which has suddenly lost its contents. The cheeks seemed to draw in, the eyes to stare with the dreadful realization of his danger.

"Tell us who might have put this on to you. You were only there with Sir Hector for a day or so—did you anger someone? Or was it somebody from your home?"

Cole took a deep breath and met the knight's gaze steadily. "It was someone in the band. I've no idea who, but it must have been one of them." Baldwin nodded encouragingly, and the youth carried on haltingly, his voice betraying his emotion.

"Sir Hector's men came through this way some five years ago. Back then I was only fourteen, but my brother Thomas was nearly twenty, and a strong, hard man. He was a good brother, and he looked after the family, four brothers and a sister, after our father died when he was eleven, working for any farmer who needed help. When my sister decided to marry, he slaved to earn enough to make her a dowry. But then our mother died, and my youngest brother with her, and Thomas had had enough. He wanted to marry, but the girl he loved was already betrothed, and the day she wed he told me he was going to go away."

"This is all very interesting, but—" Baldwin murmured.

"It's important, sir. Thomas left me in the care of John, my remaining brother, and went off. We didn't know where, all we knew was, he'd gone. Then—oh, it must have been a year later—we had a message. Someone came past our place and visited us. He told us my brother had joined Sir Hector's band, but he had died in Gascony, during a fight."

"There are lots of wars in Gascony, especially on the border with France," Baldwin said, and Cole nodded.

"Yes, sir, and I'd have thought no more about it, except this man said Thomas had been killed while fighting as an archer for Sir Hector. Now Thomas was a good fighter; known for it. But archer? He couldn't hit a barn if he was stood inside it: he was awful. No one would let him near a bow in battle. He was the sort to stand with a pike and protect the bowmen, but not ever get near a bow himself. It made us wonder."

"Many messages like that get confused, especially after a battle," Baldwin noted thoughtfully.

"I know, sir, but it still seemed strange. The messenger was very definite. When I pressed him, he insisted that he had been told Thomas had been an archer. Anyway, John was killed two months ago, crushed by a wagon at the farm. There was nothing to keep me there anymore, and when I heard Sir Hector's band were passing by again, I felt I had to come and see them to find out what happened to Thomas."

"It hardly required you to join them," said Simon dryly.

"No, sir," Cole agreed. "But when I saw them all at the inn, I guessed they might not tell me much. I thought the best way to find out the truth was to join them. Otherwise they'd just close their mouths and keep their silence, and I want to know what really did happen."

"What did you find out?" Baldwin had become interested despite himself.

"Nothing. Absolutely nothing. I asked after Tom with a few people, but they all seemed never to have heard of him. And then this happened."

~ 9 ~

Simon heaved a sigh of relief at being out of the jail. It was too small, too dark, and he had felt claustrophobic in there. The air might not be any better outside, with the stench from the street worsening as the sun warmed the waste in the sewer, but at least here there was sunlight and the noise of free people rushing about trying to earn a living. It was infinitely better than the atmosphere of the jail.

"We'd better get to the inn and rescue Edgar and Hugh," Baldwin said, glancing up at the sun. It was rising in the sky: it must be midmorning.

They crossed the street, dodging a horse and cart. To their left, the tripod still stood outside the shop, but the bailiff saw that the butcher had disappeared. Simon happened to glance in through a window, and there he caught a glimpse of the young apprentice. Grasping a massive cleaver, he was hacking at a pig's carcass dangling from a hook in the wall, splitting it in half down the spine. Every now and then the lad paused to wipe his forehead, clearing the sweat as the flies danced. Simon smiled. He could understand how tiring it must be to lift the massive axe-like tool and swing it in this heat. The apprentice would have several bodies to joint, and if he did not complete his work, his master would surely leave him in no doubt of his incapacity as a trainee. He looked young to be hefting a weapon like that, at maybe thirteen or fourteen years old, and the bailiff could not help glancing at the solemn face of the young rector, wondering whether Roger de Grosse realized how lucky he was.

It was dark in the alley inside the market entrance, which was a comfort after the furnace heat of the street where the shining cobbles seemed hotter than the sun itself. There was no breeze, and even in the shade he could feel the fresh sweat prickling under his armpits and all down his back, but he had to smile. He was calm, with no shadow of fear to darken his brow, and the fact made him proud.

So the bailiff was interested in a butcher's apprentice? What a keen mind he must have! Either keen or vacant. Better than his friend, though. Sir Baldwin de Furnshill was thought to be quick and intelligent, a cautious but tenacious inquisitor, much more of a threat than the Exeter Coroner who hardly ever bothered to travel to Crediton nowadays; with the teaming hordes of seamen at the docks, he was kept busy enough closer to home. There was no need to journey far to see death in all its forms. This Baldwin, though, was considered clever. The man in the shadows sneered at the idea. Clever! And yet now he was going from the jail back to the inn, no doubt intending to question the captain in his lair, seeing whether he might have any idea why the girl had been killed.

The two men disappeared through the doorway, and their watcher smiled again. His mind was clear once more, just as it had been the night before when he felt the knife slip so smoothly into her body; it was like pushing the weapon into an oiled leather scabbard—one especially shaped to take the thick single-edged blade. The way that his brain had suddenly been so calm, the thoughts so crystal-bright, had surprised him at first, but then he'd realized it was because he was so clever. It was impossible that the others would discover him.

A slow grin spread over his face. And now they were off to seek the man who had robbed the captain. They were bound to find suspects: only men who had something to hide would join a mercenary band.

Yes, he thought. There should be plenty of suspicious characters in a band like that. It was good to keep the King's man busy.

"Hugh, would you please stop that!" Edgar usually displayed the tolerance of an older brother toward a younger in his dealings with Simon's servant, but when the man had pulled his dagger out of its scabbard for the seventh time and scrutinized its edge as if suspicious that it had developed a fault, his temper began to fray. When Simon's servant was not studying his blade, he was whistling—a hollow, deathly sound that reminded Edgar of the wind in the branches of trees over a churchyard at the dead of night. Even when the man was sitting, his fingers would keep drumming on any convenient surface near to hand. "What is it?" he asked irritably. "Can't you just be quiet?"

"No," Hugh scowled. "I'm not used to guarding a dead body." His face reflected his mood. It was not only that he was missing Peter Clifford's hospitality, which had lived up to expectation in the excellence of his ale and the fullness of his board; Hugh had grown up on the moors, a little to the south in the old forest of Dartmoor, and his superstitious soul cringed at having to share a room with a murdered woman. The only thing that could make it worse, from his point of view, would be if she was a suicide, but even a murder victim was full of terrors. He had stayed awake all night less from a sense of duty than from a terror of the Devil coming to take an unshriven soul. Hugh might not be learned, but he knew what the priests said: if a man or woman were to die without having been given the chance to confess their sins, they could not be buried on hallowed ground. They could not go to Heaven, they belonged to the Devil, and all night Hugh had fretted, thinking that every sound he heard was Old Nick coming to take her away. Now, in the warm sunlight of a fresh morning, he had a feeling of anticlimax.

"You're a farmer's son. Surely you've had to sit up with a corpse before."

Hugh stared at him for a moment. "Of course I have! But I've never been told by my master to guard a room with a corpse in it, in case some mad bugger comes in trying to move things around." He stood and went to the chest again, looking down at Sarra where she lay on the floor.

His master and Baldwin had covered her with a bolt of cloth they had found in the chest, thus her face was hidden, but she held a fascination for Hugh. It was sad to see her dead. He was used to death in all its forms, from starvation during the appalling famines of 1315 and 1316, to those killed by swords and axes during the attacks of the trail bastons four years ago, but this little figure, whose hair tumbled silkily from beneath the cloth, seemed still more sad than all those.

"God's blood! Will you sit down and stop fidgeting! You're making *me* twitchy."

Hugh grunted and wandered to a convenient chest. Sitting, he rested a hand on another nearby and unconsciously began knocking out a rapid percussion. Edgar had opened his mouth to snap at him, when there was a tap at the door. Muttering with irritation, Edgar pulled it open.

Outside stood an old soldier. "My master has told me to fetch him some clothing." Edgar said nothing, but held the door tightly. The man glanced past him to the body and shook his head sadly. "Poor lass."

Rather than have the man stare through the door all morning, Edgar opened it wide. "Be quick. And touch nothing from the open chest."

He wandered in, going from one chest to another. Hugh saw how his eyes moved to the figure on the floor occasionally. There was no fear or horror, merely a kind of disinterested acceptance, as if it was too commonplace a sight to justify particular curiosity. This piqued Hugh. He had been quite proud of enduring the vigil by the corpse, and felt that others should be awed by the courage of two men who dared to defy ghosts and ghouls alike by sitting up with a murdered body.

Sir Hector's man walked toward him and gestured. "I've got to open that one, too."

Hugh rose, disgruntled, and waited while he rifled through the chest for oddments, selecting a short cloak and decorative belt with an enamelled buckle.

No sooner had he left than Simon and Baldwin arrived with Roger. To Hugh's disgust, neither asked how his night had been—they simply strode in and lifted the cloth from the body, so that Baldwin could study it more closely. Almost immediately his attention was drawn to Sarra's head.

Sucking his teeth, Simon moved to the tiny window and peered out. Wagons and carts passed by, interspersed with riders on horseback. People hurried by on foot. It was a busy street, and he fell to wondering again whether someone could have stood passing items out to an accomplice hidden behind a wagon. Leaning forward, he meditatively touched the frame. There was certainly enough space for a man to wriggle through if he was small enough—and if the shutters had been opened first.

Baldwin asked Edgar to help him; together, they rolled the body gently over onto its side. Over Sarra's left ear was a lump, and a crusting of blood. It looked much like Cole's wound, with one difference: hers was more like the result of a glancing blow which had scraped the skin and caused bleeding. She must have been alive when struck, for she bled, he thought. That explained a little of the mystery about her: she was alive but unconscious when gagged and bound. The next question, he knew, was *why* she had been stabbed. He studied her, then walked to the chest and looked at her outline. Where Simon had pulled the cloth aside, he carefully laid it back in place. There, where her head had lain, was a small patch of brownish black. So she was definitely alive when she was placed in the chest; dead people did not bleed, he knew. So she had been killed later.

Sighing, he rose. Simon had finished staring out of the window, and now left the room. Baldwin paused, then knelt and, using his dagger, cut off a large swatch of the material of her tunic. Stuffing it in his purse, he followed his friend into Sir Hector's room, and stood gazing round with an introspective air while Simon peered out of the window. Roger trailed in after them.

Outside, in the yard, Simon could see several men sitting at a table and drinking, laughing and joking in the shade of an old elm tree, while others worked on their weapons. Some were polishing helmets and shields until, when they caught the sun, they were painful to look at. Two men were fletching, expertly winding string round arrows to hold the feathers in place, and another was running a stone over his sword to give it an edge.

. Behind him he could hear Baldwin muttering to himself, but his attention was caught by the scene in the yard. It was rare to see men-of-war in a place like this, going about their business with a casual unconcern that made it seem normal. If they had been farmers cleaning tools and preparing for a day's work, the sight could not have been more tranquil. As if to emphasize this, the inn's hens scratched and stepped all round, their jerky motion an odd contrast to the smoothness of the armorer with his weapon. The stone sweeping along the sword's blade gave a rhythmic background to the setting, like a man scything wheat. Cloths buffing shields to a mirror-like finish added an air of domesticity which tended to confirm the impression of rustic calm.

"What are you staring at?"

Simon pointed. "You'd hardly think it was necessary to polish armor so clean, would you?"

The knight gave a small smile at the bailiff's ignorance. "Professional warriors often do that. Most armies are made up of peasants who have been ordered from their fields by their lords to go and fight for a cause they often understand only very sketchily. If they are hurled against another, similar army, they can sometimes do well, but if they find themselves arrayed against men who are clothed in armor, who shine like angels when the sun touches them, and who gleam so brightly that it is painful to look upon them, the average peasant will want to turn and run. Mercenaries are naturally warlike people because that's how they earn their living, and they practice and train to make sure that they are likely to win. After all, there is no profit for anybody in fighting if you're going to die. All soldiers intend winning, and living to enjoy their gains. A shining shield and helmet simply helps put the odds more in the mercenaries' favor."

"Whatever they do is designed to help them kill."

"Not only that: more to win," Baldwin studied his friend. "All they want is to make money, the same as any other businessman. They make nothing by killing. Prisoners who are worth money are ransomed, but in the main a mercenary army would be happier to see their poorer enemies put to flight."

"What if they fail, and they capture prisoners who are worth little or nothing in ransoms?"

"They will die," said Baldwin, his voice hardening. "But ruthlessness is not unique to mercenary bands. In any war it is the weak and poor who suffer. The same will be happening in Scotland as the army of England tries to hold back the Bruce."

Simon's eyes narrowed in concentration. "At that table—aren't they the two who found Cole last night?"

Baldwin nodded. "We have to talk to them at some point; it might as well be now," he said. He walked from the room, and with the others in tow, he and Simon led the way from the solar.

In the hall, Sir Hector was seated, complaining irritably about the quality of his food to an agitated Paul. Baldwin gave him a quick look of sympathy, and the innkeeper rolled his eyes. As they got to the doorway, Cristine was coming the other way, carrying a large tray. She stood back, out of Baldwin's path, with a respectful bowing of her head, but then he caught sight of a different emotion. She smiled with a sunny brilliance that transformed her tired visage, and when Baldwin checked, he saw that her face was turned toward his servant.

Edgar noticed his master's glance, and quickly fixed his features into their usual blank expressionlessness, but not quite fast enough. He could see that he had not fooled Sir Baldwin, and the knight had to struggle to keep the smile from his mouth. There were, he noted, depths to his servant which were still capable of surprising him.

Henry the Hurdle lounged in his seat, back resting against the inn's wall, his hands in his belt, belching softly and contentedly with his eyes half-closed. With the sun warming him, he thought he could be in France, except he preferred the drink in England. Watered wine was a pale substitute for good ale, even if it was weak ale. Margery was a very capable alewife, and her strong ale was powerful enough to put men to sleep when they were unused to it; her weak ale, brewed with less malt, had a pleasing, silky mildness, and Henry had already enjoyed three pints. He disliked the continental habit of adulterating good ale with weeds like hops; it made the drink too bitter, and everyone knew it was bad for the health, making the Flemish in northern France, who drank it in huge quantities, fat and bellicose. Beer was not as wholesome as good English ale.

His sense of well-being was rudely shattered when John dug him in the ribs. "It's the Keeper, Henry. Henry, wake up! The Keeper and his friend are here, the two who found us last night. They're back again."

Risking a quick glance from lowered brows, Henry watched the bailiff and his friend. They paused in the doorway, taking in the scene, three men close behind them, before beginning to stroll in the direction of their table. He stretched and yawned, then forced himself upright. "Let's see what they want."

Smiling cheerfully, he was the picture of relaxed honesty, but in his mind he was running through the story of what had happened the night before. Henry knew of the Keeper's reputation in the area: he was able to divine the truth in the way that people spoke, if you trusted what was said about him in the town. Henry did not believe in such powers, but he was prepared to accept that Baldwin was astute, and Henry did not want the knight guessing what had really happened the previous day, so he fixed his smile as firmly as if it had been nailed in place, and waited.

To Baldwin, from a distance they were like any ordinary pair of men taking their ease in the sun. One dozing, the other resting his elbows on the table and sipping at a large pot of ale. It was as he approached and could see their faces that he felt a pang of disgust. If his first impression of Cole was favorable, his immediate reaction to these two in the daylight was the reverse.

The night before he had thought that one was an ill-favored wretch, and now he could see that his recollection was overly generous. In broad daylight John

Smithson was as unpleasing a sight as it was possible to imagine, with sallow features, a narrow, steeply raked forehead, sharp face and light, unsettling eyes which avoided Baldwin's gaze. As they got closer, Baldwin was treated to a sight of Smithson taking a swallow of his ale. A portion fell from his mouth, and he wiped at it with the back of his hand. The knight was grateful not to have seen him eating.

There was nobody else at their table. Several other tables were filled with men from the band, and Simon wondered why these two sat alone, but the thought was fleeting, and he put it from his mind as he took his rest.

This discussion would take some time, Hugh saw moodily. He stood glumly behind his master as the inevitable questions began, Baldwin staring pensively at Henry.

"Last night we were all tired, and the excitement of the chase dulled our wits. I can hardly recall what you said about this man Cole and how you caught him. Could you run through it again?"

Hugh listened while the man told how he and his friend had noticed Cole in town. Originally they had gone after him to invite him to join them in a drink, but on approaching him, they had become suspicious at his behavior. He walked furtively, like a man who had something to hide, so they decided to follow him. He clearly knew the town, for he ducked into narrow alleys, only rarely passed where he could be seen and avoided places where the other members of Sir Hector's troop might go. They passed under lines of washing, being spattered by drips, and around filthy dumps, until they saw him drop something. They heard it rattle and spin like a coin, saw it glitter, and realized it must be a plate. With horror, they suddenly understood what must have happened: he'd stolen their master's silver and run away.

As he bent to pick up the fallen plate, Cole happened to glance behind him and—here Henry gave a chagrined smile as if he was disgraced by his stupidity—caught sight of Henry. If Henry had been less keen to see what it was he had dropped, he implied, Cole might not have spotted him. As it was, he had started to run away. They had called for help, but there didn't seem to be anyone around, and they had chased after him for miles until catching up with him some way out of the town.

Hugh's attention began to wander. He had heard it all the night before, and was not interested in the finer details of how the two heroes had managed to bring down their prey. At another table a short way off was space for three men, with a slight squeeze. He knew Edgar was committed to the protection of his master come what may, but there was little need to stand immediately behind Simon and Baldwin; a seat a few yards further off would surely be no difficulty. He indicated such to Roger, who leaned against the tree, bored, then tried to get Edgar's attention. It was only when Hugh took a step back that Edgar noticed him. Hugh jerked his head to the table silently, and Edgar looked from it to his master, then nodded.

Simon was aware of the departure of the three. He saw them taking their seats nearby, then turned back to Henry.

"I am surprised that no one heard you when you called for help," Baldwin observed.

"So was I, sir," Henry spread his hands, palms up, in a show of exasperation. "If someone had helped it would have saved us a long run."

"Yes. It seems quite clear, though, what happened." Baldwin was lapsing into the slow way of speaking which some mistook for drowsiness, but which Simon recognized as proof of extreme concentration on details. "You were after him for how long, roughly?"

"I suppose about three hours," Henry said, shooting a glance at his friend. John shrugged.

"How can I tell? It was afternoon when we first saw him, and dark when you caught up with us."

"Let us assume it was late afternoon, then. Perhaps you could tell us approximately how long you spent following him and how long chasing him?"

"I'm sorry, sir, but I couldn't say. No, I've got no idea. Anyway, does it matter?"

"Perhaps not, but I was wondering where Cole could have disposed of the silver he stole. And when, of course."

"When?"

Simon broke in, "Yes, *when. When* seems to be an interesting problem with every aspect of this matter. *When* did he get into your captain's room; *when* did he take the silver; *when* did he escape with it; *when* did he hide it? The only point of any interest apart from that is where he hid it, or with whom."

"Because, of course, there was more than one man involved," Baldwin added.

"How can you tell that?" asked Smithson quickly.

Baldwin ignored him. "Sir Hector is a cautious man, isn't he?"

"Oh, yes. Very. He has to be. In his time he has managed to annoy some powerful men, both here in England and in France. It is only natural that he should be careful."

"He must be very wary of strangers."

"Yes."

"And I suppose he makes sure that nobody he does not know, and know well, can get close to his food or drink."

Henry leaned back comfortably in his seat. "Yes. Some of his enemies might try to hurt him through poison."

"And he must be sure, really sure, of only a small number of men."

"That's right."

"Like you, for example."

"Yes. I've been with him for many years." He smiled.

"Do you remember Cole's brother?"

Henry frowned. "Cole's brother?" he asked uncertainly.

"You don't recall him? That is strange . . . Sir Hector lets you into his rooms, doesn't he?"

"He permits me to see him when I want. I *am* his deputy, you know."

"Yes, I know. He told me last night that you were one of very few men he allowed to enter his room: he trusts you. Would he have trusted Cole?"

"Cole?" Henry guffawed, and Smithson, recognizing a joke, drew his mouth into a wide, inane grin.

"What is so funny?"

"He wouldn't let Cole within yards of his door. No one who's new ever gets close to Sir Hector. Like I say, he's suspicious. After some months, maybe he would learn to put some faith in Cole, but it would take a long time."

"And all Sir Hector's men are aware of that, I suppose?"

"Oh, yes."

"How many men were in the hall last afternoon, do you think?"

"Ten or so. There would always be a guard there in case . . ."

"In case someone might try to steal Sir Hector's valuables," Baldwin finished for him. "But somehow someone *did* get in, didn't they? Someone went in, either through the door, past all those eyes in the hall, or through the window where everyone in the street could see him. Which do you think it was?"

"Me?" Henry looked dumbfounded. "I don't know. We weren't there all afternoon."

"You were there some of the time?"

"I had to speak to the captain about some problems with one of the horses. I went to see him, but he wasn't in his bedchamber so I came straight back out again. I tried to see him later on, but he still wasn't there, so I left it and went out with John."

"So it was not very important?"

"Not by then. The horse had looked lame, but by later in the afternoon when we left the inn, it seemed to have recovered."

Hugh was beginning to give up. He had tried every way he knew to engage the men round the table in conversation, but none seemed to want to talk. When he looked at them, they shiftily glanced away, and he was ready to resort to speaking to Roger. Edgar was studiously ignoring the others at the table and staring at his master.

"So," Hugh said brightly, "it was lucky that Henry and John were there when Cole tried to steal the silver, wasn't it? At least they managed to catch him." There was silence. "If he'd got away, Sir Hector would have been furious, wouldn't he?" Opposite, the man who had been in the room to collect Sir Henry's clothes hawked noisily and spat. Hugh felt his face fall. The man sneered at him, a grizzled old warrior with silver threads shining on both cheeks of his thick, curling beard. Hugh tried again. "I suppose we just have to hope Cole admits where he hid the silver, don't we? A shame about the girl, though."

"The stupid bastard. There was no need to kill her, poor lass."

Hugh turned to the man who had spat. Bright black eyes stared back confidently. "She was unlucky to be there, but I suppose Cole wanted no witnesses."

"Maybe."

"At least those two caught Cole," Hugh repeated weakly, feeling the strain of maintaining their chat.

"You reckon?"

Hugh stared. "I . . . What?"

"Cole's a fool, from what I saw. He trusted them two."

"What are you talking about?"

"Those two bastards, they always needle till they know everything about everyone, then they put the screws on. Cole had some money, but he refused to give them any, and the same afternoon, he's discovered stealing—by those two."

Roger stared open-mouthed. Edgar was sitting stock-still as if unconcerned, but he was listening to every word and nuance as Hugh stuttered, "But what . . . I mean, how could they . . ."

"Everybody coming to a troop like this has a story, right? A past. Some can't stay at home because of something that happened, like a fight where someone got hurt, or they have a girlfriend who's already married to another man—whatever. Those two bastards, they make sure they find out what a man's secret is, and then they threaten to let everyone know. 'Why're you here?' they say, all friendly-like, and 'Everyone tells us why they come here,' or, 'Nobody'll trust you unless you tell what you've done.' " He spat again and gulped ale, as if to wash away a sour taste. "And then they say, 'We need some money; we don't seem to have what we thought, and we want a drink. Why don't you give us some?' And if the new boys won't cooperate, their story gets all over the troop—and later, news might just get back to their homes."

"And they got Cole like that?"

"No, he got *them.* He lied when they asked why he was here, so when they tried to squeeze him, he told them what they could do with themselves."

"Come on, Wat, you've talked enough," said one of the other men at the table, squirming uncomfortably. "You'll get yourself in trouble—they can see you talking."

"What do I care?" The older man stared truculently at John Smithson, who was watching with hooded eyes. "They can't do anything to me, and they know it."

Edgar slowly turned in his seat, hitching a leg over the plank that formed the bench, and faced Wat. "Are you saying you think it was those two who robbed Sir Hector and killed Sarra?"

The older man took a tremendous gulp and finished his ale. "I don't know who robbed Sir Hector, and I don't know who spiked the girl." Edgar shrugged, and with a half-smile, began to move back to watch his master. Stung by his patronizing air, Wat set the pot down hard on the table. "You ignorant puppy!" He leaned forward aggressively, his voice low and coarse. "You think I'm just some old fool who's drunk too much on a summer's morning, don't you? You think because you work for an educated master you can look down on plain folk like me, because we're just dregs and unimportant. We're fools and can't know what goes on, aren't we? Well, I don't know what happened in that room, but I know that those two went into Sir Hector's chamber in the early afternoon, right? Then they went back later, and both times they were in there for some time."

"You're talking rubbish," sneered the other soldier. "You've been drinking sour ale! There were men in that hall, and they'd have seen—"

"Those drunken sots wouldn't have noticed if the King himself had passed by! I'm telling you what I saw: Henry and John went in—twice. Maybe I'm wrong, maybe they didn't do it. Maybe they just went in and got lost in all those rooms. Maybe they didn't steal the silver, and they might not have killed the girl—but I reckon they had as much chance as poor young Cole."

"But why would they put the blame on Cole? They've hardly had time to grow to dislike him," asked Edgar superciliously.

"You *pathetic* little man!" Wat sputtered contemptuously. "What about Cole's brother? You know he was in this band, and that he died in a battle—just after he'd won a hostage? And after he died, Henry and John managed to take over his prize and keep the money. If Cole hasn't found that out already, he soon will. Maybe he ain't as bright as you, little man, and maybe he'll begin to wonder whether the pair of them might have seen his brother Thomas with his hostage and decided that the profit was too much for a youngster. Maybe he'll wonder whether his brother died from a knife in the chest or a dagger in the back; maybe he'll wonder whether his new friends were lying when they said they liked his brother. And just maybe, the two of them thought their lives would be easier without him in the way."

"And maybe Cole *did* steal the silver, and maybe Cole *was* interrupted halfway through by the girl, and he did the first thing that came into his head and killed her."

"And maybe pigs will sprout wings and fly like rooks! If he did that, why did he bother to join the band?"

"To find out what had happened to his brother, like you said."

"So why did he steal the silver before he had done anything about it?"

"What?"

"You're so bright, little man, you tell me," Wat sneered. "If you'd been wondering what had happened to your brother for years, just when you had a chance to find out, would you immediately rob someone else?"

"Maybe he *had* found out."

"So he put himself outside the law before he wreaked vengeance on them. He's obviously not much brighter than you, is he?"

"So you think it couldn't have been Cole? Are you saying it was Henry and John?" Edgar demanded.

"That's for your master to decide, isn't it?"

Eyes slitted as he surveyed Wat, Edgar nodded slowly.

~ 10 ~

Simon was bored. The men were cautious in their answers, and Baldwin was having to work to tease every detail he could from them; for the bailiff, it was dull. There was no verbal interplay, just a detailed questioning, with the knight checking their story and the two giving noncommittal, one-word replies.

The bailiff found his attention wandering. At the nearest bench he could see Hugh and Edgar talking to an older man, while others looked on suspiciously. The men polishing armor had gone. The armorer was still whetting his sword with his stone, but it was a listless motion; his mind was not on the metal before him, and with the sun at its hottest, Simon was not surprised. Even under the elm it was stiflingly hot, with not a breath of air to stir the leaves.

Standing, he made his way over to the inn, intending to ask for a drink, but when he peered into the buttery, he found the innkeeper's wife asleep in a chair, head back, and mouth wide open, issuing small snores and gasps. He smiled, then left her in peace. Wondering where her husband was, he walked to the hall and glanced inside. Three men sat at the dais, playing dice.

They had been placed there by Sir Hector, and would allow no one to pass.

Simon did not attempt to test their resolve. He walked out, past the pantry and leaned on the door-frame which gave out onto the street.

The sight of Crediton High Street never ceased to give him pleasure. He had visited many other towns, even been to the city of Exeter twice, and in comparison, Crediton, he thought, was perfect. It bustled, without intimidating visitors by its size. Other places were too large, and their alleys and streets were potential traps to the unwary, but in Crediton everyone knew everybody else, and it was safe to mingle with the crowd. As he watched, young merchants and tradesmen rushed past, going about their business; canons walked by, disdainfully avoiding the manure in their path; a hunter with rough shirt and leather jerkin strode proudly with dogs at his heels; the wife of a rich burgess strolled past, her maid carrying her heavy blue cloak. Simon smiled and nodded at them, but the wife ignored him, thinking he might be drunk. The maid gave him a twinkling smile from the corner of her eye which made up for her mistress's rudeness.

He crossed his arms. At first he had thought that the killing and theft would be enough to keep his interest, but already his mind was turning from the fate of the man in the jail and moving back to his wife.

Margaret had always been all he had ever wanted in a wife. She was attractive, intelligent, and a calming influence on him in his more angry moments when he had been locking horns with the miners who had colonized the moors. He had loved her from the first moment he had seen her, and had never regretted their marriage. She had given him the two principle joys of his life: Edith and Peterkin. But now Peterkin had gone, so had much of his zest for life. He no longer had the patience he once had when Edith played in the house, and could not even speak to Margaret about his sense of loss.

It was easier, he felt, to keep his emotions locked away. He preferred to avoid discussion of Peterkin because he knew it would entail her talking and him being evasive. It would be different if they had many children, but it seemed difficult for them: two children with some years between them, and a series of miscarriages. He was not sure that she would be able to bear him another son, and it was that which hurt: not that he wanted a new wife, but he was sad not to have a son with whom he could play, whom he could educate and train.

Hearing a high-pitched scream, he sprang forward, then forced himself to relax. It was only a boy laughing. For some reason, Simon felt his scalp tingle with anticipation. When another cry of delight rang out, he followed the sound, almost unwillingly.

Giggles and squeals of pleasure issued from the alleyway down alongside the jail, and he crossed the road, shouldering people out of the way. At the entrance he stood and peered inside. Washing hung limply from tired, slack lines, and beneath, all was dark. After the bright sun in the street, he had to blink. There, a short way inside the alley was the woman and son whom he had rescued from the soldier.

Roger had seen the bailiff cross the street, and now he strolled after him. The interrogation was dull for him as well.

At the alley entrance he saw Simon hesitate. The bailiff was wondering whether to leave before the woman saw him—or to go up and speak to her. She saved him the choice. Looking up as his shadow darkened the entrance, she gave a small cry, holding out her arms, and the boy rushed to her protection, throwing his skinny arms round her neck and whimpering. Simon quickly realized that he must seem a menacing figure, with the sun behind him and his features hidden. He smiled, moving back so that the sun caught his face, and held his hands a little way from his body to show he was not holding a weapon.

She was wearing the same worn and frayed gray tunic, a cord tied round her waist to give it a semblance of shape. As his eyes began to adjust, he saw that she had a thin, ravaged face, little more than a gray skull, from which sunken eyes stared back with near-panic. Wispy strands of pale hair hung dispiritedly from beneath her wimple. Cradling her child, she stared up at him as if convinced he was about to attack her, and her fear was all too plain.

There was no reason why this woman should wish to speak to him. He had helped her during the night, it was true, but she did not recognize him. It had been dark, and he was on horseback first. Looking up at a figure some eight feet above would not give a good perspective, and she had been so scared at the threats of the man-at-arms that she might not have noticed his face.

Suddenly she leaped up, and, holding her child to her thin breast, darted away from him, pelting down the alley. He took a step forward automatically.

"Sir?"

Hearing Roger, he stopped. There was no point in chasing her; he would only scare her more if he did so. His shoulders drooped with an unaccountable melancholy, formed mainly of jealousy, as he turned to face Roger.

She ran past. It was tempting, but killing her now would be foolish. Judith must wait: he could not see to her now while the bailiff was there to hear her screams and rush to rescue her. No, he thought regretfully, and allowed his hand to relax on the knife's handle. When he looked back toward the entrance, the looming bulk of the bailiff had gone, and the watching man felt a quick resentment.

He had nothing much against the bailiff, but he was irritated by the slowness of the knight with his investigations. Why had he only arrested Cole? The man should have realized by now who was the guilty one, and that different people had performed the two crimes: one had stolen while the other had killed. If Furnshill had half a brain, he thought, the fool would have arrested the obvious one by now.

He eyed the bright opening where the bailiff had stood. It would have been a stroke of sheer good fortune, of course, had the man not turned up. The watcher had been wondering how to deal with Judith, and this would have been the perfect occasion. He hated to miss an opportunity. While he was hidden in the doorway, the pathetic woman could have run by and met her end quickly; his arm reaching out to curl round her throat as she rushed past, halting her, the quick shock freezing her for a moment, just long enough for his hand to find her mouth and smother her cry, the knife pushing through her back, near the spine, first low down for her kidneys, then higher, reaching for her heart.

He was irritated at missing the chance, but he knew

the value of patience. He was in no hurry: there would be plenty of occasions offering similar possibilities and he must take his time. Patting his knife in its sheath, he made his way to the street, and soon became lost in the crowd.

When Simon and Roger got back to the inn, Baldwin and the two servants were sitting together at a table. The two mercenaries were nowhere to be seen, and Simon felt a vague sense of relief. If he had to watch the hideous mouth of John Smithson for another second he would be sick.

Baldwin held a tankard of weak ale in his hand; he waved them toward the jug and a spare pot on the table. "I was beginning to wonder if you had gone back to Peter's."

"No, we were out in front." He did not meet the Keeper's eye. For some reason he did not want to tell his friend about the woman and her son. It felt foolish, almost, to have wanted to speak to her, and to have listened to her son playing as if it could heal the pain of his own boy's death.

Baldwin caught his mood, and guessed his friend had been thinking about his son again. He diplomatically poured ale and passed Simon the pot. "We have had some interesting information. Hugh, tell Simon what you've heard."

Leaning forward, his face once more set in its customary scowl, Hugh related Wat's thoughts, Edgar interrupting occasionally to correct a point.

As he gradually came to a halt, glowering at Edgar, Baldwin sat back on his bench and shot a glance at Simon. "Well?" he demanded, and finished his pot.

"It hardly helps us, does it?" Simon muttered, and dropped onto the bench beside his friend. "Surely he's just a man with some sort of grudge against the other two, who would like to think they were guilty. It doesn't help explain who stole the silver—or why they killed Sarra."

"Her death is the most confusing part," Baldwin admitted. "From the lump on her head, she must have been knocked out before she was gagged and bound."

"So whoever took the plate found her in the room and knocked her out, then stabbed her," said Hugh. He was rapidly getting light-headed from the ale he had drunk.

"No, Hugh," said Baldwin. "I can easily believe that she was knocked out when the thief entered the room and that she was shut away, silent, in the chest. But why would he go back later to stab her and kill her? It makes no sense."

Simon shrugged. "There might have been two men there; one was seen by her, the other hit her. The second one tied her up, but the first knew he'd been seen, so he killed her later."

"That supposes that one of them was already there, and the second came in later and gave away their intention . . . it is possible, but I find it hard to swallow." Baldwin frowned.

"Why?" asked Simon.

"One man goes into the room, then the girl enters. A second man goes in, and hits her." He meditatively swung an imaginary club with a fist. "He knocks her out, and that gives him a chance to truss and gag her. Then he lifts her . . . have you ever tried to lift an unconscious body on your own? It is like a sack of wheat;

it goes in all directions. I would think that both lifted her up and set her into the chest. But then one of them goes back and kills her."

"I wonder . . ."

"What, Simon?"

"It may be nothing, but that tunic . . . It was of exceptional quality, and very expensive. I wonder—"

"Sir, can I serve more ale?"

Simon turned a dazzling smile on the innkeeper. "Paul, thank you. Yes, we'd like more ale, but why don't you join us?"

Paul was flattered. For two days now he had been running around after the mercenaries, without a single word of gratitude. It took him little time to fetch a fresh jug and a pot for himself, and then he sat comfortably, sighing with the relief of it. His legs ached and his feet were sore from standing too long, his back was stiff from bending to pour jugs, and he had an almost overwhelming desire to shut his eyes and doze off. Margery has gone to bed; she had not been able to sleep until the early hours because of the noise from the hall, and partly from her fear of the men themselves.

"It's a shame about Sarra," Simon said.

"Yes. She was a good girl, really. Pretty, too. She never deserved to die like that."

"She was getting on all right with Sir Hector, wasn't she?"

"I think so. She was with him on the very first night, when this lot arrived, so she must have caught his eye. At the best of times she was hard enough to keep working, but after meeting him, she was impossible."

"Why?"

"She didn't want to be like the other girls, I suppose.

Wanted to get married, have children, the normal things, but with a rich man for a husband. Sir Hector was ideal for her. Money, power, the lot. He was exactly what she needed—or so she thought."

"Did she have any good clothes, like the tunic she was wearing when she died?"

"That blue one? No, I'd never seen it before. What would a serving-girl want with something like that? No, that wasn't hers."

"Where did it come from then?" asked Simon. Baldwin leaned forward, his dark eyes intent.

"I don't know."

"It wasn't your wife's—or one of the other girls'?"

"No. I've never seen it before."

"Tell me, innkeeper," Baldwin said, resting his elbows on the table. "Was she popular normally with your . . . clients?"

"Very—when she was interested." Paul smiled as his eyelids drooped with tiredness. It was hard to keep alert in the elm's shade. "She was very pretty, and she knew it. Well, it's not surprising. With looks like hers, she had all the men after her like rams after the ewe, and she could pick and choose. Why, the night before this lot got here, she had been trying to snare an apprentice to a goldsmith! He was too scared, though, from what I saw."

"Perhaps one of her more appreciative clients gave her the tunic, then."

"Could be. Poor lass. Always wanted money and marriage, and just when she got the kind of tunic she always craved, she gets herself killed."

"Was she keen to get money, then?" asked Simon.

"Oh, yes. She saw all her friends working themselves into the ground, and she was determined to be free, to have a husband who had money, so she wouldn't have to work any more."

"Do you know if she was friendly with Cole?"

"Him? No, not at all. I saw them only yesterday, arguing."

"What about?"

"Something to do with Henry and John. I don't know what."

Simon picked up a large twig and toyed with it thoughtfully. "And she was succeeding with Sir Hector."

"On the first night. Not after that."

"What happened?" Simon's ears pricked up.

"Didn't you hear? Oh, they argued. They woke up Margery, and I was really furious. It was the first proper sleep she'd had since they got here, and then just as she dropped off, there was all that shouting, and doors slamming and so on, and—"

"When was this?"

"On the day she died. She had gone to the captain during the first night, but the next afternoon, he had dropped her like a hot brick. Then yesterday they had a row!"

"What happened? Where were *you,* for example, when you heard them?"

"Me?" he said, his eyes opening a little at Simon's obvious eagerness. "Oh, I was out in the buttery, filling jugs. Cristine came through and told me something was going on, but I decided to ignore it. The last thing I'd do is stand between two soldiers in a fight—they'd probably turn on me! No, it wasn't until Margery came and told me it was him and Sarra, and how much row they were making, that I decided to go and speak to them."

"How was she? Worried? Nervous?"

"My wife? No, just irritated to be woken up, and it made her cross with me for letting them carry on. I went through the hall, and I could hear doors slamming as I got in—"

"Where? Were these doors out at the back, where Sir Hector had his room?" Simon queried.

Paul stared, forcing his mind back. "One was, I think. But the other was out at the back. It was probably the door to her room."

"That's over there?" Baldwin confirmed, jerking his head toward the block across the yard.

"Yes. Anyway, I went into the hall, and a few minutes later Sir Hector came out. He apologized, said that she had annoyed him, and that was that."

"Did he say how she had irritated him?" Baldwin said.

"Not really, no," frowned the innkeeper. "He said she had gone on about something to do with one of his men, saying Sir Hector was in danger, something along those lines."

"Which of his men?"

"I really don't—"

"*Think,* Paul! This could have something to do with why Sarra's dead."

The innkeeper recalled how he had gone to the door of Sir Hector's bedchamber, but before he could open it, the captain had emerged, shaking with rage, his face mottled. Seeing Paul he had spoken with fearsome control, as if each word was weighed carefully. "That strumpet Sarra has had the goodness to warn me that my men are plotting against me. *Me!* As if I were a puny baron! I've told her to leave my sight and not return, and I'd be grateful if you would make sure she does not come near to me again while I stay here."

Paul had nodded in astonishment, and turned to go, but he had heard the knight mutter one more word under his breath *"Henry!"*

As he told the others, Simon rolled his eyes skyward in disbelief while Baldwin closed his. Edgar winced.

Hugh looked from one to the other. "What's the matter?"

"So let me understand this, Sir Baldwin. You are accusing me of stealing my own silver and murdering a serving-girl, is that right?"

Baldwin sighed. He had known that speaking to Sir Hector again would be difficult, but he had hoped to explain himself before the captain flew off the handle. "I am not accusing you of anything, Sir Hector, but we have been told that you had an argument with Sarra on the afternoon when she died, and it might help us to find her killer if we know what you argued about." He dropped into a chair.

They were once more in the hall. Thankfully most of the mercenaries were outside. Only a few men sat nearby to protect their master. Simon lounged against a wall, idly swinging his twig. Roger was beside him, his arms crossed as he listened. The servants had remained outside at the bench.

"What has this to do with finding my silver?"

"Did you argue with her?" Baldwin continued doggedly.

"What if I did?"

"*If* you did, what was it about?"

"She had a stupid notion that some of the men were planning to mutiny, that's all."

"Who?"

"What has this got to do with—"

"Sir Hector, I am trying to the best of my ability and skill—"

"Which is limited."

"Perhaps. But I am trying to find out where your silver is and who killed Sarra."

"Then go and demand the truth of Cole. He must have done both," Sir Hector suggested with exasperation.

Simon drew his dagger and began shaving flakes from his stick. "If we question him, he could lie, especially if we were to use any force to get him to confess. He might have an accomplice, in which case even if Cole knew where it was stored, the silver might already have been moved. Cole might not know where it is now. Far better if we learn a little more about everything which happened yesterday, so we know when he lies."

Sir Hector eyed him with distaste. "If you are incapable of persuading him to tell you the truth, you don't know how to ask. If he has an accomplice, make him tell you who it is. You'll soon find out where my plate is stored when you have both of them locked up, and if you don't I can lend you men who know how to extract such facts from recalcitrant captives."

"That will not be necessary," Baldwin said sharply. His friends and colleagues had been tortured when the Knights Templar were destroyed by the French King, and the sight of their twisted, agonized bodies had persuaded him forever that torture was no assistance in an enquiry. Torture only made people answer what they thought their questioners wanted to hear; it did not force them to give the truth. "But it *is* important that we understand what happened yesterday. I cannot believe that you are trying to hide something, Sir Hector, but your refusal to answer what seems to me to be a very simple question must make me wonder what motivates your reticence."

"Are you threatening me?"

"No. But I will not be trying to discover what happened to your silver until I feel I have your cooperation."

"Then perhaps I should investigate the matter myself, with my men."

"I think," Simon interrupted, taking on a judicial air, "that would not be useful."

"Really? Well, *I* am beginning to think it might be the only way of learning what happened to my plate."

"What of the girl? You argued with her, threw her out, told everyone to keep her away from you, and then she is found dead in your room," Baldwin thundered.

"It has nothing to do with this."

"God's teeth! We will judge that, not you! I am the Keeper of the King's Peace for this town, and you are deliberately hampering my investigation. Are you aware that you are, so far, the only person we have found who has argued with her? That makes you the only man with a motive to kill her!" Baldwin paused. "Now—was it Henry whom Sarra warned you of?"

Simon looked at his friend. The knight's outburst surprised him, for he had known Baldwin to remain calm under vastly more irritating meetings than this.

"Yes," Sir Hector admitted.

Baldwin frowned. "What exactly did she say?"

"She accused him of trying to set the men against me; she thought he was a danger to me."

"You didn't believe her?" Simon asked.

"In God's name, no! She hated Henry. On the night we came here, he tried to rape her—he would have done so, too, if I hadn't intervened—and from then on she clearly wanted to get her own back. She made up this story to discredit him, and I wasn't in a mood to listen."

"So you ignored it?"

"Yes. I told her to get out and not to bother coming back. Henry the Hurdle is one of my best men."

"Did it not occur to you that he might be the man who stole your plate?"

"He's my leading sergeant! Who else can I trust if not him? He always has access to my money and silver. I can't imagine anyone less likely to have been the thief. And in any case, why should I think of other men when you have the thief already held in jail?"

Baldwin stirred. "So you ejected Sarra from your room and she left immediately?"

"Yes. She went to her own room, I suppose."

"When did you next see her?"

"When I was called to look at the open chest—when we got back from the chase for Cole."

"So you didn't see her alive again?"

"No."

"One last point, Sir Hector. The tunic she was wearing when she died—have you seen it before?"

The mercenary clenched his jaw. He had hoped that the knight would not have led on to that, but it was a natural question, he knew. The dress was far too good for a tavern slut like her. "No," he said. "I've never seen it before."

Simon glanced up at him, his dagger taking another shaving from the stick. The captain's voice had been quieter, almost contemplative, and Simon was sure he was lying.

- 11 -

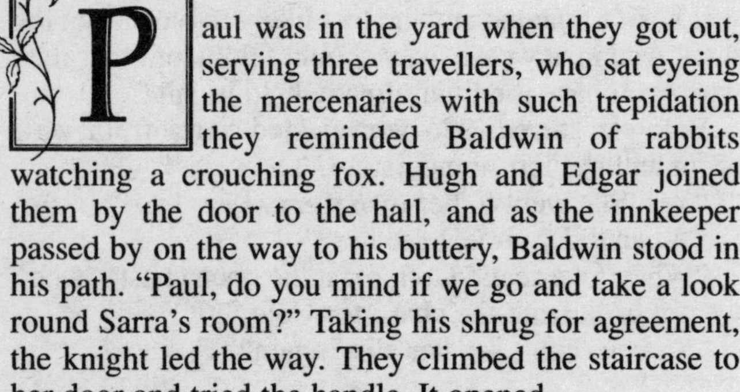

Paul was in the yard when they got out, serving three travellers, who sat eyeing the mercenaries with such trepidation they reminded Baldwin of rabbits watching a crouching fox. Hugh and Edgar joined them by the door to the hall, and as the innkeeper passed by on the way to his buttery, Baldwin stood in his path. "Paul, do you mind if we go and take a look round Sarra's room?" Taking his shrug for agreement, the knight led the way. They climbed the staircase to her door and tried the handle. It opened.

"I can see why she would prefer to get herself married" Baldwin observed.

It was a sparsely furnished little room. A palliasse lay on the floor to the right for her mattress, and a table held her few belongings. Some tunics and an apron were hooked over pegs in the timber frame of the building, but one lay as if kicked aside on the floor, and a belt rested on the bed itself.

"She must have changed into the blue tunic here," Baldwin murmured. "But where did she get it?"

"Baldwin, are you beginning to think that Cole didn't kill her?" Simon asked.

The knight waved a hand, vaguely encompassing the inn. "I don't know what to think. That lad Cole seems pleasant, while the two who caught him are . . . well, I would be happier not to have to rely on them myself. The girl could have upset them: if Henry had overheard her telling his master that he was about to try to depose him as leader, he might have lost his temper and knocked her out, put her in the chest, and then killed her, although it hardly seems likely. Why put her in the chest in the first place? Why not kill her outright?"

"Perhaps he was going to do so, but got interrupted? Someone arrived, so he had to stuff the girl into the chest and came back later to kill her."

"No." Baldwin dropped on to the palliasse and stared round the room. "That can't be it. If he was in such a hurry to hide her away, how could he find time to bind and gag her? It makes no sense!"

He opened the door and peered round cautiously. There was an odd feeling of anticipation as he went in, as if he expected her to hurl herself at him and attack. But she couldn't—not now. Still, the dream would keep coming back, and even while he was awake the memory of it lurched around in his mind like a heavy rock which occasionally bludgeoned other thoughts out of the way.

That night he had rubbed down his horse after his journey and stretched, making his muscles strain taut as he tried to ease the tension in his neck and shoulders. It was late, and he hadn't wanted to wake his staff.

Shutting the stable door quietly, he had made his way over the yard to the hall, but had then hesitated.

Before bed, he had reasoned, a last drink would be a comfort, and he had gone through to the buttery. A cask had already been broached and, filling a pot with ale, he had tipped it up to finish the last drop before opening the door and emptying his bladder onto the packed earth of his yard. Tugging his tunic back into position with a tired shrug, he had been unable to stop another yawn before going to his bedchamber.

The building was old, and he must go through the hall to get to the bedroom in the small solar block beyond. Stepping quietly, he had avoided waking the men sleeping on either side. The door beyond opened silently.

He was strong and known to be bold, but the sight that met his eyes made him stand stock-still in horror.

The fire was dying, and only offered a dull orange glow to light the betrayal. She had not bothered to pull the bedclothes back to cover herself, and her inelegantly sprawled body gleamed with a silken sheen, while beside her the figure grunted and snored in his sleep like a hog after truffles.

Standing in the doorway and staring at the two figures, his mind had worked with a fresh clarity. He could have bellowed, calling for his men to hold the man while he whipped the adulterous bitch, but they must already know of the treachery, for this libertine could only have got in through the hall, and *he* must surely have been seen by one or more of the servants.

No, he had thought: there was a better way to punish her. And him.

None of the servants had woken. Closing the door with care, stiff with the dread of being heard, he had made his way from the room and out to the stable. Nobody had expected him, and no one had seen him. He would ride away, and return tomorrow as if nothing had happened; no one would be any the wiser. And he could begin his revenge by agreeing to the plan proposed that evening.

He had calmed the tired beast, speaking low to soothe it, thrown the blanket over and tightened the girth straps, but his actions were mechanical, his mind back in the bedchamber. She was *his*. And someone else had stolen her. They must both pay—one for the dishonor, one for the theft of his woman.

And now they were going to pay, he smirked, drawing the dagger and resting the metal against his cheek. The blade sat against his belly while sheathed, and it was warm; just as it had been when he had pulled it free of her body.

Henry strolled out into the yard and walked to a table far from the inn's hall, where he could see the door. After a few minutes, John left the stables and, seeing his friend, sauntered over to join him.

The other men of the band were inside, mostly dozing after eating and drinking too much of Margery's strong ale, and this was the first time the two had been alone since their questioning about the robbery and murder. Henry found himself eyeing his companion suspiciously.

"Has anyone been talking to you?" he asked.

"Me? No—why? Someone been bending your ear?"

"No," Henry muttered, and glanced at the hall again. "But Sir Hector has been very quiet toward me. I keep seeing him staring at me when he thinks I won't notice. And I saw him talking to old Wat."

"That cruddy old bastard! He should have kept his trap shut."

"Yes, but he didn't. He shot his mouth off to the bailiff's man, and the Keeper will soon know what the old fool thinks."

"All he can say is that we sometimes fleece recruits."

"You sure?"

"Look, nobody saw anything. If they had, we'd know."

"Oh yes? How many times have we seen the captain negotiating with others who thought they were winning, only to find he'd changed sides? You know as well as I do he's able to hide his thoughts."

"Yes," John said, and stared gloomily at the inn. "What do you think, then?"

"No one knows we got the silver. I reckon we ought to get away while we can."

"Get away?" There was an unmistakable note of horror in his voice.

Henry hunched his shoulders grimly, his mouth set into a determined gash. "What else can we do? The plate is hidden well enough, but it could be found. And if anyone guesses that we had a part in the theft, they'll know who to blame for the murder."

"I suppose so," John muttered, avoiding his gaze.

Henry glanced round. Their flight would be easier if both left together. Two men could keep a lookout for pursuit more easily than one alone. He nodded, leaning closer to his friend, and they began to plan how they would make good their escape.

Baldwin was thinking of rags. They had finished their meal which, because today was Wednesday and therefore a fast day, was fish. Peter was known for the quality of his board, and Baldwin was pleased to see that he had stocked up well in anticipation of the Bishop's visit. The larder and pantry were full, and the stew pond out at the back of the garden was full of pike and bream.

He turned the patch of material over in his hands, and then cast a glance at Margaret. "What do you think of this?"

"Hmm? Oh. What is it?" she asked, and took it from him, nearly dropping it when he told her where it came from.

"Don't worry! She did not die of a contagion that can be passed to you by the cloth, unless metal contains its own poison. No, I was merely wondering what you thought of the material."

Margaret weighed it in her hand. "It's very good. The warp and weft are very fine and even, and the color is bright and fresh. I have no idea what could have created such an excellent dye."

"Could it have been produced locally?"

Margaret gave him a feeble smile. She knew that the knight had no interest in cloth or materials, even though they were so important to the town. Anybody else living in Crediton, could have given the price, and told who produced the fabric and who stitched it together. Some would claim to know almost which sheep the hair came from. "Take it to Tanner. He will be able to tell you where it came from. Why, does it matter?"

"Perhaps not, but I would like to know where it came from," Baldwin said, taking it back and giving it a cursory look before shoving it into his purse again.

Stapledon needed Roger's help that afternoon, so the others left without him. When they reached the jail, the Constable was sitting on a stool in the doorway, a wide-brimmed straw hat on his head and jug of cool ale by his side.

As soon as he was away from his wife, Baldwin saw that the bailiff recovered a little of his evenness of temper, and the observation worried him. In his experience, when a man had a devastating loss, he turned to those in whom he could trust. In Baldwin's terms that meant his man-at-arms, Edgar, who had been with him for so many years he was a close friend as well as a servant. Other similarly destitute Knights Templar had helped him to survive after the fall of the Order, giving him the aid he had needed, until he had been able to overcome his initial sense of despair; and his cure had been made complete once he had caught the man who had been responsible. In his case, he had been able to forget his grief once he had avenged his companions. With Simon, he feared there could be no similar cure. The bailiff had no enemy to catch, for it was a disease which had stolen his child. It was hard to imagine how he could find peace when he would not talk to his wife and try to make sense of their life.

Frustration at his inability to help his friend made him irritable, and when he recognized the snuffling sound as being the snores of the Constable, his anger flared. Kicking the chair, he sent Tanner sprawling.

"You are supposed to be guarding Cole, not sleeping, oaf!"

Blinking, and stifling a yawn, the Constable set his stool upright and grinned apologetically. He was surprised by the knight's mood, having always found him even-tempered in the past. "My apologies, sir. I just dozed a little."

"Never mind that. How is he?"

"I gave him some food for lunch, and he looked fine.

It's good and cool in the cell at this time of year; I expect he's more comfortable than you."

The knight had to agree with that. Overhead the sun felt as hot as a charcoal brazier, and under his tunic and shirt he could feel the sweat slowly dribbling downward. He tugged the patch of cloth from his purse. "Have you seen anything like this before?"

Tanner was a massive block of a man, tall and broad, with a face that reminded Baldwin of the wrinkled bark of an ancient oak tree. His mouth was a thin line in his face, and the lips always seemed to be pursed in disapproval, but the brown eyes were quick to smile and held a kindly light. Now he took the piece from the knight and studied it. "This is good quality cloth," he said tugging at it and pulling free a thread, rolling it meditatively between his fingers. "And a good color, too."

"It's from the dead girl's tunic," Baldwin said, and the constable frowned at it.

"You want to know where it might have come from? There's only one place I can think of round here, and that's Harry Fletcher. All the women go to him. He has the best dyes usually, but I've never seen anything this good even from him."

"I know his place," Edgar said without thinking.

His master turned slowly and stared at him. Under the astonished gaze, Edgar reddened. "Perhaps you would like to lead the way, then," said Baldwin suavely.

The shop was little more than a narrow shed, out toward the eastern end of the town, and Baldwin realized he must have passed it often, but he rarely took notice of this part of the road. He only went along it when he was on his way to Exeter, and when he returned he usually had other things on his mind, such as how he would survive the remaining miles to Furnshill.

Edgar stood a short way back, and Baldwin looked at him, intrigued. A brief glance was enough to show him that this shop was not the sort to provide a servant with the clothing he would require. Cloths of many types were displayed on the trestle table on the street, but almost all were brightly colored, and the other items for sale were designed to attract women—nets for hair, wimples, ribbons and flower-embroidered kirtles. Edgar had apparently developed a fascination in a heavy rounsey on the other side of the road. Charitably, Baldwin preferred to assume that his servant was interested in the intricately carved leatherwork of the saddle, or the gleaming blue-black coat of the heavy horse, than simply avoiding his eye.

The owner was a short, dumpy man in his late twenties. He wore a constant smile, and his twinkling blue eyes, Baldwin was sure, increased his trade significantly. They appeared to flatter and invite confidence, and the knight could well understand how Harry Fletcher managed to tempt the women of the town into his little emporium.

It appeared that he viewed himself to be the best advertisement for his goods. His tunic was voluminous, reaching down almost to his knees, and was of good quality velvet. On his head was a fine woollen coif, tied under his chin, and the cowl hanging down the back of his neck had fur lining and a long point. It matched his boots, which had the fashionable lengthened toes which were now so popular.

For all his chubbiness, the man had remarkably nimble fingers, long and narrow, and as he spoke, he toyed with the measuring string which dangled from his neck, pulling and squeezing the knots which he used for measuring like a woman playing with the beads of her necklace.

"Sir Baldwin, Godspeed. Hello, Edgar. How can I help you both?" Fletcher asked, his voice at its most servile as he looked from one to the other. "Is it something rare you are—"

"Just listen to my master and answer his questions," Edgar interjected, and Baldwin decided that henceforth he would take more interest in any illegitimate children in the area. It appeared likely that he might be able to find their father not too far from his own home.

Baldwin enjoyed the amused surprise on the man's face and the urgent flush on Edgar's before smiling and saying, "You must have heard of the death of the girl at the inn?"

"Poor Sarra? Oh, yes. Very sad. A great shame. Such a nice girl, I always thought."

"Did you see her often?"

The bright eyes dimmed a little. His eyelids had drooped, and Baldwin could see that he was assessing whether he was in any danger. It was all too common for an innocent man to be put on trial, and with ill-educated people on juries, many assumed a man accused must be guilty. It was better to be careful and ensure one was not arrested in the first place. Fletcher considered, and said, "Only occasionally."

"She came here for her clothing?"

"Sometimes."

"I do not think you had anything to do with her death, but I wanted to know whether she bought any of this from you recently." Baldwin passed over the fragment of material.

"This?" Fletcher smiled and shook his head inci-

sively. "Definitely not. Have you any idea how much this costs? No, Sarra, when she came here, mainly came just to look. She never had any money, and she already had a couple of tunics anyway. Why would she spend good money to get another? She wasn't a lady of importance."

The man's casual attitude toward the girl's death irritated the knight, and his voice took on an abrasive edge. "She may not have been a 'lady of importance,' as you put it, but she did not deserve to be murdered, either. Is there anyone else in Crediton who might have sold her cloth like this—or a tunic made from this cloth?"

"No, sir. There is nobody else in the town who could have sold such material. I had it brought here all the way from Lincoln. It is too fine for the weavers here, no matter what they say, and look at the color! Could anybody think it could be produced here? Cloth like this is only made by the Flemings, and you have to search even among them for this quality if—"

"Yes, yes, yes. All right, you have made your point. In that case, who have you sold cloth like this to? How could Sarra have got hold of a tunic like this?"

"I don't know how she got it, but I have sold one tunic. To Sir Hector, who's staying at the inn."

"Did he say whom it was for?"

"No, sir. Perhaps he bought it for Sarra. I understand he liked her."

"Where did you hear that?"

The shopkeeper's smile broadened. "Here. I have many women come here for their wimples and so on, and as soon as Sir Hector and his men arrived, the gossip increased tenfold. Everyone knows how taken he was with poor Sarra at first—until they had their quarrel, anyway."

"What quarrel?" Baldwin was not keen on inane chatter, but he knew how sometimes elements of the truth could intrude even into the malicious chitchat of an alewife.

"Sir Hector, on the day before she died, suddenly threw Sarra out and ordered her not to bother him again. He had lost interest in her."

"Who told you this?"

"A friend of Margery—that is, Paul the innkeeper's wife. She heard him shouting at Sarra. He said he had found a real woman, and didn't need a cheap tavern slut any more."

"Who did he mean?"

"Who knows? Perhaps you should ask him . . ."

- 12 -

Walking back, the men were quiet. Baldwin was sunk in gloom, wondering whether he would ever understand what was happening, while his servant was trying to hide his relief at leaving Fletcher's shop. Hugh meandered behind, as stolidly uncommunicative as usual.

The bailiff shoved his hands into his belt. They were walking up the hill now, and it was harder to push their way through the crowds teeming the roadway. The items on sale changed as they progressed toward the town center. Fish were laid out on trestles, their eyes dull, mouths gaping wide as if still straining for water, while others lay, their colors dim, in barrels alongside. The bakers were next, with loaves and rolls of bread arranged in sweet-smelling piles, ranging from good melchet, made from sieved flour to give it its pale cream color, to less fine cockets, and low-grade brown loaves made from maslin, a wheat and rye mixture for the poorer people. As they approached the shambles where the butchers had their stalls, they came to the cordwainers, with the new shoes on show. Nearby cobblers plied their trade, mending old boots. The smells increased as they came close to the tanners, who took the skins from the butchers and produced rough, dried leather which they sold to the curriers to be smoothed and shaved to an even thickness before oiling it ready for crafting. Gloves, purses, leather bottles and boxes, with patterns carved or painted on them, stood to demonstrate the skills of the craftsmen.

Simon barely gave the goods a glance, ignoring both the stallholders' cries and the young children trying to attract his attention by dragging on his cloak. The sights and sounds were familiar, and he had no wish to purchase anything.

As they came to the church, his eye lighted on a slim figure waiting at Peter's door. She turned as the four approached—it was the woman in gray.

Giving money to the poor was an important responsibility of the wealthy, and all rich men tended to provide for those less well-off in the parish. The church had an almoner whose duty it was to see to the well-being of those who could not earn their own living. For, while it was right that those who were too lazy to work should be punished, all accepted that if a man was injured and incapable of looking after himself and his family, or if a man were to die and leave his woman and children without support, it was only right that a Christian community should aid them.

As he watched, the almoner passed the woman some bread and meats. Peter, he knew, had always provided well for beggars. At his table, before food was passed even to guests, bread and other foods were put in a bowl "to serve God first." The almoner saved it to give to those who had most need. The woman held the gift in her apron, walking round to the site of the new church, and there Simon saw her kneel. Her child appeared from playing near a scaffold, and they ate with no sign of pleasure, only a kind of desperate haste, peering round as if fearing that if they did not consume it as quickly as possible, someone might take it from them.

"Simon, look—our friend," Baldwin murmured, nodding ahead. Following his gaze, Simon saw the captain.

Sir Hector stood with his back to them, near the entrance to the church. Every now and again he would peer at the inn, then round at the trees, as if measuring the time by the shadows, or searching for someone who could be hiding behind one of the heavy trunks. Simon looked up and down the street. "Is he out here on his own?"

"For a mercenary captain to let himself be separated from all his men shows a distinct lack of foresight," said Baldwin. "I suppose here in England he feels that it is safe enough. In Gascony or France he would not be so foolhardy, not with all the enemies he has there."

They continued on their way, and from the corner of his eye, Simon saw the woman walk out of the church with her child. She joined the street a little in front of him and his friend, and as he watched her, she approached Sir Hector, holding out her alms bowl like a supplicant.

"What?" Sir Hector spun as she spoke, scowling ferociously. "Who are you?"

His voice carried clearly over the hustle of the road, but the woman's response was smothered. To Simon's surprise, the knight fell back as if stunned, staring with horror. Mouth gaping, he stood transfixed. Suddenly he moved forward, struck her hand with a clenched fist, and shoved her roughly away from him. The bowl left her hand, whirling off against a wall, and clattered to the ground; a man walking by did not see it, and there was a loud crack as he stepped on it by mistake. She gave a shriek, both hands going to her head as she tried to take in this disaster. Simon thought she looked as if she could hardly comprehend such misfortune. He guessed that the bowl was not only her receptacle for gifts when begging, it was probably her sole means of gathering liquid. To lose it was an unbelievable calamity.

She sank to her knees, touching the two pieces of wood with a kind of bewildered despair, her son wailing beside her unheeded. Sir Hector watched her for a moment with a sneer twisting his visage, then turned back to his solitary vigil.

Baldwin pulled out some coins from his purse as he passed her, dropping them into her lap. "Buy a new bowl and some food," he muttered.

Seeing them, she was too awestruck to thank him, and staggered up, hauling her son with her, to the shelter of the wall. She clutched the coins to her breast, staring at Baldwin with wild eyes before suddenly darting off.

"That was uncharitable, Sir Hector."

The captain jerked around at the sound of mild reproof in Baldwin's voice; for a split second Simon thought he was going to hit the Keeper. Evidently Edgar did too, for he hastened to stand by the side of his master.

"Sir Baldwin. You always appear just as I find myself out of spirits." His tone was bantering, but to Simon he looked as if he was holding himself in with difficulty. The bailiff was not surprised. Beating a beggar was hardly the sort of behavior to enhance a man's reputation—but then Sir Hector was a mercenary, a breed of man held in low esteem all over the world. It appeared odd that the captain should be ashamed of a brief loss of temper, a trivial incident, compared with some of his previous actions.

"*You* bought that blue tunic: Sarra wore it when she died. Why did you not tell me you had purchased it?" Baldwin's face was set and angry. It was not only the beating of the poor woman, he was intensely annoyed at having to find out from the shopkeeper something which the knight could have told him that morning.

"I did not think it was something which concerned you. I still don't."

"I do. When did you give it to her?"

"*Give* it to her? You think I'd waste that much money on a—" Sir Hector's voice had risen almost to a shout, and his jaw stuck out pugnaciously. His eyes moved from Baldwin to Edgar, who had taken a short step forward, so that if the captain was to attack Baldwin, he would have to expose his side to the servant. Edgar smiled thinly and the mercenary brought himself under control with an effort.

"Sir Hector, you have made me go off on a wild-goose chase when you could have told me the truth this morning. Who was the tunic for, if not for her—and why was Sarra wearing it?"

"I have no idea why she was wearing it. She must have found it in one of my trunks. I told you we'd argued earlier. She was trying to warn me about my best men, and I told her to go . . . Well, I did not see her again. How she came to wear that tunic, I have no idea."

"Perhaps she thought you had bought it for her," Simon suggested.

"Why should she think that?"

"Women do. You had argued, then she saw the new tunic. She might have thought you had bought her a gift to apologize for shouting at her."

Sir Hector stared in disbelief. "Are you serious? Why should I do that? She was only a—"

"You have given us your opinion of her often enough before," Baldwin interrupted smoothly. "There is no need for further repetition. When did you buy the tunic?"

"Yesterday, a day after I'd argued with Sarra. I was just about to go out, and I was in a hurry, when she burst in to tell me that Henry was about to foment disorder in the troop. As if he'd dare!" He turned and began to make his way at a slow amble back to the inn, casting around as if casually, but with enough diligence to make Simon think he was alert for a threat. Or was looking for someone.

"Isn't it possible she was right?" mused Baldwin.

"No," the captain snapped. "My men are bound to me. Whether they like it or not, they know that I am a man of my word—to them at least! If I was to be deposed, the last person most of them would want in my place would be Henry. He has an annoying habit of taking on new recruits and finding out their secrets, then blackmailing them."

"You *know* about that?" Baldwin burst out, aghast.

"Of course I do. All the better for me to know I am protected. While the fool carries on like that, I am secure. The other men all hate him and fear me. He has their secrets bound in his purse, while I own their lives. All the time he does that, he costs me nothing, and yet the others wouldn't think of supporting him in any kind of coup."

"They might support another."

"No. There's none who would dare to try it. Besides, with Henry and John around, I would be likely to find out soon enough if they did. No, the idea is stupid."

Frowning, Baldwin kicked a pebble from the path. "What did she actually say?"

"That she'd overheard Henry talking to John or someone and that he was planning to form the band round himself. No, wait a moment, that's not right. She said Henry told this other person that he would not need to worry about me for long, that he would have his own band—something like that."

"And then you went to buy the tunic."

"I went out and saw the tunic, and bought it, and I said it would be collected later."

"And when you returned?"

"I told one of the men to go and fetch it."

"And you never saw her alive again, or saw the tunic until it was on her body?"

"That's right."

They were at the door to the inn, and Sir Hector stood defiantly as if daring them to enter with him.

"Out of interest, Sir Hector," asked Simon diffidently, "which man did you ask to collect it?"

"Eh? Wat, I think."

"And then what did you do?"

"I went out. I had only returned to the hall briefly. I saw Wat and went straight out again."

"Why? Where were you off to?"

"To see someone."

"Who?" asked Baldwin.

"Like I said, it is no concern of yours."

"I think it might be."

"You are welcome to think what you like."

"Sir Hector, I am trying to discover who might have murdered the girl, and you are not helping."

"I didn't kill her and I didn't see who did. Telling you whom I was about to meet will not assist you. I can only suggest you speak to someone else and try to find out who killed this Sarra."

Simon scuffed the dirt of the pavement with the toe of his boot. "One thing seems odd to me."

"The whole bloody affair seems damned odd to me," Sir Hector said heavily.

"What I mean is, her old tunic was on the floor of her room, as if she'd kicked it off in her hurry to get changed into the new one. That was why I wondered whether she might have thought it was a present for her. If she had simply seen the tunic in your room and not thought it was for her, she might have tried it on—I suppose she might even have taken it to her room to try on—but she would not have let anyone *see* her."

"So what?" Sir Hector glanced at him disdainfully, his lip curled in disgust.

"It occurs to me that she must have walked from her room, over the yard, through the hall, and into your solar. She must have known that someone could have seen her. If she was trying to clandestinely don the tunic, she picked a very public way to do it."

"So what? Maybe she wanted people to see her in a colorful tunic."

"I think most women would only behave like that if they thought the tunic was for them in the first place. She didn't see the need to hide her possession of it; she thought it was hers. That's why she changed in her room and came back by such an obvious route."

"God's blood! If she thought that, why should she

bother to go to her room in the first place? Why not simply change where she found it?"

"Absolutely right!" Simon smiled. "That's the other problem. I would have expected, if she saw it in your room, that she would have tried it on in there. She would not have bothered to go to her room to change. Of course, if she was in her room, and someone told her about the tunic, she would have gone to your room to find it, but even then she would surely have put it on in the solar. There would have been no reason to take it back to her room to don it."

"So what are you getting at?"

"This, Sir Hector. Since she changed in her room, the only reason I can see for her doing that and then going to the solar is that she thought it was hers. And logically, I think she must have found the tunic in her room, or been given it there."

Baldwin stared at his friend. "I see what you're getting at: if she thought it was a present, she would have gone straight to Sir Hector to thank him."

"It's how a woman would behave—dressing in the tunic to show how pleased she was with the gift."

The mercenary glowered from one to the other. "Are you seriously suggesting that she somehow found it in her room and rushed over here to thank me for buying it for her?"

Simon shrugged. "It's the only explanation I can believe right now. Either she found it there or she was given it there—and was told that you had bought it for her."

"Who could have said that to her?"

"That we need to find out," said Baldwin. "In the meantime, you never answered my question: for whom did you purchase the tunic?"

"That's my business. It's got nothing to do with you."

Baldwin noticed how the captain's gaze kept straying to the road behind him. He was sure that Sir Hector had been waiting for the same woman, whoever it might be, when he had knocked the bowl from the poor beggar's hand. But there was little he could do to force the man to name her—and for some reason Baldwin had an instinct not to press him. "Very well. But is there anything else you forgot to mention to us this morning?"

The captain's eyes were gray flints as he snarled, "No!"

As the Keeper of the King's Peace and his friend left the inn, it was hard for the man watching to restrain his feelings. They had found out about the new dress; that at least should put them further on the correct track, and when he saw their faces, they told him all he wanted to know. The knight, Baldwin, kept glancing over his shoulder, back toward the inn, with his features set into a black scowl of suspicion, while his friend seemed lost in thought, brows fixed into a mask of perplexity.

At last the fruits of his plans were ripening, and would soon be ready to be plucked.

When they had gone, Sir Hector stormed through the hall and into his solar like a bear with a foot in a trap. At the door to his rooms, he pointed to one of his men. "Get me Henry the Hurdle. Bring him to my solar. *Now!*"

He was seated in front of his cabinet when Henry walked in. The man looked nervous, but that was no surprise to Sir Hector. He would expect any of his men responding to an urgent summons to be anxious.

"Shut the door," he said, and waved the servant out. Henry did as he was commanded, then, darting looks all round, he sat himself on a trunk.

Sir Hector knew his men well. It was one of the basic rules of being a leader that the men under him should always feel their captain understood them and their needs. At the same time, they had to believe in his infallibility and total power. It was not kindness that had made Sir Hector the commander of warriors, but his willingness to kill ruthlessly all those who threatened him and his authority. Surveying Henry, he was aware that the man might well have thought about toppling him—might possibly even have succeeded. Henry was devious enough, though Sir Hector doubted that his Sergeant was quite clever enough to pull the wool over his eyes completely.

But he was troubled by the thought that even his most trusted man could have plotted against him.

There was nothing unusual in potential disloyalty, for that was the normal way for a mercenary band to select a new commander: he was replaced by another, stronger man, one who could instill more fear in the men beneath. The risk was always there in any group, where malcontents could easily persuade others that a better leader was available. Disaffected employers often tried to foment trouble, considering it advantageous to change commanders in order to renegotiate contracts during the interregnum. Then again, many a mercenary captain had discovered that when he went abroad without the bulk of his men, either the bulk were no longer there on his return, or they ambushed him. Loyalty was a rare commodity for a warrior! And that was what Sarra had alleged, or something similar: that Henry had plotted to oust him and take control himself.

The stupid bitch had brought her end down upon herself, he thought savagely. She had made the allegations in the middle of an inn where Henry had his spies. He was bound to have been informed and warned.

Henry shifted, waiting for his master to speak, and the movement dragged Sir Hector's attention back to the present. "Wat—is he reliable?"

"As reliable as any old bugger is who's seen too many battles. I don't know. He's certainly always fought well, but he's been moaning about things for some time . . ."

"What sort of things?"

Henry scratched his head. He couldn't see where this was leading, and he did not want to volunteer too much in case he found himself in the firing line. "Oh, about how the group is organized generally. He's always going on about money and such."

"Has he complained about you?"

"Me?" Henry decided that a little bluff honesty could do no harm. "No, but he's never liked me. Not many of the men do, they think I have too much say in things—don't like me giving orders and disciplining them. That's nothing new. But I've overheard him whingeing to others."

"Sir Baldwin reckons Wat might have told Sarra to come and see me in that tunic."

"Why'd he do that?"

"Maybe to make me angry enough to kill her."

"You'd get that angry just seeing her wearing a tunic?" Henry queried dubiously.

"I had bought it that day for another woman. If I had seen her in it, I might have killed her for polluting it with her filthy body."

Henry wondered how filthy his master had thought that same body on the night they arrived, but kept his face blank. "I don't know that Wat could have thought that out, sir. Why should he think you'd get so cross you'd kill for that?"

Sir Hector stared at him unblinking, and Henry had the grace to look away. All of them, over the course of many years, had killed in any number of battles and running fights. Henry himself had been involved in some of the vicious border wars between France and England on the Gascon marches, and none of them were free of the stain of blood spilt while their blood was up. Sir Hector knew that Henry, after the sack of one town, had found two men arguing over a captured woman. With his own rough humor he had hit upon an easy solution to their problem, and, sweeping out his great hand-and-a-half sword, had declared "Half each!" and cut her in two. No, none of them were free of the stain of blood.

"I want you to find out, Henry. Ask around. If he put her up to it, he's unreliable, and I want him gone. You know what I mean."

"Yes, sir."

"And you . . . *did* you plot to remove me, Henry?"

As Sir Hector's unnerving eyes snapped to his face, Henry felt himself go pale, as if the eyes themselves had stabbed him and let his blood run out onto the rushes. He shook his head silently, but did not trust his voice.

After he had left the room, Sir Hector sat for a long time, deep in thought. They had a long way to go before they were back again in Gascony, where the wars were, and the money was waiting to be plundered, but he was sure now that he must lose Wat before they got there.

And he must also get rid of Henry. He couldn't be trusted anymore. Sir Hector nodded to himself. He must think of someone else who could take on the responsibilities of Sergeant for the band.

- 13 -

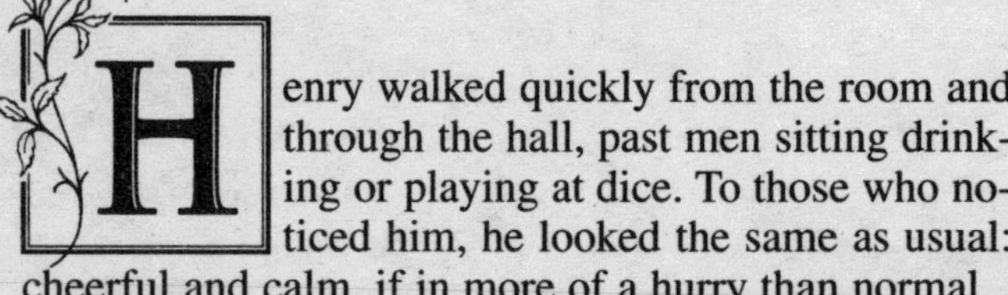

Henry walked quickly from the room and through the hall, past men sitting drinking or playing at dice. To those who noticed him, he looked the same as usual: cheerful and calm, if in more of a hurry than normal.

John was playing nine men's morris, or large merrills. It took all of his concentration to win at this. He was fine with other games, but trying to win seven of his opponent's pieces while avoiding capture himself always made him frustrated. This game was not helped by the side betting. He caught sight of Henry walking from the room, and their eyes met. Seeing Henry jerk his head, John nodded quickly before returning to his game.

Outside, Henry waited for his accomplice with his nerves fraying. It seemed like hours before John could wind up the game and leave the hall, and Henry spent the time starting at every sound as he walked up and down in the yard, trying to appear unconcerned. "What in God's name have you been doing? Didn't you see I had to talk?"

"What's the problem? I couldn't just get up and leave when there was money on the table; everyone would have known something was the matter. I came as soon as I could."

"It's not soon enough," Henry said, and for the first time John saw the naked fear in his eyes.

"What is it? What's the matter?"

"Not here. Come with me." Henry took his arm and led the way round behind the stables, to a shaded spot in the back lane where they could speak unobserved. "Sir Hector's just had me in and was asking me about Wat."

"Does he reckon Wat could have taken all the silver? The old bastard's not got the sense."

"No, he doesn't. What he thinks is: Wat took the tunic he'd collected from the shop to Sarra and tricked her into thinking it was a present for her. Wat told her to get changed into it, expecting Sir Hector to murder her when he saw her wearing it. He probably thinks Wat killed her when his original plan failed."

"Do you really think he could believe Wat killed her?"

"Yes. Right now, anyway. But if he talks to Wat, we're dead."

"He'd never—"

"He's halfway there already. Just now he asked me if I'd ever plotted against him."

"Christ Jesus!"

"Yeah."

They both contemplated their immediate future for a minute. John said, "We'd better get to Wat and silence him before he can say anything."

"That's what Sir Hector just told me to do—kill him, but what good'll that do us? You saw him talking to the bailiff's servant. Other men heard what the fool said. If he suddenly dies, people will soon put two and two together. The fact that Sir Hector told us to won't protect us. Anyway, we were seen going to Sir Hector's room and it wouldn't take much to guess we might have knocked her out. No. We've got to get away. Right away."

"What, leave the team now? Go away for good?"

Henry nodded glumly. If only John hadn't killed the bitch, there wouldn't be a problem, but now things were getting complicated. Henry had knocked her out as soon as he had seen her in the storeroom dressed in that damned tunic, and ever since then their plan had gradually unravelled like a cheap shirt. Stabbing her was unnecessary. She hadn't seen them—she could have been left there in the trunk for as long as they wanted, and no one would have cared. But once John had stabbed her, their chances of being able to enjoy the rewards of their theft were reduced to nothing. It wasn't Sir Hector, for he could hardly care less about the death of a serving-girl; he cared far more for the loss of his silver. No, it was the local Keeper, the interfering bastard! He seemed determined to find out who had taken her life. Glancing at his friend, Henry had to bite back his bitterness. John had only done what he should have done himself. It was better not to leave witnesses. It was just a shame that this time they would have been better off leaving the girl alive.

"Come on," he said. "This is what we'd better do."

That evening Simon found it hard to relax. The evening meal was heavy for a fast day, with fish fresh from the stew ponds, and barnacle geese roasted with herbs and spices. Peter Clifford was not stinting in his efforts to appear in the best light possible before his Bishop.

"Goose?" Stapledon asked, sniffing at the aroma as

the panter cut fresh trenchers and the carver sliced up the fatty, crisp and tender meat. He nodded and smiled at the page who held the bowl of hot, scented water for him to wash his hands, and then dried them on the towel while Peter washed.

"Barnacle goose," Peter agreed.

"Some say that they are not fish," Stapledon observed, and Peter was shocked.

"My apologies if it is not to your taste, my lord, but barnacle geese *are* fish. They live in the sea, growing from a worm. If you want I will have it removed and—"

"I think that would be a cruel waste of God's plenty, and as you say, they are considered by most to be fish. It smells far too good to be thrown away." He turned to Baldwin. "Have you enjoyed a productive day, my friend? Are you any nearer to finding who took the life of that poor girl?"

Baldwin dried his hands and leaned back. "I do not know who killed her yet, but I am suspicious of Sir Hector."

"Ah, yes. Sir Hector," said Stapledon, and sighed. "I wonder if he ever was knighted by an honorable man—all too often these leaders of wandering bands of soldiers call themselves 'Sir' when it takes their fancy. This man's sole claim to authority, I fear, is his ability to kill." He broke off while grace was said by one of the canons. "And it is all too natural to suspect someone who can treat life as something to be ended when it suits, rather than a gift from Our Lord which should be honored and respected."

Baldwin found himself warming to the Bishop, but before he could speak, Margaret said, "I don't understand what they are doing here. Why have they come to Crediton?"

"Apparently they were considering joining the King's army, but the pay did not satisfy them," Peter said. "I have heard that they were with the King's representatives, but decided not to go north. I think they were told they would not be wanted."

"I doubt that the King or his men would miss such as these," Stapledon said with a smile, but Baldwin was not so sure.

"Whatever their morals or the complexion of their souls, one thing the King could rely on would be their ability to fight and strike fear into the hearts of the Scottish. They may not be gentle or kindly, but they are undoubtedly soldiers, whereas most of the King's army are raw peasants, unused to killing, who are as likely to turn tail and bolt when the battle gets too fierce as remain. At least Sir Hector's men would know when to stand and when to give ground."

"If they weren't bribed at the wrong moment to change allegiance," Stapledon remarked lightly. "You almost sound as if you hold them in some esteem, Sir Baldwin."

"Not exactly, but I have been in wars where similar men have shown themselves as brave as any, and where they have been as honorable as many of their seniors should be. One thing I have learned is not to take such men for cowards or fools. They are often forced into their way of life against their judgment and will."

"They cannot be the equal of a similar troop of men with better morals and clean hearts, surely," Stapledon said.

"My lord, I fear that if you are ever in a battle arrayed with numbers of the godly on the one hand, all pure in heart and living life to Christ's own principles, who are nevertheless matched on the other side by trained mercenaries like Sir Hector's men, all well-versed in warfare and combat, you should look to your armor and ensure you have a fleet-footed destrier nearby. The mercenaries, for all their loose living, will undoubtedly win."

"I too have fought, Sir Baldwin," the Bishop said coolly. "And you may be right, but sometimes it is better to die in a good cause than live for a bad one."

"Of course," Baldwin said. "But no matter how good you feel your cause to be, you are the more likely to win your battles with trained and expert soldiers."

"Baldwin!" Peter expostulated. "Are you trying to deny the achievements of centuries of chivalry? The whole of society depends on the virtue and thence the power of our knights, and it has always been so, ever since King Arthur ruled."

"What is chivalry? It is a method of making war, and sometimes it does not work. We learned that in Outremer, in the Kingdom of Jerusalem, where all too often the Saracens beat us, even when we were strong—"

"Ah, Sir Baldwin, I think you may not understand the problems there," said the Bishop seriously. "Too many of the knights were ungodly and were motivated by the wrong things."

"Such as what? The motivation of a knight should be for glory, by fighting honorably to defend the poor and weak. Perhaps the same could be achieved by a smaller number of men better versed in the ways of warfare, and for less cost. Look at the war in Scotland. Will we win it? I have no idea, but I do know this: almost none of our men are warriors. There are well-born knights in the King's entourage, but most of the rest are lowly archers and foot soldiers. It is on them that the main fighting will fall—and how many of them are trained in anything other than the scythe and the plow? These few under Sir Hector could be worth three hundred ordinary peasants."

Simon listened to the discussion in silence. He had no wish to join in and talk about things of which he knew little, for he did not want to display his ignorance about wars and fighting. All he knew about was fighting gangs of outlaws and keeping miners away from the locals on the moors—and neither matched the experiences of a man like Baldwin, who had spent his youth fighting Saracens.

Something else made him hold his tongue. There was a niggling feeling of unease at the back of his mind, a sense that something was wrong, and he was aware of a growing anxiety.

At the end of the meal, once the warmed water had been brought for all to wash away the grease and sauces from fingers, he excused himself and walked out to the road, pleading an overfull stomach.

The sun had sunk behind the far hill, and the street was almost deserted. Buildings rose all round like the high sides of the Teign Valley, rugged and misshapen like moorstone cliffs. All the shops were blank and dead-looking, the houses had their shutters over the windows to keep out the unhealthy night air, and the only light came from louvres and trap doors in the roofs, all opened to let out the smoke from the cooking fires.

There was a curious air of expectancy. He heard a door slam, a shout of laughter and giggling, a dog bark echoing down a street, a man cursing, and the sound of revelry from a tavern. All were the normal marks of a night in a large town. A chicken murmured to itself on the other side of a wall as he passed, grumbling at being disturbed, and a lamb bleated sleepily, but over all these usual, unremarkable sounds, Simon thought there was a stillness, as if the whole town was waiting for something to happen.

Near the jail, Simon paused and watched the inn. There was a gust of raucous humor from the hall, and the bailiff felt sorry for those who lived close by. They would surely regret living so near to an alehouse, he felt, when the guests were as rowdy as these soldiers. He was tempted for a moment to join them and lose himself in drinking with men who had no fear for the future, who lived merely for the present, but he stayed outside, staring wistfully at the glimmer which showed through the closed shutters.

A gentle lowing from the shambles, and a bleating, brought him back to the present. There was no point in his joining the soldiers. They were not of his kind. If he were to go in, there would be silence followed swiftly by a general turning of backs. He was a bailiff, a man used to giving commands, but he had no authority over such as these. They were free men, free of the restraint that others might feel on seeing him. Anyway, he knew that shaking off his black mood would not be helped by going into a crowded room full of cheerful drinkers. His was a mood for which alcohol could provide no cure.

With a wry grimace he accepted that he also might not be safe alone with Sir Hector's singing and swearing force.

Simon started off toward the western end of town, but his steps faltered as he passed the entrance to the alley where he had seen the woman in gray. Something about it made him pause and frown.

It gaped like the maw of an evil creature, long and noisome as a dragon's gullet. But like prey beguiled by a tempting bait, he found himself lingering. The alley was a twisting black tunnel, in which sound was altered and the senses dulled. Here lived the poorer people of the town: those who could not afford the cosseted lifestyle of the merchants and priests farther out from the center. The tradesmen had their own rooms over or behind their shops, the smiths and carpenters above their workshops, but here, in the reeking corridor between tightly packed houses, were the families of the others who made the town what it was: tanners and curers; weavers and dyers; cooks and servants for the merchants' houses—all lived thrown together in as few short feet as possible for warmth and defense. The smell of unwashed bodies, urine, rotting flesh and vegetation from the sewer mingled with that of roasting meat and stews to form a stench which assaulted his nostrils and made him curl his lip in revulsion.

Then he froze, peering intently. There had been a scuffle and muted cry. It was not the swift skitter of a frightened rat, but a kind of shuffling and slithering. Nervously wetting his lips, he stepped in to the alley.

In the dead interior, the sound of his footsteps changed. Rather than the solid, confident ringing of his boots on the cobbles near the market, now his feet sloshed and slapped in the puddles left by people emptying bowls and bedpans. At this time of night those who lived in the alley were all in their beds, and Simon could see nobody. All he was aware of was the light above, where the moon and stars stood out with precise clarity in the deep blue-black sky, compared with the grayness of the buildings on either side.

* * *

The steps approached. He could see no one clearly yet, huddled as he was in the doorway, uncomfortable where the drips from the washing overhead had spattered against him until they formed a rivulet down his back. Now in the doorway, at least he was away from that irritation.

There was a slowness in the footsteps which annoyed him. He almost wanted to shout at the man, tell him to come along faster and stop tormenting him. His nerves were already drawn as tight as the hemp of a hangman's noose when the body was hanging. This slow, methodical sound was increasing his tension, as if he was listening not with his ears alone but with his entire body. The noise slammed into his chest and belly like blows.

And then he had passed. The hidden watcher let his breath out in relief. Soon he could escape, run away to the town and lose himself, while this fool stumbled onward along the alley.

But the unearthly wailing stopped him. It began as a low moan, a cry of indescribable suffering, which rose in gusts only to fall again, then rising and falling with increasing regularity, until it formed a steady cadence, now rising to a shriek, now falling to a disbelieving shuddering of horror.

Simon stopped dead in his tracks. The noise had put an end even to the quiet sounds in the alley, and the whole area was still, as if the very buildings were listening to the misery in the voice with hushed sympathy.

Then his legs propelled him forward. His hand snatched at his sword and tugged it loose, then swept it out as he pounded up to a slight bend in the path, feeling the blood rush in his head, his belly hollow with sudden fear, his scalp itching with icy foreboding.

The corner came, and then he was past it, and nobody had sprung out to attack him. Carrying on, the wail rose to a shriek—but now was behind him. He skidded to a halt, turned, pelted back, and saw the thin, darker hole: another alley leading from this one. He would have seen it in daylight, but in the darkness, it was all but invisible. Stopping his rush by pushing a hand out before him to cushion his speed against a wall, he caught his breath, then ducked inside.

It was a mean little dead-end. At the far side was a building with a fitful light showing between the cracked and broken shutters, and it was by this meager illumination that he confronted the bleak tragedy.

She was huddled, as if even in death she was trying to take up as little space as possible, and keen to conform to the laws that required the poor and widowed to be unseen and out of the way. At first Simon thought she was simply kneeling and searching for a lost oddment, her arms on the ground, head resting gently between them. But then he saw that her pillow was the feces flung from the upper rooms.

Her child stood beside her, a grubby cherub with spiky hair where the dirt had given it the consistency of wood. His grimy face was all mouth, bawling in his fierce grief, and Simon felt as if his heart would break at the sight of his absolute loss.

He held out his hand, his own face cracking under the massive weight of the little boy's grief, and he called out something—he would never recall what exactly—and saw the boy turn to him.

And then he saw the little face break in renewed terror. He saw the boy's mouth widen and heard the dreadful, baying howl.

And then the blow struck, and he fell headlong, clutching vainly at consciousness like a drowning man reaching for a rope lying just out of reach, as the waves of black oblivion rushed forward to engulf him.

- 14 -

Roger de Grosse was not the happiest man in Crediton that night. His errand to the merchant out to the west of the town had been dull, requiring him to confirm deliveries of wine and spices to the cathedral. It meant that he had to spend five hours closeted with the merchant's steward while he checked off all the items on the list given him by the Bishop and cross-checked them with the steward's copy; then he had to walk round the chests and barrels, sampling at random some of the wine casks, opening the chests and investigating their contents—all of which were immediately closed and marked with gobbets of wax carrying the Bishop's seal to prevent tampering.

Five hours in the chilly storeroom without an offer of ale or food had worn away the young man's normal good humor. He had expected to be back at Peter Clifford's hall long before now, while there was still the chance of spiced ale and warm food, but he had to accept that all he would be likely to find was stale bread and cold meat.

Only four months before, he would have been astonished at having been given such a task, for to be the son of Sir Arnold de Grosse was to be used to issuing orders and expecting others to leap to obey. It was demeaning to be told to go somewhere and count up barrels like an ordinary steward, but he knew the reason why. Walter Stapledon had explained at the outset that he was to be given many of the more onerous and tedious jobs, not because Stapledon disliked him, but because the Bishop had to be convinced that this new rector would be capable of humility and dedication. The Bishop, ever an astute man, wanted to make sure that young Grosse would be prepared to serve his parishioners, and his method was to test Roger's commitment; giving him the menial jobs which others tried to avoid.

The logic was simple. Roger had the chance of being given a good living; and once he was installed, removing him would be difficult, not least because his father was an important patron to Stapledon, sponsoring many services and building works. It would have been easy for Stapledon to have accepted Grosse's son and ignored the pleas of the parishioners, if only for the money. But he was a cautious man, and he took seriously his responsibilities to the souls even in the more far-flung parts of his diocese, and he was unhappy that such a young man should be installed. Stapledon wanted to test him and make sure he was fit for the position his father wanted to buy for him.

Stubbing his toe on a misplaced cobblestone and twisting his ankle, Roger gritted his teeth against the rising temptation to curse, his face a grimace of pain as he hopped, holding the offended appendage in one hand. "Cooah!" he sighed at last as the first shock and pain receded a little, and he felt able to limp to a wall and lean against it, trying to guess how much further he had to go.

He could accept Stapledon's thinking, but for now performing like a cheap servant was hard to accept. It would be different if it was regular service, if he had become the squire to a great master, serving his apprenticeship before he could earn the golden spurs and sword belt of knighthood, but all he could work toward now was the small church selected for him by Stapledon in Callington, and he was unsure he wanted it.

Setting his foot down, he wondered again about his father's plan for him. He was the youngest of the brothers, and it was only natural that his father should try to acquire a reasonable living for him—why else would a man invest so heavily in patronage if there was no reward in the end? And Sir Arnold expected his reward to be a post for any of his male children who were not to inherit, so that they might have somewhere to live. It was essential, when the eldest would take the whole of the estates, the home and the wealth accumulated over the years, to find something for the other sons, if there were any surviving.

Roger had not at first been interested in the church or in being a rector. He had wanted to be a knight.

His brother Geoffroy had been knighted some two years before, and since then had deigned to speak to him only rarely, aware of his greater position in life and knowing that he would inherit the estates while "little Roger" would remain a poverty-struck village priest—for Geoffroy had the firm, if patronizing, belief that his brother was generally an incompetent whom no amount of teaching or training for warfare could help. In Geoffrey's view, any man who was not in possession of property was weak and only existed to support those who *did* have money. Geoffroy was going to be the wealthy one, and Roger was not. Therefore Roger must accept his secondary status in life.

There was little support for Roger in the de Grosse household. Since his mother had died, Roger had relied on friends among the servants, but that had changed over the years. His father had made him give up his childish companions when he was eight. At that age he should forget foolish playing and learn his craft. Most squires were taken on by their lords as pages at the age of five so that they could be properly taught in the arts they needed to acquire in order to become good knights. The pages had to be taught the correct ways to serve, to behave politely in company, how to sing and play music, box, wrestle and fence, until finally they were instructed in the most critical art of all: horsemanship.

Geoffrey had been taken away to live with the de Courtenay family when he was six, where he was soon favored among his contemporaries. It had come as a shock to Roger when he was also sent away, for he was to be taught his letters and raised for the priesthood. He was a sad boy, constantly reminded of his weakness and inadequacy, for his peers had no hesitation in bullying him unmercifully: they were to be soldiers, strong and bold men-of-war, while he would stay at home and preach to stupid parishioners.

If he had allowed the situation to continue, Roger might have become just another lonely rector in a provincial area, but his father's blood flowed in his veins, and all too often down from his nose. He was an incorrigible fighter. The slightest hint of an insult would cause him to square up; the remotest suggestion that he was any weaker than the others led inevitably to a battle. His teachers looked on indulgently, for it was right that boys should defend themselves, and right that the strongest should lead the others, even with future priests, who would be expected to lead defenses in time of war. One boy in particular was Roger's undeclared enemy, a heavy-set youth some two years his senior, but when Roger was discovered by a Bishop, rolling in the mud and soundly boxing his ears, Roger was finally given a thorough beating.

It left him sore but undefeated. His tormentors stopped teasing and jibing, and went warily when he was near.

Yet he knew in his heart that they were right. While they went on to become squires at thirteen or fourteen, riding larger and faster horses, practicing with lance and sword, he had to sit indoors and write pretty characters on parchment, or learn how to mix the powders to produce the right level of color for the pictures, or how to read the odd language that apparently was God's own and allowed priests of all nations to converse easily.

His foot better, he hobbled along toward the church and Peter Clifford's house. The training had been hard. Each failure to understand his work, each mispronunciation and inaccurate translation resulted in a thrashing, until he was word-perfect. He was not a natural speaker, and the idea of preaching before the population in Callington filled him with dread, but the post at least offered him freedom, and that was a sweet prize, one which he felt sure he could enjoy all the more since it involved being several days' journey from any who wished to control him. It was made even more attractive by the fact that he was quickly coming to like Stapledon, who had so far proved to be a kindly and honorable man—unlike some who had trained him.

It would be lonely, though, and Stapledon had hinted that he might need help. Usually a new rector would have other staff to help, but in Callington there would be no one. Only Roger struggling to keep the congregation together.

He had to pause near the jail to rest his foot, for the ankle was swelling a little, and his toe ached horribly. Leaning against the wall, he glanced around phlegmatically. There was ribald laughter leaking out through a broken shutter at the inn, and the sound of someone singing. The pain receded again, and he tested his foot, staring at it dubiously. It should hold, he felt.

The dull thudding of hooves on dirt made him look up. From the street that led along the side of the butcher's, he saw two men appear on horseback, leading a pack-mule. They slowed as they came to the main road, then walked off slowly on the Exeter road, seeming to increase their speed as they went, until they were cantering gently at the bottom of the slight hill.

Roger watched them impassively. It was a strange time to be beginning a journey, but he was not particularly interested. He was more concerned with getting himself back to Clifford's house, so, sighing, he forced himself upright and started off again. At the entrance to an alley, he halted again. Leaning against the wall was a heavy stick; he took it and tested his weight on it. It held him, and he was about to move on when he heard noises.

The alley had no light, and in the dark he could only see for a few yards, but he was sure he could hear movement. There was a dull susurration, as of a group of people talking in whispers, nervous of being discovered.

He paused, concentrating hard, trying to see through

the gloom, but the darkness was thickened by the smoke from a multitude of fires, which hung in thin streamers like watchful wraiths.

Suddenly feeling a chill which had nothing to do with the cold of the night, he hobbled back to Peter Clifford's house as quickly as his game ankle would allow.

Margaret watched with fascination as Walter Stapledon held them to his face again, reading the paper carefully.

She had never been able to read herself: being a farmer's daughter there was no point in her father investing in her education. As soon as she was old enough she would be married and become a mother. Her training was complete by the time she was fourteen, for by then she could brew and bake, and had learned the basic skills of looking after children. Simon was able to read and write, and it was not that skill which astonished her: it was the forked piece of metal which Stapledon held to his nose while he squinted at the page.

Catching sight of her expression, Stapledon smiled as he set the paper down. "It is an old man's weakness to need help with those bits and pieces of his body which do not function as they once did."

"But what does it do?" she demanded.

"It was designed for old and feeble men like me who find their eyes are not as efficient as they once were. I used to be able to see as clearly as you can, but now I need these two glasses held in their frame to make the words look bigger."

"How do they do it?"

He laughed and passed them to her. "I look on it as

a gift from God—a miracle that makes my work easier. I do not pretend to understand *how*! I merely accept them."

The door slammed as Baldwin and Edgar returned from checking on their horses. "Is Simon not back yet?" the knight said, glancing at Stapledon with his eyebrows raised in faint alarm.

The Bishop shook his head. "Does it matter? He seems a strong enough man, more than a match for any footpad."

"Yes. He must be all right." Baldwin lowered himself into a seat and watched Margaret playing with the spectacles with the delight of a child, studying the woodwork on the table, the page before the Bishop, even the skin on the back of her hand, while the Bishop looked on indulgently.

For all his expressed confidence, the knight was concerned. Simon had been so out of sorts for the last few days that his disappearance after their meal was cause for worry. It was not that Baldwin expected his friend to harm himself intentionally. Simon was in no way capable of so foolish an act, and suicide for someone relatively God-fearing was unthinkable. No, Baldwin was not anxious on that score—but he was nonetheless unquiet. There were many dangers in a town during darkness, even at the lowest level of simply falling down in a darkened street. Baldwin had once found a man in the gutter. From the indications, it was clear what had happened: the man had tripped over a drunk at the roadside, but the unfortunate fellow had struck his head, then rolled into a ditch full of muddy water. Unconscious, he had drowned. The drunk had not even woken.

And then there were thieves. Even a tiny town like

Crediton had its undesirable element, and these were augmented at present by the mercenaries—a group who were used to killing as a way of life.

Poor Simon. He had enjoyed a life full of success and rewards, and yet the taste of all had turned sour in his mouth with the death of his son. Baldwin had seen it happen to others, but rarely so strongly as with his friend. Most, when a child died, had to shrug and try to produce a replacement. There was little point in worrying unduly about the ones who died, not when so many remained, needing help to survive.

But Simon had pinned all his hopes on the boy. After so many years of waiting for a child who could live more than a few weeks or days, for all their children apart from Edith and Peterkin had died very young, there was the double agony of knowing that his heir too was gone. Simon must have a son to allow his family to continue, and Baldwin could all too easily comprehend the agony of knowing that there was nobody to carry on the name. He had the same pain himself.

"My lord! Bishop!" The door was flung open, and now Roger burst in, wild-eyed and panting.

"Calm yourself, lad!" Stapledon ordered, staring at his young rector. "What in the Lord's name is the matter?"

"Is . . . is it my husband?" Margaret stuttered, paling with a quick intuition. "What is it? Where is he?"

"Your husband?"

Baldwin shook his head. "Simon went out to walk off his meal, that is all. What have you seen?"

"Sir, I don't know—but I'm sure something's going on in the alley by the jail. There's noise like a lot of men talking low. I really think you should send someone to investigate."

"Why?" asked Baldwin. "Maybe it was a party on their way home from a tavern."

"No, sir. They weren't walking, they were keeping quiet, like men planning a riot." Roger told them about the sounds near the alley's entrance, and Baldwin's face hardened.

"Bishop, I think I should check on this. There's no way to tell, of course, but we have heard today that some of the mercenaries might be plotting to remove their captain. If they are, I do not want them to kill him here in Crediton."

"No, of course not," Stapledon patted Margaret's hand. "See? It's nothing to do with your husband."

She smiled wanly, and looked away, but not before Baldwin had seen the fear in her eyes. "Edgar? Get Hugh. I think he's asleep in the buttery again. And tell Peter where we're going. Ask him for two of his men, just in case we need help, and tell them to bring weapons. Then come back here." As soon as he finished Edgar disappeared, and they heard a sleepy voice complaining at being woken. "You, Roger. You must come with us and show us where you heard this noise."

It was the faint awareness that something was not right which propelled him on. He had no doubt that his friend was able to protect himself: Simon Puttock, he knew, was a capable man in a fight. Baldwin had seen the proof of that often enough—usually the knight felt it was his task to control his friend when Simon became too heated, for the latter was apt to lose his temper, much like the red-headed men from the north whom Baldwin looked on as mad. The bailiff was a staunch ally in a fight, but he had been gone for a long time, and Baldwin felt the same trepidation that agonized Margaret.

It took little time to get to the alley, and Roger pointed at it with his stick. He could see that the tall knight was concerned, and his very silence indicated how perturbed he was at the disappearance of his friend.

Baldwin stared frowning into the alley, and then marched in without a word. The others followed him in silence, only to halt. Some little distance away they could hear the muffled sound of crying, which suddenly rose and was cut off.

Rollo was petrified with terror as his crying and weeping faded to a mumble. He stood, staring down at the two bodies, pawing at his mother, avoiding contact with the man who had fallen by her side. The stranger was unknown, and his mother had always told him to be cautious with people he did not know.

She had been lying for a long time, but no matter how often he prodded and nudged her, she would not wake. Rollo had seen others who had died, but he refused to accept the possibility that his mother could have. She would never have left him alone.

The alley was dark, but he was used to that. He and his mother had never had a home, and he was accustomed to sleeping outside with her, taking what meager protection from the elements they could by hanging up her cloak from a nail on a wall to form a makeshift tent and huddling together beneath it in the worst of weathers. More commonly he would find himself left alone in a room while his mother spoke to a man in a separate chamber. He had often jealously watched the children of townsfolk as they played and shouted. Rollo would never know such pleasures, because his mother had done something wrong.

He could not comprehend what it was that they were being punished for. They were both somehow guilty of a great crime, and it made them have to live apart from the other people of the town, constantly in fear. Rollo was six. If he had been the son of a merchant, he would be learning the trade he had been born to, or discovering the skills of a knight if his father had earned enough money and had an eye to the future. At the very least he could expect to be accepted into a farming community. But he and his mother were forced to beg and avoid others in case they were considered a nuisance.

And now his mother had fallen asleep, with this stranger beside her, and the other man had gone.

The sound of stealthy footsteps made him look up warily. He knew he must keep away from the men of the town—his mother had said so. She had always warned him to avoid the people who lived there, not that he had needed to be told. He had always known he was different. People looked at him, when they noticed him, with distaste, a kind of loathing. They scared him. He knew he was safe with his mother, but he was unsure of everyone else in Crediton—though he had no idea why.

Cautious, quiet noises approached slowly, and the boy's eyes widened.

The man, the odd one with the giggle who had embraced his mother and then knocked this man down, *he* had moved slowly. Rollo had seen him. As the fallen man had reached out to him, the giggling one had hit him, and the nice one had fallen. Rollo had seen the face of the odd one, and it had scared him, He did not want to see him again. Turning, he stared round with wild fear. The walls crowded in on him, dark and foreboding, but there was a hole at the base of one—the escape route for the rats that lived inside.

It took him but a moment to leap across the ground and lie down, wriggling round and shoving himself inside. A moment later a nervous group of men from neighboring houses appeared at the entrance.

Later, Baldwin peered in, his hand on his sword. He was perplexed—he could see little in the deeper darkness of the side-alley, and decided to investigate. Motioning to the others to stay, he carefully walked in. Without looking, he knew Edgar was close behind him. Edgar hardly ever left his master unprotected, always taking his place behind and to Baldwin's left where he could protect the knight from a sudden assault. It had been so now for more years than Baldwin wanted to remember, ever since their time together in the Knights Templar, when Edgar had been his man-at-arms, and there was no one Baldwin would have preferred to have beside him in a fight.

The light from the stars gave a silver sheen to the trodden dirt of the alley. This was a poor area, and the town would not spend good money on cobbles for the people who lived here. There would be no point when none of the residents could afford a horse, let alone a cart. Rubbish lay around: old staves from barrels piled into a mound for firewood, tatters and rags of cloth too worn and threadbare to be of use, a mess of bones and reeds from a hall, and odds and ends of leather tossed aside from one of the tanners' works.

Edgar wrinkled his nose in elegant distaste. "It astonishes me that people can live in such squalor."

Glancing down at something he had stepped on, Baldwin nodded. It was a dead rat. There was more scuffling ahead, from a hole under a building, and the knight irritably wondered why people didn't destroy the creatures—they caused such damage to houses and stores, chewing through sacks of grain and ruining the valuable food saved through the summer months. They should not be left to run free, doing harm wherever they went. He was tempted to go to the hole and shove his sword in, to see how many of the vile creatures were inside.

"Master!"

Edgar's hissed exclamation made Baldwin whirl round, and he quickly forgot the rats. Running to the two slumped bodies, he crouched by them. He frowned at the skinny, gray-clad woman, and sighed. Feeling for a pulse, he bit his lip. He could recognize her now, the poor woman who had begged alms from Sir Hector. "Who did this to you?" he murmured. "Was it another man you had begged from? Another man who wanted revenge for some imagined slight? A man who had waited for a woman to meet him, and who then took his frustration out on you? You lived in miserable poverty, and you have died in it."

"What, sir?"

Baldwin shook himself out of his reverie and moved on to the next figure. "God's blood! Simon, what were you doing in here? And why," his eyes moved to the woman beside him, "were you here with her?"

- 15 -

Hugh cursed as he tripped over a loose cobble. They were carrying Simon on a ladder filched from a yard nearby, and although it made a good stretcher, it was heavy—and the supports, formed from the two halves of a tree trunk which had the rungs hammered and pegged into its flats, were sharp and uncomfortable to hold. A man carried each corner, and Baldwin strode alongside, his gaze flitting to Simon every now and again.

The woman had been left with one of Peter's men as a guard. She was past help; and they would send others to collect her body, but Simon still breathed, and Baldwin wanted him back at Peter's house as quickly as possible.

For his part, Hugh had become aware how much his master meant to him; he was surprised by the strength of his emotions, seeing Simon lying flat on the ladder, an arm dangling at one side.

It was not the fear of unemployment. That was a concern for any man, but Hugh knew he could make his own living, even if it meant returning to his old village and eking out a life with relations, catching rabbits and game for his food and sleeping in a barn. There was always a place for him to live. That was not what made him silent, his eyes fixed on the still form before him, trying to avoid stumbling and tripping as he devoted himself to his master's safe delivery at the priest's house; it was the realization that the bailiff was more of a friend than a lord. For the first time, the servant understood that without Simon his existence would lose purpose. His being revolved around Simon and Simon's family, and without the man, there was nothing.

Just then, Edgar faltered, missing his step on a loose cobble, and made the ladder pitch. Hugh barely managed to restrain an impatient curse at the man for being so clumsy. They were all feeling the weight.

Seeing his white face, Baldwin walked over to him and patted his shoulder. "He will be all right, Hugh," he said, trying to sound more confident than he felt. "He's strong, and he'll soon mend."

"But what's the matter with him?" Hugh burst out. "He's breathing, but he won't wake. Was he stabbed, like that woman?"

"I don't think so. He's unconscious, so he must have been hit by someone."

"Who?"

Baldwin gave him a tired smile. "When we have found out who murdered Sarra, and that poor woman there tonight, I think we'll be nearer answering that." They were at Peter's gate now. "Someone must have hated the poor wretch to kill her and dump her there like that . . . but who? Who could have hated a beggar so much?"

Simon came to wakefulness only slowly, like a child woken after too little sleep, resentful and fractious. His head felt as if it had been scraped along the ground on one side and bumped over a series of cobbles, and his neck hurt as horribly as the time when he was a boy and had been playing at jousting with a friend. He had fallen off his horse, and the sharp crackle, like lightning exploding at the base of his skull as his head was jerked back in the fall, had shortly afterward led to the same kind of sore, red-hot sensation.

For a moment he enjoyed the comfort of the bed with his eyes shut. For some reason he knew that the pleasure would not last, but he had to force his mind back to think what was wrong, and when he remembered, his eyes snapped open. The woman, lying, her son staring, and then—nothing. Someone had hit him; must have knocked him out. Who?

His anger rose steadily. Somebody had attacked him—*him*—a bailiff! Had dared to *strike* him. Whoever had done that would dare anything.

"Are you well?"

He glanced to his side, and there he saw his wife. Margaret sat with her head resting against the back of her chair. She looked exhausted. Her head felt too heavy to lift, her neck too weak to support it after spending the whole night with her husband, hoping and praying that he would recover. Everyone knew how dangerous head wounds could be. Sometimes they looked little more than slight bumps, yet the victim could suddenly begin to have fits, and then might die. Simon's wound was only a minor scrape apparently, but he had been so deeply asleep she had wondered whether he might ever waken again.

At the first break of dawn, he had begun to mutter in his sleep, calling for her, Margaret, and then for his son. Peterkin's name was repeated over and over again, and if she was fanciful, she might have said he sounded ever more desperate, as though he was trying to call his son back from danger—or from the dead.

Then the mutters had changed. He still used Peterkin's name, but had started to call out: "Get away! Boy, come here. You'll be safe here, come to me. No! *Come away from her!*"

Baldwin had told her about the woman in the alley, so Margaret had immediately understood that Simon was dreaming about the corpse. For the rest, she had no idea what he was saying as he flung his head from side to side and moaned. To calm him and stop him from hurting himself, she had lain beside him and put her arms round him, cuddling him as she had once cuddled his son, and weeping as he wept.

"How did I get here?"

"The men found you."

"And—"

"She's dead."

"Not her—her boy! Did they find her son?"

"Son—what son?"

"Fetch Baldwin." Then, as she lurched to her feet, fatigue thinning her features and drawing her skin tight, he gave her a weak smile. "You've been here with me all night, Meg, haven't you? I don't deserve you. When you've found Baldwin, go and get some sleep. I love you."

His smile was enough to take away much of her sleepiness. She hurried to the hall, where she found Baldwin already up and talking to Peter Clifford. As soon as they heard Simon was awake, they went in to see him.

Baldwin was surprised to see that his friend looked quite refreshed. He would have anticipated heightened color, a feverish gleam in Simon's eyes and pale, waxy skin. Instead he found a bailiff who was to all intents the same as the day before. "How do you feel?"

"Irritable. And stupid to have been such easy prey."

"It can happen. Even the best knight has been known to have been attacked."

"This was different," Simon explained what he could remember. "Where did the boy go?" he fretted. "That's what I want to know. Did the murderer catch him too?"

Peter had dropped into Margaret's chair. "There was a boy there too? My God! What kind of a man could kill like that, in front of a young child?"

"Many, Peter," Baldwin said.

"Yes," Simon agreed tightly. "There are thirty or so like that who are staying even now at the inn."

"What? You think this was done by one of the soldiers?"

"Who else could it have been?"

Peter Clifford leaned forward in his chair. "He's right, Sir Baldwin. Who else but a man accustomed to rape and loot, murder and pillage, could do such a wicked, inhuman thing?"

"This woman was little more than a girl," Baldwin said thoughtfully. "Why should a man kill someone he did not know? It makes no sense."

"One of them just likes killing—that's what I think," Simon was definite. "He killed poor Sarra, now this woman. And probably her son too."

"I fear you must be right," Peter sighed. "Those poor young women. And that little lad, too."

Baldwin looked from one to the other. "No," he said at last. "I can't believe that. Suppose Sarra was murdered by one of them; why should the same man kill this poor beggar? I can see no connection. It is quite possible that a man from the troop *did* murder Sarra, I accept that, but I see no reason to suppose that the same one killed the woman last night."

"Are you saying that there might be *two* killers in the town?" asked Peter, appalled.

"Possibly."

"What about Sir Hector?" Simon said. "He could have killed Sarra, and we know he was harsh toward the beggar yesterday. Perhaps he went out again and met her, and—"

"What motive would he have for going down that alley and killing her? No, I think we need to know more facts—such as, did he go out last night?—before we begin to speculate. In any case," Baldwin made his way to the door, "I must try to find the boy."

Hugh and Edgar were waiting in the hall. Simon's servant was playing with Edith, and Baldwin left him, speaking to his own man. "We have to speak to Sir Hector. After his behavior with the dead woman yesterday, we need to find out whether he might have had a chance to kill her—though what his motive could have been, God Himself only knows. The woman had a young child—a boy. We must search for him first. He was there when Simon was attacked, and it's just possible that he saw the murderer—if it *was* the same man—who knocked him out."

Edgar nodded and left the room without a word. Baldwin knew he would be collecting their swords, and waited by the window, staring out at the town.

The attack upon Simon had upset him more than he liked to admit, even to Edgar. The fact that there were so many men who were, by their nature, uncontrollable, made him doubt whether he would be able to bring one of them to book even if he found conclusive evidence against him. Especially if it was Sir Hector . . . He had a force of thirty to protect him—sufficient to hold off all the townsmen if need be. Baldwin turned from the window, frowning in concentration. At all costs he must prevent any risk of a battle.

"Sir?"

"Yes, Hugh?" The knight cocked an eyebrow at him.

"Sir, I'd like to help this morning."

"I think Margaret will need all the help she can get. And Edith needs to be watched."

"One of Peter's servants can look after her. And my mistress will soon be asleep, as will my master shortly. I'm not needed here. But I want to help find out who hurt my master last night."

Baldwin pursed his lips. It was obvious that Hugh was deeply upset about the previous night's events. He had looked close to tears whenever Baldwin had noticed him, staring for the most part at his master's body. The knight could sense his need to try to do anything which could help bring the bailiff's attacker to justice. "Very well. You are good with children; you can help most by trying to find the woman's child. Go back to where we found Simon and her, and see if you can see any sign of him."

It was hot and clammy outside and Baldwin's mouth twisted in displeasure as he shrugged his tunic to lie more loosely over his shoulders. He had always hated muggy weather, ever since the time he had spent at Acre and in Cyprus. The air there was forever humid, in his recollection, and he disliked it intensely. He much preferred the dry heat of Auvergne and Bourbonnais. As soon as they left the cool stone building, the warm air assailed them, making the sweat tickle and itch under their arms and down their spine, and before they had gone far, Baldwin could feel that the back of his clothing was already wet.

When he threw a glance over his shoulder, staring out of town toward the east, he could see that the sky was as gray as the sea, and as intimidating. There was a subtle lightening on the horizon, but above, all was leaden, and that together with the humidity could only mean that foul weather was on its way.

The inn looked busy for so early an hour. When Baldwin and Edgar appeared, men scurried away from the door, and several of them pointed and muttered. One, who looked like Wat, grinned and leaned back against the doorframe, but the others all appeared to develop a sudden embarrassment, and none would meet Baldwin's eye. The knight waved Hugh off to conduct his search of the alley, and then jerked his head at his own man.

At the door, Wat blocked their way, "Here to see someone?" he sneered.

"We wish to see your captain," Baldwin agreed.

"I doubt he'll want to see you."

"What's that supposed to mean?"

"You'll soon find out." Wat laughed and stood aside.

Baldwin hesitated, for the expression on the mercenary's face showed something was amiss, but then he stepped forward and walked into the inn.

The hall was abustle with grumbling men, some rolling up blankets, other stuffing shirts and oddments into small sacks. Men pushed their way past him, carrying their goods out into the yard. Peering through the open doorway, Baldwin could see more men out there, tightening girths and fitting bridles to Sir Hector's horses.

"Come," he said grimly to Edgar.

They could hear him before they reached the solar block. "Dolt! Cretin! Moron! I said put it in *that* chest—that one there. Are you a fool? Are you deaf? God's teeth! Damn you, you bastard!"

All of a sudden, Baldwin felt his mood lifting.

Without knocking, he lifted the wooden latch and walked in. The captain was standing over a servant, one of the boys whom Paul the innkeeper employed to help guests. Kneeling by the chest, his face red and his eyes damp, he looked as if he could have burst into tears at any moment, and probably would have done so if it wasn't for the swearing and bellowing captain ordering him around.

"What do you want?" snarled Sir Hector.

"Why, to speak with you," Baldwin smiled, and seated himself on the edge of a closed chest.

"What if I don't want to speak to *you*?"

"You have little to lose. I only need to ask a couple of questions."

"That may be so, but I, meanwhile, have to supervise *this*," he said, kicking the boy as he spoke.

"Where were you last night?"

"What?" He stared, but after a moment his eyes slitted distrustfully. "Why?"

"Were you in the hall all night?"

"I said: Why?"

"A woman was killed. Stabbed, just like Sarra was in here. In that chest." To add a degree of emphasis, Baldwin stared at the trunk open before the boy, who snatched his hand from it in superstitious awe.

"A woman? What woman? Another tavern slut? A harlot? What's it to do with me?"

"That depends on where you were last night."

"I was out."

"Where?"

Sir Hector glowered. "There's no reason for me to hide it. I was waiting for a friend, that's all."

"Did she arrive?"

"How did you know it was a woman?"

"Who else could it be?" Baldwin said with asperity, suddenly tired of constantly sparring with the captain. "Sir Hector, the woman you spurned yesterday, the woman who was poor and begged you for alms—she was murdered last night. We found her body in an alley. She wasn't even hidden, just left where she had fallen. Do you know anything of this?"

"No."

His eyes held Baldwin's resolutely, and the conviction they carried, and the certainty in his voice, would have been enough to make the Keeper leave immediately if this was any man other than the mercenary leader. "Could it have been one of your men?"

"No."

"You seem very sure."

"Keeper, my men and I are here to break a long journey back to Gascony. We have only been here once before, and that was years ago, and right now all I want to do is get away to Gascony and earn some money."

"What of your silver?" Baldwin said, surprised that the captain could consider leaving before it had been recovered.

"I . . ." He glanced at the boy. "Leave us!" The lad was not loath to go. When he had scampered from the room, the captain sat on a trunk and stared at the other man. "The silver is gone, Sir Baldwin, but I think I know where it might be."

"Please explain."

The captain scowled at the floor. "Last night two of my men decided to leave. Henry and John, the *bastards*!" The word was spat out with virulence, but he calmed himself and continued more steadily. "They up and left last night, and nobody noticed—even though they had horses. And, no doubt, all my silver. They must have witnessed Cole hiding it, and removed the silver from his hoard."

"Why do you suppose that?"

"Because they've disappeared! It's the only thing that makes sense: they saw him steal my plate, so they knocked him on the head, took the silver from him, and hid it again. They knew if he told where he had put it, and the place was found empty, we'd assume he was *lying* and still had it all stashed away."

"There is another possibility—that Cole had nothing to do with it," Sir Baldwin reminded him. "I tend to that view."

"Why?"

"Because they went to the trouble to show it was him. They actually took two plates to prove he had taken the stuff."

"That means nothing. They could have done that to show who had really stolen it."

"I doubt it. But why should they have decided to go now? And where do you think they have gone?" Baldwin asked the disgruntled captain.

"As to the why, because they killed the girl and thought you were getting too close to them, I suppose," said Sir Hector, but he did not meet Baldwin's eye. He saw no point in letting the Keeper know how much at risk Henry and John were if they were still in Sir Hector's company when he returned to France. The knight had a long memory for disloyalty, and the suggestion that the two had plotted against him was enough to show that they were dangerous to him. They would never have made it to the French coast, to English Gascony. A channel of water offered endless possibilities for mislaying someone.

"Their running away certainly makes it look as if they are guilty," Baldwin mused. It was possible, he thought. They were the type of person who would very easily fit the mold of thief and general bad character. He sighed. So much had happened so quickly, he felt he was losing track of essentials: while following one line of questioning, he was being buffeted by gales of irrelevance.

"What do you plan to do?" he asked.

"They have gone. I cannot find them—I hardly know this part of the country. I will go to the coast and find a new lord in Gascony."

"And leave your silver?" Baldwin was struck by renewed doubt. There was something in the man's attitude that grated. He had every right to be angry, but there was a hastiness to this decision to depart which was in itself suspicious; when added to the amount of silver which had been taken, it was positively incredible. The captain could not simply go and accept his loss. No leader like him could hope to keep his men loyal if they saw comrades take his money like that and get away with it. Baldwin nodded slowly. It was apparent to him that Sir Hector was determined to hunt down the two men himself without the encumbrance of a Keeper demanding clemency.

"What could I do to find it?"

The cynical question confirmed Baldwin's conviction. "You must wait here. In my friend Peter Clifford's house is Walter Stapledon of Exeter, the Bishop. He will know every smith in the city, and he has the men to investigate. Within two days we will have your two back here."

"No, I will go now."

"Really? What could be so urgent, I wonder, that would make you leave so much money behind?"

"My silver is with those two bastards, and I want it back! There is nothing so pressing for me as getting it back again."

"Then I ask you to remain, Sir Hector," Baldwin said sternly. "I have no doubts as to your honor and truthfulness, but I must stress that others may suspect your reasons for taking so hurried a departure, when for only two days' delay you will probably be able to recover your silver."

" 'Probably,' you say! How 'probably' will I get my silver back? What is the likelihood that they will have gone to Exeter? Or they might have gone in another direction completely. What if they are heading to Bristol? I'd never get them then."

"Neither would you if you were to go on with your journey. Sir Hector, Exeter is a matter of miles away, some ten or so. If they have not been here before, save the once, they will not know any other direction to take. In Exeter, there are many roads and alleys with silversmiths. For you to cover them all would be difficult, and you would have to locate them first. Stapledon knows them all. He can use persuasion to make sure that if your men have been there, the silver is recovered. It has to be the best chance there is of recovering it. Do you have any reason to suppose that they might be aiming for Bristol?"

"No. It's just the only other large city I know of."

"It was badly devastated after the siege some years

ago; I don't know if there are any smiths there who could afford to buy the quantity of plate that Henry and John took from you. And being that much further away, they would risk being robbed themselves—do you realize how far it is to the north? If you were to wait here for two days and then leave, sending fast riders on ahead, you could easily overtake two men on horseback."

"Their horses might be fleet."

"They might," Baldwin agreed. "But they have a heavy weight of silver with them. It will be a burden to them and slow them down."

Sir Hector stared at him. He could think of no sensible excuse which would carry conviction as to why he must quit the town. From all Baldwin had said, he was right and it would be better to remain a little longer. He considered the alternatives, but he knew full well that too much suspicion must lie on his head if he were to lead his men away. Slowly, and with great reluctance, he nodded his agreement.

~ 16 ~

Sniffing disdainfully at the mess, Hugh trod carefully along the alley. There was no idea of cleanliness here. Even when he lived with his parents they had enforced the rules of keeping to their midden and not just peeing against the doorposts of the house. Here, the people didn't care. The sewers and middens were so far away that people used whatever was nearest. At least to a farmer, the nearest object was usually a tree, Hugh thought to himself, avoiding a pile of excrement, and not his neighbor's house.

Hugh turned into the side-alley with a set frown of concentration. The woman's body had been removed during the night, and there was nothing to show of the horror of the previous night. This little branchlet from the main thoroughfare faced east, and the light in the misty morning was charitable to the dirty buildings, hiding streaked and worn limewash, and dissipating the harsh light of the late summer sun so that cracks and holes could not cast such strong shadows.

He stood with his hands on his hips and squinted round the space. He had observed Baldwin often enough when the knight was investigating the site of a tragedy, but the quick eye for details that the knight possessed was not transferable to Hugh, and he knew it. Where Baldwin might have seen a dozen hints for finding the boy, Hugh only saw a mess.

Folding his arms, he leaned a shoulder against a wall and peered at the ground. His master had said that the boy had been in front of his mother, and had seen the attacker coming up behind Simon as the bailiff called the boy to him.

Casting his mind back, Hugh noted where the bodies had lain the night before. He was sure that Simon, having been unconscious for so long, all through the night, must have fallen where he had been hit. Hugh stepped to the spot where, as far as he could tell, his master's feet had been resting. There were a pair of scuff-marks, and he thought they might have been caused by the bailiff's feet jerking as he was coshed.

Nodding grimly to himself, Hugh crouched down and stared before him. The dirt had been flattened in some patches. All around there was a light coating of ash, from the many wood fires which had driven off the night's chill for the townspeople. Though behind him it had all been disturbed by the passage of the men collecting the two figures, and there were clear footprints where the man appointed to stand guard over the woman had waited, Hugh thought he could see where she had lain. As he bent lower, he caught his breath.

From the corner of his eye, he had caught a glimpse of the guard's footprints. Viewed from this low angle, he discovered he could see them more clearly. To test it, he rested his hands on the ground and held his head almost at floor-level, and found he could see the prints much more distinctly. Wriggling, he squirmed until he was staring excitedly at roughly where the woman's head had been, and gave a short exclamation of delight. He could see a series of small barefoot prints.

The ones nearest were surprisingly clear. He could make out the individual toes as if the lad had waited there for some time, and perhaps he had, Hugh reflected. After all, Simon had appeared after hearing the boy crying. He could have been there, standing beside his dead mother for an hour or more. People from the houses all round would not leave their dwellings after dark, he was sure, not to go to the aid of a brat they might not know, not when there were the sounds of misery to hint that some danger lurked.

He thought he could make out a scuffle, as if the child had retreated, then shuffled as he began to run away. More marks seemed to lead toward a wall. Rising, he followed after, every now and again lowering himself to make sure of the direction, until he came to a large patch where the muck and dirt had been flattened and dispersed. Going down on one knee, he studied it with bafflement. It was just before the wall, near a hole. Feeling a quick excitement, he dropped by the hole and gazed inside. It was dark and small, and he reached in with a hand, lying heedlessly on his back in the stinking filth. He could feel the sides and roof, and, stretching to his uttermost, he could just touch the furthest extreme. There was no child.

Standing and brushing the dirt from his shoulders, he felt a pang of compassion as he wondered whether it was here that the boy had been caught by the attacker. Maybe, he thought, the flattened patch was caused by the struggle between the two, the man catching hold of the boy who was the only witness to the attack on the bailiff, and possibly the cruel murder of his own mother.

If that was the case, he thought, resting his hands on his hips with a new determination, the people who lived closest must have heard the poor lad's screams. He stared at the walls all round. There was no doorway on which to bang, but in the alley there were several. Striding out, he turned right and beat upon the timbers of the nearest.

The latch was slipped and the door creaked open; a small, dirty, anxious young girl peeped round it. Seeing Hugh's fierce glower, her eyes widened in a panic and he realized that the door was about to be slammed. Immediately, he smiled. He also took the precaution of shoving his heavy boot into the gap. "Hello," he said.

The grubby child looked at his boot with perceptible alarm, and her mouth opened to scream, but before any sound could come out, Hugh squatted reassuringly.

"I want to speak to your mother. Is she here?"

Casting a glance behind, the small face nodded, and soon, to his relief, there was an adult with them.

She was a little under his height, but with the sallow, gray complexion of the poor. Standing in the doorway, she could have been the sister of the murdered woman, and the apron and wimple which she wore in an attempt to appear respectable only added to the impression of sad dilapidation that permeated the buildings of the little alley.

"There was a woman killed here last night."

"I know. Poor Judith."

The name meant nothing to Hugh. "She was killed down that alley, which runs beside this place. Did you hear anything?"

"There's always noises round a place like this. We heard lots of things."

"A scream?"

"Only her boy. We never heard her."

"You heard her boy?"

"Rollo? Yes. He was making enough noise to bring the roof down on our heads," she said.

"You heard him, and you did nothing?" he asked, aghast. "That child might be dead; the same man who killed his mother probably took him and killed him. If you'd gone to him when he cried you might have saved his life!"

"Yes. And I might have got myself killed," she said, wiping a grimy hand over her forehead. There was no remorse Hugh could perceive, only a weary acceptance. "What good would that have done the lad? Or *her*, come to that? I have five little ones to look after, now my husband's dead. What do you expect me to do? Run out and get myself killed at the first alarm?"

Hugh could not help taking a step back. He was not known for his courage, but he was repelled by the dour cowardice of this woman. He could understand nervous people staying in behind their doors after hearing a shriek, but not when it was a child who was being attacked! In his home village, it was the norm for all to go to the aid of a neighbor in trouble, no matter what the cause. If a man was under attack, all would help him.

"Well?" she asked at last. "Do you want to see him or not?"

"Do you know where he is?"

Eyeing him with exasperation, she knocked her little girl on the head and sent her scurrying back into the house. Soon she reappeared dragging an unwilling boy, who held back in fear at the sight of a man.

"What's he doing here?" Hugh asked, dumbfounded.

"I couldn't leave the poor bugger out in the cold all night."

"Did you see the killer?"

"No. All I saw was these two bodies on the ground, and Rollo with them, crying fit to break your heart, so I brought him in here and gave him some hot soup, and while I was doing that, men came and started clearing up."

"You could have told us you had the lad here."

"Don't grumble at me! I did what I could, and that's a lot more than many would do. I've even fed the child, and I've hardly got enough for my own, so don't try to tell me I did wrong. I wasn't going out again to speak to strangers after nightfall—how was I to know they weren't men from the inn? They could've been friends of the man who killed poor Judith and the other one."

"The other one wasn't dead. He's my master, the bailiff of Lydford."

"Oh? Well, what're you going to do with this one? He can't stay here. We can hardly feed ourselves, let alone an extra mouth."

"I will take him to my master."

She nodded, and took the boy's hand, but as soon as she tried to push him toward Hugh, the lad shook his head violently, eyes wide in the little face. Hugh held his hands out to him, but he stood his ground, lips beginning to tremble.

Sitting back on his haunches, Hugh eyed him speculatively. "He's scared of me."

"I wonder why that should be." The scorn made her voice waspish. "He saw his mother killed last night, and you're surprised he's scared of men! Here . . ." She took the boy's arm and dragged him forward. "Take him. I took him in because I thought it'd help, but he doesn't want to stay here. He won't even talk. You have him, and I hope he helps you."

The door slammed firmly, and Hugh heard the wooden bolt being pushed across. He wouldn't be speaking to the woman again. Rollo was standing as if petrified, his eyes massive saucers of fear.

The servant smiled ruefully. "Don't worry. I think I got nearly as much of a shock as you. Are you hungry? You want some food?" There was no answer. The lad was as dumb as a stone carving. "Well, I think *I* do. Let's go to the priest's house and see what we can find."

He started off, but the child was a dead weight, pulling back like a rabbit caught in a snare, his visage a picture of terrified misery.

"Look, I'm a friend. All I want to do is help you and make sure you're safe. All right? Now—when did you last eat meat?"

For the first time, the urchin's eyes met his. The little skinny body radiated hunger.

"I know where we can get you a thick slice of cold meat. Do you want some?"

Hesitantly, the child allowed himself to be steered toward the main street. Hugh walked happily, confident that he would find out who had attacked his master. This little lad had seen the blow being struck. It could only be a short time before they tracked down the assailant.

- 17 -

At the entrance to the inn, Baldwin stood taking his leave of the captain. "I will get the messenger off as soon as possible," he promised. "The men have had a good head start—are you aware if either of them knows Exeter at all well?"

Sir Hector shrugged peevishly. "I've no idea, but I doubt it. Neither of them is from these parts. John Smithson comes from the north, somewhere near St. Albans; Henry from a village near London—Wandsworth, I think."

"Good. At least they will probably have some little difficulty in finding the right smith to sell the silver to. They will quickly lose any advantage they might have had from their early departure, as their head start will be frittered away while they search."

"If they went to Exeter—" The captain broke off as an unearthly shriek filled the air. When he continued, his face had reddened and his voice shook with a bellicose resentment. "God's blood! Do they have to do it in the damned street!"

Baldwin nodded. The sound of a pig being stuck was not one which upset him unduly, being only a natural background noise anywhere in the country at this time of year, but he could see that it might be irritating. The pig was jerking in its death throes as he looked over and nodded to the butcher, who stood back watching his apprentice with his thumbs hooked into his belt. Adam nodded back happily.

Then Baldwin was jerked round by the second high-pitched squeal of terror. At the entrance to the alley opposite, he saw Hugh clutching the arm of a small boy. The lad was keeping up a constant keening ululation as he tried desperately to free himself and escape back along the alley.

Baldwin shot a glance at the captain, then gasped.

Sir Hector's eyes were fixed on the boy. His face was white with dread, and a nerve under his eye twitched as the strident wailing rose and fell. With a hissed curse, he swiveled round and marched back inside the inn.

Standing with his back to the cool wall, he waited until his heart slowed its agonized pounding.

The boy had seen him, had recognized him from the stabbing of his mother! He should have killed the little bastard when he had the chance. It would be foolish to let him live, when he had witnessed the murder . . . but before he could strike, the knight's friend, that damned Bailiff of Lydford, had appeared, and he only just had time to hide in the doorway. The boy had proved useful then, attracting the man's attention for just long enough . . . But when the bailiff fell, he had spent too long gloating at the sight of the man on the ground before he tried to catch the boy. By which time he had disappeared! He had evaporated like the dregs of wine from a goblet left overnight, except the boy didn't even leave a residue: he merely vanished.

He had looked. Oh yes, he had looked. He had searched through the rubbish, swearing constantly, picking about among the scraps of cloth and timber, muttering to himself in his futile rage as he tried to find that tragic face with the enormous eyes so that he could close them and put out the weak flame of life that burned so deeply in them . . . But he couldn't find any sign of the lad.

And then the noises had started. Subtle murmurings, the swish of feet, sibilant whispers, as people woken by the disturbance began to wonder at the sudden silence. He had heard a door being tentatively opened, and froze in quick alarm. If someone should come out and investigate, there was nowhere to hide: nowhere!

Then a door creaked, and he heard low voices, people talking in hushed, horror-struck tones. There was a pile of torn and rotten sacking nearby, and he leapt to it without a second thought, dragging the foul cloth over himself.

Footsteps had approached and faded, local inhabitants walking toward him, then exclaiming as they found the bodies and had turned back. People had seemed awed by the enormity of what they had discovered. Then there was a short pattering as those same people bolted for the security of their houses, and he was sure that he was alone at last.

Cautiously peeping out from under his covering, he had seen that the alley was clear once more. He had clambered out and quickly felt the woman. She was cooling rapidly; he knew she must be dead, for he had felt enough dead bodies in his time.

The bailiff was still alive and breathing—almost snoring, as if he had been simply snoozing after a good meal. The noise infuriated him. It was loud enough to waken the whole town! he thought angrily. He tugged his knife from its sheath, ready to stab, when the new noise stopped him. More doors opening stealthily; more voices. He had no time, he must make his escape. At least the bailiff had not seen him—he had not had the chance to spy his attacker before falling. Still holding the knife, the killer bolted, moving quietly on soft pigskin boots which made little sound on the packed earth of the alley. Only at the end had he realized he still held the dagger in his fist. He thrust it into its sheath and, with suddenly nerveless fingers, he had half-leaned, half-staggered to the nearest wall, where he stood with his hands dangling, staring over the road to where he had killed her.

She had deserved it, and so had *he*, the bastard, he reflected with satisfaction. And then a slow smile broke out across his features as he considered how his plan was going.

The same slow smile appeared now, and the thin layer of tension was banished from his face. She had deserved it, and so had *he*. And soon, surely, *he* would pay the price in full for his deeds. Unless—a frown twisted his face—unless that cretin of a Keeper of the King's Peace should realize. He was known to be clever—what if he guessed at the truth? With a shrug, he put the idea from his mind. There was plenty of proof for the knight of Furnshill. The Keeper of the King's Peace must realize soon what had happened.

Baldwin strode back through the town with no regard for the two men and child following. His stern expression matched his somber mood as he thought it all through again. Sarra had been killed after an argument with the captain. Judith had been stabbed to death after trying to beg from him, and he had refused her in no uncertain terms. The man had lost his silver, but that appeared now to have been the work of a couple of his own men, who had run away with their profit before their unstable leader could exact his own punishment. He made a mental note to free Cole: if the two had stolen the plate, surely they must also have killed Sarra . . . But although he slowed his step, he did not turn and march back to the jail. It might be better to keep Philip locked up for now, until the mercenaries had left the town. There might still be some who would be prepared to execute him in misguided loyalty to Sir Hector. Baldwin recalled how Wat had suggested that Cole had been friendly with Henry and John too; so it was just possible that Cole *had* been involved, that he had been a willing accomplice to the theft. He resolved to leave the man in jail a little longer.

Why the man had knocked Simon out was anyone's guess, but Baldwin was now of a mind to think that Judith's killer either had not wanted to kill the bailiff but had been disturbed by his blundering nearby, or had intended to kill him as well, but had been interrupted by someone else. Whichever proved to be the truth, Baldwin was certain that Sir Hector would not have balked at killing either Simon or himself.

"Hugh, could you take the boy away for a minute?"

Baldwin watched as Hugh led Rollo some feet away, then faced Edgar, standing still in the road. A rider passed, swearing at them for blocking the road, but Baldwin ignored him. "Edgar, whoever the murderer is, he has killed two women, and would probably have done for the lad as well." Baldwin gravely studied the small figure with Hugh. "He has been very brave, our Rollo. Let's hope he can be braver still and tell us what he saw last night. Simon escaped by a miracle. Next time, the killer might be more lucky—if he wants to see Simon dead."

"But surely if he wanted to kill Simon he would have stabbed him rather than knocking him cold," Edgar suggested.

"That's possible. But he knocked out Simon after he'd killed the woman, I assume. She felt quite cool to the touch, so she'd been dead some time. It's quite likely he only struck Simon because he wanted to silence him. Perhaps he would have stabbed him as well but he was stopped by other people approaching."

"So you think he might still try to kill Simon? That'd be a little irrational, wouldn't it?"

"It's hardly the behavior of a rational man to kill two women, is it? There's nothing I'm aware of which links them: a girl from an inn and a beggar. And if he is not rational, he might come to the conclusion that Simon could have seen him. He might decide that it is better to make absolutely sure of Simon's silence—that's why I want you to look to our friend's protection. Don't let anyone near him while he's unwell."

Edgar nodded. Hugh returned when Baldwin beckoned.

"Hugh, I want you to stay with your master all the time he's ill from this blow to his head. I think he might be in danger. Edgar will help you."

Simon's servant glowered truculently. Jerking a thumb at Rollo, he was about to speak out when Baldwin hastily cut him off.

"Right, let's get back before anything else can happen."

The last thing he needed was for the boy to be even more scared than he already was. Baldwin did not want Hugh to point out that, of all of them, Rollo himself must be in the most danger.

Walter Stapledon pulled the spectacles from his nose with a wry smile and sighed. There was no doubt that the two discs of glass helped enormously, and with them he could see as well as he ever had, but they were tiring for his eyes. Roger was reading at another table, and he looked up on hearing his Bishop's despairing exhalation. Stapledon was staring up at one of the windows as if for inspiration, his brow furrowed with affairs that Roger could only guess at.

The matters which were causing so much distress to the Bishop were not simple issues about the cathedral, or the founding of Stapledon College at Oxford; nor were they to do with the grammar school the Bishop was bent on creating. They were affairs of state.

This letter was from his friend John Sandale, the Bishop of Winchester and, more recently, the King's Treasurer as well. John had written to tell him of the appalling state of the Exchequer's records. There was no classification of records—most were not even dated. The staff were being smothered by their work, and had little, if any, guidance as to what they were expected to achieve.

Standing, Stapledon stretched and went to the screens. He stopped a passing servant and asked for wine, then returned to his desk. Soon the jug and a large goblet arrived, and he sipped sparingly.

The trouble was, the King was weak and ineffectual. He could be too easily swayed by any man with a persuasive turn of phrase—or a man who was too pretty, he admitted, sourly staring into his drink. That was one piece of information the country would be happier not to know. In general his friendships were passed off as being the natural desire of a young man to meet with others of his own age, but there was no way to hide his more flagrant affairs from closer members of his household, and, reading between the lines of Sandale's letter, Stapledon knew that the King had set his hopes on yet another man. How the Queen could tolerate such behavior, he had no idea.

If the King was not careful, he might lose his crown—and his head. It would not be easy to force some of his more strident critics, especially those who also enjoyed positions of power, to restrain their public condemnation of him. No, it was beyond the Bishop how the poor Queen could bear to be near him, and if she were to lose her reserve, the King's fate would soon be sealed.

Hearing the stamp of approaching feet, he looked up. Soon the door was thrown open and Baldwin and the others walked in. Smiling his welcome, Stapledon put his letters aside, folded, to be free from prying eyes, then froze at the sight of the expression on Baldwin's face.

"Hugh," the knight said, and gestured curtly. "I'm sure the lad would like to see the garden. And might enjoy playing with Edith—uhn, after he's had a wash, perhaps. Oh, and give him some food. See to it that he's comfortable."

Stapledon watched as the servant took the boy out, then turned enquiringly to the knight. Baldwin sat on a bench at his table, and explained who the boy was, then told of his fears for the lad's safety since the screaming fit in the town.

"And there is more," Baldwin went on. "Two of the mercenaries have run away."

Roger sat open-mouthed while Baldwin told of his discussion with the captain until he could not help bursting out, "They must have been the men I saw last night!"

"What? Where?" Baldwin frowned.

"Two men on horses, with a pack animal on a long line. I saw them just before I heard the commotion in the alley, and it put them from my mind."

"Where were they heading?" Baldwin asked keenly, suppressing his excitement, and when Roger told him, he gave a groan of delight. "Then I was right! They *are* going toward Exeter. Bishop, could you send a messenger to alert your men at the cathedral? Have them check on all the silversmiths and find out if they've had a large amount of plate offered to them? Much, if not all, will be foreign, I would imagine. It must be easy to tell."

"I can try," the Bishop said, "but are you sure? They might simply have gone that way as far as the first village, then turned north. There's nothing to suggest that they would definitely have gone to Exeter."

"No, but I'm sure they will have done, nonetheless. They have no local knowledge, and would expect their captain to be after them at the earliest opportunity. Where else could they go, other than to the nearest city where at least they could try to hide themselves in the crowd, and where there would be many ships and other roads to take? These men, from what I saw of them, have a certain cunning, but I doubt whether they'd be able to think up a more detailed plan."

"But they might have been planning this for months."

"Possibly, but I doubt it. Sir Hector and his men have been up north. They were trying to get themselves recruited by the army. John Smithson comes from near St. Albans, while Henry the Hurdle is from Surrey, near London. The mercenaries passed nearby both places, once while they were going northward, to offer their services to the King. If they were going to steal all this stuff, surely they'd have done it near one of their homes? Then they'd know people to sell it to, people who could hide them until the fuss died down and their captain had gone. No, the robbery was perpetrated here because of something about this place. I just wish I knew what it was."

"Roger—could you fetch me Stephen, please. And tell the groom to prepare his mare. He will be leaving as soon as possible." The Bishop turned to Baldwin. "Now, would you like a little wine?"

"No, thank you, my lord. I must see that child and make sure he is all right, and I want to see Simon too."

"I suppose I should return to my work as well," the Bishop muttered, throwing the papers a look of repugnance so virulent that Baldwin laughed.

"It is our duty to work, my lord."

"Yes. Strangely, though, I sometimes wonder what made the Good Lord decide to inflict papers on us. We must have done something appalling to have deserved such a punishment."

Simon was not in his bed. Leaving his chamber, it was only when he reached the garden that Baldwin could find him.

Immediately outside the house, on a terrace, Peter had created a pleasing display of medicinal and culinary herbs. Below it, beyond a group of massive oaks and elms, was a large meadow, and in here Baldwin saw Margaret playing with Edith. Judith's son was nearby, sitting on a bench with Simon, while Hugh hovered, scowling distrustfully at the world at large.

To Baldwin's relief, apart from a certain pallor, Simon looked fine. While the knight had been at the inn, Peter Clifford had asked one of the canons who was well practiced with medicines to come and see Simon, and he had impressed the priest with a professional display, holding up a number of fingers before Simon and asking him to confirm how many, inspecting the wound itself and smearing egg-white over it to cleanse it, and making sure Simon's tongue had not gone black. Peter had no idea what this last could possibly show, but he was prepared to take the word of a trained man when he was told that Simon was fit, though he might be prone to headaches for a while to come.

Baldwin took a seat next to his friend. "How are you?"

"Grim." Simon winced. "And this weather doesn't help."

Baldwin nodded. The damp heat smothered everything like a blanket, and he was already sweating profusely after the cool of the hall. "How is your head?"

"I feel as if I've spent the whole of last night drinking with Sir Hector's men, matching each of them pint for pint individually, before being used as a football. And every time I speak, someone hits me again, from the feel of it."

"It will improve." Baldwin smiled. He had little sympathy with small knocks. Now he was sure Simon was to recover fully, he saw no need for excessive compassion. Men had suffered from worse, and would continue to do so.

"I am grateful for your sympathy," Simon said ironically. "Margaret told me about last night. Thanks for coming and fetching me. So! What happened this morning?"

Baldwin told him, beginning with Hugh finding the boy and then recounting his interview with the captain. "And Roger saw them riding off, so we know where to search."

"It shouldn't take long," Simon said speculatively. "There aren't all that many silversmiths in Exeter."

"No. We should have an answer—or a pair of prisoners—tomorrow evening."

"With any luck, we can put them straight behind bars."

"But what are we to make of the other instance? The boy clearly identified the captain, albeit unintentionally."

"The two in Exeter must have stolen the silver."

"*Probably* stole—not *must have* stolen. After all, it could still have been Cole who took the plate, and they saw where he hid it."

"True, in which case either Cole or those two also murdered Sarra."

"Yes . . ."

"Baldwin, you've gone into one of your ruminations. You're staring out over the meadow and frowning, and that means something doesn't strike true to you."

"I was merely thinking: it seems unlikely that there should be two murderers stalking the town, and yet the boy showed terror when he saw Sir Hector. If Sarra was killed by whoever took the plate, it was not Sir Hector—he would hardly take his own silver. So, if he killed Judith, the two murders must be unconnected, but what possible motive could Sir Hector have to kill this woman Judith? The most obvious suspects for the murder of Sarra were Henry and John, as their rapid departure showed. And yet—"

"Could they have killed Judith and knocked me out?"

"I don't know. It's possible. We cannot tell how long you were unconscious there. It is feasible that they struck you down, saw who they'd hit, and left quickly to ride from town."

"But why would the boy have reacted as he did when he saw Sir Hector, unless he saw his mother's murderer?"

Baldwin sighed with vexation. "Perhaps the murders *were* nothing to do with the robbery. Maybe there's something we've missed. In any case, we should have the captain watched. The boy certainly shrieked at the sight of him, and that seems to imply he must have had something to do with Judith's death."

"That's easy to arrange. Tell Paul, on the quiet, that we'd like to know if the bugger decides to leave in a hurry."

"That should be easy enough. Paul has several lads there to help serve customers and do odd jobs. One of them was packing for Sir Hector this morning."

"I wonder why? He has all those men with him. Didn't Hugh say Wat was his servant? I seem to remember Hugh saying it was Wat who went into the room when they were looking after Sarra's body."

"Perhaps Sir Hector has lost faith in Wat—maybe he thought the inn's lad would be better trained at such things than a soldier. And I very much doubt whether one of the other girls would want to be alone with him. I get the impression they all distrust him after Sarra's death."

"That'd be no surprise."

"After young Rollo's reaction to seeing the bastard, I rather tend to agree with the girls. Rollo's shock was terrible. And the captain's response was just as marked. He went straight back inside, and I saw him leaning against the wall as if he was about to die."

"I hope not," Simon said darkly and touched the lump over his ear. "If he did this and killed those girls, I want to see him hang."

"Well, we shall know either way when the two are brought back from Exeter."

"Yes—*if* they are."

- 18 -

That night was a long one for Sir Hector. He had no wish to remain in the hall with his troop after learning that the two men he had trusted most, though mainly from reasons of their own self-interest, had left him. Especially since he was quite certain in his own mind that they had stolen his silver. Henry and John had robbed him. It was impossible to believe, but futile to try to deny. Their disappearance was their confession.

At his board, while he was being served, he caught a knowing look from Wat. When the knight stared, his man-at-arms smiled and looked away; Sir Hector knew what that meant. Wat had been in the band for almost all the time Sir Hector had controlled it, slightly longer than Henry or John. They had proved to be disloyal, and now Wat was as well. Sir Hector had hoarded any rumors or unwary comments like a miser cosseting his money, and he was sure that Wat was plotting against him. That fool thought he could lead the company as well as his master. Sir Hector kept his face impassive, as though unconcerned. Wat would not survive the sea-trip to Gascony either. On that the knight was determined.

It was ever the way with mercenary bands. Sir Hector had taken over when the time was propitious. Old Raymonnet was tired after running things for too long. He had become slack and let his greed get the better of his good sense, taking the best-sounding offers and forgetting to see which side was the more likely to win; he'd even committed the cardinal sin of waiting until it was too late before deciding to switch sides on one occasion! That had cost the band dearly.

No, it had been clear that Raymonnet had to go, and after the miserable affair between the French and English in 1295, Raymonnet was as much use as a broken reed in a fight. The French and English were arguing—once again—over who should control Aquitaine. The French had taken large areas, and in 1294 the old warrior Edward, the present King's father, had sent his men in. Raymonnet and his band had joined them, and had helped in the taking of Rions. Afterward, seeing how fertile the land was and how wealthy the towns were, they decided to stay, to accept a payment to help protect the town and do garrison duty.

The armies sent over the sea by King Edward I were large, but the land they were going to protect was vast. While the French could quickly concentrate forces wherever they wanted on the border, the English had to rely on men from England to come and defend it. It was a costly exercise, and one in which the English responded only slowly. The money flowed like rock from merchants unwilling to be taxed, and it soon became obvious to Sir Hector that the French were more likely to pay for useful allies than his own King.

Raymonnet could not see it. He was convinced that the English were the more secure of the two—after all, the English lands were under the direct control of the King, whereas the French monarch depended on all his allies and vassals; his own territory was small. It was in vain for Sir Hector, increasingly desperately, to argue that the French had the military muscle, while the English barons had no wish to fight. The result could only be a French victory; they had the soldiers and the most efficient and powerful army in the world.

In March 1295 the French were at the gates, and after carefully bribing some of the garrison, Sir Hector was able to effect the takeover he needed. There was a mutiny, the English troops were killed, and on Palm Sunday the French King was able to enter the town.

Raymonnet was never seen again. He had been stabbed in the back at the beginning of the mutiny, and Sir Hector had tossed his body over the wall, to lie among the besiegers' dead. From then on, Sir Hector was the leader of the company.

Now he wondered how much longer he could remain so. The knight was no fool; he knew he might never get to the English provinces if someone was to talk. How much had Wat said? The man looked so smug and arrogant at his table, taking generous portions of salt, accepting the comments of his neighbors like a lord receiving praise from subjects—just as Sir Hector had expected his men to behave toward *him.* It was his right as the leader to be granted full honors, for he was the ruler of this tiny, mobile fiefdom. They lived by martial law, and his word was the only one which counted.

For now, but not for much longer if Wat talked to the Keeper.

If Wat were to talk, only one man's word would matter: Wat's.

Sir Hector met Wat's eyes again, and this time neither man flinched.

Paul was aware of undercurrents of tension all night. Something was wrong, and he was not sure how the evening would end. If matters got worse, he would have to send for the Keeper and the Constable, for he wanted no bloodshed in his inn.

There was a muted hubbub not like the previous nights on which the men had made merry the whole time. Tonight all was subdued and moody, like the sky had been all day, gloomy and threatening.

The girls felt it too, he could see. Cristine weaved her way between the beckoning hands with her usual skill, but even her face was set and drawn, with no sign of her customary smile. Paul went back to the buttery and filled more jugs. He was hoping that if all the men quickly got drunk, they might merely fall asleep as they had done for the previous two nights.

Young Hob was asleep in there, curled up in a corner, and Paul was tempted to kick him awake, but it was only a reflection of his own anxiety and tension. The lad was exhausted, no less than Paul himself. Especially since he was not yet ten years old, and had been up since daybreak. Paul filled his jugs as quietly as possible and made his way back to the hall. If the captain tried to leave, Paul had been instructed to send Hob to the priest's house to tell the Keeper. Hob could sleep until he was needed. With any luck, he wouldn't be.

Wat took another refill, acknowledging the gift with a nod and grin of thanks. He concentrated on the men near him. There was no point in glancing at Sir Hector;

both men knew that the fight had begun. The question now was, who would be strong enough to win? Wat was determined it would not be the man on the dais.

He had no personal dislike for Sir Hector; this was merely a matter of business. Sir Hector had produced good contracts for them over several years, had kept them all clothed and fed, and supplied with women. There was no cause for him or any of the others to complain, for all had shared in the general wealth created.

But Sir Hector was no longer the capable, astute man he once had been. One thing he could never understand was how a group of soldiers melded together. There was a sense that all belonged to the same family; *esprit de corps* counted for a great deal, but for it to work properly, their leader must be strong and seen to be fair. In his dealings with Henry the Hurdle and John Smithson, Sir Hector had demonstrated lousy judgment. He should have punished them for taking advantage of their fellows before matters got so out of hand. That way, the company might have held together, the men staying loyal. Sir Hector had forgotten that he depended on *all* of the men in the band; thinking he could rely on two to keep the rest in line, he unwisely hadn't heeded the mutterings of dissatisfaction. It was foolish, Wat knew, for a leader to trust in a small number of advisers, for those plotting mutiny would carefully avoid talking to such men and would ensure that any reports getting to the leader through his nominated sergeants would be favorable. His gullibility had cost him the faith of the group.

Matters had come to a head after the robbery. When John and Henry were seen to be subjected to only a mild enquiry and, at least in the view of most of the company, inadequately interrogated, the men began to look askance at their leader. A captain who could not protect his own goods was not to be trusted with another's life. How Sir Hector could expect them to put their confidence in him when he could not control two petty thieves who made money from blackmail, Wat could not understand. But there was more. Since losing his silver, the captain seemed to have withdrawn into himself, as if he had already accepted defeat. The men had noticed—and drawn their own conclusions. Their leader was grown insipid; he no longer had the edge he once showed.

Whereas Wat had the trust of *all* the men, and the support of over half of them in this battle for the leadership. He had always stood up against the two blackmailers and supported any new member who was persecuted by them. Gradually, he had found a following among his colleagues, for he was a man who could hold his tongue when told a secret. He had skills as a warrior, could fight with bow or sword, and knew how to motivate men who were almost at their last gasp to leap to their feet and follow him up the siege ladders.

He drank deeply and cast a cautious eye toward the man at the dais. Sir Hector had had his day, and now it was past. Even his title was fiction . . . "Sir" Hector, Wat thought, his lip curling. Most of the other members of the company didn't realize he had given himself the title after a clash in Bordeaux. A knight had refused to fight him, saying that to draw sword against a commoner would be an insult to his chivalry and honor. Sir Hector had ambushed him the next day, killing the knight in a bloody ambush, then appropriating the man's belt and spurs. He was no more chivalrous than Wat.

And now Sir Hector was to be retired. Whether he wished it or not.

Looking round the room, Sir Hector was aware of the eyes on him, and for a while he could not think what they reminded him of. He was so used to his absolute authority in all matters, that he had long since stopped taking notice of the opinions of his men.

There was a uniformity among them now, he noticed. Occasionally he would observe a covert glance, a fleeting expression upon a grubby visage, which he was sure did not augur well for his future. It was as he came to this conclusion that he could suddenly name the look on their faces: speculation.

His hand, as he reached for his tankard, was steady, he noted with inner satisfaction, and he brought the cold pewter to his lips with no sign of his sudden shock.

Not for many years had he seen such feral expectancy. His men displayed the same impassive interest that a wolf pack showed toward an intended victim, when the prey was slowing from cold, terror and hunger, freezing to petrified languor as it waited for the final attack, the sudden rush which would end in the kill.

He set the tankard back on the table. Outwardly calm, his brain raced with near-panic. It wasn't only Wat he had to contend with, but the whole company. He must set his stamp on them all, and quickly. Otherwise there was no point in planning future campaigns.

If only she was still here, he thought regretfully. Then she might help him to make sense of it all. But she wasn't, and that was that.

Rising, he made his way to his solar and shut the

door, locking it securely with the heavy bolt. He gazed at the symbol of safety with a wry twist to his lips that was nearly a smile. Before, he had always been safe because of the strength of his little force, secure in the knowledge that any attack must first beat through his men before reaching his solar. Now his safety depended on locking himself away from his own troops.

As the first clap of thunder exploded overhead, Margaret leapt upright, eyes wide in alarm. She had never grown used to the fierce demonstrations of the elements. Edith, sleeping by her bed, began to wail, and Margaret forgot her own fear enough to climb from her bed and step cautiously through the rushes to collect her child, holding her close as she crawled back between her sheets, pulling them up close round her daughter's body while trying not to disturb her husband.

A fresh blue-white flare lanced through the gaps in the wooden shutters, closely followed by another report, and Margaret heard a hound set up a mournful howling. The dismal sound made her shiver—it reminded her all too well of the wolves on the moors, and she recalled the stories of how the Devil rode with the wolves, pointing out the houses which held the youngest children for the beasts to devour, while he took the innocent souls.

Edith murmured drowsily, comforted by her mother's warmth, but at another crackle she stuffed her thumb in her mouth, squirming furiously.

"Has she only just woken up?" Simon asked.

"Yes. I tried to keep her still so she wouldn't stir you, but—"

"Don't worry, Meg," he said, and she nearly gave a

groan of relief, it was so good to hear the gentleness in his voice. She smiled as he rolled onto his back. As the lightning flickered, illuminating the room with its cold blue-gray light, she could see his face.

Hearing a low moan, which rose to a keening scream, he half-rose from the bed, and only subsided when her hand took his shoulder. "There's nothing you can do to help him, Simon. Let him be."

She was right, he had to admit. The boy was inconsolable—and seeing the bailiff, a man he associated with his mother's death, would certainly not help him. Then Simon heard a stealthily opened door, a faint creak as someone stepped out into the hall . . . followed shortly by the clatter of a falling polearm and a muttered curse. He could recognize the voice of Stapledon's rector. It was typical of the young man that he would want to go to the aid of a scared child, and equally typical that the three-footed clumsy fool should wake the household in so doing.

"Will he ever get over it?" he wondered aloud.

"Of course. We all do."

He studied her profile. Her face glimmered under the benign glow of the dying fire, giving her an orange-pink flush, and he smiled when she looked at him with feminine confidence. "You have great faith in his powers of recuperation, but I'm not so certain. He's seen his mother slaughtered before his eyes, and that's something I don't think many children could cope with."

"Really? And do you not know that all the people in those alleys are as poor as beggars? How many of them have had to watch their mothers and fathers, children, wives and husbands, as they died?"

"That's not the same! Someone dying of natural

causes is hard to take, but it's not the same as seeing someone stabbed to death in the street."

"No. If the boy had seen his mother fail slowly, if he had seen her fade with weakness over weeks instead of falling quickly, he might have been torn by disgust. He might even have come to hate her, if he had to wipe her wounds, wash her, feed her, clean away her soiled bedclothes, and still try to find food to feed himself. He would have hated her all the more for the food and water he had wasted on her, just keeping her alive for an extra day or two, when that same food might have fed him instead of her illness."

"You think him seeing his mother die quickly is better?" he frowned.

"Yes. In time he will know that nothing he could have done would have saved her. He will not hate her; he will remember her as a caring mother who never begrudged him a mouthful of her food or a sip of her water. Judith gave him life, and for that he will always be grateful. And now, because her death was unnecessary, he can enjoy the satisfaction of seeing her avenged. Not only that, he can participate in condemning her murderer." Her voice was quiet, but absolute in her conviction. "And in years to come he will feel stronger for having helped bring her killer to justice. His healing will begin when he sees the killer hang, for then he will see that the fears of his boyhood are unfounded."

"And he will forget his pain and his mother that quickly?" Simon asked patronizingly, and she responded as if stung.

"No, of course not! He will always miss her, and always regret not having had her with him for longer. No man can lose his mother without feeling the misery of the loss. But that does not take away from the inner strength he will gain from this. All I said was, it is better for him that she died this way."

"Is it the same for others?"

She turned away. The hurt in his voice told her clearly enough of the turn his thoughts had taken. "How would you feel if your Peterkin had been murdered, and you knew who the killer was, Simon? How would you feel if you could capture him and have him arrested, put in front of a court and accused? When you saw the man hang, you would know you had done everything you could for your boy."

"We *did* everything we could—so why does it hurt so much?"

"Because we couldn't do enough. And we cannot get revenge for him. All we can do is try to have another Peterkin."

"No. Not another Peterkin."

His firmness made her glance round, but there was no harshness in his voice. "Another son, but not another Peterkin. Maybe," he gave a self-conscious chuckle, "maybe a Baldwin. Ah, you're tired. Give me Edith for a little while. You try to rest."

"She is all right here."

"You spent all last night with me, Meg," he reminded her, and smiled. "Let me help you. I can at least look after our daughter."

The thunder was abating as she passed the sleeping girl to him, trying to control the sudden rush of burning hope. This was the first time he had spoken to her of Peterkin since his death, the first time he had mentioned his pain at the hole in their family . . . And the first time he had raised the idea of a new son.

As she languidly curled and felt herself slipping toward sleep, she could feel the bed shaking with his gentle sobs, but she could not help the smile of relief which broke out on her face. Her husband had returned to her at last.

The scraping noise was an irritation at the edge of Sir Hector's hearing. He could hear it through the deep fogs of sleep, and while his mind tried to thrust it away and return to unconsciousness, docketing it as the feet of a mouse or another nightly creature, some extra sense made him waken.

His room was in darkness, and his eyes snapped open as the storm broke overhead. The concussion of the thunder relaxed him for a moment, making him think it had been this which had woken him, but then he heard it again: the small, slow, squeaking sound which his ever-wary ears had noticed.

Moving with the stealthy patience learned over many campaigns, he rolled silently to one side until his knees were off his palliasse and on the ground. His great sword was in the storeroom, but his lighter travelling sword, built for only one-handed use, was by the bed, and he picked it up still sheathed, holding it in his left hand ready to be drawn, as he faced the door.

Before sleeping, he had taken the precaution of sliding a heavy chest in front of it, and now he lifted it at one end and hauled it away with painful slowness, making as little noise as possible. The scratching continued, and he cautiously raised the latch on his door and stepped into the corridor before standing stock-still.

He saw the blade jutting through the shutter, the splintered wood, and the oh-so-faint glimmer of light from a candle. An electric blue light outlined the window, and then a clap of thunder rattled the doors, and still he stood watching as the fine blade of the knife wobbled from one side to the other, trying to force up the timber that locked the shutters closed.

The wood moved a little, and he quietly crept forward. If he was quick and lifted the balk out of the way, he could kill the first assassin, and probably hold the window. He wondered dispassionately how many there would be outside, but he reckoned that there could only be three at most. Wat was bound to be there, and he would hardly attempt to kill Sir Hector on his own, but he could not count on the help of too many of his comrades in murdering his captain. More than two would be a risk—there was always the possibility that someone might decide Sir Hector was a safer master than Wat and take it into his head to warn him. No, if he was Wat, he would have arranged for two accomplices, no more.

As the blade twisted and a crack appeared in the shutter, running upward with the grain, Sir Hector decided to act. He walked into the storeroom and selected a crossbow. Hauling with both hands, forcing the blunt wooden butt into his belly until it felt as though it was going to stab through his skin and into his guts, he managed to pull the string back until the sear caught and held it in place.

There was another splintering from the shutter. He snatched up a heavy metal bolt and fitted it to the grove, then walked out. Taking careful aim, he fired.

The iron bolt struck the wood to the right of the wriggling blade, and disappeared. Simultaneously there was a shrill cry of pain, and the knife was dragged back. Sir Hector heard someone sobbing in fear and pain, and he smiled grimly to himself, cock-ing the bow once more and taking another bolt. He was sure that there would be no more attempts on his life tonight, but he still slept very lightly, sitting in a chair with the crossbow on his lap.

It was impossible to stay inside. While the rain lanced down, he had to go out and stand in the yard, the drops pelting on to his upturned face so hard it was like being hit by gravel. Giggling, he held his hands over his head and let them slowly fall in reverence to the cleansing water.

His mind was clear now. The lightheadedness of the last few days had gone, as if the killing of *her* and poor Judith had finally cured him of a fever. He felt as if he had been suffering from some sort of illness, and now, under this rain, he had been redeemed, absolved and strengthened in the one heady downpour.

With the disappearance of the other two, he could finally bring his plan to fruition. Now was the time for the last throw in the game. And after that *he* would see whether it was sensible to cuckold him.

19

Baldwin grunted, sipped at his water, and then belched volcanically. Peter Clifford threw him an admonishing look.

"Peter, I know. My apologies, but the meal last night was rather rich for my constitution," the knight said, and burped once more. Grumpily he sat at the table. "Be grateful. It could be the other end."

"I'm no longer surprised that you were so off-hand about knights and the very concept of chivalry the other night, Sir Baldwin," the priest admonished him testily.

Baldwin grinned, but soon his features had fixed themselves into a frown of concentration, and the priest sighed. Crediton was an important town for the diocese, bringing in a good income each year, and Peter had wanted to be able to impress the Bishop during his visit. Instead, the conversation invariably revolved around the murders in the town. The plans Peter had set in place to impress had all gone awry: the visit to the hospital, the tour round the recent work on the church, the plans for celebrating St. Boniface's birth, all were overshadowed by the killings.

Though Exeter was nearby, it was rare for Stapledon to come this way. His business was conducted more often in London, Winchester and York, wherever Parliament met or in the fine homes of other bishops. Stapledon was not by nature a greedy man; he believed in trying to help the souls in his diocese, but Peter knew that the state too often intervened, forcing him to set his religious responsibilities aside and shoulder the burden of civil service.

For many, becoming involved in politics was solely a means of self-advancement, and Peter, being realistic about the motivations of his colleagues in the Church, could see that the Bishop was not averse to extra power and authority, but Stapledon did not have the urge to seek power alone. Much of his efforts were directed toward making the kingdom stable, and to that end he spent weeks in discussions and negotiations, trying to make the King and his enemies see sense.

Peter supposed that, for a man involved in such weighty affairs, the unpleasant, even banal, pair of murders were almost a welcome relief from the petty disputes and arguments which could embroil thousands if the Bishop's fears were realized. Certainly his interest in the two deaths had been surprising; a wealthy cleric was not usually the kind of man who would show fascination with the dealings and deaths of the poor.

Just then there was a knock at the door, and Peter saw Baldwin spin to face it. When the servant opened it, he was surprised to see the old mercenary, Wat.

Peter made a muttered apology and left the room while Baldwin invited the man to be seated.

Studying him, Baldwin was struck by the demeanor of his visitor. Wat had lost his coldness and truculence and appeared almost meek in the way he entered, his eyes cast demurely downward like a young virgin.

The curtain to the screens rattled, and Baldwin glanced up to see that Simon had entered. Baldwin was pleased to note that his friend appeared fully recovered, and walked in with a steady step, sitting beside the knight.

"You wanted to see us, Wat?" Baldwin asked.

"Yes, sir. I thought you ought to know."

"Know what?"

The soldier looked up and held Baldwin's gaze. "My master," he said simply. "I think *he* must have killed those women."

Ignoring the bailiff's quick intake of breath, Baldwin leaned forward and nodded encouragingly. Wat pulled a grimace, as if any discourse with officers of law was loathsome, but then he began to speak.

"You see, I've been with him for longer than most. I know all his ways, and I know how he works. He's not just an ordinary lord, he's too used to killing. Far as he's concerned, the only thing that matters is him. Nothing and nobody else."

"That's fine, Wat, but I didn't realize you were a monk," said Simon caustically.

The tired old eyes faced him. "I'm not, but when I kill, it's for a reason. It's for money or gold or food. It's not for nothing."

"Go on, Wat," Baldwin said quietly.

"Well, sir, like I say, I know him. I've been with him so long now, over ten years, that I know some things about him. Has he told you we came through this town before? That young lad, Cole—his brother joined the company then, some five, maybe six years ago, when we were last here. That was when Hector met with Judith."

Those few words made Baldwin and Simon sit up

and listen carefully. "Met Judith? You mean your captain knew her back then?"

"Oh yes! She was a tavern-girl at the time, as young and fresh as a new primrose. Pretty much like that Sarra. He took her on his second night, and she went along to his chamber like it was her bridal bed. Silly cow. Two mornings after I saw her, she was weeping like a child. I don't know why, but he'd beaten her. She looked like he'd whipped her before he threw her out."

"Was this at the same inn?" Simon asked.

"Yes, sir. But it was a different owner then."

Baldwin nodded his head. Paul had taken up the inn a little over four years before. He did not know who had run it until then. "You think he killed Judith?"

"I can't say. All I know is, Sarra upsets him and she dies. Then he sees Judith again, and she dies."

"Why should he kill her? It makes no sense."

"It makes sense to me."

"Why?"

"She was killed, but her son was left alive, wasn't he?"

"Yes."

"Like I said, we were here five or six years ago. How old is the lad?"

Simon stared. "You can't mean . . . If she was his son's mother, he couldn't kill her, surely! How could any man, especially a knight—"

"Oh, Hector's not a knight. He was never given his belt and spurs—he took them from a man he killed."

"Not a knight?" Simon burst out. "Now you're raving! Of course he is. He must be! No man can bear knightly arms without being able to prove his right."

"And how do they prove their right, sir?"

"By force of arms . . ." Simon said, trailing off as he

peered with bafflement at the calm soldier before him. "But there is more, surely. Someone could apply to discover where he was knighted, and by whom."

"Hardly," said Baldwin, keeping his eyes on Wat. "The man might have died by now. Or Hector could say it was a French knight, or a Teutonic one, who knighted him. Who could tell whether it was true or not?"

Wat nodded. "And right now, with the French trying to weaken the King and take over ever more of his lands, how could a French knight be found to confirm that he had dubbed Hector? He's safe enough."

"But that's outrageous!" Simon exploded. "A man can't just *call* himself a knight."

"Of course he can. Men often do," Baldwin said mildly.

"Especially in companies like mine," Wat agreed.

Simon looked from one to the other, disbelief clouding his features, but their calm and factual tones disconcerted him. "All right, but even so, how on earth could someone kill a woman after she had borne him a son?"

Wat's eyes were lidded as he surveyed the bailiff. "It's been done before. Sometimes by kings, sometimes by ordinary men."

"I see." Baldwin gloomily rested his chin on his palm. "So you think he killed both of them, though you have no idea why."

Wat moved uncomfortably on his seat. "I think Sarra was trying to win him back. You see she was wearing *that* tunic . . . And I know he'd bought it for someone else."

"Who?"

"I don't know, just someone in the town."

"Why do you say that?"

"It was after he'd spent that first night with Sarra, the Monday morning. He left her and went into town. When he came back, he was really happy, laughing and joking. Next day, he bought the tunic. He told me to go and fetch it from the shop, as it was being finished off. He went out again, didn't get back till afternoon. I think he found Sarra in his room with the new tunic on, and he killed her for wearing it."

"Just for wearing it?" Simon asked dubiously. "He could kill just for that?"

Wat ignored the interruption. "I reckon he had met a woman while he was out. It was someone he liked, and he bought the tunic for her, ready for seeing her again later."

"Later?" Baldwin frowned.

"He was out most of the night after his meal. I think he was with her."

"Who? Judith?" Simon was beginning to flounder.

The look he received was withering. "No. Whoever the third woman was."

"And who was the third woman?" asked Baldwin, sipping at his water and wincing as he suppressed a fresh belch.

"I don't know, but I think it was someone he had met when we came through this town last. After he'd thrown Judith out that time, he met another one, and wouldn't tell us who she was, either."

"Was he normally so reticent?"

"No."

"So why do you think he kept her name secret?"

"I've got no idea. Maybe she was important, or had powerful friends."

Baldwin scratched at his head. "And you believe he killed Judith too? Why should he murder her?"

"Oh, I think she must have asked him for money. My captain is not happy to give, as you may have noticed."

So news of Sir Hector's attack on Judith had spread, Baldwin noted. He sat back and folded his arms. "Why do you tell us all this now, I wonder. You have known these things for some time. Why come forward now?"

But Wat stood, smiling patiently. "I had no idea he was so dangerous. How can we, his men, rely on someone who can go abroad of a night and murder a woman just because she asked him for charity? Or another because she put on a new tunic he didn't intend for her? The man is erratic, and we can't trust to his judgment."

"So you feel able to accuse him?"

"Oh no, I can't accuse him, for I did not see him do it, but I felt sure you would want to hear about him." He smiled at them, then bowed and left.

Outside, he stopped. They had appeared to listen carefully to what he had said, and he only hoped it was enough. He could have cursed Will for his stupid attempt at assassination. There was no need to kill the man! Hector was already finished. This pair of murders was more than enough to seal his fate, whereas if he was murdered, the whole troop could be held up while the Keeper tried to figure out who was responsible. It was stupid to have tried to break in like that. It had taken all Wat's self-restraint to prevent him punching the wounded man who lay on his blanket whining about the pain from his side, and he had relished the lad's agony as the old bolt was jerked from his wound, the bright crimson blood flowing in a steady tide down his flank.

Wat grinned to himself and set off back to the inn. His plans were almost complete. He would be surprised if he was not captain within a week.

* * *

Simon frowned after him as the mercenary left the room. When they heard the door slam he faced his friend, his perplexity making him sound peevish. "What's he on about? Does he really think Sir Hector did it, do you reckon?"

"Yes, I believe he is fairly sure that his master did kill the women, but that has very little to do with why he came here."

"What was he doing here, then?"

"He was forcing us to arrest his master."

"Baldwin, it may be my head, but I cannot see what you are—"

"Sorry, Simon, I was thinking out loud." Baldwin smiled at his friend. "I have known such bands of wandering soldiers in the past, when I was in Rome and France, and they have one principle which seems the same for all of the companies: there is an election of a leader. The man in charge is always the strongest, the one most likely to win the money and women for the rest."

"So Sir Hector is the strongest among them?"

"*Was.* That, I think, is soon to become his problem. He was the strongest and most ruthless, and because of that his men feared and respected him. Now, though, it would seem that he has sunk in Wat's estimation. He is prepared to come here and give several hints that his master could be capable of the two killings, and give us motives for them both. Sir Hector should tread carefully when he goes down any quiet streets. He may find someone waiting with a drawn dagger."

Simon puffed out his cheeks. "What on earth makes a man seek power like that?"

There was a chuckle from behind them. "Are you referring to me?"

"Bishop, of course not! I . . . My apologies if you thought . . ." Simon stammered.

"It is my fault for listening without permission. I confess to my sin," Stapledon chuckled, peering at him shortsightedly. He motioned to Roger to fetch wine, and sat with them, "But you look troubled, my friends. Can I help? Is it something to do with the two men in Exeter?"

"If," Baldwin said heavily, "I was right, and that's where they've gone. You are partly right, my lord. It is to do with them and their kind."

"The murders?"

"Yes." Baldwin sighed. "There seem to be so many men in that little band who could kill, and several who might have been involved, and still worse, now it seems there is some rivalry going on within it, so we have a man come here to denounce his leader."

"Ah, I see. You are looking for a murderer, and rather than the normal situation where there is a body and a dearth of possible killers, you have been presented with a pair of dead women and an embarrassment of potential murderers. Not to mention," he mused, "a poor lad who is now without a protector."

Simon rubbed his eyes. They felt gritty from lack of sleep the night before. "And a robbery."

"Yes." Baldwin glanced at Simon. "And now we think that the two mercenaries were the thieves, I suppose we should free young Cole, though we might as well wait until we have had a chance to speak to the other two."

"Yes. I'd leave Cole there for a little longer. Apart from anything else, he's safer there from Sir Hector's men. One or two of them still might try to curry favor by hurting him."

"If my men do bring Smithson and the other one back from the city, what then?" asked Stapledon. "Will you arrest them for the murder as well as the robbery?"

"I suppose so," Baldwin said doubtfully

"Could they have killed Judith as well?"

"I can see no reason why they should. What connection could there be between her and them?"

"Is there any need for any connection? Surely men such as these need no excuse to kill?" Stapledon asked.

"There's always a reason to kill, even if it is simply a fit of anger. I cannot believe that these two men happened to see Judith in the alley and decided to murder her."

"In that case, look for men who knew her and had a reason."

"We have one," Simon said. "Sir Hector." He explained to the Bishop what they had learned from Wat.

"I see." Stapledon primly pursed his lip. "I should have thought that would be enough to arrest the man. One woman, lately his lover, has been found dead in his room, and from what you say, wearing a tunic he had purchased especially for another. Then a second woman demands money from him because she has borne him an illegitimate son, and she too dies. It seems more than a coincidence to me."

"Yes," Simon agreed, but his eyes were on Baldwin.

The knight sat staring into the middle distance, a twist of his mouth giving him a sardonic smile. Coming to, he stood. "Bishop, you are right. We have to find out who had a link with the two women and stop simply listening to the views of others. That is why we're being blown with the wind, first taking one man's word as true, then taking another's."

There was an animation about him which suggested

to Simon that he had an idea he wanted to test. "What do you mean?"

"I mean, there have been various men coming here and trying to influence us. Now it is time for us to find out what we need, rather than waiting for others to tell us what they want us to know."

"Fine," Simon said sarcastically. "And where do we start?"

"First with the people in Judith's street. But this time, I want to know about *her*. So far we have been tied up, thinking about all the killers in town, but the people who knew her, and who knew Sarra too, live here, in Crediton. The motive for the murders is here. The theft of the silver was here, the women lived here, the killings were committed here. Surely if we can find a connection between them, all will become clear and we will discover who the murderer is."

Hugh was not happy about leaving his master to the care and protection of Sir Baldwin and Edgar, but when he saw how tired his mistress looked, he could understand that she would need a rest from her boisterous daughter.

But though Hugh was forced to remain, he made his feelings plain that Simon too should stay behind. There was no point in his leaving, the servant felt, and he watched the three men's departure with simmering resentment.

It was also impossible for Roger to leave the house. Whenever he left the orphan, the boy set up such a screaming that he had to return. Rollo would not accept anyone else being near him unless Roger was there, a situation which seemed to have been reinforced when the rector had gone to him the night before. The mad, terrified panic had driven the child from his comfortable palliasse, and when Roger had entered, he had found the boy curled in a fearful ball in the corner of the room farthest from the window. As the thunder crackled and boomed, Roger had turned his eyes upward. The storm sounded like ten thousand moorstone slabs being fractured all at once, and he was convinced that the roof must collapse. He was unpleasantly reminded of the walls of Jericho as he listened to the immense power of the storm. Rollo had whimpered, trying to squeeze himself away as Roger went in, but when he squatted nearby, there was a sudden splintering crackle overhead, and the boy had leapt into his lap.

They were soon at the alley where Simon had been attacked, and it took little time for them to find the door on which Hugh had knocked to find Rollo. Baldwin beat upon it and stood back.

It was the mother who opened it. She stood wiping flour from her hands while she surveyed them with the truculence born of poverty. Baldwin noticed that she was tall, and apart from the lines caused by worry and poor diet, would have been handsome. But the vertical slashes at either cheek, the bruises under the eyes and the nervous tic were proof of her mean existence.

"You are the woman who looked after Rollo, Judith's son, the night before last," Baldwin said. It was more a statement than a question, and she stopped wiping her hands, suddenly still as she stared at him. He continued gently: "We are trying to find out what happened that night, to seek her murderer. Will you help us?"

Slowly, holding his gaze, she nodded. She had heard

screaming, and been too scared to go and find out what had happened. Some from the street had gone, and she had heard them muttering anxiously, talking about a body. That had decided her to remain safe indoors. She had heard footsteps, running away, and the arrival of a company, which Baldwin decided must have been himself and the others. Later there was a terrible sobbing, and, there being no other noise, she had dared to go out.

Rollo had been standing alone, fists clenched, staring at the ground. From what she said, he must have been staring at the spot where his mother had lain. She had brought him home, but had been unable to get a word out of him. He had simply sat and wept silently, starting at every new sound, allowing her to feed him some thickened soup, and gradually he had succumbed to his exhaustion and fallen asleep in her lap.

"I don't see the man who took him away," she finished suspiciously, her eyes going from one to another as she looked for Hugh.

"He is with Peter Clifford. Tell us, how well did you know the boy's mother?"

"Judith? Not well. She was just always around, you know? Poor girl got herself pregnant when she was only eighteen or so, and that was that. The innkeeper, that's old Dan, before this new one, was a hard man to work for. He tried to make the girls be friendly to the customers, but with Judith, he threw her out. Called her a slut; no better than a Winchester Goose."

Baldwin nodded. Prostitution was common, for there were few other ways for a woman with no man to look after her to survive. If she had not been fortunate enough to be trained for weaving or embroidery, and could not get a job working as a huckster on the streets, there was no other way to support herself. In London, all the prostitutes were forced to live within Cock Lane, part of the Bishop of Winchester's lands; he benefited from the rents, and they were commonly known as "Winchester Geese."

"What did she do then?"

"Lived up to his view," she said shortly. "Or down to it. Nothing else for her."

"Did she have any friends? Family?"

"If she had any family, she'd have had a chance, poor girl, but no. Lots of people knew her, but I wouldn't say she had friends. Only a few of us who used to give her the odd crumb when we had something to spare. For her boy, mainly. Rollo was always hungry; the little fellow never had enough."

"Are you aware of any enemies she might have had?"

"That bastard who put her where she was, the one at the inn. I hope he rots for what he did to her."

"Yes, but what about others? Were there many people who seemed to hold a grudge, or bear her ill-will generally?"

She thought a moment. "Several wives. They always had something against Judith; whenever their husbands were late home they'd blame her. Usually it was just that the men had drunk too much and had to sleep it off for a while, or they'd fallen down in the gutter. It wasn't Judith's fault."

"Any in particular?" Baldwin probed.

"I don't know. Widow Annie, over at New Barton, she has always resented Judith, but that's because she has a thing with the Constable, and Annie never believed him when he said he was late because of some other reason. Annie was always the jealous sort."

Baldwin thought of the widow—he had met her a few times—and shook his head. Annie was too respectable to think about murder, though her bitter tongue and taste for gossip and malicious rumors could shock sometimes. "Anyone else?"

"Only—" She stopped and frowned. "Mary Butcher, I suppose. She was always spreading nasty tales about Judith. And you know what they say."

It was a confident comment, issued with a knowing look and prim wink, but Baldwin was lost. "No, I do not," he said simply.

"Oh! Well, this captain, the one who did that to Judith—they say he met with Mary too. Seems like it was *that* close . . . Could have been Mary, not Judith who was with child."

"Ah! Really?"

- 20 -

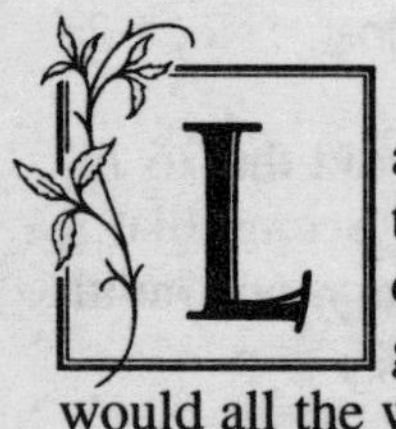

Later, as they made their way back through the dirty alley toward the welcome brightness of the road, Baldwin glanced thoughtfully at his friend. "Why would all the women hate her so much?"

"I think it's partly because of the chance that their husbands might bring home diseases, but also because prostitutes are seen to be evil. Why else would they not be permitted burial in consecrated ground? This poor woman will be buried out of the town somewhere. Everyone is a little scared of them in a small place like this, because they represent something different."

"Not that different, surely?" Baldwin was puzzled. "Many women must have understood that she had no other way to support herself."

"They would expect her to prefer to starve."

"Her boy as well?"

"Yes. These people," Simon said, stopping and staring about him, "have so many children, they place little or no value on an extra mouth. A death means more food for the survivors, and they can become quite hard about it. It is the way of the poor."

"I suppose so."

They had come to the street. Turning down it, they crossed over and walked to the butcher's shop. The apprentice sat on the stool in the doorway, plucking chickens and stuffing the feathers into a small sack. He looked up as they approached. Picking up a knife, he broke the legs of the fowl in his lap and sliced round them before pulling the feet off, drawing the long, white tendons with them. Then he cut the head off and pulled the skin back to expose the neck.

"Where is your master?" Simon asked as they got to the doorway.

The boy looked up. "He's out, sir," he said, and bent back to his task, cutting quickly round the vent.

"When will he be back?"

"I don't know, sir. He's often out collecting beasts. Sometimes not back until late." He pushed a finger inside the neck cavity, loosening the organs, then hooked two fingers in from the vent and drew the entrails free, dropping them on the roadside. "Today he's delivering."

"What of his wife . . . Are you going to clear this mess away?" Baldwin could not help himself asking it; the flies were maddening.

"She's staying with her sister in Coleford. Left on Tuesday, sir."

"Tuesday?" Baldwin frowned.

"Yes, sir. She had a blazing row with my master, and left just after."

"When will she be back?"

"I don't know, sir."

"You don't know much, do you? Do you know that you *are* going to clear up this mess?" Baldwin said pointedly.

"Yes, sir."

"You ought to have all this meat in the cool, too. It'll fester out here in this heat."

"As soon as my master is back, he'll put it all in the store."

"Why don't you put it there?" asked Simon.

"My master thinks he's been robbed recently. Some meat's been disappearing. I think he blames me, because he's locked the storeroom. I can't get in."

"Well, when your master gets back, tell him I want to see him," Baldwin said. "I will be at Peter Clifford's house."

They left the apprentice languidly reaching for another chicken corpse, and made their way back across the road to the jail, silent as they mulled over the boy's words. Tanner was awake this time, and stood quickly when he realized that they were going to enter.

"How is he, Tanner?" Baldwin asked.

"Fine, sir. Nervous, but that's no surprise. You want to see him?"

Cole had reduced. His frame, once so large and powerful, had shrunk, and his shoulders were bent as if from hard effort. The eyes which Simon had first been so impressed by were now sunken and had lost their glitter.

Seeing his emaciated appearance, Simon shot a glance at the Constable, but the look of compassion on Tanner's face showed that it was not caused by maltreatment; it was simply the effect of days of not knowing what might happen, the fear of pain and death.

The knight recognized that look only too well. So many of his friends had carried the same unbearable torment etched hard into their features as they underwent the agony of watching comrades suffer torture, knowing that the same pressure would be brought to bear on them when the inquisitors lost interest in their present target. Baldwin had hoped never to see such anguish again.

"Be seated, Cole," he muttered. "We have some questions for you."

"Is this my trial?" The young man's eyes flitted from one face to another, desperately seeking assurance.

"No. We are merely continuing our enquiry. Have you heard about Judith?"

"Who?"

"Another woman has been killed."

"But I was here! I couldn't—"

"Be still! It might mean you are free from suspicion of the murder of Sarra, but it does not mean you are innocent of the robbery of Sir Hector's silver. Just answer our questions honestly, and tell us all you know."

Cole nodded glumly. "I'll tell you everything."

"Good. You joined the company on Sunday, yes?"

"Yes. I found them there when I arrived in the evening."

"It was the Tuesday that you were attacked, and that night when we found you with Henry the Hurdle and John Smithson?"

"Yes."

"What had you been doing that morning?"

He screwed his face up. Of all the things he had considered during the long hours of darkness in the dank little underground cell, those few last, precious hours of freedom before the momentous event of his arrest had not been uppermost in his mind. He had concentrated on the afternoon. Now he tried to remember what had happened before. "I was awake early—Henry woke me—and spent some time with him after breakfast, learning what the company had in the way of weapons. Then he sent me to the stables to help with the horses. He said, 'A good soldier always looks after his horses better than himself, especially when the horses are owned by Sir Hector.' I was there almost all the time."

"You had no break?"

"Yes, a couple. We had lunch just as Sir Hector was going out."

"Had he been out already?"

"Eh? Yes. The first time he'd come back and had some words with Wat."

"Where were you when he left?"

"In the buttery. I saw him leave."

"Did you watch him in the street?"

"Only a moment."

"What did you see him doing?"

Cole shrugged. "He walked out and went off toward the west."

"On his own?"

"There were no soldiers with him, if that's what you mean."

"No, it is not what I mean. Did you see anybody with him?"

"As I said, I only watched him for a moment or two."

Simon cleared his throat. "What about the other soldiers? Were any comments made about him as he walked away?"

"The usual sort, I imagine. I got the impression that he's not the most popular man in the world." Cole fell silent, then: "They were all saying how he'd beaten the serving-girl, Sarra. Most of them were not even surprised; it wasn't something that upset them, it was just something to chat about, the way that the young girl had been thrashed."

"Did anyone say *why* she had been so poorly treated?" Baldwin pushed.

"Someone said he'd found a new woman."

Their sudden stillness made him look up, baffled. Baldwin said, "Try to remember anything you can about this woman, Cole. Did anyone say who she was, where she came from, how the captain had met her, anything?"

"She was local. I know that much, because one of them said he'd seen her the time before when they'd stayed at the inn. One of the others laughed, and muttered something, but I couldn't hear it. Then somebody said she was married to a man in town, and he winked, and the others all guffawed."

"She was a married woman?" Simon pressed him, his dark eyes intent. "You are sure of that?"

"Yes. They seemed convinced. And . . . one of them said she didn't like the meat she got at home—she preferred steak to bacon."

Baldwin studied him. As before he was struck with the impression of honesty. "One last thing. We have heard you argued with Sarra. What was that about?"

Cole reddened. "She wanted me to perjure myself. Henry and John had upset her, and she wanted me to swear that they were plotting against Sir Hector."

"You refused?"

"Of course I did! I'd not seen anything to suggest they'd been planning Sir Hector's downfall. She wanted me to lie so that she'd find her way back into his favor, and I said no."

While Tanner put the prisoner back in his cell, the three stood huddled near the open door, staring at the butcher's shop. The apprentice still sat unperturbably plucking chickens, small clouds of tiny feathers whirling occasionally as the breeze caught them, floating and spinning until they touched the damp soil of the street and stuck, soaking up the mire and becoming part of the road's surface.

"What do we do now?" Edgar asked.

Simon cocked an eyebrow at him. "We find out where the butcher's wife has gone, that's what we do."

"But how?" Baldwin gazed up the road toward Coleford and the west. "Edgar, you seem to know many of the women in this area. Can you find out where she originally came from?"

His servant cleared his throat. "I suppose so. Mind, Tanner might know more; he comes from that way himself."

"Ask him, then. Meanwhile, we shall return to Clifford's house to get our horses. The weather looks good, and it is time we had some exercise," Simon said.

Tanner did know Mary's family. They owned a smallholding which they had won from their demesne lord some generations ago when an ancestor had provided some useful service. It was, as Tanner explained it, a mixed blessing, for the others in the locality were still villeins, owing their livelihood to their master, receiving food and guaranteed work in exchange, while the free family sometimes suffered, having no protection or support when the harvest was poor. Many thought they would have fared better if they had remained villeins like their neighbors.

The road climbed a short rise after the town, and Simon enjoyed the ride. His bay rounsey was a good, solid horse, built for covering long distances, and had a pleasant, mild temperament. Baldwin, he noticed, was on his Arab, a beautiful white animal with a high-stepping gait and what to Simon seemed an incredible turn of speed.

As they crested the first hill and dropped down the other side, the sun broke through the clouds. All at once the sky showed clear and blue in the gaps, and the men began to feel the warmth. Here, on the western side of the town, the trees were thick and covered much of the landscape, except to their left where Simon could see the blue-gray mounds of Dartmoor crouching on the horizon. Above it were thick storm-clouds, and from the mistiness the bailiff was sure that it must be raining hard. He never could understand why the moors had their own weather, and today he was glad to be away from it.

As the sun touched the soil and heated it, it gave off a refreshing scent. The smell was of vigorous, healthy earth, rich and loamy, filled with rotted vegetation. It was impossible for Simon not to compare it with the desolate plains where he was bailiff. There the earth was so filled with moorstone and peat that only stunted trees and the poor grasses could survive. This part of Devon was where he had been raised, and here everything seemed full of vitality and energy. Even the very color of the soil was different. On the moors it was almost black, while in other areas, he had been surprised to see how dull and brown it looked, especially during the hot weather, when it appeared anemic.

Here, near Crediton, it was a uniform bright red, hearty and bursting with goodness; plants absolutely thrived on it. No matter whether they were trees, vegetables or herbs, all grew and blossomed with a vitality that was rare in other parts even of England.

After three or four miles, the lane curved round to

their left, and started down the long, gently-sloping hill into Coleford. Simon remembered it as a pleasant little vill, with four or five cottages and houses on the busy road from Exeter to Plymouth. Some monks had a place there, too, he recalled, and would offer sustenance to travellers, but today they were not going so far as the vill itself. At the top of the steeper part of the hill, they turned off left to a small hamlet, and here they found Mary Butcher's sister.

Ellen, who was married to Hal Carpenter, was a happy-looking, chubby woman in her late twenties. As the three men rode along the lane and into her yard, scattering the chickens and making her goat bleat in irritation, she was kneeling by a large stone, kneading dough. Hearing them, she sat back on her haunches, wiping strands of hair back under her cap as she surveyed her guests.

As Simon smiled and dropped from his horse, she stood and smiled back. "Are you lost, sirs? This isn't the road for Plymouth."

"No, we are looking for Ellen Carpenter."

"That's me," she said, and gave him a smile so welcoming, he felt as if he had known her for years. "Can I offer you something to drink? I have ale."

When she had fetched a jug and three wooden cups, they squatted with her round the stone while she continued kneading. Her children, of whom there were five that Simon counted, though they moved around so much there may have been more, peeped round tree trunks at the three important guests.

"You are sister to Mary Butcher, who lives in Crediton?" Simon asked, once the preliminary greetings had been offered and received.

"Yes, sir."

She had the rosiest complexion, Simon thought, that he had ever seen. Hazel eyes with green flecks sparkled in the sun, and auburn tints in her hair glittered like gold. "Is she here? We would like to speak to her."

She smiled at him, a little puzzled. "No, Mary's not here. Why—isn't she at her home in Crediton?"

"No," Simon said disconcertedly. "We were told she was here."

Baldwin asked, "Was she due to visit you here this week?"

"No, not especially. She usually turns up when she feels like it. I don't know in advance. It's not so easy to send a message from Crediton to here."

"She often comes here, then?" Simon asked.

"Oh yes, fairly often. I don't get to see her over there, mind, as I have all these to look after." She waved a proprietorial hand at the animals and children all round. "She likes to get away from the smell and noise of the town and back to the country every so often, so she walks out here when she has the time. Her husband doesn't mind."

"That's Adam Butcher?"

"Yes. Adam married her four years ago, just as his business was growing. It was a relief to us, I can say. We were beginning to think she'd never get a husband. She was already twenty-three by then. Now, me, I got wed when I was eighteen—a much better age. I had four children by the time I was twenty-three."

"We were told she had come here on Tuesday, but you say you haven't seen her?"

Her eyes became anxious. "You mean she's disappeared? No one knows where she is?"

"I doubt it," Baldwin said reassuringly. "I expect the

apprentice—it was he who told us she was here—got confused. He did not strike me as being of the brightest. Do not worry. She will have gone to a friend, or maybe another sister?"

"No, sir. I am her only sister," Ellen said, and her eyes held a haunted look.

"I can see why she would want to come here," Baldwin continued. "It is a good little estate you have here."

"Not bad, sir. The beans are good, and the peas did well. Better than last year, anyway. And my husband, he's a good worker, and he's often busy with the manor, mending carts and barrels. It keeps us in wheat and barley."

Baldwin nodded. Peas and beans were plentiful at this time of year, and the chickens scratching in the dirt at his feet were all young, most looking only a few months old. They were fresh this year, so she and her husband were surviving well as free people. "Tell me, Ellen, how long has Mary been living in Crediton? Someone told me she was there some five or six years ago, before she married."

"Yes, sir. She used to work in the cloth trade, weaving and doing some needlework. She stopped all that when she married, of course."

"Of course. So she was living in town for more than six years?"

"Nearer eight, I should say. Since she was eighteen or nineteen."

"How did she come to meet Adam?" Baldwin was watching her face intently, Simon noticed, and he wondered what the knight was driving at.

Ellen clearly felt she had no secrets. She gave a loud guffaw. "She didn't; he came to meet *her*! The way she tells it, she was walking along the road one day, when he threw out some offal from his shop and spattered her all over. Well, she went mad, and stormed inside, and gave him a piece of her mind, threatening him with all sorts, saying she'd get the Constable on him, and the Keeper of the Peace, and just about threatening him with the posse of the county. She can be hard when roused, can young Mary, but glorious in her rage. Poor old Adam was smitten: never stood a chance. He was infatuated from the first."

Smiling, Baldwin said, "He is more madly in love with her than she with him, you mean?"

"Oh yes," she said absently, her mind still on the whirlwind romance and wedding, and then her eyes sharpened, and she gave him a quick look that he could not read.

"Does she love him, do you think?"

She gave this consideration, the smile still playing round her lips, but it had faded, and there was a touch of sadness as she nodded. "A little. But not enough. No, it would have been better if he didn't love her so much. Then at least there would be some equality in their house. The trouble is, she's not the sort to be excited by living with a man like him. He adores her, but she was always the sort to bore easily, and that leads to nagging."

"Is she a nag, then?"

"With poor Adam, yes, though I daresay he'd deny it. He always was a poor fool. I expect he thinks she's just being precise, and he isn't. She tells him where to put his things—even his tools in his shop—and he won't argue. He doesn't want to upset her."

"Not a solid foundation for a marriage," Baldwin observed.

"No, sir. Not at all. But, to be fair, they both seem happy enough."

"Yes, of course. Tell me, are you good friends with your sister?"

"There is none better. Whenever we have troubles, it is to each other that we turn."

"Rather than your husbands," Baldwin guessed conspiratorially.

"Certainly rather than them!" she laughed gaily. "There are some things which only a woman can understand."

"And some secrets which can only be shared with another woman."

"Oh, yes!"

"Such as men."

She was suddenly quite still. Though her hands carried on, carefully turning and kneading the dough, the whole of the rest of her body was unmoving.

Baldwin stared at the ground pensively. "Ellen, have you heard about the company of mercenaries in Crediton?"

She looked up. Her smile did not alter one jot, Simon saw, but there was a fixity in her face now as she looked at his friend. Some of the friendliness had gone. "Mercenaries?"

"Yes. The same troop which your sister noticed so many years ago. The same captain, Sir Hector de Gorsone, the same men in the band. She knew them, didn't she? She knew him, Sir Hector, better than any, didn't she?"

"I don't know what you mean."

"Yes, you do. It was because of her that Sir Hector threw out another wench, Judith. She's dead now, you should know that. So is your sister's latest replacement, another poor girl called Sarra. Both dead, and neither for any good reason." Baldwin sighed heavily.

"If your sister comes here over the next few days, send a message to us, Ellen. We have to speak to her. Otherwise, I think she might be in danger."

"Danger!" she scoffed. "What sort of danger?"

Baldwin looked at her long and hard. "Did you not hear what I have been saying? This knight has had three lovers in Crediton: the first is dead, the third is dead; the second is your sister. Tell me when you hear from her."

- 21 -

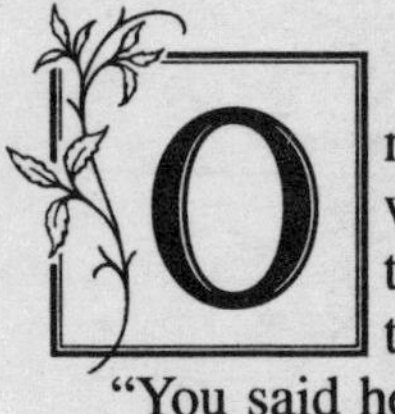

On the ride back to Crediton, Baldwin was deep in thought. When they reached the top of the hill leading down to the town itself, Simon turned to face him.

"You said her sister could be in danger, Baldwin—but why? Why on earth should this bloody man want to kill all the women he has known in this town?"

"That's not necessarily the way to look at it, Simon," Baldwin said. He patted his horse, then irritably waved away the small swarm of flies he had disturbed before continuing, "This knight may not have harmed any of them. It is startling how clear the links are to Sir Hector, isn't it? Two women die, and both were short-term lovers of this knight. Both times there happen to have been arguments or rows with him. Sarra at the inn had a shouting match with him, and was shortly after found in a chest in his very room; Judith bumped into him in the street, and got herself stabbed."

"Yes, so there's a clear link to him."

"True, but then, if you reverse the perspective, who would benefit from these women being found and their attachment to Hector being discovered?"

"Nobody, surely?"

"I can think of several. The mercenaries themselves. Take Wat: he wants to get rid of his master; I think that is plain enough. Otherwise he would not have been so forthcoming about Sir Hector's relationship with Judith."

"Maybe he wanted to see justice done."

Baldwin gave him a long, intense stare. "Justice done—Wat? I think you mistake him for a pleasant man, for a gentleman, Simon. He is not; he is a mercenary—a ruthless, dedicated killer and despoiler. A knight should fight for Christianity, for the greater glory of his name and reputation in this world and the next. He should defend the weak and unfortunate, showing courtesy and largesse. Have you noticed any of these attributes in Hector or his men—Wat, for example?"

"I'm sure they—"

With an uncharacteristic burst of anger, Baldwin reined in his horse. "Simon, don't try to be their apologist. They are *evil*, nothing more. Men like them ride where they will, offering allegiance only to those who pay them, and no one else, but even that is only for as long as it suits them. They have no conception of honor or largesse; all they want is the next sum of money, and they are casual about how they receive it."

"Calm yourself, Baldwin," Simon said soothingly. "I accept that you understand more about such men than me; I've never come across them before."

"My apologies, Simon. This whole affair is starting to make me smart, and like a bear baited at the pole, I turn on whoever I can reach."

"When we came out today, you were thinking that the matter could be resolved by looking at the local situation. Surely that has worked, in the main? Now we have learned that the butcher's wife was also known to Sir Hector. It seems fairly clear that he threw over Judith for her, and quite probably the same thing happened to Sarra when he met Mary Butcher again in town."

"Yes. And now she too has disappeared," Baldwin said grimly.

"She may not be dead, Baldwin. Think on this; if she was intelligent, as soon as she had heard about Sarra and Judith dying, she might have put two and two together. Maybe she's run off to protect herself?"

"It is possible, certainly."

"In terms of this whole affair, though, let's just hope that Stapledon's men catch the two thieves. At least they might be able to shed some light on the thing."

Bishop Stapledon wandered out into the garden with Peter Clifford and expressed his delight at the mixture of plants. Peter, he knew, was very keen on his herbs and spices. Several plants he had arranged to be delivered from far afield.

Irises were among Peter's favorites. As he explained—at some length—the plant was an almost perfect example of God's bounty. The roots could be crushed for ink, the flower yielded a juice which could be used as a salve for teeth and gums, the leaves thatched for mats or patching roofs, and if it was needed for none of these purposes, the flowers were both beautiful and sweet-smelling.

The Bishop smiled and nodded as Peter led him round the garden, keen to avoid hurting his host's feelings by letting his boredom show. Lilies and roses were pointed out to him—they filled a bed near the house—while further on, toward the orchard where the apple, pear, cherry and nut trees grew, was the herb garden. Rue, whose smell the Bishop cordially detested, flourished here, but there was also sage, chamomile, lavender and other attractively perfumed plants. After an hour, even the enthusiastic Peter began to observe the Bishop's attention waning, and they walked over the lawn, full of daisies, violets, primroses and periwinkles to create an aromatic and attractive cover, to the shelter of an oak where there was a bench.

Here they found Margaret and Hugh. Edith was a short distance away, playing a game with Rollo which seemed to involve pulling flowers from the lawn. Hugh stood as the two approached, but the Bishop waved him back to his seat. "May we join you?"

"Of course, my lord." Margaret moved along the bench and Hugh stood again resignedly and went to station himself behind her. From here he could see the children. Rollo had frozen at the sound of men's voices, but seeing two men he recognized, and after a brief confirmatory glance at Hugh, he resumed his game. Hugh suspected he was so used to seeing the priest dispensing charity that he knew he had nothing to fear from men in holy garments.

The men sat, and Stapledon looked at Margaret. "I hope you do not mind me noticing it, but you look very refreshed. Are you feeling somewhat better?"

She could not hide her pleasure from him. "It is not just me," she confided. "My husband was very sad over the death of our son, but he has almost recovered from it. These last weeks have been difficult, but I think we have got over our pain. Peter's kindness has helped so much."

The Bishop nodded gravely. "Your husband was extremely upset. I know how hard it can be. I suppose all of us in the Church are aware, for we see so many tiny coffins being interred, and death can strike the richest as well as the poorest in the land."

"We shall have another son, God willing," Margaret said.

"Yes." Stapledon was watching Rollo. "That young fellow likes playing with your daughter."

"Edith likes his company too. They are not so very different in age, and where we live she does not have many friends. It is pleasant for her to find someone with whom she can enjoy a game."

"Yes," he repeated, then frowned, lost in thought.

"Bishop? Bishop!"

Stapledon looked up, jerked back to the present, to see Roger running over the lawn. The Bishop forced down a sense of annoyance. At last he had begun to relax, and Roger's bursting in on his pleasant mood of calm was vexing. By the time the rector had approached, however, the Bishop had managed to dispose of the exasperation and had regained his equanimity. "What is it, Roger? Is the house on fire?"

"No, sir. But a messenger has just arrived from Exeter. They have found and captured the two runaway mercenaries, sir, and are bringing them here."

"Excellent!" said Peter, and rubbed his hands together with satisfaction. "Then we should soon be able to put this sorry affair behind us once and for all."

"Yes," said Stapledon, but again his eyes moved to the small figure only a few feet away. "Most of us will."

When Simon and the others arrived back in Crediton, they were hot and dusty. The moisture on the road from the night's downpour had splashed and spattered their legs on the way to Coleford, and red-brown splotches marked their hose and tunics. Returning, the dampness had been driven off by the sun, and instead of soggy droplets they had been assailed by a clinging mist of fine reddish powder which had risen as their horses' hooves had disturbed the road. Now, looking at Baldwin, Simon could see that his hair had a wiry firmness, his face had darkened, with paler streaks where the sweat had run, and his tunic was, instead of white, a dull ochre at the shoulder and dark orange-brown at the hem. It made him look as if the color had run from the top down in a rainstorm, the bailiff thought with a grin, which faded when he looked at the state of his own hose.

The powdery dust had not only affected their clothing. Simon's eyes felt as if they had gravel in them, and his throat was as sore as if he had swallowed a pint of sand. As they passed the inn, he croaked, "Let's wash away a little of the road with some of Paul's ale. His wife is a better brewer than Peter's bottler."

Baldwin nodded, and they were soon out in the yard behind, gripping quarts of ale.

Simon glanced round after taking a long pull at his drink. At another table were a group of soldiers from Sir Hector's troop, all studiously avoiding the bailiff's eye. He recognized none of them, and was about to turn away when he saw Wat.

The mercenary was standing out toward the back of the yard, near the stables, talking to someone Simon could hardly see. Only two boots protruded beyond the stable wall, and a hand which rose and fell in emphasis. Wat was staring with what looked like horrified fascination, occasionally shaking his head in quick denial or nodding in grave agreement.

"Baldwin," Simon said, hiding his mouth behind his jug, "Wat is over there, in deep debate with someone, and it looks as if it's a serious matter."

"Eh?" Baldwin surreptitiously glanced over his shoulder. "I wonder what—"

Catching their eyes on him, the mercenary made a quick gesture to silence his accomplice. He was in two minds whether to speak to the Keeper immediately about this latest discovery, but he could not see how to avoid the unpleasant revelation. It would soon come out anyway, and he saw no way to gain more capital from it. Nothing he could do would reduce the impact of the news.

All of a sudden he felt tired, worn out from his recent planning and manipulations, from his devious trade-offs in the attempt to win the favors of the stronger elements of the troop. The stage had been set ever since Hector had failed in his bid to win a position with the King, for once his attempt to get a new contract had been summarily dismissed, it was obvious to all the others that his leadership was questionable. His fighting ability was never doubted, but the main responsibility was to find contracts and money for his men, and he had fallen short of their expectations. They could now see that he was ill-considered by recruiters. He had turned his allegiances once too often. Now even a King desperate for aid would not employ Sir Hector and his men.

They had discussed this, the men of the band, when they had been told of his lack of success. Some had wanted to keep him on, thinking that he could lead them back to France and a new role, but others were so thoroughly disgruntled with his organization and his reputation for losing contracts that they wanted a change.

It had been this which had prompted Wat to move, to test the water with his colleagues to see whether he could tip the balance and make them all lose their trust in Hector, but this was not how he had intended things to go. From the first, he would have preferred to save his company from any association with murder in England. It would be different if this was France, where killings were sanctioned with the full authority and severity of the power his group could wield, but in England they must live within the law without upsetting too many people, and the spate of murders was impossible for even the most incompetent and corrupt of officials to ignore. In Wat's estimation, most officials were corrupt, but he was not sure if Baldwin was incompetent.

The Keeper's dark eyes were fixed on him, gazing intently with that little frown Wat had come to recognize as curiosity, and Wat did not enjoy having the man's attention for the second time that day. But he had little choice.

"Come with me." Leading the way to their table, Wat gave a curt jerk of his thumb over his shoulder. "This man has found something you should see."

"What?" Baldwin said, turning his face to the newcomer. This was another of the mercenaries, but not one he had spoken to as yet. The man named Will was short and very thickset, with a neck like a bull. His round face was pocked and scarred, and he wore a bristle over his jaw to show he shaved but rarely, but he was surprisingly well-spoken. He appeared to have hurt his right arm, for he had it supported in a simple sling, but Baldwin noticed he was stiff in his body too, and wondered whether he had been stabbed or wounded in some other way.

"Sir, I've found a body in the stable. A woman's body."

Baldwin and Simon stared, then leapt to their feet and pounded to the stable.

Simon was aware only of a kind of desperate yearning for the man to be wrong. He had seen too many deaths over the last week. Two dead women, both stabbed, both for little or no apparent reason, was as much as he felt he could cope with. For there to be yet another was incomprehensible.

As he entered, he slipped on the hard-packed earth of the stable floor, and nearly fell. The hay was stored on a raised floor, with the horses beneath in their stalls. To reach it they had to ascend a ladder. Simon waited while Baldwin, looking more tired than he had ever seen him, slowly went up after Wat and Will, and then Simon followed.

As he reached the top, there was a scurrying and skittering through the hay. Wat curled his lip. "Rats. They get everywhere."

The hay lay all about in an untidy mess, intermingled with the clothing and accoutrements of the mercenaries, for those who could find little space in the hall were accustomed to the comfort and warmth that the hay could offer.

"I was just getting my gear ready for cleaning," Will said in a choked voice; looking at him, Simon could see that he was as shocked as the bailiff himself. He stepped forward and pointed.

At first, all Simon could see was the paraphernalia of warfare. A short sword, a bundle of bolts for a crossbow, a stout leather cap and a chainmail habergeon lay in a bundle on top of a heavy blanket. Nearby was a cup lying on its side. The ale which it had contained had dribbled onto the hay, the beery smell intermingling with the wholesome scent of the dried fodder.

The cause of the man's shock was right there in front of them. The blanket, which looked as though it performed the function of bedding for him, had been lifted at one corner and thrown aside. Beneath it, a hole had been scraped in the hay, and some crimson cloth was visible.

"When I sat down, it felt lumpy and uncomfortable, so I dug around. Then I felt something, and wondered what it was," he explained. "I pulled at it, lifted the hay, and found . . . *that.*"

Baldwin knelt and gently eased the hay from the crimson dress. It lifted easily to reveal the body of a young woman. Her eyes were dim as they stared upward through a layer of dust from the hay. A thick coating of the same dust lay upon her, but when he touched the cloth, the tiny particles of grass and seed did not move, for in places the material was quite damp.

"I must have slept right next to her all night," the mercenary said, with a stricken wonder in his voice.

"More than one night," Baldwin remarked callously. "This woman has been dead some days."

Simon met the soldier's horrified gaze for a moment, and then the man was sick.

Paul brought their ale and stood with them as they stared down at the body. They had put her on the ladder and, using this as a stretcher, had carried her over to the hall. Baldwin had spent some time digging through the hay, but could find nothing else. There was no sign of who might have killed her.

"You are quite sure?"

The innkeeper threw Baldwin a testy glance. "She was my neighbor. Of course I'm sure! This is Mary Butcher, all right."

"I had to ask. When did you last see her?"

"Oh, Monday, I think. She was outside when Sir Hector left, and they walked off together."

Baldwin sighed and looked at Simon, "It seems fairly consistent."

Simon nodded as the landlord walked out. "With Sir Hector having killed her? Yes. Just like the others."

"The stab-wounds are the same as those which killed Judith. Two cuts in the back."

"They're the same as the ones that killed Sarra too. She had two wounds, didn't she?"

"Yes, but she was stabbed in the chest; from the front."

"That was because she was in the trunk."

"Yes. The killer could merely open the lid and thrust down," Baldwin commented, motioning with his fist, but then he stopped and stared down at the body again.

"Something wrong?"

"Hmm?" Baldwin shook his head. "No. I was just thinking: Judith and this woman were attacked from behind. I daresay the murderer put his hand over her mouth to stop her screams, and then . . ." His hands performed the actions as if rehearsing the sequence of events which led to her death. He let his hands drop and stared down at the body meditatively. "I wonder why that seems important to me?"

"What I don't understand," Simon said thoughtfully, "is who he was waiting for."

"What?" Baldwin shot him a keen glance.

"The day when we saw him with Judith. We thought

he was waiting for someone, and after today, I assumed it must be Mary; but she has been dead for some days."

"Yes. Certainly she has been dead some time," Baldwin mused. "Which does seem strange. Unless he was trying to establish an alibi—pretending to be waiting for her when he had killed her. Another thing, the rats were all over the loft, and yet there is hardly a mark on her."

Simon raised his eyebrows, then peered at her. "You're right. There's hardly a mark on her—only at her fingers and toes."

"I have never known rats to avoid fresh meat." Baldwin pondered. "I would have expected more damage."

"More to the point, though, is why on earth Sir Hector would have put her there at all."

"It is incredible."

"Incredible? Bizarre. The man has gone from hiding one corpse in a chest, leaving a second lying in an alley, and now he's deposited this one under a thin layer of hay where his own men were sleeping. It's bizarre, all right."

"Yes," Baldwin agreed, and turned his solemn eyes back to the woman before him. "She cannot have been there in the hay for long, though. Feel her dress—it is damp. She must have been moved to the stable some time after she died. Before that she was stored somewhere else."

"Why is she damp?" Simon asked as he gingerly touched the cloth.

"It was raining last night. Heavily. Surely it is not difficult to conclude that she had been secreted away somewhere else, and was then moved to her new hiding place last night during the storm." Even as the knight spoke his eyes were moving over her body, seeking any further hints as to how she came by her death. She would have been an attractive woman in life, he thought. Slim and well-formed, with large blue eyes and thick brown hair. Her wrists were tiny, and her ankles too, and she had a waist so slender he could have encompassed it with both hands. On her front there was no mark, but for the nibbles of the rats at her fingers and toes. Her back too showed little mark, but they could see where the cloth of her dress had been sliced by the blade which had killed her.

He sighed. It was incomprehensible that someone should snuff out the life of such a dainty young woman. Still more so that this should be merely the third in a sequence.

"Where else could she have been stored?"

"When we know that, Simon, we shall know who killed her, and why!"

"Do you think he will confess?" Simon ignored the other's brief display of irascibility, and dropped onto a seat. Leaning forward, he studied Mary Butcher.

"I see no reason why he should. Do we have any proof that he was the murderer? All we know is that he was seen with her before she died. It is a tenuous link to this corpse. By the same token, almost anyone could be accused of the murder."

"Maybe so, but surely we have to arrest him. What if it *was* him, and he goes on to kill others? He's killed three already; we can't take the risk he might kill a fourth."

"Can't you?"

Simon whirled round. Sir Hector had entered the hall from behind them, taking even Edgar by surprise. The soldier walked slowly and deliberately over to them, his hand resting on his sword, but not in a threatening way. He scarcely glanced at them, but went to the table on which Mary Butcher rested, standing by her and looking down at her with what Simon could only think was sadness.

"Poor Mary. Poor unhappy, dissatisfied Mary," he murmured, then faced Baldwin. "I did not do this. I could not have dreamed of hurting her. She was my love, the woman I wanted to take with me."

"She was having an affair with you." There was no need to ask it as a question; Baldwin stated it as a fact.

"We met years ago," the captain agreed. "I wanted her to join me then, but she wouldn't. She knew little about a mercenary's life, but Mary always enjoyed her comforts. She liked being able to get the choicest cloths, the finest skins and furs, and I would have given her plenty of these things, but she could have them here too, from her husband, without the risks of losing me through fighting, without her needing to travel constantly, without the fear of being hunted by enemies, without constantly wondering whether the allies of the day would turn on us tomorrow and become our foes."

"She would not go with you."

"No." It was said with blank finality.

"So why come back here?"

The captain turned his disconcerting gray eyes onto Baldwin. "Because I have thought about her every day for the last few years. Because I missed her, and wanted her, ever since I last saw her. Because I felt I had lost a part of me since I left her behind. I had to exorcise her from my soul, and I thought if I were to see her again, I might be cured."

"So that is why you came this way after being refused a contract with the King?"

"Yes. I thought I might have got over her, and even

took the servant-girl to divert me . . . But it was no good. A servant is no more than that, merely a servant. What I wanted was here, in Mary."

Baldwin nodded, inwardly wondering how a man could take one woman to try to forget another. And if he could, Baldwin reasoned, would it be so great a step to kill the one who could not match the expectation?

His visage must have betrayed his doubt. The mercenary curled his lip. "You think I would simply have murdered the tavern slut for not being Mary? She was nothing to me! I kill those who harm or threaten me, those who thwart or betray me—the wench did not deserve to die for not being the woman I desired. And I certainly could never have killed my poor Mary, whatever she had done. I loved her with all my heart."

"When did you last see her?"

"On Monday night. Her servants, and her husband's apprentice knew I was there, but they didn't care. They watched me enter her chamber, and they saw me leave in the morning. They all felt I was better for her than her husband."

Simon doubted that. Any number of servants could be relied on to keep their silence if talking might involve annoying a mercenary captain.

"You are sure that was the last time you saw her?" pressed Baldwin.

"Yes. I tried to many other times . . . You saw me on one occasion, in the town. I was waiting for her then, that was why I was so irritated by that other slut."

"Judith?" Baldwin asked.

"Was that her name? The beggar."

"Did you recall her?"

"Recall her?" Hector's face showed no emotion, but Simon saw that he had paled.

"Yes, Sir Hector: recall her. She was the woman you took when you last came to Crediton, wasn't she? Before you met Mary."

"I . . . I don't think so." He licked his suddenly dry lips.

"You had forgotten her? The woman whom you had enjoyed for a night or more, but whom you evicted from your side once you had met Mary for the first time."

"No. I . . . No."

"And then there is her son, of course. Born a little while later."

"No!" The captain's features had paled to wax-like translucency, and he picked at his lower lip as if in an attempt at memory.

"Was he your son?" Baldwin threw out the question swiftly and harshly.

"No, he can't have been." The anguish in the captain's voice was almost tangible.

"I wonder. In any case, Sir Hector, I think I have more than enough reason to suspect you for the murder of these women."

"Why would I have killed them? What reason could I have had?"

"The first because she stole, you thought, a new dress bought for your lover, the second because she shamed you in the street, telling you she had borne your son." Baldwin watched the captain narrowly as he guessed at this, and was satisfied to see the dart strike home. Sir Hector flinched. "And then Mary, I assume, because she refused to leave her home and her husband to run away with you."

"No, that's not it at all. It's all wrong, completely wrong."

"She wouldn't go with you, would she?"

"If that was all, I'd have killed *him*, not her! It had nothing to do with—"

"She wouldn't go away with you, so you decided to kill her instead. You decided that if you couldn't have her, nobody else would either. Even her husband."

"That's nonsense. Why should I do that? I couldn't have hurt her, not my Mary. I loved her."

"Yes," Baldwin said, resting himself against the table and crossing his arms. "But I have to wonder what that word means to you. You are a soldier, Sir Hector. You are used to taking what you want. You wanted Mary Butcher—and you took her. You had no thought for her husband, her reputation, or for anything else. You wanted her, so you had her."

"That's a lie!"

"Is it? Do you really understand what the truth is, I wonder? Your whole life is a series of thefts. You agree terms with a lord or baron, and then ravage a whole area. You take what you want—isn't that how your band survives? And then you come here and try to carry on the same way. A woman here, a woman there. Sarra, and Judith, and Mary. All of them were yours until you became bored with them. And then you killed them. All of them, all stabbed twice, all killed the same way."

"Even Mary?" His voice had fallen to an awed horror.

"Even Mary," Baldwin agreed mercilessly. "You killed them all, didn't you? Why did you do it?"

Simon watched as the two men confronted each other. Sir Baldwin seemed to grow in stature as he spoke. It was as if he was trying to convince himself that he did not truly believe his own words, that the concept of such hideous crimes was so awful that he could not credit anyone with the ability to commit them. His face was hard with a kind of desperate urgency, like a man who wanted to be proved wrong, but who was convinced nonetheless that his worst imaginings were shortly to be confirmed.

But while they spoke, Baldwin found himself becoming more sympathetic to the captain. It was not that the Keeper was gullible, or that he was prepared to condone the mercenary's life, but the man appeared to shrink even as Baldwin, alive with a new strength, invigorated with his disgust and revulsion at the crimes, railed at him.

To Simon, Sir Hector looked as if he was shrivelling in on himself, reducing to the scale of one of the hill farmers whom the bailiff saw every week; old beyond his years, worn and ravaged by cares and ill-health. Simon nodded. There was all too often no way to prove who might have committed a particular crime, but in this case he was convinced that he and his friend had caught the correct man, and it gave him a fierce pleasure to see the effect of Baldwin's words.

There was something in Sir Hector's haggard visage which made Baldwin study him hard as he spoke. Something about the man's manner made his voice soften a little. It was not the immediate sympathy which a man felt for another accused of heinous offences, for the Keeper had become hardened to seeing criminals suddenly realize the degree of their crimes as their doom approached. It had often occurred to Baldwin that nothing was better capable of assisting a poor memory and inducing contrition than a rope. But if his sensitivity had become blunted after years of prosecutions, his empathy remained, and with this captain, he was sure that there were signs of his pain.

That itself was no proof of innocence. Baldwin had known of cases where men had killed women they loved: from jealousy, from sudden rage, from any number of reasons. All had expressed their shame, and appeared honestly devastated by their actions. It was not rare. But as he mentioned the name of the latest victim, he was assailed by doubts. The captain stood, head bowed, shoulders sagging, and hands limp by his sides, the very picture of misery. This was not the arrogant warrior-lord, ready to quarrel with anyone, and to back up his argument with the point of his sword; this was a man who had lost everything he held dear. His life, his posture suggested, was at an end. There was nothing more for him.

Baldwin ground to a halt and viewed Sir Hector pensively, his head on one side. The captain made no gesture, spoke no word of denial, gave no statement of outraged innocence, and suddenly the knight was doubtful. His mind ran through the evidence, and he was forced to admit to himself that the only links which connected the captain to the dead women were tenuous.

"Sir Hector, you are free for now, but I demand that you do not leave this inn. I will speak to your men, and make sure that they do not abet you in an escape, but I see no reason to lock you in a cell. You may remain here."

The man nodded, and walked away, through to the solar, and Baldwin's keen stare followed him until the door had shut. "Edgar. Fetch me Wat, and the man Will who found this woman today."

- 22 -

at walked in with a rolling swagger that put Simon in mind of the sailors he had seen in Plymouth and Exeter. The old mercenary wore a grave expression, but Simon was convinced that a grin of sheer exultation was battling for dominance, and it was no great surprise. He had wanted the leadership of the company, and his master had allowed it to slip from his grasp and fall into Wat's lap almost unnoticed. It made Simon glower with disapproval, to see a man so pleased by the results of three deaths.

"Wat," Baldwin said, once the man had entered and Edgar had closed the door behind him, "we are holding your captain here. I place him under your control. Do not you, or any of the other men in the group, try to leave Crediton, or let Sir Hector go. He is your responsibility, and you will answer for it if he escapes. Is that clear?"

"Absolutely clear."

"Now you," Baldwin said, and turned to the man called Will, who glared back truculently. "How did you notice the body there today?"

"I told you. I sat down and it felt hard and nobbly, so I tried to see what I was sitting on."

"And you uncovered her tunic?"

"Yes."

Baldwin nodded as if to himself. "And that was right where you have been sleeping for how long?"

Swallowing, Will was a little gray-faced as he responded, "All the time we've been staying here."

"So you think you have been sleeping on top of her every night?"

He nodded, aware of the nausea returning.

"I think you did not. If she had been there, you would have felt her," Baldwin sighed. "It seems to me that someone must have hidden her there only recently. Last night, in fact."

"Eh?" sputtered Wat with a start. "What do you mean? No one's going to dump a body like that—it's asking to be found out. No one would commit murder and then make sure their crime's found out!"

"Did you leave your bed last night?" Baldwin asked.

The man shot a look at Wat, then gave a shrug. "Yes. I was there until the storm, but then I got up . . . just as the rain started."

"When did you return?"

"I didn't. I . . . hurt myself, and a couple of the men took me into the hall."

Baldwin nodded, his eyes going to the wound, and Will reddened.

"This is mad!" Wat burst out.

"Some would say that any man who decides to kill must be mad," Baldwin said evenly. He had the impression that the mercenary was trying to distract him from his study of the wounded man. "Even if it was for money."

Wat made a gesture of rejection. "That's got nothing to do with it. Why should Sir Hector dump the body there? He'd know it'd be found. And when it was, the trail would lead right to him."

"Perhaps Sir Hector did not put her there."

"Then who did?"

"That is what we must discover. She was not there at dark last night, I assume, for she was not noticed. If a man could feel her when he sat on her, she would surely have been felt by someone lying on top of her. Her dress is wet in places, too, which tends to show she was being carried around last night."

Simon stood and paced the room, then stopped and faced Baldwin again. "There are only two explanations why someone should have put her there. One is because another hiding place was unsatisfactory; the other because, as you say, the body was *intended* to be discovered."

"Yes. I can see no other reason."

"But the first is inconceivable."

"Why?" demanded Wat hotly.

Simon threw him a contemptuous look. "Why? Think, man! If you were to kill someone, would you leave the body in an accessible place?" The mercenary was silent, and Simon suddenly realized that he might well have been in such a situation in his past. "Er—anyway, if somebody murders, they try to hide the corpse far from prying eyes. The last thing they'd do is keep a body in town. They move it out into the country, if they have the chance, and dump it in some quiet spot. Oh, the run-of-the-mill killings, the arguments over ale or gambling, get finished and resolved quickly; two men fight and there's one dead afterward, and the killer is soon found, but in a case like this, where there would seem to be some kind of plan being followed, to judge by the fact that three are dead, the thought uppermost in the killer's mind is how to cover his tracks, and that means concealing the death. If a corpse cannot be found, no man can be prosecuted."

At this, Will gave a puzzled frown. "You think Sir Hector killed her, then moved her to my bed in the hay? He can't have, he was in his rooms all night."

Baldwin stared at the confused mercenary, then at Wat, who was grimly studying the floor. "Is that true?"

"I had someone outside his door all night," Wat admitted ungraciously, mentally cursing Will. He had no wish for Baldwin to hear about the attempted assassination. "It seemed a good idea after I heard about Judith being found. If he had tried to collect this woman and hide her, he'd have been seen."

"Ah," said Baldwin quietly, and Simon wandered to a seat and dropped into it, gazing up at Wat.

"That, Wat, was rather what I expected," he said. "Unless we can prove that Sir Hector had an accomplice, I think we might be forced to assume he is innocent."

Wat stared from one to the other, mouth open in astonishment. "You're both mad!"

Simon rested his chin on his fists. "No," he said tiredly. "But I think someone is."

He was suddenly exhausted. The day had begun so hopefully, with their questioning of the woman in the alley, and then had taken a positive turn when they discovered the identity of Sir Hector's lover . . . but now their hopes had been dashed. That was the bewildering thing about these killings; as soon as they felt they were getting close to seeing a pattern and could put their hands on the killer, something else happened to throw them off. The robbery had at first appeared to be a simple affair, and then they had found Sarra; Judith's murder had apparently placed suspicion firmly on Sir Hector's shoulders; finding Mary under the hay had initially appeared to confirm the guilt of the captain.

The door banged as Wat and his companion left. The older mercenary strode out angrily, probably, Simon thought, because he could see his independent command being stolen from him even as he tried to grasp it.

"Could it have been him?" he wondered.

"Who? Wat? Possibly. He wants his master ousted hard enough, that is for certain," Baldwin said, stretching and groaning before slumping back in his seat. "His whole ambition is tied up with getting himself the leadership of his group."

"It's strange how everything seems to point to Sir Hector. Wat could have killed the woman, then tried to make it look as if his master was guilty, so that he could take on the captainship."

"Yes. But there are so many others in the band—did one of them do it?"

"Wat was Sir Hector's servant when Sarra was killed. He might have given her the dress and stabbed her, hiding her in the chest to make it look as if his master was responsible."

"It is possible, but I find it hard to believe. Wat could have told her to wear the tunic, and made sure that Sir Hector saw her in it, relying on his master's anger to cause her death, but I doubt that he himself killed her and hid her. Why should he take the risk? And the second woman, Judith. How could Wat have known about her? I suppose Sir Hector might have mentioned seeing her that day, but it seems unlikely. Sir Hector never struck me as being the sort to require a *confidant*, and in the mood he was in that day, I doubt whether he would have wanted to more than bark at his men for looking sloppy after being, as he saw it, stood up by Mary for some hours."

"If what he said about her being supposed to meet him there is true . . . I must confess, I believed him when he said that."

"Yes, so did I."

"Was she avoiding him, do you think? Sir Hector might have made himself so much of a pest to Mary Butcher that she kept away from him. That in itself could have angered him so much that when he *did* get her alone, he did away with her."

Baldwin eyed the body on the table before them. "It is possible," he agreed. "But anyone can see that he is sorely affected by her death."

"True. I thought the same. His pain was all too apparent."

Slamming a fist into the palm of his hand, Baldwin stood irritably. "This is ridiculous! Three women are dead, a serious robbery has been committed, and yet we are nowhere near resolving any of it."

They made their way from the room, leaving instructions that the body should be kept until the priest could arrange for its collection, and paused outside, staring toward the butcher's shop. Baldwin frowned. "We should see if Adam is back yet. It would be best that one of us speaks to him before he hears of his wife's murder from another."

Simon agreed. They walked to the shop, but the apprentice, who was preparing hams now, said that his master still had not returned. Baldwin asked him to make absolutely sure that the butcher went to Peter Clifford's house the minute he got back, then they fetched their horses and carried on to Peter's.

* * *

He rubbed vigorously at his temples. It was incomprehensible. They had found her, but he was still free. Surely they could see that he must be the guilty one? Who else had any kind of an attachment to all three of them? The Keeper and his friend must be blind or incompetent.

Then his eyes cleared, and the fog in his brain began to dissipate as he realized at last what it must mean. Slowly, he raised his head and stared at the wall opposite. *They had been bribed.*

It was all too common. All over the country, men involved in the legal system were taking money to line their own pockets; sheriffs, bailiffs and reeves were regularly purged in order to control their worst excesses. For a fee, the right witnesses could be found to bolster any dispute, and if the price was high enough, an entire jury could be guaranteed to provide the right result.

That must be it, he thought, and his eyes glittered with righteous fury. To be denied justice was an insult—and after so much planning, too. His lips set into an indignant sneer. And it was all because the Keeper was corrupt.

But the Keeper had a reputation for honesty, he knew, and a puzzled frown overtook his petulance. All in the town spoke of his determination to seek justice for plaintiffs, and if he were so corrupt, surely he would have given himself away before now? The Keeper was involved with almost every important case, and yet there were no slanders about his character or fairness. He was always considered reasonable and wise, finding the common ground and resolving issues often before any lawyers could get involved. Why should he suddenly have become dishonest?

Then he drew in his breath with the realization of who must have betrayed him. The Keeper was fair and honest, a kindly man known for fair dealing, but perhaps he was too gullible. A devious and unscrupulous man might be able to pull the wool over his eyes with great ease, especially a man who was used to manipulating the system and other people. A man who was himself involved in the law, who knew how to alter the facts, or, at least, could change how those facts were perceived, could easily make the Keeper confused enough to leave free the wrong man.

His face was white now as he saw his error. It was not the Keeper who was his enemy: it was the Keeper's friend—the bailiff of Lydford Castle.

Quickly now, he ran through how Simon Puttock must have deliberately misinformed the Keeper. First he must have taken money from the captain, for no one deliberately changed the outcome of a trial for nothing. Sir Hector must have bribed him, then, and the bailiff accepted the money to protect the mercenary. From then on, he would have prompted people to change their evidence, making them think they were helping justice as they tried to please him, lying . . . no, not necessarily lying. Some of them probably thought the bailiff was right and they had been mistaken. It was so easy for an uneducated man to be confused with legal prattle.

No doubt some had been bribed to lie. That Wat was untrustworthy; he had always thought so. The mercenary looked like a friendly old man, until you stared hard into his eyes, and then you could see how the resentment flickered and burned. Of course, the man was safe from most, but not from someone who understood how dark the soul could be; not from someone who had learned how evil even those whom one had trusted completely might become. For nobody could be trusted; only oneself and one's dagger were certain.

But what could he do about it? His eyes were haunted as he considered his awful predicament. Clearly the main obstacle to justice was the bailiff. Simon Puttock must be forced to admit his complicity with the captain, or suffer.

Then his mind, with a wonderful clarity of insight, focused on how he might force the duplicitous bailiff to confess his guilt.

And he smiled.

Peter Clifford watched as the two men were helped from their horses. Bound at the wrists, they were uncomfortable and peevish, but though both sulked, neither attempted to deny their guilt. The packmule loaded with its three heavy sacks told its own tale.

Sighing, Peter went back inside to wait. Baldwin and Simon had arrived a little earlier, and the bailiff was out in the garden with his wife and daughter, while Baldwin was ensconced in a large throne-like chair, his fingers steepled together, head bowed as if in prayer.

Hearing the priest enter, he glanced up. "They're here?"

"Yes." Peter crossed the room to another seat. He had just settled himself when Stapledon's men entered with their prisoners. Others trailed along behind and dumped their sacks with a merry clanking that sounded like hundreds of horseshoes clattering on the rush-covered stone floor.

Baldwin studied the two men for a moment, then gestured at the sacks. "Do you deny the theft now?"

Henry looked up sulkily. His eye was blackened,

and his hair was matted over his forehead where he had been struck with a cudgel when he tried to make a run for it. He met the Keeper's gaze with as much dignity as he could muster. "Look at us, sir. We've been beaten, bound, and hauled back here against our will, and—"

"Silence! Don't think you can brazen this out. You were caught with the stolen goods on you, trying to sell them for the best possible price. I am sorely tempted to throw you to your captain for him to mete out justice, for I think he would be keen to exact his own price on you for your disloyalty. Tell me now, what happened on the day you stole all this plate."

It was at this point that Simon entered. He walked in with Hugh, and they moved quietly along the wall to seat themselves at a bench a little way behind Baldwin.

Simon was surprised at the anger in his friend's voice. He had often seen Baldwin interrogating people, but never had he witnessed the knight in such a state of complete cold fury. From where he sat he could not see Baldwin's face, but the chilling tones obviously reflected his temper perfectly.

It was rare for Baldwin to feel like this, and he was himself a little shocked by his mood, but to his way of thinking, the robbery had sparked off the series of murders. He had an urge to blunt his bitter rage at so many pointless killings on the two men who had begun the chain of events.

"Sir, all we have done was take some things from our captain because he owed us money."

"You robbed a man of his own possessions. And killed a girl, an innocent little girl who had done you no harm—"

"That's a lie!" John Smithson declared hotly. "We never hurt her. She was just—"

"Shut up, you idiot! Do you want to wear a hemp necklace?" Henry snarled.

"*You* shut up. I won't swing for what Hector's done!"

"Tell us what happened, I am sick to death of the lies and innuendos I have been given by you two and the others in the gang. There have been three deaths now, and I want to know what's been going on."

"*Three* deaths?" Henry repeated. He was quieter now, his eyes wide with horror. "But we've had nothing to do with them." Then, a little bolder, "They must have been after we left. You can't say we did them."

"I can say a lot," Baldwin said pointedly. "I can say that one happened during your robbery, another on the night you left town. We don't know when the third murder took place, but it was quite likely while you were still here."

"Who? Who were they?"

"Sarra you know of. The night you left, a poor beggar woman called Judith was murdered in an alleyway, and today we have found the body of Mary Butcher."

"Why would we kill a load of women we knew nothing about?"

"You knew Sarra," Simon interjected. "You tried to rape her the night you all got here."

"That wasn't rape! We thought she was just a tavern-wench; we never thought she'd be worried. Anyway, we left her alone when Hector told us to."

"But you wanted her, didn't you?" Baldwin continued. "And you killed her later—from jealousy, maybe, or perhaps just because she was there and saw you stealing the plate."

Smithson shot a look at his confederate. "No," he said wearily. "That's not how it was."

His quiet tones were in contrast to Henry's outraged protestations, and Simon breathed a little easier. While Baldwin had been examining the men, Simon had been unsure as to how the two would react, but John Smithson's change of temper heralded a change in the wind for the pair.

"That's not how it was at all," he said again, his head downcast. "We had nothing to do with the killing. It was like this. We were here five or so years ago, staying in the same inn for a while. Me and Henry met Adam then, and we all got on. He was a bully man, keen on a joke and having fun, and had a good stock of comic tales. It was fine to sit up with a jug of strong ale with him of an evening. Of course, then he had been apprentice to his old master, who still has his shop in the shambles with the other butchers. Adam managed to get his new place three or four years ago."

"Do you know how he managed to afford it?" Simon interjected.

"No, sir. But I could guess. Adam was never one to quail from risks if the money was good. He was always prepared to take a gamble if he could see profit, and I expect he won the money."

"Or fooled someone into giving it to him," Baldwin guessed.

"Maybe, sir. Anyway, Henry and me have been with Sir Hector for many years now. Earlier on it was fine, with good profits and the chance to rule ourselves as we liked, but things have been getting slack recently. Sir Hector's become too easygoing. He used to be a strong man, able to bend anyone to his will, but times have changed. For the past year we've not won a single contract, and the money's been hard to come by. It was late last year that we decided there was nothing worth doing in Gascony. We'd heard there were good sums to be gained out in Morocco, fighting with the Moors to protect their lands from their Eastern neighbors, but Sir Hector was against the idea, and others backed him up. So we set off to return to England.

"The grumbling began almost as soon as we landed at London. The prices there are insane! It's a wonder that anyone can afford to live there, the way that the citizens have tied everyone into their guilds and clubs. Anyway, it wasn't long before we heard about the war in the north, and the King's new army, so we set off to join him.

"But even the King turned us down. For experience, for training, for determination, he could not ask for better troops, but Edward did not want us."

"Perhaps," Baldwin remarked, "he had heard tell that you had changed sides before."

John stared with open astonishment. "But anyone would do that when his side begins to lose! It's only common sense."

Baldwin said nothing, eyeing him grimly, and the man continued defensively: "When Edward's commissioners rejected us, the complaints became near to outright rebellion. Some of the lads were suggesting that the captain should be chucked. It was his responsibility to keep the men together, his job to find us new contracts, for there is no point to our way of life if we have no one who wants us, no one to pay for us. We might just as well be villeins in another's army. And the trouble was, we were always seen to be loyal men of Sir Hector's. None of the others trusted us because they thought we were with him.

"It came to a head some miles from Winchester, on our way back to the coast. We approached Wat to join his side. The last thing we wanted was to be killed for being too loyal to Sir Hector. But he refused to listen—denied any scheme to oust Sir Hector. So it was obvious we no longer had any safety in the company. We thought we'd better run—and the silver would make life easier for us.

"When we got back here, and met with Adam again, the idea of getting away seemed like the best one for us. If we stayed, we would get killed; if we left, we could find another company or do something else. Try farming, make a new assart: anything.

"We saw Adam on the way into town, and later that afternoon, he came to us at the inn and suggested we should meet the next night, when all the men would be a bit quieter. We couldn't see him that night, because Sir Hector was set for a good banquet. As you know, our captain went out next morning, told us later he'd met with his woman again—"

"Mary Butcher," Baldwin observed.

"Yes, sir. Like you say, Mary, Adam Butcher's wife. We were horrified."

"And you told Adam?"

"God's blood, no!" The exclamation was too emphatic to be false. "Don't you know what his temper is like? If we'd done that, Adam would have been in there straight away with a cleaver. No, we didn't mention her at all."

"But I suppose your master was pleased to hear you would be drinking with his lover's husband?"

John bit his lip sheepishly. "He asked us to take Adam away for a bit, said we'd be well rewarded if Adam could be made to have an accident, but we refused."

Henry butted in. "We wouldn't just kill a man for another's passion."

"No, I daresay you wouldn't," said Baldwin pensively. "Not when you could see a way to winning all Sir Hector's money without risking a rope."

"We never risked the rope," Henry declared with passion. "Look, we went out with Adam, and we talked, but he refused to consider it at first. We rode to the old inn toward Sandford, and spent most of the night there, chatting about things, and we raised the idea of taking Sir Hector's plate, but Adam wouldn't hear of it. He left us, to return home early in the morning, but changed his mind, and came to meet us, and then we agreed what—"

"He changed his mind?" Baldwin interrupted.

"Yes, sir. He left the inn before us to make his way into town. By the time we were up at the cross on the Barnstaple road, he came haring back. He said he'd been thinking, and that he'd be mad not to accept. It was rare enough that a chance to get hold of so much money came along, and he couldn't throw over the opportunity."

"I see. Continue."

"It was easy," said John. "Sir Hector was out first thing, and came back in the afternoon, leaving again later on. Our only fear was Wat, because he might have enjoyed seeing us flogged, but Sir Hector had told him to collect the new dress for him. We knew we had plenty of time without interruptions—all we had to do was make sure we were out before Wat came in to fetch the salt for Hector's meal—so we went to the captain's rooms, pretending to want to see him. We knew he wasn't there, but it gave us time to open the shutters to the yard. Then we left; and I kept a lookout while Henry climbed in through the window. He closed the shutters, and I walked out to the front. He started passing things to me there."

Henry spoke up sulkily. "John was pretending to be helping Adam. The butcher had sent his apprentice inside to see to the meats there. I passed the things out to John, and he shoved them all into a sack in the back of Adam's wagon. Adam kept a lookout on the main street and up the hill beside, and John could see up the other way."

"Why go through the charade of entering to open the shutter, leaving again, and climbing in from the yard? You were inside already, so what was the point?" Simon asked.

Henry threw him an astonished glance. "We went in to see him—we were pretending we thought he was there. How long would it have been before one of the others came in to find out what we were doing if we'd stayed there longer? No, we went in to unlock the shutters, and then we knew we could get in through the yard and spend as long inside as we liked."

"Weren't the men in the hall suspicious?" Baldwin asked.

"Well, we don't speak to them too much. No, they said nothing. Someone sniggered when we came out, sort of thought it was funny we'd been searching for the captain. Later, when the silver was all out, we did the same again. John came round to the back and tapped on the frame when it was all quiet, and I got out. Then we went back pretending to see if Sir Hector had returned yet, and locked the shutters again."

"Didn't you fear someone walking along the street and seeing you during this exercise?"

John Smithson smiled slyly. "We'd thought about that. Adam had gutted some calves that morning and left their innards like ropes all over the pavement. Nobody came close, not with the smell of that lot fester-ing in the sun for five hours—even the horses went on the other side of the street."

"So you cleared out all the plate?"

"Yes, and then Adam took the wagon round to his shed and stored the silver in his hayloft. At the same time Henry climbed out and we went back inside to shut the window again."

"The girl," Simon muttered. "What about the girl?"

John looked at Henry, who was pale now, with a light sheen of sweat over his features. "I swear," he said, and his voice was a croak, "I never killed her."

"But you knocked her out? And stuffed her into the chest?" Simon said, rising and standing beside Baldwin. "Why?"

"When I climbed inside, through the window, it was empty. Later, I heard her approaching the room. She was calling out, happy. I just had time to nip behind the door, and when she came in I clouted her with my cudgel. She went down like a squirrel shot by a slingshot from a tree. John was at the window by then; I don't know whether she saw him before she fell. I just trussed her up and dumped her inside the nearest chest. That's all, and I'll take my oath on the Bible for it."

"You may have to," Baldwin said quietly. "And that in front of a Bishop."

Henry squared his shoulders. "It's the truth."

Glancing at John, Simon saw him purse his lips. "What about you, John?"

"Me?"

"Somebody returned to the body and stabbed Sarra twice. When the lid lifted, she must have thought it was someone coming to free her but, instead, she saw that person thrust down with a knife. She couldn't even scream, with her mouth gagged. Was it you?"

"I said: I was outside."

"Yes, but Henry has just pointed out that you were at the window when she came in; she might have seen you."

"I don't think so. I—"

"Were you prepared to take the risk? If she *had* seen you, she could tell her master what you had done, couldn't she? You couldn't afford to leave her alive. She was a witness to your theft."

John stared at Henry. "Was I there on my own for any moment?" he demanded.

"No." The other's voice allowed no doubt. "Neither of us were. We were together all the time we were in there."

"How so? What about when you, Henry, were inside, and John was out? When you had finished passing the plate out and went to the back of the inn, it would have been easy for John to slip inside and murder the girl, wouldn't it?"

"He couldn't have, sir," Henry stated. "I thought he had at first, but he couldn't. When I left that room, I barred the shutters. The only way in was through the window of the back room or the door. No one could have got in from the front."

Baldwin stirred. "You realize the difficulty," he remarked. "You confess to striking the girl, and to putting her into the chest, and then expect us to believe you when you say you had nothing to do with her death. Nobody else knew she was there."

"One man did," Henry muttered, and Baldwin groaned as he realized.

"Of course!"

"He was there when I told John about the girl, and he was here in the town after we'd left. I don't know why you reckon the other girls got killed, but I'd be willing to bet it was him as killed them all."

Simon met Baldwin's gaze with a perplexed frown. "The butcher—Adam?"

"He was the only one," Baldwin said slowly. He wondered why he had not seriously considered the man before.

"But why should *he* kill them all, though?"

"Because he knew that each of these women had a link to Hector. Every one of them was associated with him in some way—the serving-girl Sarra, Judith because she had been a serving-girl years before, and Mary because she had been his lover. Perhaps he killed her because of jealousy, for no other reason. She had been dead some days. I think he murdered her as soon as he could after finding out about her infidelity. He heard about Sarra from Henry, so he stabbed her—"

"Sir, he couldn't have," Henry said.

"Why not?"

"Because he wouldn't have been able to get into the solar. We could do it only because we were known. A stranger like him would have been stopped at the hall."

"Sarra got in," Simon said. "And obviously didn't leave. The guards didn't stop her, or look for her when she didn't come out."

"That's different! They all knew she had been sleeping with Sir Hector. They would have assumed she was waiting for him inside. Adam would never have got in."

"I think you miss a point here," Baldwin said languidly, sipping from a goblet of watered wine. "You departed by the window, then went back inside to lock it, to make it look as if no one could have got in that way, yes? You had told Adam about the girl already.

Right, then. I think he saw a wonderful opportunity. You told him, and went to go inside: through the hall to the solar. Meanwhile, he clambered in through the window to the yard, threw open the lid, stabbed her, dropped the lid, and was out again, before you had gone through the hall."

"He could have, Henry," Smithson said in awestruck tones.

"It meets the facts as we know them," Baldwin asserted. "Except there is still one thing. The man whom you intended to be captured . . . What happened to Cole?"

All at once Smithson's eyes shifted nervously, while Henry sighed. When he spoke, it was with a kind of sullen defeat, as if he accepted at last that he was convicted and might as well confess all in the hope of leniency.

"It was me. He'd been asking about us all day, trying to make out we'd killed his brother. We hadn't, for we were nowhere near him on the day he died. We were on the flanks, while he was with Sir Hector in the center of the troop. But Cole was wary of us, and it seemed to me to be a good thing if we could get rid of him. I waited till he was out alone in the yard, and then kicked over some harness in the stable. He came up quick enough, and as soon as he was inside, I threw some horseshoes over to the other side of the door. When he turned to the noise, I clobbered him. I dragged him over to the back, and then had the idea of putting the blame on him. Nobody in the company would miss him, for he was new to us, so people could be suspicious of him. I tied him, and left him at the back of the stable. Adam brought his cart round, and we hid Cole between two calves' carcasses, took him out to the south, and left him tied to a tree. Later, me and John walked there. John had fetched a couple of items from our hoard to leave on him, and then we waited. He didn't wake while we were there."

Baldwin rested his chin on his fist as he looked from one to the other. "I see. Your openness does you some credit, I suppose. At least after this, we now know that Cole can be freed."

"Yes, and Adam Butcher should be taken at once," Simon agreed.

"Be careful," Henry said. "He always was a hard man but now, since he's learned of what his wife got up to, I think he's more than a little bit mad."

"Come, Simon," Baldwin said, getting up. "Let us visit the butcher and see what he has to say for himself."

Hugh and Edgar in tow, they made their way to the door, while Stapledon's men remained with the two prisoners. Baldwin was about to go out through the front when he heard the scream.

- 23 -

argaret had not felt so happy for weeks. Simon appeared to be getting over the shock of poor Peterkin's death, and the return to Crediton after so many months up in the bleak countryside of the moors seemed to have done him good. She preferred not to consider how much of his returned color was due to the excitement of having another murder, or series of deaths, to investigate. It was more comforting to ignore that side of his nature, even though she was fully aware how much he enjoyed being involved in such enquiries. He was almost another man when there was a serious affair to be tried and justice to be sought.

There was no doubt in her mind: he was improved. It was there in the way he smiled at her again—he had stopped doing that after Peterkin's death. In some way she knew that a part of this was due to the boy.

Rollo and Edith were playing together, their heads so close that they looked like a single creature. Every so often the boy threw a glance over his shoulder to make sure that Roger had not left him. Sitting on a low log which had been cut from an oak and was waiting to be separated into pieces for the fire, they looked like two small, and grubby, angels. The sun shone through their hair, making it flame into reddish halos with iridescent fringes; all they lacked was wings.

The poor boy, she thought, had little chance in life. Orphans like him were all too often without hope, relying on the charity of the parish for survival. Even the most basic requirements for life were often refused to a lad with no family. Others reasoned, with cause, that the cost of an extra mouth represented in food was not worth the possible reward later. Those who could afford to look after such a waif preferred to give their money to institutions for the general good rather than dissipating their efforts in looking after a single person who was likely, in any case, to die. What was the point of seeing to the worldly needs of a single child, when the same money could go to a church or abbey where the monks would be able to say prayers which would protect the souls of hundreds or thousands?

She mulled over this dilemma as she watched them constructing daisy chains, Edith giggling to herself while the boy seriously threaded one stalk through the next. Children should be protected and looked after, like any precious goods, but their value was regularly ignored. When a villein's family suffered a lack of food, it was all too often the children who must do without, for their father needed the sustenance to be able to work his land and produce food for the future. Sometimes mothers would starve themselves in an effort to keep their children alive, but this was frowned upon. If the children could not survive, such was God's will, whereas the mother should keep herself fit to look after the others and in order to be able to produce more. There was no sense in her killing herself to look after those who were unproductive.

Margaret knew it was sensible, but she did not like it. It would be impossible for her to watch her Edith die for want of food, for the young life possessed by her daughter was more precious to her than her own. The view that only adult life mattered because it was productive was incomprehensible to her.

Yet she did not want to have this extra little life attached to hers. It was difficult enough knowing that she had failed her husband by not producing the heir he needed so desperately to take the family forward, without accepting defeat by inviting a cuckoo into her nest. She knew of many families who were apparently plagued, like them, with an incapacity to breed their own boys. They were able to produce strong herds of cattle and flocks of sheep, their dogs and cats multiplied easily, and yet all too often there was this fundamental weakness: no sons to carry on the family name.

Rollo was a likable boy, and Edith thought he was the perfect playmate, but Margaret could not take him into her family. She would always be expecting him to meet her own exacting standards, and if he failed, she might lose her temper and remind him he was motherless. In any event, if she were later, as she hoped and prayed, to be able to conceive and bear a son for Simon, he must feel deserted again. The cuckoo would be supplanted.

"May I join you?"

"Of course," she smiled, and patted the bench beside her. Stapledon dropped gratefully on to the log, and studied the children with interest.

"They appear to get on very well together," he mused.

"Yes. It is nice for Edith to have a child of her own age to play with. I think she was bored before."

"How is he?"

"He obviously isn't over it, I would hardly expect him to be, but he seems calm enough so long as someone is with him. It's when he's alone that the fear comes to him again."

"Yes." Stapledon gave a grimace. "One shudders to think of what he saw. It would be enough to break the mind of many."

"He's young; youth often helps. There is a resilience in children which we adults often lack," she said indulgently.

"Perhaps. But I cannot help but wonder what may become of him."

In the pit of her stomach she felt the trembling nervousness. She dared not look at him, fearing that her eyes would give away her innermost thoughts. "Er . . . No, neither can I," she said.

"It would be best for him to be looked after in a family, I suppose."

"Yes—ideally, anyway."

"But the right sort of family . . . It is hard to find parents who would be suitable."

"Very hard."

"Not, of course, that there aren't many very deserving people in this town. Very deserving, indeed . . . But so much more could be made of him."

"Er . . ."

"And then there's the financial aspect. Few in Crediton could afford an extra mouth, one would imagine."

Margaret nodded glumly, steeling herself to reject the suggestion.

"So tell me, Margaret. What do you think of this for an idea?" Stapledon turned to face her, his brow wrinkled in thought.

And then the cudgel struck him and he crumpled at her feet.

Baldwin's hand was already tugging his sword from its scabbard even as the shriek shivered and died on the late afternoon air. His eyes went to Simon. The bailiff shoved him aside as he began to run for the garden. "That was Margaret!"

He and Hugh rushed out into the garden. Simon felt his heart pounding as his sword came free of its sheath with a slithering of steel. His wife needed him, and he would not fail her. Not this second time. For weeks he had avoided her when she needed him; he had tried to escape his own sadness by excluding her and thus preventing her from reminding him of his loss. The shame of his behavior, freezing out the woman who depended on him alone for her life, when all she wanted was to give him her support and offer her comfort to him, burned in his veins like molten lead.

There was another sharp cry of fear, then a keening wail of absolute, chilling terror, and Simon felt his scalp contract in reaction. He gripped the hilt of his weapon and led the way down the short staircase to the herb garden, past the trellis up which the roses climbed, and through to the lawn overlooking the meadow.

Here they found the children. Stapledon lay sprawled beside the oaken log, and Baldwin ran to his side. He looked up at Simon, relief plain on his face. The Bishop was alive.

Simon went to Edith. She stood, shocked, staring at her playmate, and was pleased to be able to plunge her face in her father's tunic to hide from the piteous child.

Rollo stood, eyes wide, mouth gaping, as scream

after scream issued from his frail little body. He was incapable of speech, unconscious of the others all round. His whole being was one long, solitary screech of loss and despair. First the man had killed his mother, and now the kind lady who had looked after him had been taken away as well. Roger stood nearby, wringing his hands, unsure how to calm the child.

Passing his daughter to Hugh, Simon went to the little boy, holding him tightly in his arms, trying to control the crying with the strength of his own body, as if he could pass on a little of his own self-restraint by doing so. Gradually the sobs faded until, shaking and groaning with his misery, eyes streaming with tears, the little boy allowed himself to be taken by the rector.

But Simon did not feel his anguish dissipate. His wife had been here, and now she was gone. Stapledon, who was moaning to himself as he tried to sit upright, had been knocked down with as little compunction as Simon would expect in a man swatting a fly, and not treated with the respect accorded to a man of God.

"Roger, what in God's name has happened?"

"Bailiff, I—"

"Where's Margaret? She was here, wasn't she? Where's she gone?"

"Bailiff, it was the butcher, Adam. He struck the Bishop, then took your wife—"

"Where, man! Where did he go?"

A hand shot out, pointing the way. "There, toward the church. I saw him take her that way. To the church."

"Daddy!"

He heard the terror in his daughter's voice. "Come here, Edith. It's all right."

She rushed into his arms and he held her close for a moment, but then he lowered her to the ground. "You stay here, my love, you understand? I'll go and get Mummy. We'll come back here."

Simon set off at a run. He was unaware of the others, of the way that Hugh thrust Edith into the arms of the dumbfounded Peter Clifford before chasing after him, or how Baldwin made haste to follow; he was only aware that Margaret was in mortal danger, in the clutches of a murderer who appeared able to kill without compunction and for no reason. Simon was determined to save her.

Up the garden he pelted, then into Peter's hall and along the screens, his boots slapping hard on the flags. If Adam was heading for the church, this was the quickest way there. Out into the yard he ran, scaring a horse and making it rear so that the ostler cursed as he tried to bring it back under control. He skidded over the cobbles of the outer yard, and across the grass of the old graveyard, toward the scaffolding which encompassed the new building like a haphazard fence.

Vaguely he was aware of figures running behind him, but his concentration was fixed on the red stone edifice in front. He pounded over the turves and rubbish of the works, until a pair of figures up at the top caught his attention, and he stopped dead.

One he recognized immediately. With her golden hair, strawberry-tinted in the late sun, streaming behind her, her cap dangling from a string, Margaret was carefully ascending one of the topmost ladders. Behind her, as nimble on the slender planks, as sure-footed as a cat, a long dagger in one hand, was the butcher.

This would make them regret their corruption. They would know from now on that if there was one man they could not cheat, that man was him. He would make them realize that they could not avoid their duties. They would have to arrest the captain of mercenaries. He was obviously guilty. Adam had made sure that the evidence pointed to him, and they could not possibly have missed the proofs.

At the top of the highest ladder he halted, breathing deeply. It was strange that he felt so little fear. Usually he would be nervous standing on top of a small stool, but today he was up here, on top of a tall scaffold, with a view over the whole of the county, as far as he could tell. To the west were the hills rolling toward Barnstaple and the sea, while eastward the road disappeared on the way to Exeter.

He sighed with contentment. This was wonderful: marvellous! He felt superhuman, capable of anything. The dagger was as light as purest down in his hand, his feet were assured on the narrow boards which the builders used as flooring, and his mind was perfectly clear. He was rational and more aware of himself than ever before.

A workman sauntered round the scaffolding from the other side and stopped, open-mouthed, at seeing the two. "What are you doing here?" he demanded, but then he saw the knife. Snapping his mouth shut, he turned and fled.

Smiling at his captive, Adam tied her hands tightly, then motioned vaguely with the knife toward the men below. "Do you know who they are?" he enquired. "They know who I am, but I have only met a couple of them before now. Curious, how lives can become intertwined. Theirs and mine, and all because of a man who was prepared to steal my wife. There was no reason for him to do that; he just took her because he could. Why did she want him? She didn't fight, you know, she just accepted him into her bed—my bed!—when she thought I was out. But I surprised them." He gave a chuckle. "Oh, yes. I surprised them."

Margaret stared at him. "Did you . . . kill them?" she managed.

"Kill them? No, that would have been foolish. I would have had my revenge, but where would the justice have been? No, I wanted *him* to suffer for what he had done. I could have stabbed him there, while he lay in my bed, but he wouldn't have had the expectation of his agony; it would have been a quick and easy death, and I didn't want that for him, not for the man who ruined me and my Mary. Poor Mary." He broke off and frowned at his long knife, and when he continued it was with a contemplative quietness. "She was my life, my whole life. All I ever wanted. I would have done anything to make her happy, yet she betrayed me; I gave her presents and toys, but she went to another man. She never hinted that I had failed her, there was not an angry word between us, but she preferred this *mercenary.*"

Below, Margaret could see the small knot of men swelling as others joined, all pointing up at her and chattering. She could just make out her husband, and imagined his stark horror, almost convinced she could see the expression on his face. He would be terrified in case he lost her too. Peterkin was bad enough, but to lose her as well, she thought, would be likely to unbalance his mind. She wanted to kiss him, to smile once more into his serious gray eyes and hug him, and wondered whether she would be able to ever again.

"Down there, they all think I simply went mad. They think I killed the women for no reason. What do they know of love, of loss?" he sneered, gesticulating, then shouted, waving his blade derisively. "What are you all staring at? Come up here, if you wish to talk, you cowards. *I'm* not corrupt. *I'm* not false or devious. *I'm* not a lying official lining my own pocket at the expense of justice!"

Margaret remained silent, staring down at her husband with a strange sense of serenity. Her hands were bound, and she could not try to run from this odd little man with his terrifying prattle, inconsequential yet deadly. There was no point in trying to escape, since if she were to keep from his clutches, she would surely fall in the attempt. The planks up here on the highest level were thin boards of split timber, roughly cracked away from boughs in lengths by wedges hammered in with the grain of the wood, and they had all warped and twisted in the sunlight as they dried. Some had been lashed to the scaffolding, but much of it was loose, the workers relying on their own skill and surefootedness for their safety.

She let herself slide down until she was crouched on a plank, hands gripping a vertical scaffold pole before her, and began praying. Her only regret was, if she were to die here this afternoon, that she had not been given a last chance to tell her husband how much she loved him.

Baldwin put a hand on Simon's shoulder. "My friend, come away. There's nothing else for you to do here. Why not—"

"Leave me be, Baldwin. You would not have me desert my wife while there's still a chance I might be able to do something."

"It would be better if you were to go."

"Why?" Simon shrugged the hand from his shoulder, but when he turned, his face was not angry, only sad and anxious. "So that if she were to die, I would be spared the sight? Come now, what about *her*? Do you think she would be happier to see me leave her all alone, or would she be better pleased to know that I am here, and will do all in my power to save her? She may not want me to see her die, but she'd be devastated if I was to disappear. It would be the last indignity, to see me run when I might be able to help her."

Baldwin felt the unfamiliar sting of dampness at his eyes, and he wordlessly rested a fist on his friend's shoulder and nodded.

"In the meantime," Simon muttered, "tell someone to get all the workers away from the place. The last thing we want is the bloody fool to become scared by them and kill Meg and himself."

"Master?" Hugh came and stood beside them, squinting up at the figures high above. His voice was calm and quiet. "There's a second set of ladders on the other side of the church. I think I could get up there."

"Are you sure?" Simon's face showed his desperate hope, and Hugh nodded.

Ever since Simon had rescued him from the tedium of life as a sheep farmer on the northeastern limits of the moors, out at Drewsteignton, Hugh had been devoted to Simon. When he married, Hugh had quickly grown to adore Margaret, and his feelings for Edith and Peterkin had bordered on adulation. It was impossible for him to stand by and watch the woman die and then, as must inevitably happen, the ruination of his master: the idea was unimaginable. "I can do it," he said confidently.

"It's a long way up," Baldwin said uncertainly. He knew only too well that Hugh was terrified of heights, and had only recently overcome his fear of being as high as on horseback.

"I can do it," Hugh repeated stubbornly.

"Very well," Simon said. "Show me where it is. I'll—"

"Simon, no!" Baldwin interrupted. "You mustn't! You must remain here and talk to Adam, try to distract him so he doesn't see us approaching."

"I must do something. Hugh here can show me how to get up there, then I can try to save her."

"Master, Sir Baldwin is right," Hugh said urgently. "You have to be here where she can see you. Like you said, how will she feel if she sees you going?"

"And how will I live with myself if I do not try?" Simon asked, but he was cut short by the butcher, who began waving his arms and bellowing. Simon watched, hardly heeding as his wife slipped down to sit, exhausted from exertion and fear.

"Bailiff? You can hear, can't you? How do you feel about *your* wife being killed, eh? How would you like to see *her* down there with you right now? Shall I push her, make her fall? Or should I stab her first, so she's dead before she lands? Which would you prefer?"

"Baldwin," Simon muttered, "I have to go up there."

"You cannot. I shall go in your place. No, Simon, no arguing. You *must* remain here: the man clearly knows you and is trying to get at you for some reason. Listen to him—he is mad, but not stupid. If you disappear even for a moment, he will notice, and what then for Margaret's chances? This is not a matter of honor, any more than disputing a path with a rabid wolf is honorable. Both are situations which call for serious actions. With a wolf one must kill it or die; here we must kill Butcher before he can harm Margaret . . .

"Simon, you *must* stay here! Occupy him—keep him talking. Hugh, you come with me," Baldwin commanded. He made his way back toward the road, Hugh and Edgar following. Once in the street, they went a short way west, until they were hidden by a tall hedge. "Now, Hugh, lead on. But remember, be quick!"

- 24 -

She shivered. It was not because of any inclemency in the weather, for she could feel the warmth of the late-afternoon sun on her right shoulder. Ahead of her was a high hill, for Crediton and the church lay in a valley, and all she could see was the tips of the trees rising up the hillside and over its summit. This late in the year, their leaves were yellow, brown or red, and the gold of the dying sun's light tinted them with a roseate hue. Each individual plant seemed to glow with an inner glory, and she found herself wondering in awe at such beauty. It was as if she had gone through her life without noticing such things before, and seeing these colors for the first time made her appreciate how precious such simple sights were. The rich gorgeousness of the picture pulled at the strings of her heart, and a quick sob surprised her, as unexpected as a sudden sneeze.

Squaring her shoulders, she looked away. She refused to allow the butcher to think her scared.

But Adam was paying her no heed. Leaning over the low railing, he leered down. "You thought you'd fooled me, didn't you, Bailiff? Thought the wool was pulled over my eyes. But I'm not a *cretin*, I can see things when they face me, and I could see you'd taken the mercenary's money to prevent him being arrested."

"I have taken no money from him," came the bewildered protestation from below, and Adam snarled in disbelief.

"No money? No bribe? You, an official, refused to take a bribe to defeat justice? You must be an honorable, virtuous man, Bailiff, a truly *perfect* gentleman. You expect me to believe that, when after all the proofs you refused to have him arrested? He was guilty of adultery, of murder, and all the women who died were associated with him, weren't they? Who else could be suspected?"

Simon stared up at the man. The little rotund face which the bailiff had previously thought to be practically comical in its good humor, was strained, and the features worked uncontrollably. "Please, God, hear my prayers. Let Baldwin reach him before he can hurt my Meg," he breathed.

The wall led round the perimeter of the church, and out to an alley behind, and it was here that the three men paused. They could discern shouting from the front, but there was no sound from here, at the back. With a short nod, Baldwin led the way at a run. They crossed beneath some huge trees, to the yard behind the church.

Here massive blocks of red stone lay in orderly piles, while chips and fragments crunched under their boots, strewn all over as liberally as clitter on the moors. Tools lay all around: sledgehammers and chisels, saws and drills, buckets and ropes, windlasses for pulling heavy loads up to the highest levels, anvils and braziers, all rested where they had been dropped by the startled workers.

To their left was the first of the ladders. Baldwin looked at it apprehensively. It seemed strong and heavy, constructed to take the weight of many men and their loads. Its solid rungs were hardly worn, and he noted that it must be of fairly new construction, but as his eyes followed its path skyward, he swallowed. It was a very long way to the top.

Forcing down his fear, he cautiously made his way to its base, standing with his hands on either rail, and steeling himself, began to climb.

The first quarter of the ladder was little problem. He refused to glance down, keeping his eyes fixed firmly on the wall in front, and found that the mechanical effort of lifting one foot, setting it down on a rung, then repeating the operation for the other foot, was relatively simple and painless. Then he approached the middle, and things got a great deal worse.

It was the rhythmic bumping that did it, he thought as he clung to the wobbling woodwork, eyes wide in horror. He felt as if he was moving yards at a time, in toward the wall, then away, with such force he was convinced the top of the ladder must spring from the scaffolding and hurtle away, pinning him and the other two underneath it as it fell.

"What is it?" he heard Edgar hiss, and with a supreme effort he managed to raise a foot carefully and plant it once more on a rung. He dared not look down at his servant, or speak in case his voice carried to the other side of the church. And from that moment until he came to the top of the ladder, he loathed Edgar.

At the top, he sidled sideways to fetch up on a plank, and here for a moment he allowed himself to catch his breath, still staring at the wall of the new church. He became aware of the two men coming up, and soon his heart lurched as the planks bounced under the weight of the others. Stifling a curse, he turned to motion to them to keep still, when he caught a glimpse of the scenery, and was held spellbound with fascinated terror at the height. He felt paralyzed, like a mouse freezing into immobility under the gaze of a cat. It was only when Edgar tapped him on the shoulder that he came to and prepared himself for the next stage of the climb.

This ladder was lashed loosely to the scaffolding at its base, which at least offered some degree of security to the quailing Keeper. Once more the center section rocked and bounced, filling him with dread, convinced now that the whole structure, not merely the ladder but the entire scaffold, must collapse. He clenched his teeth as he crossed the threshold of panic and continued upward.

There was only one more ladder, and this was shorter, but smaller in size, and considerably older. Hugh was after him, and he tugged his dagger free and tested the blade meditatively while they waited for Edgar.

Hugh had never felt so cold and pitiless before. He had been involved in fights often enough, especially when thieves tried to steal his lambs for the pot when he had been a boy, but this was not the anticipation of a fight, this was the righteous determination to seek justice. Nobody had the right to take captive his mistress, yet this little man was holding her and threatening to kill her. Hugh was determined to protect her, and in so doing, the family of the master. If he had anything to do with it, Margaret would be safe, and the butcher would die for what he had done.

It was not something in his blood which made him murderous; it was the memory of what had happened to Rollo after his mother had died, and the thought of how poor little Edith would react to hearing that her mother, her devoted mummy, had died. This made him tingle with animal anticipation, pricking the ball of his thumb on the point of his blade to see how sharp it was.

Edgar looked from him to his master with a blank expression. Hugh, he could see, was in a black mood, a killing mood, while Baldwin was close to shivering with fear. He stepped so slowly and carefully he looked as if he thought he was going to fall through a plank at any moment. It almost made Edgar want to laugh—or weep with frustration.

"Why didn't you arrest him?" The thin voice floated down in the stillness before twilight with a curious calmness. "I tried to help you, you know. I tried to show you what he had done. First adultery, then the girl in the chest. The pauper was an old flame of his, and then my wife was a lover of his as well. I mean—it could hardly have been more obvious, could it? But you ignored all the hints. He *must* have paid you a fortune to keep away from him! That's what you do, isn't it? Take money to make sure that those who can afford it, avoid the rope. How can you justify your corruption?"

"We didn't know, Adam." Simon cried, aware of the desperation in his voice. "We thought the first girl died during the robbery, and the second we just weren't sure about. Then, when we found your wife, we were right to think it wasn't him, weren't we? It was you all along, after all. But this has nothing to do with my wife, has it? Why not let her go?"

"NO!" The scream made the blood turn to ice in Simon's veins. "Why should I, eh? Why should I let you have a life again? Why should I let you enjoy your

woman again, when mine has been taken from me? Why should *you* deserve her when my own angel, my precious darling, is dead? Why should I let her live when you have ruined my life?"

"But I haven't," Simon protested desperately, his hands held out. "All I did was try to help my friend seek out the truth. It wasn't a deliberate attempt to hurt you, just a seeking out of the facts—"

"*Liar!* You took his money to protect him, you can't fool me!" To Simon's horror, he began to edge his way nearer Margaret. "The Keeper is known to be fair and decent, I can't believe he'd have tried to cheat me of justice, so who else could it have been, eh? Who else was with him day after day, investigating the affair, poisoning his mind by lies and treachery? There was nobody else—but *you*! You made him believe Sir Hector was innocent, that he was not the killer, that he hadn't enjoyed my wife. It was all *you*!"

"Adam, look, why don't you let me explain, let me tell you how it really was?" Simon pleaded.

"You—explain? But you're a liar! How could I believe a word you told me?" Adam jeered. "The only one I could believe is the Keeper. He's at least honorable, and maybe he should know the truth, so he can hold you in . . ." His voice faded as he surveyed the area before the church. "Where is he?" he screamed suddenly. "Where is he, the Keeper? He was here before, I saw him. Where's he gone?"

"Nowhere. He just went to—"

"Now you're lying again! You always lie—you're corrupt! He's gone, hasn't he—but where to? Is he false too?" The tone of his voice had risen, and now he was screeching like an alewife. "Is he corrupt as well? He is, isn't he?"

With mounting despair Simon saw his wife give him a wan smile as the butcher got behind her, and put the point of his knife at her throat.

"Please, *please* don't hurt her! Look, I'll come up myself—take me instead, don't hurt her. She's done you no harm, it's me you want, so take me! Let me come up, I'll bring no weapon, and you can do what you want with me. I'll—"

"No! No! No! I want to see you grovel, I want to see you in agony. I want you to realize what my life has become, to suffer like I'm suffering. My wife is ruined and dead, and the man responsible is free still, and it's your fault—all your fault! Well, watch this, Bailiff. Let's see how bravely your own wife dies!"

From the bottom of the ladder, Hugh heard the conversation. Ignoring the others, he rushed up it; reaching the planking, he sprang forward, his dagger grasped firmly in his fist. He took in the situation at a glance; the butcher stood with his back to him on the opposite wall. Hugh sprinted to the corner, and then approached along the shorter wall. He was too far to attempt to throw his knife yet, so he grabbed his purse, sliced through the cords which bound it, and hurled it with all his might at the butcher's back.

Adam snarled like a terrier distracted from its prey, and turned, his teeth bared. He shook a fist, and was about to turn back to Margaret, but Hugh now was close enough. He tossed his dagger up lightly, catching it by the very tip of the blade, then hurled it, roaring as he pounded along the ramshackle planking.

Dropping his own knife, Adam stared angrily at the bone handle which protruded from his breast. He muttered, and caught at the handle, as if to tug it free, but a thin dribble of blood spat from his lips, and he seemed to have lost all energy. His fingers were heavy, so very heavy, and it was hard simply to grip the knife. He gibbered in impotent rage, letting his arms fall as Hugh came closer, and took a step back. With a hideous screech of blind terror, he stumbled too far and fell over the edge.

Margaret watched his body fall. It took a long time to strike the ground, she noticed unemotionally, and his cry went on for ages until it suddenly stopped with a dull thud.

She was aware of Hugh at her side, his hands taking her by the shoulders and turning her to face him, while he studied her throat anxiously, giving a huge sigh of relief when he saw that there was no damage. She stared up at him lethargically, wanting to stand, but the effort was too much, and even when he offered her his hand, she could hardly grip it. He had to heave her up to her feet, and even then she found her legs simply could not support her. She had to lean against him for fear of following Adam over the edge.

Soon Edgar and Baldwin were there with them. Baldwin cut the thongs binding her wrists, and between the three of them they managed to get her to the ladder and gradually helped her down with the aid of a rope.

At the bottom, Simon groaned as he caught her up in his arms and buried his head in her shoulder. Baldwin and the others left the couple to themselves.

- 25 -

"As to why he killed them, I suppose we'll never know," Baldwin said.

They were back in Peter Clifford's hall, drinking Hippocras. The strong fumes of the wine, mingled with the ginger, cinnamon, nutmeg and cloves, gave off a scent which dispelled their fears and calmed their nerves.

Simon needed it. He sat by his friend, but still held the hand of his wife firmly. Right now he felt that he would never dare leave hold of it. He had learned in a very short space of time how much he adored her. The events of the afternoon had nearly shattered his mind, as the butcher had hoped. Glancing at Margaret and squeezing her fingers affectionately, he noted the lines on her brow, the heavy bruises under her eyes and the paleness of her face. It was only with an effort that he stopped himself kissing her.

Stapledon frowned. "From what you say, it was all done in an attempt to frame the mercenary."

"Yes, as far as we can tell. From what he said, it was in order to put the blame directly on Sir Hector that he murdered the women, including his own wife."

"A hideous act."

"As you observe, an appalling deed. By all accounts he was very much in love with Mary, and when he discovered she was having an adulterous affair—and there appears to be no doubt whatever on that score—he went quite mad. To kill two innocents, and his own wife . . . Well, it beggars belief."

Simon nodded. The little butcher must have been quite demented. He picked up his goblet and sipped, then froze. "Baldwin, have you given any instructions for releasing Cole or Sir Hector?"

"Oh . . ." Baldwin met Peter Clifford's eye shamefacedly and decided not to curse. It always offended the priest. With a slight grin, he continued, "No—thanks, for reminding me."

"I should send someone to invite them both here for a celebratory drink. Wat is still holding Sir Hector, isn't he? Let the message go to him. Ask Wat to bring his master under guard."

"Simon, are you planning something?" Baldwin asked suspiciously.

"Me? Of course not. The very idea!"

Stapledon watched them bemusedly. What were they planning now? It was hard to tell, but he thought he could discern something in their bantering tones, though they were too far away for him to see their expressions.

He was staggered that Margaret Puttock had been prepared to remain with her man. If he'd been her, he would have retired immediately to his room and slept, he was sure, for the story of how she had been captured and hauled aloft had been told and retold many times already, and all the servants in the house were treating her with huge respect after her ordeal. He was surprised that she had not lost her sense after such a trial, and was uncomfortably aware that his own conduct in similar circumstances might not have been so praiseworthy.

Now the two men were talking in undertones, nodding as each confirmed points with the other, and Stapledon strained his ears. They were not being quiet to hide anything, but more because their speech was an extension of each other's thoughts. For these men, talking to the other in a low voice was indistinguishable from carrying on a sequence of logical mental processes, Stapledon thought to himself. They were almost as close as a husband and wife in the way that they appeared to be able to anticipate the words of the other and counter an argument before it had been fully expressed.

Accepting a fresh goblet of Hippocras, he wearily sank back in his chair. His head still hurt abominably, but he had suffered no long-term damage, as the surgeon had assured him. There was no loose bone where he had been struck, and for such an old man, the surgeon had implied, it was a miracle that he had suffered no worse injury. He curled his lip wryly as he recalled the highly *un*-Godly words he had used to drive the skinny medico from his room bawling the man out for his nerve.

The first of the two men to arrive was Cole. He looked dreadful, with his greasy hair flat on one side, and almost vertical on the crown where he had run his fingers through it. His complexion was pale and he looked as if he had been suffering from a fever, his skin was so waxy, and the general impression of illness was added to by the nervous twitch at the corner of his mouth. Tanner stood behind him, waiting for confirmation from Baldwin that he was permitted to free his prisoner, and he cut the thongs that bound Cole's hands as soon as Baldwin nodded to him. Thankfully, and for the first time in many days, Cole dropped onto a stool, wondering what had happened to cause his miraculous release.

Less than a quarter of an hour later Sir Hector arrived with Wat and another guard. His appearance was in every way the reverse of Cole's, making the distinction even more marked. His face was ruddy from exercise, his eyes clear and steady, his stance firm and assured.

"You asked me to come and celebrate. I understand you have ended this unhappy affair, and that Adam Butcher is dead?"

"Yes," Baldwin smiled. "He fell from the church's scaffolding . . ." He glanced at Margaret, and chose to forego a more precise description of the afternoon's events.

"It is good to hear. I will drink to celebrate with you. Here's to the end of a murderer!"

Simon watched him speculatively. "Would you drink the same toast for any murderer?" he enquired.

"Of course. Anyone like that is a loose brick in the wall of our society; they can bring the whole building down around us all. Society needs protection from such as they."

"Hmm."

"Do you know why this madman decided to kill the women? Did you discover it?"

"Ah, yes," Simon cleared his throat. "I forgot you wouldn't have heard. Basically, he was trying to set you up as the scapegoat."

"He intended that?"

Baldwin nodded. "Very definitely. He wanted to ensure that you were arrested, and hanged."

"You see," Simon continued, before his friend could carry on, "he knew you were having an affair with his wife, and he wanted revenge."

"He would kill all those women just to get at me? It seems hard to believe!"

"Nonetheless, it is true. He killed Judith because he knew you had . . . er . . . been her lover when you were last here."

"It is true," Sir Hector admitted. "She even alleged that her boy was my bastard!" He laughed, but nobody joined in.

"Quite," Baldwin said. "Anyhow, Butcher saw you having your altercation with her, we think, and could see that we had witnessed it as well, so he stabbed her, knowing that this second murder would be bound to make us think you were the guilty party. After all, most murders are committed by men who kill their lovers or their wives—just as Butcher himself did with his own wife."

Sir Hector sipped his Hippocras, nodding. "I see. And he knew I was not at the inn because I was waiting to meet his wife. He must have found out we had planned to meet. The evil devil must have forced her to tell him where and when, so that he could make me look suspicious."

"Very likely," Baldwin agreed. "The murder of his own wife was intended, I think, to be the sweet glazing on the fruit, the crowning proof which would lead us to arrest you. It was meant as the final evidence, and it certainly was compelling. Yet we had doubts, for she must have died some days before, and we had seen you waiting for her. You might have been trying to establish your innocence, but it did appear odd. You would have been better served to make sure that everyone knew where you were all the time."

"I am glad you realized," said Sir Hector gravely. "Knowing I was suspected of killing my Mary made a bad situation even harder to bear."

"What about me?" Cole demanded. "I've been locked up for days, held under suspicion of murder as well as theft. What happens now? Am I truly free?"

"Oh, yes," Simon smiled. "Our apologies for your confinement, but the evidence was extreme against you. You were new to the group, and at first all we knew of you was that you had been found with incriminating items on your person. It was natural to suspect you. Then we learned that the men who had found you were the two whom the company generally mistrusted and despised, and it was better, it seemed to us, to leave you in the jail for your own safety. You had been picked out, if you like, by two who were capable of stirring up others against you and causing your death."

"And, of course, we had to wonder whether you might have killed Sarra," Baldwin murmured, pouring more drink into his goblet. "There was no reason to suspect you in particular, except we had heard about you arguing with her. The only evidence, likewise, against Sir Hector at first was that he had argued with Sarra and forced her from his presence."

Stapledon felt his brows rise. Being too myopic to see people's expressions, he often had to rely on his impressions . . . and the feeling he had now was that there was a certain stillness in the room after these words. He had no idea what had caused it for a moment, but then he stared at Sir Hector. The implication of Baldwin's words was that there was other evidence, surely.

"There was the matter of the blue tunic, for example," Simon said easily, taking up the baton again. "Wat always said that you had an evil temper, and that you might kill her if you saw Sarra wearing it when you had not given her permission. We thought he might have tried to oust you from leadership by sending her to you wearing it. He had been planning to supplant you for some time, according to Henry and John."

"He would have been capable of it," Sir Hector agreed, glancing at his guard. Wat shrugged.

"But even if he did, you would have been wrong to react to it by murdering her. No, this is what happened. The two men, Henry and John, stole the silver. Henry was inside, and Sarra arrived when he was in the middle of the robbery. He heard her approach, concealed himself, and then knocked her down. There being no other place to hide her, he shoved her into the chest, and got on with his task. Later, he left."

"We thought," Baldwin reflected, "that Adam then managed to climb in through the window and kill her before Henry and John could return to lock the window, but there is another possibility."

Simon leaned forward, elbows on his knees, smiling, his goblet held negligently in one hand. "It's this: *someone else* returned to the room, and Adam, waiting outside, heard him. He heard the chest lid being lifted, the murder taking place."

"If he had, he would have told you," Sir Hector objected.

"No, possibly not. After all, he had a dislike of officials that was close to a madness. He distrusted any man in a position of authority, as we discovered. And I suppose he might well have thought that it would be easy for you to accuse *him* of bad blood because of your affair with his wife. You had the perfect response to any accusation he made. I think it was that, more than the adultery itself, which unhinged his mind. The knowledge that there was no one who would look after his interests made him seek a more drastic means of redress. He killed his wife—well, he was going to anyway—and perhaps it was during a flash of rage that he regretted later. But he murdered Judith simply to add weight to our suspicion of you. The sad part is, he wasted a life for no good reason. All he achieved was to divert attention from you. When we found the body of Mary as well, it was clear that some devious scheme was in progress."

"Do you mean to accuse me?" Sir Hector thundered, standing suddenly. "Do you dare to suggest that I killed the tart?"

Baldwin eyed him coldly, then meditatively refilled his pot. "Adam was sure you went back in and stabbed the girl. Why? He would recognize you on sight, wouldn't he? But if he was outside, Henry and John had barred the shutters giving on to the road. Adam *could not* have seen in. All he knew was that someone was there, and he had heard that only you, Sir Hector, and your most trusted men were allowed into your private rooms. He heard a noise—Henry and John had gone and were not yet inside—so whoever it was, it must be *you.*"

"But that's rubbish!"

"Yes, it is," Simon agreed.

"What?"

"Adam didn't know that someone else could also get in—the man who had to fetch the salt for your meal. Your servant, Wat."

Sir Hector's mouth fell open, then he turned to face his guard.

Wat was immobile for a moment. He wetted his lips, whirled, and took a half-step toward the door, but his way was barred by three of Peter Clifford's men, all with stout cudgels in their hands. Tanner stood with them, grinning, his hands in his thick leather belt.

"Wat," said Baldwin solemnly, "I accuse you of the murder of Sarra, a worker at the inn. You will be taken to the jail until you can be tried. If you resist . . . Well! I almost wish you would!"

The blustering mercenary had to be bound and led away, furiously rejecting all responsibility. It took the combined efforts of Stapledon's men and Tanner—Hugh gave encouragement from the fringes of the melee, but managed to avoid participation—to restrain him, but at last he could be removed by a gleeful Sir Hector. While Baldwin went with them to the jail, Simon and his wife retired to their chamber.

"How are you?" he asked as she sat on the edge of their mattress. She looked dreadfully pale, and her eyes were half-closed, though the room was dark with the shutters barred against the cold darkness outside. He squatted by her and gently held her hand to his face.

"I am fine, now. Honestly."

"You are safe, and that's all that matters to me."

"I thought I was going to die, for a while."

"So did I. I hated standing there. Baldwin wouldn't let me try to help you, and I—"

She shut his mouth with a finger. "It is over now."

"I thought I wouldn't be able to hold you again. I thought I was going to lose you. I love you."

She smiled at the whispered words. "I love you too. I promise I will not leave you until you have a son."

"I do not care about that right now. All I want is to see you well again."

Margaret's eyes closed, but then she remembered the conversation in the garden, and she sighed.

"What is it?"

"The Bishop was talking to me about Rollo when that man attacked us. Simon, I want us to have our own boy, not another's. Is that selfish?"

"Selfish? Perhaps—but if you think I want any reminder of this afternoon, you are wrong. I couldn't bear to have him in our household either. Don't worry, I shall tell the good Bishop."

When he returned to the hall, Baldwin was already there, seated near a frowning Stapledon. Peter was at the church exhorting the workmen to continue, and the three were alone for a while. After sitting in silence for some minutes, the Bishop peered at them. "Sir Baldwin, Simon, I must be more dense than I had realized, for I still cannot see how you have arrived at this conclusion."

Baldwin smiled at the peering bishop. "It is a great deal more simple now, dealing with the matter in retrospect, because we actually have the sequence of events."

"It's hard," Simon said, pouring himself more wine, "when you begin an investigation like this. At first everyone is trying to help, but all that means is you've got to try to isolate what is important from the mass of details which are uncovered. All too often there is so much which is irrelevant."

Baldwin held his hand over his goblet as Simon offered more wine. He had already drunk far more than usual. "As you know, it looked bad for Cole from the first," he began. "A new man joining, who was found after a couple of days with silver on him when Sir Hector's plate had all been stolen, and then the girl was discovered . . . It was apparent that he must have been discovered in the course of this theft, and had killed Sarra before she could raise the alarm."

"But," Simon interrupted, waving his goblet so freely that wine slopped on to the floor, "How could Cole have known that he would have time to rob Sir Hector? He was too new to be trusted by most of the men there. And how could one man have carried off so much metal? If he was involved, he would have needed an accomplice."

"Simon is correct. It was obvious to me that others should be sought. Another thing was that the girl had been stored in the chest unconscious, and killed later. That indicated to me that the murder and the robbery were not necessarily connected. Thus, although Sir Hector could hardly be implicated in stealing from himself, he might have had a hand in killing Sarra."

"Then there was the question of whether Cole would have robbed the mercenary." Simon smiled.

Stapledon put his head on one side. "What do you mean?"

"If you were desperate, would *you* steal from a mercenary warrior? From a captain, at that?" Simon asked, then, seeing the Bishop's rueful shake of his head, pounced triumphantly. "No, of course not! Why? Because a man like that would scare any but the most hardened warrior. Is it likely that a youngster fresh from a farm would dare to challenge him?"

"Perhaps he was too unworldly . . . ?" the Bishop murmured, but Baldwin smiled and shook his head.

"It will not do, Bishop. He had seen Sir Hector at

close quarters for more than a day, and in any case, he knew of such men—his brother had died, and one who had known him had returned to tell Cole *how* he had died. Cole could not have been so stupid or naïve as to have missed how dangerous Sir Hector was. It was one final piece of evidence which convinced me though."

"What was that?"

"When I thought about it, there were two pairs of assaults. Cole and Sarra were struck by someone with a club or similar weapon, both hit in about the same place; Judith and Mary both had stab wounds in the back. The only different wounds were young Sarra's: stabs to her chest from having a knife thrust down at her—so forcibly that the knife penetrated the cloth behind her. Cole and she had both been knocked out with blows to the left side of the head. It was not proof on its own, but it was quite conclusive when all the other points were taken into account."

Simon rested his elbows on his thighs. "Cole was unlikely to have been the thief, and equally unlikely to have killed Sarra. If we accept that people would prefer to rob anyone other than a mercenary leader, who would have dared? Surely only another mercenary!"

"It is clear now what happened," Baldwin said. "Henry and John knew Adam from the last time they were here. When they met and drank again, the two told the butcher how sick they were of their master's overbearing manner. They had worked out the details of their theft in advance, and asked Adam if he would help them, but he refused. However, they knew something he didn't: his wife was having an affair with their captain. Maybe they told him, maybe they didn't; but he assuredly went home and found his wife in bed with Sir Hector, and that sealed the pact. He went back and saw Henry and John once more, and agreed to help them."

"I expect they thought he'd just beat his wife, which was no more than they believed she deserved for her whoring around, and would agree to help them just so that he could get even with their master," Simon said.

"Sir Hector trusted them most of all," said Baldwin. "He told them he had an assignation with Mary that afternoon, and they made their plans accordingly. He went out, as they saw, and they visited his chamber a little later, on the pretext of seeing him about a horse. They unlocked the back shutters—it was more private than the front—and then left. Once they were outside again, while John stood guard, Henry climbed inside, opened the front, and began passing the plate out to the others. Adam was needed to repel unwelcome witnesses, and he managed it by eviscerating some animals. That, in the heat of the afternoon sun, was enough to scare everyone away. People in the streets tend to keep moving. They do not hang around in one place too much; they have errands to run, messages to deliver, or some other purpose. The men could pass the silver out, stow it in the wagon under sacks or something, and remain undiscovered."

"And when they were done, John helped Henry out again," said Simon, "before they went inside once more to lock up the shutters."

"Meanwhile, Wat had given the dress to Sarra to try on. He was hoping it would anger his master so much that Sir Hector would kill her—his rages were known well enough—but she arrived too early. Henry knocked her out and stuffed her into the chest to hide her."

Simon nodded. "But while they were outside, before

they could get back in to lock the last shutter, Wat entered. He was hoping Sarra would be dead. He had given her the dress, taking it to her room and letting her think it was a present from his master, knowing it would enrage Sir Hector to see it on another. Wat was sure the captain would do for her.

"He was acting as servant to Sir Hector, so he was often in and out of the solar, fetching things from chests. That day, he went to the chest and there he found the girl. I suppose he must have been confused at first, staring down at her and wondering what she was doing there, but I imagine he quickly thought that his master had put her there for some reason. It was a heaven-sent opportunity. Sir Hector had not killed her—but everyone would think he had! Just to make sure, Wat was prepared to spread the story of how angry Sir Hector would have been to find his dress on another woman. So he stabbed her, and slammed the lid down."

Baldwin continued: "All this time Adam was outside, keeping an eye on things for his friends to make sure they were all right. He heard Wat in the room before Henry and John closed the shutter at the back, and assumed it must be Sir Hector. When he heard about the murder, he was sure Sir Hector had done it."

"But in that case, why did he not merely tell you?" Stapledon frowned.

Baldwin shrugged. "I think he saw a way of disposing of his wife at the same time. How else could he get rid of the woman who had cuckolded him? It must have seemed an inspired plan to kill Mary and put the blame onto Sir Hector."

"When did he kill his wife?"

"I have no idea. Probably during Tuesday. He was

heard rowing with her then. She has certainly been dead some days."

"Where could he have hidden her?" Stapledon wondered. "It is not easy for a man to conceal a corpse for long."

"It is easier for some than for others," Baldwin smiled dryly. "For example, Adam had a cool room to store his meats and carcasses. His apprentice has been refused permission to enter it just lately. I think we can assume that her body was secreted there for a few days."

"The only question remaining is, who killed Cole's brother?" the Bishop said.

Baldwin allowed himself to sink down further in his seat. "I am glad I have no jurisdiction over that matter. The death—if it *was* a murder—happened over the sea."

"But do you know who did kill him?"

"I have little doubt it was Henry and John. According to others, they profited by his demise, but equally he may well have fallen in the battle. I fear I do not care: he was a mercenary himself, and knew the risks of joining such a company."

"So," the Bishop sighed, "we are left with the poor victims of this series of tragedies."

"You are thinking of Rollo?" Simon asked tentatively.

"Yes. The poor lad needs to be looked after."

Baldwin frowned. "I suppose we might find a place for him."

"But we have a solution here," Stapledon exclaimed.

Simon drew a deep breath. "I am afraid not, Bishop. Much though I'd like to help, I fear I cannot take the lad with me."

"But—"

"No, we have lost a son, and it would be cruel to expect an adopted boy to take Peterkin's place. He would upset us whenever he misbehaved or got something wrong, and if he was good and obedient, he'd be doing no more than what we'd expect. His life would be a misery, with no comfort or joy."

"Simon, I think—"

"And I wouldn't be prepared to allow Margaret to suffer it. Every time she looked at his face she would be reminded of her ordeal today, and that's a slow torture I'm not going to expose her to."

"Bailiff, if you would let me speak," Stapledon smiled. "I wouldn't dream of forcing the lad on you. I had thought of a much simpler solution—*I* shall take him to Exeter with me. He may be useful in the kitchen or stables, and if he shows an aptitude I can teach him. Who knows? If he shows any promise, in years to come he might be able to go to my college at Oxford. He can be assured of food and drink and shelter in any case."

Simon sagged with relief, "Yes, yes. That would be perfect."

Stapledon nodded happily, but then a small frown crossed his brow. "I wish I knew why that murderous fool had to kill Judith in the first place. It was such an evil act! How could he deprive Rollo of his mother, purely to create a spurious connection with Sir Hector in the hope that it would lead us to arrest him?"

"I think it might be simpler than that," Sir Baldwin said gently. "You recall I said that people tend to hurry along a street? Well, there is one class which does not."

"What do you mean?"

Baldwin took the jug and topped up his goblet. "One

group in particular will stand in a certain place for a long time every day: beggars. Judith may have spotted something odd on the afternoon of the robbery, and when she heard of the theft, realized that she actually knew someone who had been involved. We shall never know for certain, but she may have mentioned the butcher to Sir Hector when we saw him knock her down. He might have thought she was threatening him. I have often noticed that guilty men hear what they expect to, rather than what is actually said. In this case, any mention of his lover's husband would very possible make him leap to the wrong conclusion. Yet all Judith was doing was trying to curry a little favor after so many years of neglect by him—especially since most people believe Rollo was his son."

"Talking of Rollo, didn't you tell me he screamed when he saw the knight, when Hugh brought him here?"

Baldwin smiled. "Certainly. But then again, right next door to the inn is the butcher's and Adam was there at the time. I think Rollo saw Adam as he came into the street. For Sir Hector, it was simply the first time he had ever noticed the boy, and he was a little shocked to be confronted with a son who shrieked like a banshee at the sight of him. I don't know but that I wouldn't blanch myself if that was to happen to me. Anyway, to return to Judith for a minute, I think it is fair to assume that any loyalty or softer feelings she may once have held for the knight dissipated quickly after he struck her. I expect she went to Adam to ask him for money afterward. What could be more natural than that after her attempt to help Sir Hector had been so publicly scorned, she should go to the other protagonist and demand compensation from him? From Adam's point of view, killing Judith was not merely useful in forming a link in the chain of evidence against Sir Hector, it also removed someone who could have proved to be an embarrassing witness."

~ 26 ~

Paul woke to the sound of shuffling feet and banging, and rolled over wearily. After the late nights and forced early mornings of the last few days, he was unwilling to leave the warmth of the bed. Cuddling his wife, he screwed his eyes tight shut and let the noise wash past him, determined to grab a little extra peace before beginning a new day.

Though he sought sleep, it evaded him, and he was forced to lie half awake, his brain meandering indolently. It was typical, he thought, that the mercenaries should not only expect him to continue serving them until past midnight, but that today they should be determined to wake him before dawn as well. It was a measure of their ungenerous attitude to others, he thought sourly. They held the world in contempt.

A loud thud made the building tremble, and young Hob, on his truckle bed nearby, grunted and whimpered in his sleep. Paul swore and got up resentfully. He could not rest with that row going on. Scratching, he made his way to the window, tugging the knotted string free from its notch to let the shutter fall.

Below him the road was clear. The sun had not risen

high enough to chase away the shadows, and only an occasional passer-by strolled in the darkness. Two hawkers stood sorting items in baskets ready for the day's trade. Beyond, over the roof of the jail, he could see the long coils of smoke rising from freshly lighted fires. Soon the town's women would be warming their pots and making breakfast for their families.

Beyond the bulk of the new church, the mist lay like a sheet of snow, hiding the valley in the chill morning air. He could only tell where the river lay from the trees which lined the far bank, and from the view he knew that the weather was changing at last; winter was approaching. A sudden gust blew along the street and Paul shivered, drawing back into the room. He pulled the cord, yanking the flat wooden board up until the knot met the notch in the timber above and he could let it hang. Only a small gap remained, and the draft from that should not wake his wife.

Pulling on his hose and a jerkin against the cold, he slowly negotiated the ladder to the buttery. When he opened the door, he stopped, his mouth gaping. The hall and screens were the picture of bedlam.

Mercenaries swore their way past him, stumbling under the weight of chests. Others dragged sacks out to the yard. Paul had to wait in the doorway as a pair of soldiers strained by, grasping leather-covered polearms tied in thick bundles. Behind them another trooper wheezed along in their wake, querulously complaining about the pain in his head. Paul was not surprised that the soldier should feel fragile—it would have been a wonder if none of the men had felt sickly. Almost all of Margery's ale was gone, most of it over the last two days, since the arrest of Wat and the thieves.

Spying a gap in the stream of porters, the innkeeper

stepped quickly into his hall. He was determined that Sir Hector would not leave before the bill was settled.

There were fewer men leaving the solar now. Most of the valuables and stores had already been taken to the yard and loaded on to the wagons. From the clattering of iron on stone, the horses were skittishly expectant as they stood by, knowing they would soon be leaving and anticipating the exercise. In his mind's eye, Paul could see the massive black beast Sir Hector had arrived on, and he gave an involuntary shudder. Proud and arrogant, the horse terrified him.

"You rise early, innkeeper."

Paul smiled and ducked his head. To Sir Hector he looked at his most obsequious, and the captain was sickened, convinced that, like all innkeepers, all he wanted was his money. Curtly he asked for the reckoning, and the two of them began to negotiate. Paul gave his figure; Sir Hector registered shock and suspicion. Evidence was proffered in the form of empty barrels in the buttery, and rejected on the basis that they might have been half-empty when the mercenaries arrived. Eventually they settled on a sum which satisfied both. If Paul was convinced it gave him only a little profit, at least there was *some.*

The knight too was content. It had cost him more than he would have hoped, but the charge appeared fair. He carefully counted the coins, sniffing at the expense, then left, striding out to the yard. Ignoring the men standing all round, he stepped onto the mounting stone, and swung his leg over his horse's back. Once there, he studied his men.

It was a sadly depleted band. When Sir Hector had arrived in Creditor, it was as the leader of a united, battle-hardened force. Now his two sergeants were in jail after stealing from him, his most experienced man was with them awaiting justice for murdering Sarra, and Will had disappeared after the abortive attempt on Sir Hector's life. Will knew the price for disloyalty. He wouldn't dare show his face again.

The others stood by sullenly. None wanted to meet his eye, and he considered them silently for a moment. It would be easy to leave them, and the idea was tempting. All he need do was send them away and walk back inside the inn. They would go. One or two might wish to remain, but most would be glad of the opportunity to be free of him, and he could find a new life amongst the merchants of the town.

But fighting was all he knew. What could he do in a small town like this? Crediton was a quiet, profitable place, ideal for the new breed of trader. The mills were rarely silent, the farmers thrived, the cloth industry was booming—but what work was there for a mercenary? Sir Hector had no skills other than those of a warrior, and they were not in demand. He could not find peace here.

Abruptly he pulled his horse's head round and urged him on.

Paul watched the men file out of the yard, the wagon lumbering after them, and went back to the hall, sourly eyeing the mess.

"They've gone?" Margery yawned as she came in.

"Just now, yes," Paul confirmed, and went to the front door. Soon the troop appeared, coming past the butcher's and marching off past the inn to the west. Sir Hector stared ahead fixedly, refusing to acknowledge the innkeeper and his wife. Margery shivered as the men moved on: their silence was even more oppressive than their rowdy displays in the hall. She was glad to see them go.

"Good," Paul said, and smacked his hands together. "Now to clean the hall, and then to rest. I feel like I've not slept in a week."

"Yes," his wife said listlessly.

Paul put an arm round her shoulder. She was worn out after the last few days, and even after a night's sleep she looked ready to drop. "Why don't you go back to bed and rest a little longer? I can get the girls to help me down here."

"No, I'm fine."

Her fatigue showed in the bruises under her eyes. Looking at her it was hard to imagine she had recently risen from her bed. She shrugged Paul's arm away, not unkindly, and fetched a besom, beginning to sweep away the old rubbish and reeds from the hall's floor.

Paul stood watching for a moment, but his attention wavered, and soon he was peering up the road to the west. He felt curiously empty. In the space of a few short days he had been bullied and threatened, lost a number of honorable clients, witnessed a near-rape in his own hall, had poor Sarra murdered and an assassination attempt on the mercenary captain. And all there was to show for it was a small dust cloud disappearing on the horizon, accompanied by a faint musical tinkling of armor and harness.

Rousing himself, he went to help his wife. There was a sense of sadness for Sarra, but death was common enough. Paul had a business to run.

He did not see the limping figure scuttling from the shadows of the jail and hurrying after the band.

At the top of a gentle rise Sir Hector found he could see clear to the hills of Dartmoor. The sky was a light gray, gleaming brightly; it should clear before long as the sun's heat burned through. The land undulated softly, a series of rounded hillocks with swift-moving streams between. He could remember it from his last visit.

Then, when he had first met Mary, he had experienced a poignant melancholy at leaving the town. He had discovered for the first time that it was possible for him to want to give pleasure to someone else, and that feeling had lasted until now. Losing Mary, seeing her lifeless corpse, had killed something inside him.

For a moment he allowed himself to confront the possibility of how his life would have been had he stayed here after that first visit to Crediton. He might have been able to set himself up as a merchant. Certainly he had possessed the money at the time. The wars in Gascony had been profitable, and he had made a small fortune from taking hostages and demanding payment for release. There had been enough profit from his ventures to guarantee a comfortable retirement.

But Mary had been unwilling to accept him. She had known that Adam was interested in her, and she had thought that a butcher would be a safer husband than a soldier.

"Then I will give up warfare," he had declared on that last evening when they lay together on her bed.

"You? Forswear your career for a mere woman?" She had sat up then, looking down at him playfully.

"For you, Mary," Her name was perfect, he had felt. She looked like a Madonna squatting above him, smiling as she toyed with her hair.

"No. You will get bored. One woman for a bold knight? You would fret and go mad with the dullness of life in a little town like this."

"Mary, I mean it! I will marry you."

"No," she had said, laughing and turning away, avoiding the arm which tried to encircle her. "You are a soldier. I am to be a butcher's wife. I will sit, and cook, and sew, and breed little butchers while you travel and capture your prizes. We couldn't live together, you and I. We're too alike. Someday you would anger me and my tongue would lash you, then you would beat me and I would hate you. I need a husband I can control."

Now, surveying the road ahead, Sir Hector murmured, "You couldn't control *him*, though, could you, Mary?"

Without her, he felt no desire to return. There was nothing to attract him. The vision of peace and comfort he had dreamed of during his travels had been cruelly shattered. All that was left to him was war.

The Bishop had almost made him laugh aloud when he had visited the night before. His expression of stupefaction had been comical, but Sir Hector had no regrets. Stapledon had suggested that Sir Hector might want to take the lad with him: "Rollo *is* your son, after all."

"What if he is? Can he hold a sword? Can he fight? Does he know how to storm a wall? What would I do with a child?" Rollo was too heavy and useless to take on campaign. He had not even received training as a page—he would be so much useless and expensive baggage. "You keep him, Bishop. You look after him. I didn't know I had a son before I came here and I want to leave in the same happy ignorance."

"He is your flesh and blood."

"Perhaps. And perhaps if I was to buy a manor here and settle with a wife, I might think of giving him a home, but as things are I cannot take him with me."

"But he would be happier with you. You are his father."

"His father?" Sir Hector had rasped, his eyes snapping to the Bishop's face. "You think that blood will make the boy happy? Do you truly believe that being with me will make his life more pleasant? All I will see in him is a reminder of his mother, when all I want is a memory of my Mary. I cannot show him any affection, for I feel none toward him. To me he would only be a thorn in my brain, constantly making me think of this town and the woman I have lost. No, Bishop. *You* keep him."

The knight shook his head. Stapledon had no idea what a mercenary's life was like. He was used to living in his palace and could have no idea of the struggle involved in keeping a company together and trying to earn enough to live.

As the road dropped down, following the line of a hill, he smiled again. It was good to be on horseback. He patted the light sword at his hip. While he wore steel and owned a warhorse, he was a man. Only old women sat indoors and planned meals. His life was that of a warrior, and it was all he needed. A quick regret touched him as a memory of Mary's face flitted across his mind, but then it was gone and he gave himself up to enjoying the ride.

The further from the town he travelled, the lighter his heart, and as if to emphasize his rising spirits, the sun burst through the gray skies, a finger of light burning through the clouds ahead and shining on the damp roadway.

When he felt the thump on his back, his first reaction was to wheel and glower behind him. It felt as if someone had thrown a rock at him. "Who—?" he began, but then, seeing the man before him, he was silent.

Will had returned. He had hurried after the mercenaries, catching up with them a mile outside the town, and grabbed at the weapons in the wagon. Now he stood in a huddle of men, a crossbow in his hands. Seeing Sir Hector turn, he let the crossbow fall, awestruck. At his side, the other men gawped at their leader.

"Well, little man? Are you brave enough to shoot me, then?" Sir Hector bawled, and made to turn his horse and ride down the man—but found his arm was unaccountably weak.

"Load another, Will. Shoot him again. *Quickly!*"

The captain noted the speaker down for punishment. Egging on a mutineer would cost him his tongue. But Sir Hector felt feeble; his usual strength had failed him. Beneath him, his horse moved nervously, making small, dancing steps. It was all the knight could do to stay mounted. As he watched, Will picked up the bow, tugged on the string, and dragged it back to cock it. Dully, as if through the fog of sleep, Sir Hector saw a man pass Will another bolt. Though Will, his face red and sweat pouring from him, was clearly in pain, it did not look as though this was owing to the hole in his side. His hasty fumbling was more from fear of his master.

Sir Hector spurred his horse, but found he could not keep his seat. The great black beast moved again, jerking his head up and down quickly, and Sir Hector almost toppled over. A quick stab of pain between his shoulders made his eyes widen. He had been shot!

Will raised the weapon a second time and fired, and Sir Hector saw rather than felt the bolt strike his chest. His head was an insupportable weight, and his chin fell to his breast. Slowly, as the animal under him walked on, he slid from the saddle. As his back struck the ground, he gasped with the agony.

The men continued on their way. For the most part none glanced in the direction of their leader, but one kicked him, pushing with his foot until the knight rolled into the ditch. There he lay, staring after his company while they carried on. Sir Hector swallowed, but the liquid in his throat would not clear, and he recognized the clattering sound of his breathing: he had heard it before. He tried to sit up, but the pain stopped him. It would be better to rest, he thought, and let his head drop to the grassy bank beside him. He had an urge to retch, but knew he couldn't.

When the men reached the next bend in the road, one of them turned to stare. He could see a splash of color by the roadside where the captain had fallen, and hesitated a moment, then ran back.

He could hear the breath rattling in Sir Hector's lungs as he drew near. The knight was lying as if asleep. The approaching figure was a blur to him, and he tried to smile—at least one of his men was loyal—but his mouth would not respond. "Help . . . me . . ."

Will crouched and drew his dagger. "We need a new leader," he said simply.

If you enjoyed
THE CREDITON KILLINGS,
turn the page to explore
the first three books in the intriguing
Knights Templar Mystery Series
from Michael Jecks

THE LAST TEMPLAR
THE MERCHANT'S PARTNER
A MOORLAND HANGING

*In **THE LAST TEMPLAR**, Simon Puttock has just been appointed bailiff of Lydford Castle, when he's called to a village where a charred body has been found in a burned-out cottage. Unaccustomed to violence in this peaceful area, Simon assumes it's an accidental death—but his partner, Sir Baldwin Furnshill, quickly convinces him that the victim had been killed before the fire began!*

When Tanner and the others arrived, the constable was surprised to find the monk and the bailiff sitting by the side of the road in front of a small fire. The monk rose immediately and ran to greet them, his nervous features cracking with an expression of desperate relief, and when Tanner caught a glimpse of the bailiff he began to understand why he was grateful for the new arrivals. Simon did not move. He sat still and quiet with his cloak wrapped tightly around him as he stared into the fire. Tanner dismounted and walked over to him.

"Thank God you've arrived! We were wondering whether you'd all wait for morning before coming and we didn't want to stay here alone all night," said the monk, breathlessly, as Tanner walked to the bailiff. The constable nodded absently and continued on, leaving the monk to welcome the others.

"Bailiff? What's wrong, bailiff?"

Simon could only slowly bring his eyes up from the

fire. After the horror in the woods he felt more tired than he had ever been in his life before. The nervous energy and the anger that had kept him going through the woods had drained him, and the horror of the sight in the clearing and his mad rush back to the road had finished the job. Now as he looked up he seemed to the constable to have aged by twenty years since the afternoon; his face was gaunt and pale and his eyes glittered as if he was in a fever, and Tanner crouched quickly beside him, his face full of concern. Simon hardly seemed to notice him. Almost as if he waned not to see the constable, he turned his gaze back to the fire and stared vacantly into the flames.

"Bailiff? What's happened?" said the constable in shocked amazement.

"We got here just before dark," Simon said quietly. "We found it easily enough. David—that's the monk—he found it quite quickly. The tracks were clear, going off into the woods over there." He pointed briefly with his chin to the opposite side of the road and returned to his solitary stare, talking softly and calmly while the constable frowned at him in anxious concern. "I told David to wait here for you and I went in alone. I must have been going for over an hour when I found a small clearing. One horse at least had been kept there; there was a fresh pile of shit where it had been tied."

Simon looked up suddenly and the constable felt the pain in the bailiff's eyes as they searched his face for a moment before returning to their introspective study of the flames. "The abbot was not far away. I carried on and found him. He had been tied up—tied to a tree. Someone had gathered up a load of twigs and branches and piled them underneath him." Tanner saw him shudder once, involuntarily, but then his voice continued calmly. "Then set light to them and burned the abbot to death."

Tanner stared at him steadily. "What? He was burned at the stake?"

"Yes," said Simon softly, almost wonderingly. "He was burned alive." Then he winced, his voice strained and harsh with the horror of it. "He must have been screaming when he died. Oh God! Stephen, you should have seen his face! It was dreadful! The flames were not hot enough to burn the top of his body, it was like he was staring at *me*! It felt like the devil himself was looking at me through his eyes, I could see his face clearly. God! It was awful!"

"But who could do a thing like that? Who would do that to a man of God?" said Tanner with a frown of consideration. Of course, outlaws were known for their brutality, exceeding even the viciousness of the pirates from Normandy, but neither French nor English bands were known here in the heart of Devon. Tanner was older than the bailiff and had served in the wars against the French, so he had witnessed the cruelty that men could show to each other, but even in war he had never heard of a monk being killed in this way, like a heretic. He was puzzled rather than horrified.

But he was worried too—if these two outlaws could do that to an abbot, nobody could be safe until they were caught. He looked up at the other men as they hobbled their horses and came forward to the fire, laughing and joking as they came. Their humor seemed almost sacrilegious after what he had just heard. and he had to bite back a shout at them.

Tanner was a calm and stable man. As a farmer he was used to the changing seasons and the steady march of the years as he watched his animals and plants grow, flourish and eventually die, but he was also used to the cruel and vicious ways of the wild, where the stronger creatures survived and the weaker died. Even so, to him this crime seemed strange in its barbarity. Animals could do that to each other, killing for food or pleasure, but for men to do this seemed curious in his quiet rural hundred. Constables in towns might be more used to cruelty of this type, he reflected. He had seen such acts at time of war when he had been a foot soldier for the king, but he did not expect them here, not during peace. Why should they do this to an abbot? He sighed and looked back at the bailiff, sitting silently absorbed beside him.

"You need to rest, sir. Lie down. I'll organize a watch and get the men sorted out."

"Yes," said Simon heedlessly, nodding slowly. He was gradually losing his feeling of horror under the stolid gaze of the constable and it was slowly being replaced by a distracted confusion, as if he had seen the whole of his world toppled. He had lived here all his life and in that time he had never seen a murdered man—or any man who had died in such an obscene manner. It seemed as though all that he had ever believed and known about the people who lived in the shire had suddenly been destroyed, and that he must reconsider all of his deepest held convictions in the light of this single, shattering event. A tear slowly dribbled from his eye and ran down his cheek, making him start, and he wiped it away angrily.

As if the gesture itself had awoken him, he looked over at Tanner, who was staring in his turn at the flames. "Right. Tomorrow we start the hunt for these killers, whoever they may be. I want them brought to justice," he said, almost snarling as he felt the disgust and hatred rising again. He was angry, not for the crime alone, not just for the hideous death of the man in the woods. It was for his own heightened sense of vulnerability, for the feeling that the men capable of this act could kill others, and would. They must be destroyed, like mad bears—hunted down and slaughtered with no compunction. "You get one of the men to ride on to Buckland and let them know what has happened here. The rest of us will follow the tracks and see if we can find them."

*In **THE MERCHANT'S PARTNER**, the mutilated body of a midwife and healer is discovered one wintry morning, and at first it appears that a lack of clues will render the crime unsolvable. Soon suspicion falls on a local youth. But Sir Baldwin has doubts about the boy's guilt, and enlists Simon in a hunt for the real murderer. And the truth, which lies beneath layers of jealousy, suspicion, and hatred, could prove fatal to anyone who disturbs it.*

Six miles to the south the Bourc was glancing up through the trees as he rode, retreating into his cloak in the bitter cold. On either side the trees rose stolidly impervious to the weather, but high above he could catch occasional glimpses of the stars, shining as tiny pinpricks of light which flared and were hidden like sparks from a fire. They glittered briefly before being smothered by the ghostly clouds rushing by, clouds that made him frown with wary anxiety. They raced by as if fearful of the weather that he knew must chase hard on their heels.

Hearing hooves, he stopped and stared ahead cautiously. It was late to be traveling. Soon he saw a man riding toward him. Showing his teeth in a short grin, he nodded. The other man, dressed warm and dark for hunting, nodded back and hurried on. The Bourc smiled ruefully to himself. He was muddy from splashing through puddles, and he knew he was hardly a sight to inspire confidence in a stranger. At a sudden thought he turned, and saw that the man was staring back with frank interest. The Bourc smiled ruefully as he kicked his horse and ambled off toward Wefford.

He had travelled far enough tonight. At the first clearing that looked hopeful, he pulled off the road. Through the trees he could see a cabin, a simple affair of rough-hewn logs. Part of the roof was gone, and it was in a sorry state, but for all that it was a refuge from the worst of the wind. He led the horses inside and saw to them before starting a fire.

Chewing at some dried meat, he considered his options. His business was finished now, so there was nothing to keep him here. The sooner he could get home the better. If he continued this way, heading to the west and retracing the route he had taken from the coast, he should arrive within a couple of days, but it would surely take a lot longer than necessary. The journey west to Oakhampton and then south was quite out of his way, working its way round the perimeter of the moors. It would be more direct and quicker to cut straight south, over the moors to the sea that way.

It was still dark the next morning, Wednesday, when, over to the south of Furnshill, Samuel Cottey harnessed his old mule to the wagon and prepared for his journey, cursing in the deep blackness before dawn as his already numbed fingers struggled with the rough brass and leather fittings, pulling hard at the thick leather straps.

"Sorry, my love," he muttered as he occasionally caught a flap of skin in the buckles, making the old animal snort and stamp. "Not long, now. We'll soon have you done."

All set, he stood back and surveyed his work, rubbing the bandage on his arm that covered the long gash. It was a week ago now that the branch had dropped from the tree he was felling and slashed the flesh of his arm like a sword, but, thanks to God, the old woman's poultices seemed to be working and it was healing. Sighing, he stretched and then walked back to the cottage, stamping his feet to get the feeling to return to cold toes. Inside the smoky room, he warmed himself by the fire in the clay hearth in the middle, smiling crookedly from the side of his mouth, the lips pale and thin in the square, ruddy face under the hatch of gray hair. Sarah, his daughter, smiled back into his light brown eyes as she handed his mug full of warmed beer to him and watched carefully as he drained it, smacking his lips and wiping his hand over his mouth, then burping appreciatively. Giving her a quick grin, he passed back the mug.

"That's good," he said, then kissed her cheek briefly. "Be back soon as I can—I'll try to be home before dark, anyway."

When she nodded, he left, stomping quickly to the wagon and clambering aboard, whistling for his dog. After a quick wave, he snapped the reins and began to make his way from Wefford to Crediton, the dog barking excitedly behind.

As he left the light from the open doorway behind, his mind turned back to their problems. This last year had been the hardest he had known, especially since his brother had been killed by the trial bastons, down far to the south on the moors. Now the family relied on him alone to keep both farms going. His sister-in-law was right when she said that the two families could not live on either holding: both were too small to support them all, and neither could be expanded without a deal of work, hacking down the trees that fringed them. No, the only way to continue was by keeping both going.

But how to do that? There was only him, his daughter Sarah, and his brother's son Paul. There was too much work for them, now that they had to try to keep both properties working. Maybe they should do as Sarah suggested, and buy more pigs. At least they could often feed themselves; they did not need grain like cows.

The sun was lighting the eastern sky as he rattled and squeaked his way down the track into the village, head down, chin on his chest and shoulders hunched in an effort to keep the bitter cold from his vulnerable neck. Samuel had been a farmer for many years, and he was used to the cruelty of the wind and the freezing snow that attacked the land every winter, but the weather got worse with each passing year. Glancing up, he saw the sky was lighted with a vivid angry red, and sighed. The sharpness of the air, the streamers of mist from his mouth, and the red sky could only mean one thing: snow was on its way at last.

Passing the inn on his left, he glanced at it with longing, already wishing he could stop and warm himself before the great fire in the hall but, shuddering and shivering, he carried on, rubbing at his arm every now and again. Beyond was the turn he needed, and he made off to the right, toward Crediton, where his brother's farm lay, between the town itself and Sandford. He had to collect their chickens and take them into the market. Paul was still too young to be allowed to go to market on his own.

It was hard, he thought, sighing again. If only poor Judith had lived longer. But his wife had succumbed to the pestilence that followed on the tail of the rain that killed off the harvest two years ago.

The trees suddenly seemed to crowd in around him, their thick trunks looming menacingly from the thin mist that still lay heavy on the ground, almost appearing to be free of the earth, as if they could move and walk if they wished. It was this feeling that made him shiver again, peering up at the branches overhead. From somewhere deep in the trees came the screech of a bird, then some rooks called overhead, sounding strange and unnatural.

All he could hear was the clattering and squeaking of the wagon, with the occasional dull, deadened thump as the iron-shod wheels struck stones or fell into holes, and it felt impossible that any noise could be heard over the row he made, but still he caught the sounds of the waking forest, and his eyes flitted here and there nervously, as if fearing what he might see.

Then, all at once, he was out of it. The track led upward here, to a small hill where the woods had been cleared, and he drew a deep breath of relief, blowing it out in a long feather of misted air. The feelings of dread left him, and he squirmed on the board that made his seat, telling himself he was a fool to be fearful of noises in the woods.

Cold-blooded murder has transformed Simon's official obligation into something horrid—and he will need the assistance of his friend, Sir Baldwin, to draw a criminal out.

In ***A MOORLAND HANGING****, justice must be served even if their search exposes extortion and foul corruption, and killers willing, even eager, to shed more blood.*

—

"They are certainly very curious. All the branches point in the same direction—had you noticed that?"

"It's as if they're pointing to something, isn't it? There are rumors I've heard . . ."

"Yes?"

"Well, you remember the stories, don't you? About the Devil and his pack of wish-hounds baying after lost souls? This is where those stories come from, Baldwin, out here on the moors. They say that the wish-hounds are heard here when the winds blow hard."

Baldwin gave him a sour stare. "I suppose you think the hounds come here to piss on the trees? Diabolical hounds peeing on the branches kill them off, and that makes the oaks die on one side? Really, Simon, I—"

"No, of course not," said Simon, hastily holding up a hand to stem the knight's ironic flow. 'But I know *I* wouldn't want to stay here after dark."

"No, I can see why," said Baldwin reflectively, gazing at the trees. The atmosphere was oppressive, he thought, and it was easy to understand how people could imagine the worst of such a place, especially if the wind howled among the boughs as night fell. Baldwin did not believe in old wives' tales himself, but it was natural for anyone to be affected by the menacing power of a place like this.

"The people here think there's some kind of strangeness about it," Simon continued. "Maybe that's where the names come from. Round here, 'wisht' means uncanny, or weird. Certainly these trees look it."

"Yes, they do. But I think these trees grow this way for some mundane reason. Wish-hounds!" His voice betrayed his amusement, and the bailiff shot him a suspicious glance.

Another mile southward, after they had breasted another hill, Baldwin at last understood why Simon had brought him this way. He reined in his horse and stared.

"This is what I wanted you to see, Baldwin. Welcome to the tin mines of Dartmoor!" Simon announced as they came to a halt.

Baldwin found himself staring at a wide encampment on a plain surrounded by low hills, the whole unmarked by wall or fence. Dotted here and there stood small, gray turf and stone cottages. One, larger than the others and set in their midst, gave off a thick plume of smoke which straggled in the slight breeze. The broad area was pitted and scarred with holes and trenches. Through the middle trailed a narrow but fast-flowing stream, from which sprang several man-made rivulets, and there was a large dam over to their right. Other leats were fed by this, tailing off into the distance, and Baldwin guessed that they led to other workings.

"With all these houses, there must be many men here," said Baldwin, eyeing the area speculatively.

"An army. Over a hundred in this camp alone," Simon agreed, and kicked his horse on.

They had only traveled a short way when they saw a pair of men at the outskirts of the vill, and Simon smiled with sardonic amusement at their reaction—it was all too typical of the attitude of miners out here that they should be suspicious of strangers. One pointed in their direction before running off, while the other man grasped what looked like a pick and faced them resolutely. By the time the bailiff and his friend had come closer, there was a group waiting for them, looking like trained soldiers to Baldwin's military eye. The man who had run for help had returned, joined by a thickset character who looked as if he was in charge.

Simon rode up to him, smiling in a friendly manner until the tinner snapped: "Who're you? What d'you want here?"

The bailiff sighed. It was infuriating that these miners should feel free to be so arrogantly discourteous—even more that they had the right and strength to behave so. He heard Baldwin's intake of breath and could almost feel the waves of disapproval from the knight.

"Good day," he replied pleasantly. "We're on our way to visit a friend, to the east. My companion here hasn't seen how tin is farmed, and—"

"He won't find out today, either," said the man firmly, and Baldwin moved his horse a little closer to Simon. The miner was short and sandy-haired, with skin tanned by the sun and wind to the color of old saddle leather. Though he looked quite old, Baldwin could not be sure whether that was a sign of the harshness of life on the moors or an indication of his age. If fitness was anything to go by, the man was not ancient. His belly was taut, the breadth of his shoulders was almost the same as his height, and the knight quickly came to the opinion that he would not want to fight such a man without a superiority in weapons. As it was, the man merely carried a long dagger at his waist, but Baldwin could see that he was wary in the way his hands rested close to its haft, his thumbs hooked into his thick leather belt.

"At least tell us how far it is to Sir William Beauscyr's Manor," Baldwin said sharply, and was pleased to see a quick flicker of doubt in the miner's brown eyes.

"You're friends of Sir William?"

"Not quite," Baldwin said, then glanced at Simon. "But the bailiff of Lydford and I are on our way to see him."

"The bailiff?" His gaze moved suspiciously back to Simon.

"Yes, I'm the bailiff," said Simon, exasperation beginning to take him over. "And yes, I'm on my way to see Sir William. Now answer my friend's question and tell us how much farther it is to the Manor."

Directions were grudgingly given while the other men watched, hands fiddling with mattocks and spades, and Baldwin was glad when they could finally set off once more and leave the tense little knot of miners behind. Once they had passed by the village and were making their way up the slope at the far side of the camp, he glanced back and was disturbed to see the sandy-haired man standing motionless in the same place, his eyes still fixed on them.

***NEW YORK TIMES* BESTSELLING AUTHOR**

BERNARD CORNWELL

"PERHAPS THE GREATEST WRITER OF HISTORICAL ADVENTURE NOVELS TODAY."

Washington Post

The Grail Quest series

THE ARCHER'S TALE

0-06-050525-7/$7.99 US

A brutal raid on the quiet coastal English village of Hookton in 1342 leaves but one survivor: a young archer named Thomas. This terrible dawn sets him on a path toward his ultimate quest: the search for the Holy Grail.

VAGABOND

0-06-053268-8/$7.99 US

Five years have passed since Thomas began his quest for justice. Now, as England's army fights in France, her Scottish foes plan a bloody invasion that will embroil the young archer.

HERETIC

0-06-053284-X/$7.99 US/$10.99 Can

In the flames of unceasing war, Thomas' heart, will, and courage will be supremely tested in the conclusion of an epic quest for vengeance and the greatest prize in history: the Holy Grail.

www.bernardcornwell.net

Visit www.AuthorTracker.com for exclusive information on your favorite HarperCollins authors.

Available wherever books are sold or please call 1-800-331-3761 to order.

BC 1005